C000144666

Spider World

THE DELTA

Fiction by Colin Wilson

Adrift in Soho
The Black Room
The Glass Cage
The God of the Labyrinth
The Janus Murder Case
The Killer (Lingard)
The Man without a Shadow (The Sex Diary of Gerard Sorme
    and The Sex Diary of a Metaphysician)
The Mind Parasites
Necessary Doubt
The Personality Surgeon
The Philosopher's Stone
The Return of the Lloigor
Ritual in the Dark
The Schoolgirl Murder Case
The Space Vampires
Spider World: The Tower
Spider World: The Delta
Spider World: The Magician
The World of Violence

Spider World

THE DELTA

Colin Wilson

HAMPTON ROADS
PUBLISHING COMPANY, INC.

Copyright © 2001
by Colin Wilson
All rights reserved, including the right to reproduce this
work in any form whatsoever, without permission
in writing from the publisher, except for brief passages
in connection with a review.

Cover design and photo by Grace Pedalino
First published in Great Britain in 1987 by Grafton Books.

For information write:

Hampton Roads Publishing Company, Inc.
1125 Stoney Ridge Road
Charlottesville, VA 22902

434-296-2772
fax: 434-296-5096
e-mail: hrpc@hrpub.com
www.hrpub.com

If you are unable to order this book from your local
bookseller, you may order directly from the publisher.
Call 1-800-766-8009, toll-free.
Library of Congress Catalog Card Number: 2001091201
ISBN 1-57174-273-5
10 9 8 7 6 5 4 3 2 1
Printed on acid-free paper in the United States

Acknowledgements

As with the first volume, *Spider World: The Tower*, I owe a considerable debt of gratitude to my friend Donald Seaman for comments and suggestions. My children, Sally, Damon, and Rowan have also provided some useful guidelines. David Ellis made some interesting and useful suggestions for the Delta section. And I should like to acknowledge—somewhat belatedly—that the original idea of writing a "children's book" came from my friend Roald Dahl, who will no doubt be appalled at the outcome of his rash suggestion.

Cornwall, 1987

Contents

Introduction

For as long as men can remember, the earth has been dominated by giant insects and ruled by poisonous telepathic spiders who breed human beings for food. The Spider Lord Cheb is reputed to be a hundred-eyed monster tarantula who is virtually deathless. The few humans who remain free live in underground lairs in the desert and are continually hunted by the death spiders, who float overhead in silken balloons, and whose willpower probes the desert landscape like searchlight beams.

Niall and his family live in an underground lair that once belonged to a tiger beetle. From his grandfather Jomar, Niall hears tales of the days when human beings were masters of the earth but finds them hard to believe. He also hears stories of the underground city of Dira, the largest colony of "free" humans in existence, and of the Great Delta, the area of jungle inhabited by man-eating plants and deadly insects.

When two members of the family are killed in the Delta, Niall and his father set out across the desert for the underground city of Dira to escort the beautiful Ingeld—now a widow—back to her own people. On the great plateau, they take refuge in an immense ruined citadel, and for the first time, Niall begins to believe that men once ruled the earth. In Dira, Niall meets his attractive cousin Dona. But it is with Princess Merlew, daughter of King Kazak, that he falls in love. He is tempted by Kazak's offer to settle in the underground city, until he realizes that Merlew regards him as little more than a child. Angry and disappointed, he sets out with his father on the long return journey. On the way, they take refuge from a sandstorm in the ruins of an ancient city, and there find a strange machine that dates from the twenty-first century. Inside it, Niall finds a telescopic metal rod which he can use as a spear. And it is with this rod that Niall kills a death spider, and so brings upon his family—and upon Kazak's underground city—the wrath of the Spider Lord himself. One day, he returns to the burrow to find his father dead, and the remainder of his family kidnapped by the spiders.

He follows them, hoping to find an opportunity to free his mother and sisters, but is himself captured by the spiders. They take him across the sea to a great city that was once inhabited by human beings. Now its buildings are crumbling, and vast spider webs stretch between the skyscrapers. There he learns that human beings are less badly treated than he supposed. The human servants of the spiders are ruled by women—since females are the dominant sex among spiders—and they live in communes. Men and women are strictly segregated. Only the slaves—who are little more than imbeciles—are eaten by the spiders.

In the center of the spider city stands the mysterious white tower constructed by men of old for some long-forgotten purpose. Every attempt by the spiders to penetrate its smooth, glass-like walls has been unsuccessful. Niall witnesses the latest attempt by the servants of the bombardier beetles—led by the sapper Bill Doggins—and comes close to being blown to pieces. The tower evidently holds some important secret.

In the spider city, King Kazak has once again established himself as a leader of men and is collaborating with the spiders. When Niall again encounters Merlew, he begins to believe that she may be in love with him after all. From Kazak, he learns the horrible truth about the fate of the spider-servants and is strongly tempted by an offer to become the King's ally. But another glimpse into Merlew's true feelings drives him to escape.

With the aid of the telescopic rod, he learns the secret of entering the white tower. It is a time capsule, left there by the men of old before they left the earth in giant space transports. And during the next few days, Niall learns the past history of the human race from a humanoid computer called the Steegmaster. There is only one secret that the computer refuses to divulge—how human beings can conquer the spiders. This is something Niall has to learn for himself.

Hunted by the spiders, he takes refuge in the slave quarter of the city. He succeeds in becoming the overseer of a contingent of slaves whom he leads to the city of the bombardier beetles, known to the slaves as Crashville. Because the beetles have always defended themselves with detonations of hot gas, they adore explosions—the bigger and louder, the better. Niall has arrived on Boomday, their festival of explosions, organized by the chief explosives expert, Bill Doggins. During the festival, Niall gains an unexpected ally in the beautiful Odina, a guard Commander who has fallen in love with him. And, when Boomday in Crashville culminates in unforeseen disaster, Doggins also agrees to become Niall's ally in exchange for Niall's agreement to lead him to the Fortress, a disused barracks in the slave quarter where Doggins hopes to find explosives.

He finds far more than he expected; not only explosives, but "Reapers," the deadliest weapon—apart from the hydrogen bomb— ever invented by man. Trapped by the spiders, they escape back to the city of the beetles in stolen spider balloons; but Doggins is forced to use his Reaper to destroy the army of spiders besieging the city. Their escapade has started a war between the beetles and the spiders.

They are taken before the ruler of the beetles—the Master—to answer for their insubordination. There they are confronted by the Spider Lord speaking through the mouth of Odina, whose brain he controls. The beetles agree to hand over Doggins for punishment, but have their doubts about the legality of handing over Niall, a free human being who had every right to escape. The Spider Lord, enraged at the thought that his prey might elude him, tries to strangle Niall. In the ensuing struggle, Odina is killed. And the beetles, incensed by this attempt at treachery, decide that Niall shall remain free. As he tries to express his gratitude, Niall loses consciousness . . .

PART ONE

The Councils

The first time Niall woke up he was in agony. His throat felt as if he had swallowed a red-hot sword, and his eyes were throbbing with pain. He tried to sit up, but a cool hand rested on his forehead and gently forced him back onto the pillow. The pain seemed to dissolve away.

The next time he woke it was daylight, and the room was full of pale blue light. He was lying in a wide bed, with his bare arms on the coverlet. Through the transparent blue wall he could see a large tree with yellow flowers; it shaded the room from the sunlight. The ceiling was covered with a pattern like rippling green leaves.

He raised his hands to his throat, and his fingers encountered a hard shell. His neck was completely encased in a substance that looked like dried clay, held in place by bandages. Suddenly he realized that he was naked, and that the thought mirror was no longer round his neck. He sat up in alarm, then saw that his clothes were on a chair beside the bed, and that the thought mirror lay on top of them. Beside it lay the telescopic rod. He sighed with relief.

The door opened and Selima came into the room. She smiled when she saw that he was awake. "Are you feeling better?"

"Much better." But his voice was unnaturally hoarse.

She laughed. "You sound like my grandfather." She sat beside him on the bed and placed both hands on his cheeks. He immediately felt the pleasant, cool sensation that he had experienced in the night. The ache in his throat vanished.

He asked her: "How do you do that? Do you have something on your hands?"

"No." She showed him her palms. "It is a power that comes from my mother. Our family has the gift of healing."

Niall felt as though he was floating down a slow stream, under green overarching branches. He allowed himself to sink into sleep.

When he woke again, Doggins was standing by his bedside. The window was open and he could hear voices of children playing in the fountain. Behind Doggins stood an old man whose sunburned face was covered with wrinkles and lines; the penetrating gray eyes were sunk deep in their sockets. He wore a shabby tunic of a dull green color, like dying moss, and was carrying a bag of the same material.

Doggins said: "This is Simeon. He's our medicine man."

Niall nodded and said hello, but his voice still sounded as if it was being strained through dry leaves. Simeon stared at him intently with his strange gray eyes, which seemed to contain points of light, then took his wrist. After feeling the pulse and placing his hand on Niall's cheek—there was a brief, tingling sensation as he did so—he rested his bag on the bed and took from it a short knife with a pointed, heavy blade. With this he began to cut delicately at the plaster round Niall's throat; after a few long, deep incisions, he was able to pull it apart. The air felt unpleasantly cold on the exposed skin. The old man reached out and touched Niall's throat with his forefinger; it made Niall wince.

Doggins asked anxiously: "What do you think?"

"He was lucky. Another inch to the right and he'd be dead." Simeon had a deep, throaty voice that was almost a growl.

Niall tried to peer down at his own neck, but it was impossible. Doggins picked up a hand mirror from a dressing table and held it out. Niall was shocked at the blotchy travesty of his face reflected in the polished steel. The eyes were bloodshot and the cheeks were covered with red and purple marks that looked like bruises. His throat was circled by yellow and purple finger marks.

He asked Doggins: "What happened to Odina?"

"We buried her this morning."

"This morning?"

"That's right. You've been here since the day before yesterday. You were in a fever."

From his bag, Simeon took a phial of a brown liquid. "Open your mouth." Niall obeyed, and he felt a few drops of cool liquid on his tongue. "This will burn. Close your eyes, and try not to swallow."

As the liquid spread through his mouth, it seemed to turn to fire. It reached the back of his throat, and the pain was intense. He closed his eyes and rested his head back against the padded headrest. After a few moments, the pain turned into a pleasant, warm sensation. He was unable to prevent himself from swallowing; as he did so, the warmth soothed the bruised sensation in his windpipe. Then, suddenly, his whole body felt relaxed. He said dreamily: "That's a wonderful medicine."

"It's called Jackal Bane, and it comes from the Great Delta."

Niall opened his eyes. "You've been to the Great Delta?"

"Many times."

"Will you tell me about it?"

"Yes, but not now. You must rest."

They went away, leaving him alone. But although he now felt deeply relaxed, and the pain had turned into a distant ache, he was no longer sleepy. Instead, he thought about Odina, and allowed himself to experience the misery of losing her. When he thought of the last kiss he had exchanged with her, as he left the house on his way to the spider city, he felt the tears welling from his eyes; he made no attempt to stop them or to brush them away as they ran down his cheeks. The death of his father had been a hard blow, but his anguish had been the distress of a child who suddenly feels alone. Now he felt the heartache of an adult who has lost someone he loves. It seemed an outrage and an affront that anyone so beautiful should be consigned to the earth, and for the next half hour Niall allowed himself to sink into a condition of profound melancholy and pessimism. In this state he concluded that all life is a tragic mistake, and that the invisible powers who control our destiny regard us with a kind of bored contempt. These reflections left him deeply shaken, as if he had looked into an abyss. Finally, worn out with a sense of life-weariness, he drifted into a doze.

He was awakened by Selima, who was carrying a tray. She smiled so dazzlingly when she saw him that he found his heart lifting in response.

"You look much better."

"Do I?"

She held out the mirror, and he saw that his eyes were no longer bloodshot and that the hemorrhages had almost disappeared from his face. The purple bruises on his throat had faded into a brownish-yellow.

She sat on the bed and placed the tray on his lap. "Try this."

He tasted the thin broth and found it delicious. To his surprise, he was able to swallow without pain. A thick, granular brown bread, covered in pale yellow butter, caused a twinge of agony, but the relief of his stomach was so great that he ignored it. As he ate, the rising tide of physical satisfaction swept away the last remnants of his earlier melancholy.

He asked Selima: "Were you frightened when the spiders surrounded the city?"

"Of course. Some of the others were not frightened because they were certain the beetles could protect them. But I was brought up among the spiders. I know how dangerous they are."

"How *did* the beetles prevent the spiders from overrunning your city?"

She seemed surprised. "You don't know? They use willpower. I forget what it is called, but it means that they lock their wills together into a kind of mesh."

"I understand. The spiders do the same thing. But how did the beetles know they were going to be attacked?"

"They expected it. As soon as they learned that you had gone to the spider city to steal explosives, they knew the spiders would come."

"And do you think they will attack again?"

She shook her head, smiling. "Oh, no. Not now we have the Reapers."

"Ah, you know about the Reapers."

"Of course. Everyone knows." She took his tray. "Now you must rest again."

As she was opening the door, he asked: "Has there been any sign of the men in the other balloons?"

"Yes. They have all returned safely. Hastur's balloon came down in the river, but they swam ashore. And Milo brought back some children he found in the forest."

"What children?"

"Some children from the spider nursery."

He asked eagerly: "Do you know their names?"

She gave him a strange, enigmatic glance.

"Your sisters are not among them."

He gazed at her in astonishment. "How did you know about my sisters?"

Again she gave him the curious, doubtful look. Then she went out, leaving the door open. He stared after her, wondering what was to come. There were footsteps in the corridor, and a blue-clad girl stood in the doorway.

"Dona!"

She flung herself onto the bed and clasped her arms round his neck, giving him a long kiss. He had forgotten the pleasant warmth of her lips, and it took his breath away.

Selima, who had returned, said with mild reproof: "You must not excite him. He still needs a lot of rest."

"No, I promise I won't." Dona released him and sat down at the foot of the bed. They stared at one another, smiling, hardly able to believe they were together again.

Selima said: "I will be back in a few minutes." She left the room, closing the door quietly behind her.

Niall asked eagerly: "What has happened to my sisters?"

Her smile vanished. "They were taken away two days ago. The commander who came for them said they were being taken to their mother."

"That was on the day of the explosion?"

"About two hours before."

The news was not entirely unexpected. Two hours before the explosion, they had been bargaining with Kazak. His sisters were intended to be part of that bargain.

Dona reached out and touched his hand. "I am sorry."

He shrugged. "It may be for the best. If the spiders are holding them as hostages, then they probably won't harm them." He deliberately closed his mind to the fears that tried to invade it. "But tell me how you escaped."

"When the explosion came, I was out on the lawn with some of the children. Then the earth began to tremble and I thought it was an earthquake—we had an earthquake once in Dira, and some of the walls fell down. So I told the children to sit on the ground and not to be afraid. But then the spiders seemed to go mad. They all began running about in a strange way, as if they didn't understand what they were doing—one of them even ran into the river. Do you know why they did that?"

"Yes. The spiders are telepathic. So if one of them is hurt, the others can feel it. They were experiencing the death agonies of the other spiders. But what happened then?"

"Then the sky became dark with black smoke, and the children began to cough. The windows of the nursery were all broken but no one seemed badly hurt. And then the commanders left—they took the boats and went back across the river. The smoke was getting worse, and I thought we might all choke to death. So I told my children to follow me and we walked out. No one tried to stop us. All the streets were empty. So we walked towards the hills."

"But where did you hope to get to?"

"I didn't care. I just wanted to escape from the spiders. So we simply went on walking until we were out in the countryside. After a while, the children became tired and hungry. But we found an orchard with apples and plums, and a stream, so we all rested for an hour. Then one of the children told me that she had seen a spider balloon, and I crept to the edge of the orchard and looked out. And I saw there were men in the balloon—men in yellow clothes. I knew they were the servants of the beetles. We watched the balloon until it seemed to sink into some woodland. Then I made the children walk across the fields until we came to the woods. We all shouted, and the three men came and found us. They brought us back here."

"Was it a long journey to the city of the beetles?"

"Not very far, but it took a long time because we had to keep hiding from the spiders. We saw lots of spiders in the fields, and at first we thought they were looking for us. Then we almost walked into one of them—it came suddenly from behind some trees—and it didn't even see us. I think there was something wrong with it."

"In what way?"

"It was walking as if it was dazed or wounded. Or perhaps just very tired . . ."

The door opened and Selima looked in. "I think you ought to let him rest now."

"All right." Dona gave him a quick smile and went out. It was only then that Niall realized how tired he felt. He tried to think about what Dona had told him, but it was impossible to focus his mind. Yet the knowledge that she was safe filled him with a sense of well-being; he was thinking about her as he drifted into sleep.

Then he was dreaming that he was floating above the spider city in a balloon. There was a smell of burning in the air, and he could see smoke drifting up from the smoldering houses in the slave quarter. The devastation there was appalling; street after street had been leveled into rubble. The town hall square was clearly visible, with its green lawns, but the building itself was a ruin, with only two broken walls left standing. To the south, where the barracks had stood, there was now a wide expanse of water joined to the river by a broad and irregular channel. As Niall drifted over it, he could see the bodies of spiders floating upwards in the brown water.

The balloon had crossed the river and passed within a few feet of the white tower. Most of the buildings in this part of the city seemed to be undamaged, but the streets were strewn with broken glass. He passed close to Kazak's palace and leaned out of the undercarriage, trying to see in through its windows. As he did so, he heard his mother's voice calling his name. He cupped his hands and shouted: "I'm here! Where are you?" Her voice called back: "Here, in the bedroom." It was so clear that she seemed to be only a few feet away.

He woke up with a start and looked round the room, expecting to see her. It was dusk, and the room was empty. For a moment he felt like bursting into tears of sorrow and disappointment. Then, as he stared at the purple sky out of the window, he suddenly became aware of her presence. As soon as he closed his eyes and focused his mind, he could see her sitting cross-legged on the floor of her bedroom in Kazak's palace; her eyes were also closed. Their minds made contact, and he experienced joy and relief as he received her message that they were safe. But as he tried to send her a picture of his own situation, his concentration wavered; his brain was still numb with sleep. The contact was lost and he was alone.

A few minutes later, Doggins peeped in through the door. "Feeling better?"

"Much better, thanks."

"Well enough to attend a meeting?"

His heart sank. "Another council meeting?"

"No—just human beings this time. But I'm going to need your support."

"*My* support?" The idea surprised him.

"It's our stadion—that's a kind of civic council. I'm told they intend to try and pass a motion of censure against me."

"Would it matter?"

"Oh, yes. They could order me to destroy the Reapers."

"Wouldn't that be rather stupid?"

Before Doggins could reply, there was a tap at the door and Selima came in carrying a light whose brilliance filled the room. She placed it on the table and went out. Niall stared at it with astonishment.

"What's that?"

"A simple pressure lamp. It's a kind of family secret. My grandfather invented it eighty years ago, but we've never been allowed to use it."

"Why not?"

He shrugged with disgust. "The crawlies say it's a machine."

"How does it work?"

"This contains oil." He tapped the shining metal globe at the base of the lamp. "A pump forces it up this tube and it's vaporized as it strikes this ceramic mantle. Simple, really."

Niall stared at it with fascination. It was not simply the design that intrigued him, but his sense of being perfectly familiar with it already. Then a flash of intuition gave him the answer. Like his ability to read, this knowledge had been implanted in his memory by the Steegmaster. As this insight came to him, he experienced a glimpse of many other items of knowledge that lay slumbering in the depths of his memory; for a few seconds he experienced a bewildering sense of double-exposure, as if his identity was suddenly in doubt.

Doggins reached into a drawer.

"Here's another item of forbidden knowledge."

He tossed a book onto the bed. Niall looked at the title: *The Principles of Electronics*.

"Why forbidden?"

"Because books are forbidden. Paragraph twenty-two of the Peace Treaty: 'There shall be no printing or circulation of books on pain of death.' So most of the books are in museums, locked in glass cases."

"But you can read?"

"Of course. Most of us can. It's a secret we pass on from father to son. But if the spiders found out, we'd be in trouble. Twenty years ago they discovered that one of our people could read—an old man of ninety—and insisted on having him executed."

"And the beetles agreed?"

"They had no alternative—it's in the treaty."

Niall was turning the pages of the book, baffled by the mathematical symbols. Doggins asked casually: "Who taught you to read?"

It took Niall a moment to register the question. Then he looked up, startled. "How did you know I can?"

"I could see your eyes moving. Who taught you?"

Niall grinned. "A machine."

Doggins looked at him from under lowered eyebrows. "The same machine that gave you the food tablets?"

Niall laughed at his penetration. "That's right."

"And where is this machine?"

"In the white tower."

Doggins' eyes widened. "Are you serious?" Niall nodded. "Have you been in there?"

"Yes."

Doggins' face had suddenly become pale. "How did you get in?"

"With this." Niall leaned over and picked up the telescopic rod which was lying on top of his clothes. He pressed the button and it expanded. He handed it to Doggins. "Can you feel anything?"

"A kind of a tingle?" Doggins was trying to keep his voice level, but the shaking of his hand betrayed his excitement. "Where did you find it?"

"In the desert." Niall described how they had taken shelter from the sandstorm, and how the wind had uncovered the desert city. When he described the glittering machine, Doggins nodded.

"That would be a Grasshopper. It was the chief mode of long-distance transport at the end of the twenty-first century." He looked at the rod in his hands. "But I've never seen one of these before. Sorry, go on."

As Niall described how he had found himself inside the tower, Doggins' excitement became intense; he obviously found it hard to sit still. His face lost its paleness and became flushed. What intrigued Niall was that he seemed to be able to feel this excitement radiating from Doggins like a physical force; he found it curiously disturbing and tiring. It was almost a relief when, as he was describing the Steegmaster, Doggins interrupted him.

"That proves I was right! Glorfin says we ought to be contented to stay as we are . . ."

"Glorfin?"

"Our civic leader, head of the stadion. He says we ought to be contented to serve the beetles and live peaceful lives. But why did the men of old store all that knowledge if they didn't intend us to use it?"

"They *did* intend us to use it—when we're ready for it."

Doggins said impatiently: "We're ready now. I've been ready all my life."

Niall shook his head. "The old man said there were some things he couldn't tell me—things I had to find out for myself . . ."

"What kind of things?"

"For example, how to defeat the spiders . . ."

"We already know that." Doggins was in the full flood of excitement. "What else?"

Niall shook his head. "I can't remember. But he seemed to feel that there were certain things I had to learn for myself . . ."

"Of course!" Doggins was now walking up and down the room, and the lamp gave his black shadow a life of its own. "It's the same with everything—we don't appreciate anything we get too easily. But I've been waiting for this all my life . . ." There was a knock at the door, and he said: "Damn!"

Selima looked into the room; she was obviously wondering what all the shouting was about.

"The members of the stadion have arrived—they're in the dining room."

Doggins groaned. "What a moment to interrupt us!" He made an effort of control. "All right, tell them we'll be there in a few minutes." As Selima went out, he pulled open a drawer. "Here, wear this." It was a yellow tunic of the beetle servants.

Niall dressed quickly and hung the thought mirror round his neck. As he did so, he noticed the cord around Doggins' throat.

"What's that?"

Doggins gave him an odd, twisted grin. From inside his tunic, he pulled a thought mirror. It was almost identical to the one Niall was wearing, except that it was silver in color. Suddenly, Niall understood.

"*That's* why I could tell what you were feeling. You'd got that thing pointing at me."

Doggins weighed it in his hand. "I borrowed it from the museum. Tell me something. Do you find it makes you tired?"

"At first. You get used to it."

"Thank God for that. I've been feeling worn out all day. Did you get yours from the tower?" Niall nodded. "Let me try it, would you?"

Niall handed over his thought mirror and accepted the other in return. As soon as he hung it round his neck, he sensed the difference. At first, this one seemed far more powerful; then he realized that it was not simply a question of power. Like his own thought mirror, it could concentrate the will into a beam of intensity when turned inward; turned the other way, it broadcast the intensity outward. But there was something coarse and brutal in its power, like someone screaming a command. He found that wearing it for only a few moments made his head throb with exhaustion.

Doggins said: "This one doesn't seem as strong." He tossed it back. But instead of hanging it round his neck, Niall dropped it into the pocket of his tunic. An instinct told him that, while he was in this condition of weakness, the thought mirror would be an obstacle to his recovery.

As he followed Doggins down the corridor, children peered at him out of doorways, and made him conscious that he was an object of intense curiosity.

They entered a large room, whose main item of furniture was a polished oval table. It was large enough to seat about twenty people, and most of the chairs around it were occupied. Niall recognized only three of the faces—Milo, Ulic, and the doctor who had treated him, Simeon.

Everyone stood up as Doggins entered the room; but Niall could sense that it was a purely formal gesture. Doggins took his seat at the end of the table, and indicated that Niall should sit next to him. A small, gray-bearded man sitting at the other end cleared his throat.

"Pardon me, but are strangers permitted at official council meetings?"

Doggins said: "Glorfin himself said he wanted to question our guest. That would hardly be possible if he was not present."

The little man flushed. "Is there any reason why he should not wait outside until we are ready to question him?"

Doggins colored and glowered angrily. "Yes, Pybus, there is a reason. He is a free man and he does not have to submit to our questions. He can walk out and tell us all to go to the devil. Apart from that, he is a guest in my house . . ."

The little man had become red with embarrassment; he dropped his eyes before Doggins' angry glare. The man who sat next to him—a tall, bald-headed man with a cadaverous face and lantern jaw—cleared his throat and said shortly: "The point is taken. Let us proceed." But he was obviously displeased.

Doggins lowered his eyes to the tabletop, as if he was accepting the rebuke; but the lines of his mouth made it clear that he was in an unconciliatory mood.

The bald-headed man said: "Before we begin, perhaps you would introduce your guest?"

Doggins said: "His name is Niall and he comes from the desert region of North Khaybad."

"Am I correct in assuming he is the runaway slave the spiders were searching for?" The speaker was a fat man whose head was covered with tight blond curls.

Doggins gave him a hard stare. "Wrong on both counts, Corbin. He is not a slave because he was born free. And he is not a runaway because he was brought here against his will, and therefore had every right to escape."

Corbin gave a faint smile. "Is that not prejudging the issue?"

Doggins shook his head. "No. It is you who are prejudging the issue."

The bald-headed man interrupted impatiently: "Let us stop wrangling. The question we have to decide is perfectly simple— whether you have broken the law. Do you answer yes or no?"

Doggins looked at him steadily for a moment before answering: "No, Glorfin, I haven't."

Glorfin stared at him reprovingly; it was obvious that he disliked his tone. "It is hard to see how you can maintain that position. Did you not lead an expedition to the city of the spiders?"

Doggins nodded. "Yes."

"Did you have the permission of this council or of the council of our masters?"

"No."

"In that case, you broke the law."

Doggins shook his head firmly. "I cannot agree. Two hours before we set out for the slave quarter, the deputy chief minister placed his hand on my head and told me that he now regarded me as one of themselves. That means that he had raised me to the rank of honorary Saarleb. And that meant I had a right to make my own decision without consulting this council."

Pybus interrupted: "Did that mean you had a right to commit an act of war against our allies?"

"There *was* no act of war—only an act of self-defense. Milo and Ulic can tell you what happened."

Glorfin said: "Milo and Ulic have told us their story. It is your story we now wish to hear and judge."

Doggins said: "Very well. You are all aware that my entire stock of explosives was destroyed by an accident?"

A little, sharp-faced man interrupted to ask: "This was the accident that led to your promotion?"

"Yes."

"So your promotion was obtained on false pretenses?"

Doggins seemed completely unperturbed. "If you wish to put it that way, Zorab, yes."

The little man nodded. "Very well. Please go on."

"Thank you. I found myself in the position of Blaster-in-Chief without any explosives to maintain it. And at that point I made my decision to explore the barracks in the slave quarter because I knew that where there is a barracks, there is usually an armory." He looked blandly around the table. "And that was my sole motive in leading the expedition to the slave quarter. It was, I agree, an impulsive decision, but I felt I had the right to make it. I didn't believe there was any danger. If we were caught, we would reveal ourselves as servants of the beetles, and accept any punishment that they decided to impose. Everyone who came with me accepted that before we set out.

"It went seriously wrong, and I am willing to take the blame for that. And in order to escape, we had to defend ourselves against the spiders. I regret that, but it was necessary. It was my job to make sure that no more of our own people were killed. We'd lost three and I didn't intend to lose any more." He sat back in his chair, and again lowered his eyes. There was a long silence. The others looked impressed. Even Niall felt convinced, although he was aware that the force of the argument was due to the thought mirror rather than to the words that conveyed it.

Glorfin sighed. "Then it seems that our chief problem is to decide how to convince the spiders that it was not a deliberate act of war."

Zorab asked dubiously: "Do you think that is possible?"

"I don't know." Glorfin was obviously deeply troubled. "We can only try."

His eyes were resting on Niall. Corbin also looked at Niall.

"Of course, it may be necessary to begin by handing the runaway slave back to the spiders. That would show our good faith."

Doggins glared at him icily. "The Master himself refused to do that. What makes you think you can reverse his decision?" Corbin flushed and dropped his eyes.

Glorfin shook his head. "Nevertheless, we must reach some decision. We have to be realistic. At the moment, we are virtually at war with the spiders. That cannot be allowed to continue."

Doggins looked at him, smiling. "You mean you intend to throw yourself on their mercy?"

"Do you have any better suggestion?"

Niall had to admire his patience and restraint.

Doggins looked round the table. "Yes. I suggest we begin by accepting the present situation."

Glorfin—and most of the others—looked horrified. "You want us to stay at war?" He obviously thought Doggins was mad.

"No." Again Doggins looked round the table, and Niall was aware that he was using the power of the thought mirror to undermine their resistance. "I want us to make peace. But not on the same terms as before. You know that the Peace Treaty gave all the advantage to the spiders. I want us to regain that advantage." He turned towards the door and called: "Selima."

The door opened—it had evidently been prearranged and Selima came in carrying the pressure lamp. Its dazzling white light filled every corner of the room and made the tiny flames of the oil lamps seem absurd. Selima placed it in the center of the table and backed out of the room.

Pybus stared at the lamp in horror. "Are you mad? You are breaking the law."

Doggins smiled mockingly. "A law against light?"

"You know it is against the terms of the Peace Treaty."

Doggins sighed. "Then perhaps it is time we renegotiated the Peace Treaty."

Glorfin stared at him severely. "You hardly seem to understand the situation. Our problem is to persuade the spiders to make peace and . . ." He struggled to find the word.

Doggins grinned maliciously: "Forgive us?"

Glorfin said defiantly: "Yes, forgive us. We have committed a horrible offence against our allies. And you want to make it worse by trying to force them to change the treaty. That is completely out of the question." But, with Doggins' eyes on him, his voice lacked conviction.

Doggins shook his head. "I don't see why."

Corbin said irritably: "Perhaps you could explain what you have in mind?"

"Yes, with pleasure." Doggins leaned forward, his hands spread out on the tabletop. "You ask me to be realistic. Very well, I will be realistic. You are looking for ways to put back the clock. You want to return to the situation as it was a week ago. And I am telling you that is impossible. The spiders aren't going to forgive and forget. They'd be ready to make peace, of course—they don't want war any more than we do. But it wouldn't be real peace. Now they know we're dangerous, they won't rest until they've either killed us or enslaved us. They'll simply wait for another opportunity to attack us. And we'll hand them the opportunity the moment we destroy the Reapers. As soon as we do that, we're defenseless."

Glorfin was shaking his head. "They have far more reason to attack us if we *don't* destroy the Reapers."

Doggins grinned sarcastically. "More reason, perhaps. But they won't dare."

Glorfin looked shocked. "You are suggesting we should remain enemies?"

Doggins stared at him. "Let me be quite clear about what I'm suggesting." He paused, and allowed the silence to lengthen. "The spiders treat the beetles as their equals. I think it's time we persuaded them to treat us in the same way."

Pybus shrugged. "That is impossible. Do you expect them to free all their slaves and servants?"

Doggins regarded him seriously. "They don't have to—their servants think they already have freedom. But you and I know what happens when they're sent off to the great happy place, don't we?"

Pybus shook his head. "That is only a rumor."

"You mean you prefer to believe it's only a rumor. You know as well as I do that it's true."

Pybus looked unhappy; Niall could see that he was unconvinced, but was allowing himself to be swayed by Doggins' conviction.

Doggins said soothingly: "But let's not argue about that. I'm not talking about the servants of the spiders. I'm talking about us. You've all been breaking the treaty since you were five years old. You can all read and you've all got books hidden in your cellars. That's against the treaty. Wouldn't you like your grandchildren to be able to learn to read at school, instead of having to be taught in secret?"

Glorfin said firmly: "You seem to me to be exaggerating. Does it matter where we learn to read, provided we learn? Do we really want lamps like that one, when we can have as many oil lamps as we please? We already have as much freedom as we want."

Doggins said: "As *you* want."

"Yes, as I want. And as my family wants. Why can't we leave things as they are?"

Doggins' smile was conciliatory. "I agree with you. I'd like to leave things as they are—or rather, as they were. But we can't. Things have changed, and we have to recognize that." He lowered his voice and tapped the table with his fingertip. "Look. The spiders are going to have to make concessions merely in order to make peace. We've killed dozens of their people, perhaps hundreds." Glorfin winced. "According to their law, we should all be handed over to them for execution, and our wives and children as well. And even that wouldn't be enough—the spiders say that one of their lives is worth a hundred human lives. If they're going to make peace, they'll have to forget all that. So why not use the opportunity to make them change the Peace Treaty?"

There was a silence; Doggins kept his eyes on them to press his advantage. Then Glorfin looked at Niall.

"I would like to hear the opinion of our guest."

Niall was startled; he looked questioningly at Doggins, then realized with amusement that, like the others, he was beginning to treat him as a leader. He said: "I'm not sure my opinion would be of any use to you. I have spent most of my life living in a hole in the desert, hiding from the spiders. They killed my father and took my family into captivity. All I want is to see the overthrow of the spiders . . ." He was about to add: "so that men can be masters of the earth again," but he sensed that this would shock them.

"Yes, I can understand that." Glorfin looked at Doggins. "And is that what you would also like to see?"

Doggins thought carefully. "Ideally, yes. I've never liked the spiders. But I know it's not practical. So I'm only suggesting that we ask them to change the Peace Treaty."

Glorfin looked round the table. "How many of you support that view?"

Milo and Ulic raised their hands; so, to Niall's surprise, did Simeon, who had been listening to the discussion with an inscrutable expression.

Glorfin asked: "Against?"

18

The others all raised their hands. Glorfin said: "Seventeen to three." He looked at Doggins. "I'm sorry. You put your case very well. But the majority of the stadion finds it unconvincing. We shall now have to decide what action to take."

Some of the council members began to push back their chairs. Doggins said: "One moment, please." All waited. "I have a suggestion that might solve the dilemma." Again, he allowed a long pause, and Niall realized that the arts of oratory came naturally to him. "You want to persuade the spiders to forget what has happened. I believe that is impossible. In any case, I have no wish to forget. Like Niall, I believe that men should be free. I could not live here if we surrendered to the spiders. So I believe that the best solution would be for me to leave."

"Leave?" Glorfin looked as if he could hardly believe his ears.

"That's right. Leave this community and go elsewhere. I know many places overseas where we could be safe from the spiders. I'd be willing to take anyone who wanted to come with me." He smiled at Milo and Ulic.

Pybus said: "And you would also take the Reapers?"

"Of course. We'd need them to defend ourselves."

They were silent as they absorbed this startling idea. Niall could see that, as it sank in, it struck them as the ideal solution. Although they were inclined to conceal this—in case Doggins used it to his advantage—their eyes betrayed their enthusiasm. With Doggins gone, there would be no obstacle to making peace with the spiders.

Glorfin asked cautiously: "Do you wish us to consider that as a concrete proposal?"

Doggins nodded. "I do."

Glorfin rose to his feet. "Then unless someone has something further to say, I suggest we conclude this discussion until I have had a chance to speak to the Master." No one spoke. "Good—the meeting is ended." He gave Doggins a smile of genuine friendliness. "Thank you for being so candid with us."

As they left, several council members paused to shake hands with Doggins; it was obvious they felt they were saying goodbye, and experiencing sentimental regrets. Niall watched them ironically; he could see that Doggins was impatient to see the last of them.

Only Milo, Ulic, and Simeon remained behind. While Doggins was seeing the council members off the premises, Niall could sense that they were contemplating the strange and frightening prospect of leaving the community in which they had lived all their lives, and hoping secretly that some other solution could be found.

Doggins said: "Shall we move to somewhere more comfortable?"

In the room in which Niall had eaten lunch, Lucretia and two of the other women were carding flax; when the men came in, they stood up without speaking and left.

Doggins took his place in an armchair. "Simeon, you haven't said a word all evening."

Simeon grinned mirthlessly: it made his hard, old face look like wrinkled teak. "You did very well without me."

Milo said: "I don't know how you did it. They'd already made up their minds before the meeting began. Pybus wanted to order you to destroy the weapons, then hand you over to the spiders."

Doggins shrugged. "They're all fools and cowards."

Simeon said mildly: "That's not quite fair, Bildo. They *had* got a point. Think what might have happened if you hadn't found the Reapers. You might all have been killed, and our city would have been starved into submission."

Doggins said soberly: "Do you think I don't know that? When I think of what might have happened it makes my hair stand on end. But it didn't happen, and that places us in an entirely new position. And these fools on the stadion won't see that. They can't see that there's no going back."

Simeon nodded. "Which is why I have decided to join you. But that still leaves us with the main problem. Which way do we go forward?"

Doggins said: "Before we discuss that, there's something you all have to know."

At that point, the door opened; two children came in carrying trays which they placed on the table. One contained food, the other a large earthenware jug with five earthenware goblets. When Doggins tilted the jug, Niall was delighted to see that it contained the clear, golden liquid he had drunk on the boat. But as he tasted it, he was overwhelmed with sadness at the thought of Odina. Suddenly, he felt many years older.

Ulic asked: "Were you serious about going to another country?"

Doggins nodded; he was tearing at a leg of roast pheasant. "If necessary. But it may not be necessary."

Ulic's eyes gleamed with hope. "Why not?"

"Because of something I learned only just before the meeting." He turned to Niall. "Tell them."

Once again, Niall repeated his story of the white tower, and this time he also described what had happened as he lay under the peace machine. As he spoke, he felt again that strange sensation of being in two places at once: in this pleasant and comfortable room, and in the colder and yet more exciting world of reality. He experienced the overwhelming conviction that human beings live in a world of sensory illusions, but that their minds are capable of penetrating through to the objective reality behind them. He was so absorbed in this inner vision, and in his new understanding of it, that he scarcely noticed the effect he was having on his hearers. It was only when he finally stopped and moistened his dry throat that he realized he had been speaking for half an hour, and that no one had interrupted him with so much as an exclamation.

Doggins was the first to break the silence. "Now you see why I don't want to leave. We can't leave all that knowledge behind."

Simeon started, as if waking from a dream. "My grandfather used to say there was a time when men were the masters of the earth, but I thought it was just a fairy tale."

Niall regarded him curiously. "Why? The spider city proves that men were once far greater than they are now."

"True. But the beetles and spiders must also have existed in those times, and I find it hard to believe that they were once the size of my fingernail. As a doctor, I find the idea absurd."

"But the comet Opik was radioactive . . ."

Simeon nodded. "I know all about radioactivity. It might cause a few minor variations. But it wouldn't create a world full of giant insects."

Niall asked: "Then how *do* you explain it?"

Doggins interrupted impatiently: "What does it matter how we explain it? The spiders exist and we've got to decide what to do about them."

Milo said hesitantly: "May I speak?"

"Of course."

"I take it that our real aim is to gain free access to the white tower?" Doggins nodded. "In that case, we surely have no choice? We have to drive the spiders out of the city."

Doggins said: "How?"

"There are many possibilities, but the simplest way would be to use the Reapers."

Niall observed the touch of grim satisfaction in his voice as he said this; Milo was obviously thinking about his dead comrades.

Doggins said: "I agree. With the Reapers, we could blast the city into the ground in half an hour. But we'd also kill a lot of people."

In the silence that followed, the force of his objection sank home.

Ulic said: "Suppose we destroyed only the part of the city around the tower? There are few human beings in that area."

Simeon intervened. "Whatever you do, you'd have to kill a lot of human beings. The spiders would order them to attack us if we tried to invade the city."

Milo said thoughtfully: "Suppose we tried to win over the human beings? We all have many friends among them. If we explained that we only want to give them their freedom, surely they would not be foolish enough to throw away their lives?"

Niall shook his head. "That is impossible. The commanders are completely loyal to the spiders, just as you are loyal to the beetles. And the others do what they are told. They would never disobey orders."

There was a silence. Then Milo said: "In that case, we have to decide which is the most important: the death of a few human beings or the destruction of the spiders."

Simeon shook his head violently; Niall could see the idea appalled him.

Niall said: "I think there may be one other way." All looked at him. "To destroy the Death Lord himself."

Doggins frowned. "And what about all the other spiders? We'd still have to fight them."

"Not necessarily. You have seen what happens when the spiders are attacked. When they taste defeat, they panic. They are used to being the masters. If we destroyed the Spider Lord, it would be like cutting off the head of a serpent. The rest would be harmless."

He could see that they were unconvinced.

"Let me explain why I think so. When I arrived in this country a week ago, I knew nothing about the spiders, except what my grandfather Jomar had told me. He told me the legends about Vaken the Wise and Skapta the Cunning and Ivar the Strong, and how they fought against the spiders." Their expressions told him that they had never heard these names before. "And he also told me the story of the Great Betrayal—how the traitor Prince Hallat went to the Spider Lord Cheb, and offered to teach him the secrets of the human soul in exchange for Cheb's help in capturing the Princess Turool. My grandfather told me how Cheb had human prisoners brought in front of him, and how he read their minds until he knew every detail of their lives. After this, Cheb ate them because he felt that this was the only way to truly understand them.

"Now, although I failed to realize it at the time, my grandfather had given me the key to understanding the spiders. We know that eating someone doesn't help you to understand him. But the whole instinct of a spider is directed towards eating. They spend all their lives sitting in a web, waiting for food. Now the death spiders no longer have to worry about food. But they still spend their lives sitting in their webs. You see, the spiders have no *imagination*. And this is something that I failed to understand until I first encountered a spider—it was a wolf spider, in fact. I found it hard to understand how a creature can be so dangerous—in some ways so intelligent—and yet so stupid. Then, little by little, I began to understand. Spiders have never had any purpose except to catch food. So they have never had any need to develop imagination.

"That is why the life of the spiders is based on obedience. They have no imagination, so they naturally obey orders."

Simeon nodded. "I've often noticed that the spiders cannot think for themselves."

"It's not that they *can't* think for themselves. It's that they can see no reason to think for themselves. Why should they? They have a regular food supply. They have no need to be afraid of enemies. What would they think *about*?"

Doggins shook his head. "They *must* be able to think. Somebody has to organize the city."

"That is true. The Spider Lord has to think. He is like the queen in a nest of ants. He gives the orders and everyone else carries them out. But if the queen is killed, the ants are thrown into confusion. And if we killed the Spider Lord, the same thing would happen to the spiders."

They looked at one another and at Niall. Doggins said finally: "You could be right." It was clear that he was still troubled by doubts.

Milo's eyes reflected his excitement. "I think he's right."

Simeon said: "But would we be right if we killed the Spider Lord? In the long run, no one can benefit by an act of treachery. And while there is no official state of war between the beetles and the spiders, any attempt to kill the Spider Lord *would* be an act of treachery."

Niall asked: "And was it not an act of treachery when the Spider Lord tried to kill me?"

"Of course. But two acts of treachery do not cancel one another out."

"But would you agree that it gives me the right to try and kill the Spider Lord?"

Simeon frowned and took a deep breath. "Yes, I suppose it does."

Niall said: "Then why not leave me to decide what should be done?"

"You'd do it alone?"

"If necessary."

Milo interrupted: "This is wrong! We would be guilty of cowardice if we allowed Niall to act alone. I, for one, am willing to help him."

Ulic said: "So am I."

Doggins interposed soothingly: "Let's not argue about it. We don't have to make a decision tonight, do we?" He laid his hand on Milo's shoulder. "Let's wait and see what happens. If I'm not mistaken, the spiders will make the next move. We can afford to wait." Milo smiled, deferring to the older man's authority; but he was obviously unhappy about it. Doggins squeezed his arm. "Don't worry, you'll get your opportunity to fight the spiders."

"I hope so."

Doggins reached for the jug and refilled their cups. "Let's drink to it." They raised their cups. "To the destruction of the spiders."

But although Niall raised his cup to his lips, he made no attempt to drink. The smell of the liquid reminded him of Odina, and he experienced sudden revulsion at the thought of associating her memory with the idea of destruction.

In the early hours of the morning, Niall had an appalling nightmare. He was alone in the spider city; it was night and he was on his way to kill the Spider Lord. As he crossed the square towards the headquarters of the Death Lord, he held the Reaper in front of him, his finger on the trigger. But the square was deserted and there were no guards on the door. When he kicked the door, it flew open; the hall beyond was empty. Keeping his back pressed against the wall in case of a sudden attack, he mounted the stair. Everything was silent. On the third floor, he felt the soft carpet under his feet, and found himself facing the black, leather-covered door that led into the hall of the Death Lord. He approached it cautiously, convinced that it was a trap. He listened outside; there was no sound. Then he kicked open the door and pulled the trigger of the Reaper. As he did so, he realized with a shock that he was firing at his brother Veig. It was too late; Veig's body dissolved into a blue mist. There was a cry of despair, and his mother came running out of the shadows, shouting, "What have you done?"

Niall woke up with a shock; his heart was beating hard and he was covered in perspiration. It was an immense relief to realize that he had been dreaming. He pushed back the blankets and sat up, fighting off a choking sense of despair and guilt. As his senses returned, he began to feel better. But the dream had puzzled and frightened him. Why should he dream of destroying his own brother?

The room was dark. Long curtains had been drawn, covering the outside walls from floor to ceiling. But through the circular window he could see the gray light of dawn in the sky. He sat staring at it, emptying his mind of all thought and feeling until his breathing returned to normal. Then he deliberately concentrated his mind, inducing that glowing point of light inside his brain; for a moment, the room became strangely silent. He relaxed so suddenly that it was as if a trapdoor had opened under his feet.

It was as he was sinking into this effortless calm that he noticed the shadow that had appeared between himself and the lightening sky. It sloped across the circular windowpane at an angle of forty-five degrees, like the branch of a tree. He stared at it curiously and without alarm, trying to determine precisely what it was. The window opened on pivots at the top and bottom, and stood slightly ajar. As he watched, there was a faint creaking noise as it opened further; then he saw that the branch-like shadow was moving. With mild astonishment, he realized that it was some large insect, like a caterpillar, and that it was crawling in through the widest point of the open window. But, for a caterpillar, it seemed surprisingly long. Then something about the wriggling motion struck him as familiar, and he realized that it was a millipede or centipede.

In the total silence, he could hear the brushing of its body against the window frame. It was so long that, as its tail finally wriggled through the gap, its head must have been close to the floor. A moment later he heard the soft impact as it lost its grip on the wall and landed on the carpet.

It was only now, when he could no longer see it, that he experienced a sense of danger. Quietly, he reached out and placed his hand on his tunic, which lay on the chair beside the bed. Underneath it, he could feel the hard outline of the telescopic rod. As his hand gripped the cold metal he was surprised at the electrical tingle that ran through his fingers. With the solid metal tube in his hand, he ceased to feel vulnerable.

He could hear the slight rustling movement as the centipede crossed the floor. For a moment he was afraid that it would disappear under the bed, forcing him to search for it; then a faint tug at the bedclothes told him that it was climbing upward. He stared intently at the foot of the bed, watching for the first sign of movement.

It was only when something brushed his foot that he realized it had crawled inside the coverlet. His instant reaction was to withdraw his feet and scramble into a sitting position on the pillow. Then, as he saw the movement of the coverlet, he struck again and again with all his force. The coverlet rose as the creature thrashed in agony; Niall held it down with one hand while he continued to strike with clenched teeth. The tail, which was still unencumbered by the blanket, twisted upward and struck him on the head; but he ignored it. He knew that the centipede's poison, like that of a spider, is contained in venomous claws just behind the head. With each blow he could feel the yielding of the soft body. Yet the creature seemed to be surprisingly strong, writhing like a snake. He went on beating frantically until the tail collapsed onto the floor; the coverlet was so wet with blood that it covered both his hands.

In spite of his excitement, he was feeling strangely cold, as if the temperature in the room had dropped to zero. His teeth were chattering as he climbed off the bed and stood upright on the carpeted floor. Softly, afraid of awakening the rest of the household, he drew back the curtains; pale morning sunlight streamed through the blue-tinted walls. With the cylinder raised above his head, he drew back the coverlet with his left hand, then jumped back as the blood-soaked body gave a violent jerk. A moment later it collapsed and he realized that this was a purely reflex movement.

He pressed the button that caused the rod to expand, and cautiously poked the dead centipede. Then he pulled the bed covers onto the floor and used the rod to lift the broken body clear of the bed. As it hung there, he could see that it was a gray-green centipede with black bands. It was about as thick as a child's forearm and more than four feet long. The legs, like plump fingers, were spread out on either side of the body; the long jointed antennae had both been broken by his blows. It was these that had brushed his foot and given him warning. Drops of clear-colored venom dripped from the fangs and fell on the bed. He pushed open the window and dropped the centipede out onto the flowerbed.

Quite suddenly the room was no longer cold. He felt strangely tired—so much so that, if the bed had not been covered in blood, he would have climbed back into it and fallen asleep. Instead, he pulled on his tunic and pushed his feet into sandals. Then he tiptoed out into the corridor. He knew that Doggins' bedroom was next to his own. Very slowly, he raised the wooden latch and pushed open the door. The room was in almost total darkness, but when his eyes became accustomed to the gloom, he could see that Doggins was sleeping alone. Niall shook him softly by the shoulder. Doggins woke with a start. Niall said: "Something's happened."

Without a word, Doggins clambered out of bed, struggled into his tunic, and followed Niall back to his own bedroom. He closed the door carefully behind them. When he saw the bloodstained bed he gave an exclamation of astonishment. "What was it?"

Niall took him to the window and showed him the dead centipede lying among the snapdragons. He described briefly what had happened.

Doggins said: "We've got to get rid of it before the others wake up—especially the children. Get those bedclothes off the bed . . ."

He went out and returned a few minutes later with an armful of sheets and blankets. The bloodstained bedclothes already lay on the floor. Fortunately, the blood had made only a small stain on the flock mattress; together, they turned this upside down. Then, as Niall remade the bed, Doggins vanished with the bloodstained sheets. Soon afterwards, Niall saw him outside the window, lifting the dead centipede with a pair of wooden tongs. Ten minutes later, billowing clouds of woodsmoke blowing past the window indicated that the incinerator behind the house was in operation.

When Doggins came back, Niall was cleaning the blood off the telescopic rod.

Doggins said: "Don't mention this to the women."

"Of course not. But how can we be sure that it didn't wander in by accident?"

"No. It was a messenger from the Spider Lord."

"How can you tell?"

"It was a hunting centipede. The spiders breed them to hunt wild rabbits in the foothills—they put them down the hole to drive the rabbits out. But that's the biggest I've ever seen. You'd better sleep with your window closed from now on."

"I ought to leave your house. The others might be in danger."

"We'll talk about that later. Get some sleep."

But now he was no longer feeling tired. When Doggins had gone, Niall climbed back into bed and hung the thought mirror round his neck. He immediately experienced a flash of pain that seemed to divide his skull like a hatchet blow. It was so intense that he had to clench his teeth and place both hands over his eyes. After a few seconds, it became a headache that throbbed in the back of his head. He resisted the temptation to remove the thought mirror, and tried to accept the pain and to merge with it, as if it was as natural as pleasure. As he did this, he made an interesting discovery: the thought mirror could provide the concentration to resist the pain that it caused. When he concentrated, the pain increased, but so did his power to fight against it. This pain, he now understood, was due to physical exhaustion; the attack of the Spider Lord had drained his vital energies. Yet there was also a curious satisfaction in defying his own fatigue. As he increased his concentration, the pain became so agonizing that he felt droplets of sweat running down his face, and his pulse beat inside his skull like a hammer. But, underlying the discomfort, there was a sense of power and exultation.

Then, at a certain point, the pain itself became an ally, increasing his ability to focus. It was not unlike squeezing a handful of broken glass and deliberately trying to crush it into a powder. He sat with his fists clenched, his eyes screwed up to exclude the light. Quite suddenly, he was in control of the pain; it was a curious sensation, as if he was pushing himself up from the ground with a heavy weight on his back. One more convulsive effort of will and he was standing upright, swaying slightly, and astonished to find himself in this unusual position, as an animal might feel if it succeeded in standing on its hind legs.

He opened his eyes and looked around him. The room seemed unchanged; yet, in another sense, it had become quite different. His concentration had achieved an intensity that he had never experienced before. Everything he looked at seemed deeply interesting; even the wooden latch on the door was so fascinating that he felt he could stare at it for hours, exploring its possibilities. It seemed self-evident that every object in the room concealed a thousand meanings that he normally overlooked.

He had never been so conscious of his freedom. He was aware that he could *choose* what to do with his mind—whether to think about his past life, about the problem of the spiders, or whether to simply allow himself to explore this strange, exciting world that surrounded him. Now he could see quite clearly that our human senses are blocked by curtains, and that it was within his power to open or close them as he wished. When he focused his attention to admit more light, he experienced an excitement that was like a breeze blowing against his face. This soon expanded into a feeling of almost magical sensitivity. He could see that the branches of the tree outside the window were responding to the dawn wind like a cat purring with pleasure, and that the leaves were not merely rustling, but were speaking a language of their own.

As the sun rose, he was intrigued by a curious distant sound that seemed to rise and fall on the breeze. It was a faint ringing noise, which might have been compared to the ringing of a million tiny bells. He went to the window and pushed it open. Then he realized that it was not a sound, but some kind of vibration that seemed to be induced in the flowers by the sunlight. They were throwing off a sparkling shower of energy, which surged out of them like sparks from a firework, and then rained gently down to the earth. It was an astonishing sight. Many of the flowers were still in the shade, and these were throwing off only a few random sparks of energy. As the sun reached them, this turned into a soft rain, like water from a fountain; then, as the full light of the sun fell on their open petals, the sparks became more energetic, and blazed upward so that the air above the flower bed was a glittering mass of colored light.

The grass of the lawn was giving off a gentler, softer vibration, and seemed to be covered in blue mist. As his eyes became accustomed to this, he was interested to see that the tall red houses of the beetles were surrounded by the same blue color, whose outlines moved like a slow burning flame. Now he could see that the purpose of the spiral design was to prevent this energy from flowing directly upward and dissipating itself in the atmosphere; by forcing it to flow into a spiral that was closed at the top, the houses were given more time to absorb this living current.

By comparison, the human dwellings seemed somehow lifeless and sterile. Some of the energy was absorbed by the blue walls, but most of it was simply reflected back and lost in the atmosphere.

As he turned away from the window, he experienced a momentary dizziness, and had to lean back against the wall. His body was unaccustomed to this richness of sensation and his senses were flagging. With a deliberate movement of his will, he drew the inner curtains to block out the intensity. The ringing sound immediately faded away and the room became silent. A feeling of relief was succeeded by deep weariness. He walked back to the bed with heavy steps, like a drunken man, removed the thought mirror, and lay down on his back. Then a wave of deep peace washed over him and carried him into sleep.

When he opened his eyes, there was a tray of food on the chair beside the bed, and the sun was high in the heavens. As he ate the white bread with honeycomb, and drank cold milk, a sense of well-being told him that his strength was beginning to return.

The door opened a few inches and Simeon looked in. "Ah, you're awake. Are you all right?" He took Niall's wrist and felt his pulse.

"Much better now."

He laid his hand on Niall's forehead. "You feel better. But I think you'd better stay in bed for another day."

Niall said: "That's impossible. I must leave here today."

Simeon looked at him with amazement. "Leave? What are you talking about?"

"Hasn't Doggins told you what happened?"

"I haven't seen him today—he's in the town hall."

As Niall described how he killed the centipede, Simeon's face became grim.

"Was it gray with black bands?"

"Yes."

"That's a hunting centipede all right. Their venom could kill an elephant. You were lucky."

"I might not be so lucky next time. Or it might get into one of the children's bedrooms. That's why I can't stay here."

Simeon shook his head. "You don't have to worry about that. It wouldn't attack anyone but you."

"How do you know?"

"They hunt by vibrations. It's like a very fine sense of smell."

"But how would it know my vibrations?"

"That's something I don't understand. I'm told there used to be an animal called a bloodhound. It could track anybody down once it had been given a sniff of something that belonged to him. These hunting centipedes can do the same kind of thing. But I don't know how they pick up the scent in the first place—perhaps by some form of telepathy."

"So I have to sleep with the doors and windows closed?"

Simeon smiled suddenly. "I don't think that will be necessary." He stood up. "I think I can give you something to solve the problem. Finish your breakfast."

When Simeon returned ten minutes later, he was carrying a large wooden plant pot; the plant was concealed by sacking. He placed it under the window, then removed the sack. Niall stared with curiosity at the bright green plant whose sinuous tendrils seemed to be drooping with exhaustion. The plant was about five feet high, and it had a peculiar but not unpleasant smell, sweet and slightly medicinal. Apart from the tendrils, there were also fleshy yellow-green stalks, each one surmounted by a yellowish head; the shape reminded Niall of the head of a snake. Niall leaned down to look more closely, then jumped back with an exclamation. Some of the green tendrils had moved towards him, like the pseudopods of a squid fungus.

Simeon laughed. "They're quite harmless to human beings." He reached out towards the plant; one of the tendrils moved hesitantly, then curled round his finger, as if caressing it.

"What is it called?"

"I don't know. My wife used to call it the viperweed. We brought the seeds back from the Delta. Watch."

From his pocket Simeon took a large pillbox; a buzzing sound revealed that it imprisoned a fly. Making sure that the door was closed, Simeon removed the lid. The fly, a shining green bluebottle with a two-inch wingspan, immediately buzzed up to the ceiling. For a few seconds, it flew furiously around the room, bumping into the walls. Then, at last, it detected the breeze from the window and flew towards it. What happened next was so swift that Niall was unable to follow it. The plant moved with the speed of a striking snake, and the fly vanished. Only a frantic and muffled buzz revealed that it was now inside one of the snake-like heads. The buzzing ceased almost immediately.

Simeon looked at it with a proprietary smile. "They're fascinating little things. With one of those near the window, you never have an insect in your house. Look."

From his pocket he took another pillbox; he removed the lid and inverted it on the floor. A brown dung beetle fell out on to its back; Simeon turned it over with his fingertip. "No, not that way." He prodded the beetle until it walked towards the plant. While it was still more than two feet away, one of the green tendrils swooped down on it, and a second later the bewildered dung beetle was being lifted through the air, the end of the tendril coiled round its midriff like a python. It raised the beetle up to the head of the nearest stalk. This time, Niall was watching so closely that he was able to see what happened. The top of the head split open, revealing what looked like two rows of pointed white teeth. The tendril seemed to flick the beetle into the open mouth with a movement like a whiplash. Instantly the mouth closed, although a slight movement of the green skin revealed that the beetle was struggling frantically. Then, once again, the tendril drooped, and the whole plant became so totally immobile that it looked incapable of movement.

Niall said: "Do you think it could stop a four-foot centipede?"

"Certainly. I've seen it eat a large rat."

Niall stared at it with morbid fascination.

"Would it be dangerous to a human being?"

"In the Delta, perhaps. Not here."

"Why in the Delta?"

"They grow to four times the size there."

"Why?"

Simeon shrugged. "The soil, perhaps. The place is seething and swarming with life, like a cheese with maggots. It's as if nature had gone mad." He gave the plant an affectionate pat. "But they're quite pleasant creatures once you get used to them."

When he had gone, Niall went and stood close to the plant. It cost him an effort not to flinch as the snake-like heads moved towards him and the tendrils reached out and caressed his legs. It was a strange sensation, like being sniffed by some curious animal. After a few minutes, the plant seemed to lose interest and once again became immobile. But when Niall reached out and scratched one of the heads, it seemed to press itself against his hand. There was something about this movement that Niall found deeply disturbing and puzzling, although he found it hard to pinpoint the source of his disquiet.

He was aroused from these reflections by the sound of metal-rimmed wheels on gravel. Out of the window he could see a cart drawn by four charioteers which came into the square at a brisk trot and halted in front of the town hall. The cart contained two people: a woman in the black uniform of a guard commander and a blond-bearded man who wore the yellow tunic of the beetle servants. As Niall watched, they mounted the steps and disappeared into the town hall. The charioteers pulled their cart into the shade and sat down on the steps, mopping their foreheads.

Niall left the house by a side door and crossed the grass towards them. As he came closer he realized, to his delight, that one of the charioteers was Massig. Massig recognized Niall at the same moment and jumped to his feet, staring with open-mouthed astonishment.

"What are you doing here? I thought you were dead!"

Niall laughed. "You can see I'm not. Where did you hear that?"

"From one of Kazak's charioteers. He said you'd died with the king."

"So Kazak is dead?"

"Yes, he died in the explosion."

Niall experienced a twinge of sadness. In spite of a certain feeling of mistrust, he had always liked Kazak.

They sat down together on the step. Niall asked: "Who was that bearded man you brought?"

"That was Captain Manetho. He sailed in this morning with a cargo of explosives."

Niall lowered his voice. "The spiders didn't try to detain him?"

"Detain him?" Massig looked puzzled. "Why should they?"

Niall shrugged. "The beetles seem to think the spiders want to pick a quarrel."

Massig shook his head. "That's the first I've heard of it."

"Were the spiders very angry about the explosion?"

"Angry?" Massig obviously felt that Niall was speaking in riddles. "Why should they be? It was an accident." He gave Niall an odd look. "Wasn't it?"

Niall said quickly: "Oh, yes, I imagine so."

At that moment, to Niall's relief, they were interrupted by a girl who came out of the town hall; she was carrying a tray with refreshments for the charioteers. While Massig was drinking deeply from an earthenware vessel full of fruit juice, Niall seized the opportunity to slip away.

He stepped into the cool twilight of the town hall. It was full of beetles and human beings hurrying about their business. As he stood there, waiting for his eyes to adjust to the dimness, someone slapped him on the shoulder. It was Milo.

"Hello, Niall. You're too late for the meeting of the stadion—it's just finished."

"What happened?"

Milo leaned forward and said in a low voice: "They backed down, just as I expected."

"Why?"

"The story got around that they were forcing Bildo to leave our city. You know many people regard him as a hero. So half the young people announced they'd go with him if he went away. That made the stadion think twice . . ."

"So what will happen now?"

"I don't know. That depends on Bildo. Why don't you ask him yourself—he's over there."

On the far side of the hallway, Doggins was deep in conversation with the blond-bearded man. When he saw Niall, he broke off.

"We were just talking about you. This is Manetho, my chief mining engineer."

Manetho and Niall clasped forearms. Manetho was a squarely built young man with a broad, good-tempered face that was reddened by the sun and wind. He had immense, muscular arms. Niall took an instant liking to him.

Doggins said: "Manetho sailed into port this morning. He's been away for the past three weeks."

Niall asked Manetho: "Did you have any trouble with the spiders?"

The young man grinned. "Not a bit. I didn't even guess there was anything wrong. They detailed a squad to help me unload and sent me back here in a chariot. Now the cap'n tells me we're supposed to be at war with them."

Doggins shook his head. "I don't know what's supposed to be happening. I'm not even sure that I want to." He placed his hand on Manetho's shoulder. "You go and report to Mostig, then get yourself a meal. After that, come over to my house."

A s they emerged into the sunlight, Niall saw half a dozen members of the stadion, including Pybus and Corbin, standing in a circle, obviously engaged in a heated discussion. The hostile glances they cast at Niall and Doggins revealed that they were the subject of the conversation.

Doggins took Niall's arm. "Feel like a walk?"

"Of course."

He led Niall behind the town hall to the road that led out towards the quarry. Many people greeted Doggins, who was obviously a popular figure; even beetles saluted him respectfully. But Doggins responded with an air of abstraction; he was obviously worried. It was not until they were alone, beyond the last of the houses, that he finally spoke.

"It's worse than I thought. The spiders are sending two ambassadors to meet the Master and the full council. That means they're determined to make peace."

"Is that so bad?"

"Bad?" Doggins stared at him in amazement. "It's a bloody disaster. It means they're going to order us to destroy the Reapers."

"What makes you so sure of that?"

"It's common sense. They allowed Manetho to come through the port without any trouble. In the spider city, he saw the results of the explosion—it's flattened half the slave quarter—but they told him it was an accident. Nobody even mentioned our raid on the barracks. That means they're trying to show us they want to forgive and forget. Their ambassadors are going to say: Everything is back to normal, so let's discuss our disagreements."

"Perhaps they really want peace." Niall was surprised by his own words; they seemed to have emerged without his volition.

Doggins snorted. "Of course they want peace—on their terms. They'll try and persuade the Master to order the destruction of the Reapers and to hand you over."

"They may not want me handed over. I've just talked to one of the charioteers and he says everyone thinks I'm dead."

"What?" Doggins looked at him sharply. "Did he tell you why?"

"He said he'd heard it from one of Kazak's charioteers."

Doggins frowned, biting his lip. "That's interesting. So the Spider Lord thought he'd succeeded in strangling you the other day. But he wouldn't have tried again today unless he'd discovered that he'd failed. That means he knows the beetles won't hand you over and he's determined to get rid of you any way he can. . . . And that can only mean one thing—his main demand is going to be the destruction of the Reapers."

"But surely the Master wouldn't agree to that?"

Doggins shrugged. "He's a wise old bird, but I don't think he even begins to understand the crawlies. He assumes everybody's as decent as he is." He lowered his voice, although it was obviously unnecessary. "Between you and me, I've never understood how anyone so wise can be so stupid."

These words aroused in Niall a sudden insight, accompanied by a curious sense of excitement. It was the recognition that there were certain matters upon which Doggins was completely blind. This blindness made him an admirable servant, for it enabled him to concentrate his full attention on practical problems. But it meant that he would never even suspect the existence of a world in which trees enjoyed the caress of the wind, and flowers threw off sparks of living energy.

They had arrived at the top of a low hill. The grass on its far slope was brown and withered, and beyond that, there was no grass—only blackened earth. This was the area that Doggins had blasted with his Reaper. A few yards down the slope there was an object that looked like a large boulder; on closer inspection, Niall saw that it was a dead spider, lying on its back, its legs bunched up on its stomach. He touched it with the tip of his sandal; the charred flesh felt like wood.

They walked a dozen yards further across the hard-baked earth. Then, suddenly, the ground at their feet seemed to disappear; they were standing on the edge of a sharp drop, about twelve feet deep, which extended for hundreds of yards on either side of them. At first Niall took it for some natural feature; then, when he saw melted rocks, realized that it had been caused by the blast of the Reaper. It had literally vaporized the earth, as easily as it might have melted ice.

For the first time, Niall understood the terrifying destructive power of the Reapers. He drew a deep breath. "No wonder they're afraid of us."

Doggins said grimly: "You know what the crawlies are like. Do you think they'll be in a hurry to forget this?"

They walked along the edge of the depression. Niall was astonished and shaken at the sheer size of the devastated area; it was at least half a mile in diameter. It was easy to gauge the precise position of the balloon when Doggins had pulled the trigger; the blast had struck the ground like some immense jet of water, cutting a deep valley for several hundred yards from the point of impact. Then, like a jet from a hosepipe, it had spread out sideways, hurling a wall of rocks and loose earth in front of it. Everything around the point of impact had been destroyed or completely vaporized while further away, the sheer force of the blast had preserved objects by driving them like leaves before a gale. In this area, bodies of spiders lay among uprooted trees and fragments of rock. There was an unpleasant smell of decaying flesh in the air.

As they walked around the circumference of this area of charred earth, neither of them spoke. It was Doggins who finally expressed the thought that preoccupied them both. He pointed towards the buildings of the spider city on the southern horizon.

"Just one Reaper could destroy that place in less than a minute."

"And all the human beings in it."

Doggins glanced sideways at him. "Almost worth it, wouldn't you say?"

"No. My family happens to be among them."

Doggins shrugged. "Oh, I wasn't serious. Just a thought . . ."

Niall's foot slipped on something soft. It was a small squid fungus which had been squashed flat by his sandal. He gave an exclamation of disgust. Then, for the first time, they both noticed that there were dozens of the creatures crawling towards them like gray slugs. One of them reached Niall's ankle and extended its gray tentacles to try to climb on his foot. He kicked it away.

"Strange. I wonder where they came from?"

Doggins pointed. "They're attracted by the dead spiders."

It was true. A dozen yards away there was the decaying corpse of a spider, the entrails protruding like balloons from the open belly; hordes of tiny squid funguses were feeding on the flesh like an army of grubs.

Niall kicked away a fungus that was trying to crawl up his leg. They made a wide circuit around the dead spider, and the funguses that had been crawling towards them seemed to lose interest. As they drew close to the point where they had started, Niall paused to look at a charred, rock-like corpse that lay on its back. For a moment, his eyes had deceived him into thinking that it was trying to turn over. A moment later, another movement made them halt again. The body had undoubtedly given a faint jerk. Then, as they both watched intently, a split appeared in the belly. It opened slowly like a wound and a squid fungus crawled out, dragging a fragment of entrail behind it. Doggins grimaced and started to walk on.

Niall said: "Wait a moment." He walked slowly round the blackened corpse, trying not to breathe in the stench.

Doggins stared unbelievingly. "What on earth are you doing?"

"I can't understand how it got in." He gave the body a heave with his foot, and half-turned it over; the back was shiny, like burnt wood.

"Through its mouth."

"Impossible." Niall pointed. In fact, the spider's jaws were locked in the agony of death.

Doggins grinned. "Maybe the other end."

Niall suddenly experienced a prickling sensation in his scalp; the idea that flashed into his mind seemed so absurd that he felt reluctant to put it into words. He said finally: "I wonder if it's possible . . . that the spiders are turning into squid funguses?"

"Doesn't sound likely to me."

Making a conscious effort to suppress his disgust, Niall peered into the open belly. Now he could see that the impression of seething movement was due to thousands of tiny creatures like maggots; but when he looked more closely, he could see that each one was a tiny squid fungus. Some of these—the larger ones—were attacking the others and apparently eating them. And the attackers were growing so fast that they were expanding in size as he looked at them.

The largest of the funguses was roaming over the backs of its fellows like some brooding monster and as it moved on, it left an empty space on the gray intestines which was quickly covered again with smaller squids. In less than five minutes, the fungus had increased in size until it was as large as the palm of his hand.

Niall pointed. "Look. It's absorbing them like one raindrop absorbing another."

Doggins gave him an odd look and shrugged. "What difference does it make?"

"It means they must be made of the same substance."

The cannibal fungus had started to heave its way out of the belly; both watched with a mixture of disgust and fascination. It made straight for Doggins and tried to crawl onto his sandaled foot. He kicked it away violently, but his foot sank into it and it clung to his toes. He brushed it off with his other foot. Again it tried to return.

Niall said, laughing: "You don't have to kick it. Order it to go away. Use the thought mirror."

"How?"

"Look, turn this side inward. Concentrate your mind. Then use the other side to direct your energy outward. That's what it's for."

Doggins held the mirror in his hand and turned it over.

"Concentrate—as you did on the glue flies."

Doggins stared at the fungus and a furrow appeared between his eyebrows. He shook his head. "It doesn't seem to work."

"That's because you're not doing it properly. Gather your energies *inside* you. Then project them outward."

Again, Doggins frowned with a kind of concentrated fury. Niall could see that he was failing to grasp the potentialities of the thought mirror. Instead of using the subtle energies of the heart and solar plexus, he was trying to use the crude force of his brain, exactly as if he was holding a Reaper. He reminded Niall of a man shouting at the top of his voice.

The fungus was still crawling towards Doggins' foot and he was forced to step backwards. Then, suddenly, the fungus halted. It tried to move forward, reaching out with its pseudopodia; again Doggins frowned and it halted. A look of delight appeared on Doggins' face. "It worked."

He scowled at the fungus and after a moment it began to move away. Doggins made a visible effort of concentration, and it halted, then moved towards him. Doggins shook his head. "That's unbelievable!"

He bent until his face was within two feet of the fungus, evidently under the impression that this would somehow increase the power he was exerting. At first nothing happened; then the squid began to push itself up on two pseudopods, as if trying to stand upright.

Doggins grinned. "I'm trying to make it turn over. Oh, no you don't!"

He frowned at the squid in time to stop it from moving away. He touched the thought mirror with his fingertips: "You know, with enough of these things, we wouldn't need the Reapers. We could beat the spiders at their own game." Niall could sense his excitement.

The squid was now moving away fast. Doggins followed it, frowning. It halted. Then, once again, it began to move away, this time with unusual speed.

Doggins looked puzzled. "What the hell happened there?"

"Why?"

"It didn't work." He frowned again, standing over the fungus; again it halted, then moved on again. "I can make it stop, then it seems to change its mind. . . . I must be getting tired." He looked suspiciously at Niall. "Are you doing it?"

Niall shook his head. "It's not me. It's the force."

"What force?"

"I don't know what it is. But it's some underground force that seems to control the squid funguses." When Doggins looked at him blankly, Niall said, "Can't you feel it? That's what's making it resist you."

"I can feel something . . ." Doggins took several strides until he was ahead of the fungus, then went down on his hands and knees. He scowled at it with the look of a demented gargoyle. The fungus started to move away, then halted. Then again, it began to slither away. Doggins screwed up his face until the veins stood out on his forehead and his eyes were almost closed. Suddenly, the fungus began to move back towards him. His face relaxed into a smile.

"That's better!" He turned to Niall. "Now it's stopped resisting."

"Yes. The force seems to give up after a while."

"How did you find out about this force?"

"I felt it the other night when that fungus was eating poor Cyprian."

Doggins made the fungus turn over on its back where it lay helplessly, its pseudopodia writhing. With an effort, it finally succeeded in turning itself over again. Doggins made it turn back again. It was obvious that he was delighted with his new-found power. He said thoughtfully: "I'd like to know more about this force."

Niall shrugged. "It seems to spread out like ripples on a pond. Haven't you ever heard of it before?"

"No." As the squid struggled upright again, he made it turn over. "Although Simeon's wife used to talk about something of the sort."

Niall asked eagerly: "What did she say?"

"I don't know. I never paid much attention."

"Can we go and ask her?"

"Unfortunately no. She's dead." His eyes widened. "Hello, what's happening now?"

Like an army of ants, squid funguses were suddenly converging on them from all directions. There was nothing menacing about their movement; they seemed to be impelled by curiosity. But it was clear to Niall that, if they stayed where they were, they would both be overwhelmed by sheer numbers. He said: "Let's go."

But as soon as they began to stride towards the hillock from which they had started, the funguses moved faster. Their speed was astonishing; they seemed to move over the ground like a gray tide. Soon they were surrounded by funguses on three sides. As they started to run, the gray tide flowed in towards their feet. A moment later they felt the soft bodies squelching under their sandals. Doggins slipped and fell forward on his hands; within moments squid funguses had covered both hands, and were moving swiftly up his arms. He shouted with anger and disgust, and began brushing them off; they left small red marks behind. Niall halted for a moment, and in this time the funguses began crawling up his legs; they felt cold and soft, like a slimy caress.

Both of them began to run towards the line of scorched grass that marked the limit of the devastation. Ahead of them lay the almost vertical bank that had been carved out of the earth by Doggins' Reaper; they tried to scramble up, but slipped back. Doggins began plucking frantically at the squids that now covered his arms and shoulders. Fifty yards to their right, the bank was less steep. They ran towards it, slipping on the soft bodies. A few more strides carried them beyond the tide of squids; Niall gained the top of the bank with a headlong rush, then turned and helped Doggins. He saw, to his relief, that the squids had halted at the foot of the slope and were making no effort to climb it.

Doggins had succeeded in pulling off most of the funguses and trampled them violently underfoot. Niall preferred to use the power of his mind; one intense burst of concentration caused the gray bodies to retreat down his legs, leaving shining trails behind them.

Doggins began to scrub off the slimy deposit with handfuls of withered grass; he was cursing with disgust. "Filthy creatures. I wish I'd brought the Reaper."

"You've got the thought mirror."

"True." He suddenly became cheerful again. "But it's not as fast." He looked down at the army of funguses; they were beginning to drift back towards the dead spiders. "I wonder what made them attack us?"

"The force. It doesn't like being overruled."

"But what is it?"

"Your guess is as good as mine."

As they walked back towards the town, Doggins was silent and thoughtful. He asked Niall finally: "You say you noticed this force when that fungus was eating Cyprian?"

"Yes."

"How?"

"I could feel it."

"And can you feel it now?"

"I could if I made myself relax deeply enough."

"Is it some kind of willpower?"

"I don't think so. Not exactly."

"Could it be due to the Spider Lord?"

He shook his head. "No. It's too strong."

"But suppose the spiders did it with MRI?" Niall looked at him blankly. "You don't know about MRI? Multiple reinforcement interaction? That's how the beetles kept the spiders from invading the town. They can lock their wills together to form a kind of barrier."

"And can the spiders do it, too?"

"Of course. But the defenders have the advantage. The only way to break the barrier is to break the will of the defenders."

"You mean that a group of spiders—or beetles—could exert more willpower than one alone?"

"Oh yes, far more—a hundred times more." He took out the thought mirror and held it in the palm of his hand. "Men could do the same if they had enough of these."

They were now passing the house that was being constructed by the glue flies. Their bright gold bodies, tinged with a faint sheen of pink, covered its upper half with a dazzling cloud. At close quarters, their buzzing was almost deafening. They halted inside the earth bank, and Doggins stared at the flies, his forehead wrinkling in a frown of concentration. The effect was startling. The buzzing ceased immediately, bringing a strange silence. Then the golden bodies of the glue flies began to rain down like hail at the foot of the half-built wall. Others settled on the walls, then fell off, or blundered into one another. Doggins stared with astonishment.

"This thing's more powerful than I thought."

They hurried across the grass. At close quarters it was clear that the flies were only stunned; they were already moving groggily. Doggins stirred some of them with his foot.

Niall said: "Why don't you see if you can wake them up?"

"All right." Doggins concentrated, wrinkling his nose and forehead. Then he leapt backwards as a swarm of glue flies buzzed up from the ground, some of them flying under the skirts of his tunic. Doggins began slapping his legs and cursing.

Niall found it hard to control his laughter. "Don't kill them. Order them to go away."

Doggins concentrated again, and half a dozen bewildered flies blundered out from under his garments. He grinned at Niall, looking like a delighted schoolboy. "This thing's amazing. And to think it's been sitting in the museum for all these years . . ."

He made the flies return to the top of the building, and hover round it in a dense but silent cloud. His power obviously astonished him. He made them settle on the walls, then vanish inside the half-built house. Then, becoming more ambitious, he made the flies form into a swarm like a comet's tail and circle around the house in a glittering spiral.

Watching him, Niall was again aware that he was failing to make full use of the thought mirror. He held it in his hand and turned it from side to side, as if directing its energy beam. And instead of using its concave surface to concentrate his inner powers, he was using a crude, aggressive will-force that came from the head. The power he was able to exert by this method was impressive, but the effort was obviously exhausting; Doggins' face was soon covered with a film of sweat. Niall's impulse to explain all this was checked by an instinctive realization that it would be a mistake; Doggins would feel he was being patronizing.

There was something else that intrigued Niall. In spite of the direct contact between his own will and that of the glue flies, Doggins seemed unaware that he was driving them to exhaustion. Entranced by his power to control them, he was making them fly faster and faster, until they looked like a ring of gold-colored smoke, circling the house in complex gyrations like some aerial ballet. At any moment, Niall expected him to stop and allow the flies to resettle on the walls; instead, like a man in the grip of some intense pleasure, Doggins continued to concentrate, increasing his own effort as the flies became exhausted. As Niall was about to interrupt, he was checked by the light of sheer joy in Doggins' eyes.

Quite suddenly the golden spiral dissolved; once again bodies rained down on the ground. Doggins looked puzzled and hurt, like a child whose toy has broken. He went over to the flies and stirred them with his foot.

Niall said: "I'm afraid they're dead."

Doggins muttered: "Damn."

"Can you get more flies?"

"Of course. We breed them." He shrugged and turned away. "But what we really need are more of these." He gave the thought mirror an affectionate pat and dropped it back inside his shirt.

They were halfway back to the town when they both saw the spider balloons. There were two of them, and they were approaching fast from the direction of the spider city. For a moment Niall experienced panic and a desire to hide.

Doggins said: "I was afraid of that."

"What?"

Doggins made no reply; he stood and stared at the balloons with an expression of brooding hostility. Within less than a minute they were over the spire of the town hall, descending at a steep angle. Then they vanished from sight.

"You think it's the ambassadors?"

Doggins took a deep breath. "It couldn't be anybody else. I'd like to know why they're in such a hurry."

"I suppose they want to reach an agreement."

"That's what worries me." He touched Niall's elbow. "We'd better get back."

The half-collapsed balloons were lying on the lawn in front of the town hall. They were surrounded by a crowd of children, who watched with fascination as the balloons slowly deflated, and were obviously totally unconcerned at the presence of the brown wolf spider who stood on guard. A girl in the yellow tunic of a beetle servant hurried towards them; at close quarters, Niall recognized Dona.

Doggins asked her: "What's happening?"

She looked in the direction of the town hall. *"She's* there."

"Who?"

Dona lowered her voice. "Princess Merlew."

Doggins asked: "How many spiders?"

"Just one."

Niall and Doggins looked at one another. Doggins said: "That means she's one of the ambassadors. Cunning."

At the mention of Merlew's name, Niall had experienced a mixture of excitement and foreboding.

Dona was looking at him with troubled eyes. "You won't let her persuade you to go back?"

He stared at her in astonishment. "Of course not." He was about to add, "Do you think I'm mad?" but felt this might hurt her feelings.

A beetle guard came towards them from the town hall; Dona watched with apprehension as it addressed Doggins with movements of its feelers and with curious rustling sounds. Doggins turned to Niall. "He says we're to follow him. We've been summoned by the council."

Dona touched Niall's hand. "Please be careful."

"Don't worry." He squeezed her hand. But his smile expressed more confidence than he felt.

They followed the guard into the entrance hall. Here the bustling activity seemed so normal that his tension began to subside; the cool semidarkness exerted a curiously soothing influence. He even began to experience a pleasant anticipation at the thought of seeing the Master again. But at the head of the ramp that led to the underground chambers, their guide halted and made more signals. Doggins pointed to the door. "He says you're to wait in there."

Niall pushed it open and found himself in an empty room. The light was brighter than in the hall and a faint breeze came through the open window. The room was furnished with a few simple chairs and a divan in the shape of a crouching beetle. Niall sat down and leaned his head back, closing his eyes. The couch was covered with a smooth, silky material that was cool against his skin.

It was pleasant to be alone. Niall liked Doggins, but there was something oddly exhausting about his company. All his thoughts, all his feelings, seemed to be directed towards completely practical ends. For Doggins, the world was not a place that existed in its own right; it was there to be used and manipulated. After an hour in his company, Niall felt a powerful need to forget the outside world and sink inside himself.

The room was pleasantly cool. Through the window came the distant splashing of a fountain and children's voices; a fly buzzed drowsily overhead. He took a deep breath and relaxed as if sinking into a couch of fragrant leaves. He resisted the urge to sleep, concentrating his mind enough to become keenly aware of the depths of silence inside him. The point of light glowed momentarily inside his skull, and as he relaxed beyond it, he became aware of the rippling flow of the force, beating gently like wavelets on a beach.

Then, quite suddenly, he became aware of a nagging tension in the depths of his mind. It was not a feeling of danger, but simply a warning. He had experienced it once before, when confined in the cell in Kazak's palace: the realization that he was being watched.

He took care not to betray this knowledge by the slightest movement of his face; anyone watching him would have assumed he was asleep. Lying on his back, breathing regularly, he scanned the room with his mind. It took only a moment to establish that the hidden watcher was observing him through the window. Then a slamming door provided him with the excuse to stir and open his eyes; he yawned and sat up, glancing at the window. To his surprise, there was no one there; nothing was visible but the cloudless sky. He stood up and strolled to the window, then reached out as if stretching and pushed back the curtains a few inches. A fly buzzed past his head and settled in the corner of the ceiling. Niall closed his eyes, breathing in the cool air; his inner-monitor now told him that he was being observed from overhead.

He walked casually back to the divan and caressed the smooth material of the cushion. Then, with a sudden movement, he grasped it by the corner and skimmed it sideways and upwards across the room. The skill of the born hunter ensured its accuracy; the insect met the cushion in midflight and was knocked back against the wall, then to the floor. In a single stride Niall had crossed the room; he felt the armored body crunch under his sandal. It was a small fly, with a wingspan of less than two inches. Niall wiped the sandal clean on a rug, then went and closed the window. When he closed his eyes again, the sense of being observed had vanished.

The feeling of grim satisfaction was checked immediately. It was a frightening thought: that he could be observed through the mind of an insect. It meant that he could never feel certain of his privacy. It also meant that the Death Lord might be aware of everything he had done or said within the past few days. And although, on reflection, he dismissed this possibility—confident that his unconscious alarm system would have given him warning—he was still left with a disquieting sense of insecurity. It was no comfort to reflect that this was precisely what the Spider Lord wanted him to feel.

In his abnormally sensitive state, the click of the door latch made him start. Merlew came into the room and closed the door behind her, inserting a wooden peg above the latch to prevent it from opening. She was wearing a short dress of a red, silky material, which left her arms bare; the red-gold hair descended smoothly to her shoulders. As she turned to smile at him, Niall's heart contracted; he had never seen her looking so beautiful.

She said nothing, only stood looking at him, with her arms by her sides. Then she came across to him, looked into his face for a moment, then put her arms round his neck and kissed him. Her bare arms felt cold against his flesh, but her mouth was warm. In that moment, he knew that he had been mistaken to think he no longer cared about her. As he held her tightly against him, he experienced a sense of incredulity that she should now be kissing him, and that she seemed to want him as much as he wanted her.

She was the first to break away. She ran her fingers through the thick hair behind his ears and pressed her cheek against his neck. She said: "I've come to take you back with me."

He tried to shake his head, but the pressure of her face made it impossible. "You know I can't do that."

"Don't you want to stay with me?"

"Of course I do. But I want to stay alive, too."

She placed her lips against his ear, and their softness induced a sensation so powerful that his body stiffened. "Let's not talk about it now. I want you to kiss me."

She took him by the hand and drew him towards the couch. With mild astonishment, he watched her check the door to make sure the latch was secure before she lay down and drew him down beside her. Then, once again, they were both absorbed in the sheer delight of physical contact, drinking one another's essence as if impelled by physical hunger and thirst. Now, once again, Niall became aware of her internal reality, of the practical woman of the world who knew precisely what she wanted and was not afraid to try and take it. This no longer repelled him; his desire made it unimportant. He was even aware that there was something impersonal about her desire: that she was bored and frustrated and wanted to lose herself in a man's arms. This was also unimportant compared to the sheer pleasure they were now giving one another, as his male life energy passed into her and he absorbed her female energy. This was a simple physical transaction, like eating; but they seemed oddly fitted to satisfy one another's hunger.

Merlew was the first to disengage; she pushed him gently away, then sat up on the edge of the couch, brushing back her hair. She smiled down at him and rested her palm against his cheek. "I want you to come back with me." As he started to shake his head, she placed her hand over his mouth. "I promise that they won't try to harm you. I won't let them."

He moved her hand away gently. "He tried to kill me today."

"I know."

He stared at her in astonishment. "You do?"

"Yes. I have spoken to the Spider Lord. He told me he tried to kill you."

"And you still want me to go back?" He looked into her eyes with a certain mistrust; but their expression was clear and untroubled.

"That is why I want you to come back. The Spider Lord could kill you any time he wanted to. He has many servants."

"Did he tell you to say that?"

"No. I am saying it because it is true."

Niall pushed her away and sat up. "If I have a choice of dying among friends or among enemies, I would prefer to die among friends."

"But you wouldn't be among enemies. You would be among people you know—your mother and brother and sisters, and Ingeld and Massig. Did you know that my father is dead?"

He nodded. "Yes, I'm sorry."

"That means that I am no longer a princess, but a queen." She spoke proudly. "You would be my husband. Therefore you would be king."

He asked gently: "Do you think that would protect my life?"

She shook her head impatiently. "The Spider Lord wants peace. I *know* that. The spiders are not like human beings. They are not dreamers—they are realists. I understand them because my father was also a realist. They know that the servants of the beetles could destroy their city and everyone in it. That is why they are willing to do whatever is necessary for peace. And that is why they want you to come back with me. They know that the beetles can control their own servants. But you are a free man, and they cannot control you."

Niall smiled. "So they want you to control me for them?"

She shrugged, laughing. "Of course, why not? We have to be realists, too. If you are my husband and you are living in the spider city, you are no longer a danger to them."

"But I would still be at their mercy. The Spider Lord could break his word to me."

She smiled confidently. "Perhaps. But not to me."

"You believe he trusts you?"

"Of course."

"Then why does he send his servants to spy on us?" He pointed to the dead fly. "That was a servant of the Spider Lord. I killed it just before you came in."

Merlew stared down with curiosity at the dead insect. He could see she found it hard to believe him.

"How can you be certain?"

"I can sense these things. That is why the Spider Lord wants to kill me."

She came back and sat beside him, taking both his hands in hers. She gazed into his eyes and spoke with great conviction: "If you were my husband, he wouldn't need to be afraid of you." She leaned forward so that her mouth came very close to his. "Please trust me."

A knock at the door startled them both and they moved guiltily apart. She called imperiously: "Who is it?"

"Billdoggins." He pronounced it as one word.

Merlew crossed the room, removed the sliver of wood from the latch, and opened the door. Doggins looked down at her with intense appreciation; she stared back coldly. He said: "You're wanted in the council chamber."

She turned and looked questioningly at Niall. Doggins said: "No, just you." Niall could sense that, in spite of his admiration, Doggins regarded her with a certain hostility.

"Very well." She turned to Niall. "Wait here for me."

She went out without looking back. Doggins closed the door behind her. "She certainly likes giving orders."

"She's a princess—in fact, a queen."

Doggins grunted. "And doesn't she know it. What did she want?"

"She wants me to go back with her."

Doggins stared at him with raised eyebrows. "She must take you for a fool."

"No. She believes I would be safe."

"Then *she* must be a fool."

Niall decided not to argue; he could see that Doggins was tense and anxious. "What happened in the council chamber?"

Doggins shrugged irritably. "Things are going badly. The first thing the spider ambassador demanded was the return of the spider balloons. That seemed so reasonable that the council agreed at once. That means they've got us pinned down."

"We still have our feet. But what about the Reapers?"

"They're discussing that at the moment. The ambassador wants them destroyed."

"And what do you think will happen?"

Doggins shook his head gloomily. "I'm afraid the decision may go against us. The beetles dislike the Reapers as much as the spiders do. But at least they seem to agree that they're our property, since we found them. They've told me to go and discuss it with the others."

"That sounds hopeful."

"The final decision rests with the council."

"What do you suggest we should do?"

Doggins said: "There's one thing we've *got* to do—that is, stay one jump ahead of the spiders." He went to the door and quietly opened it; there was no one there. He closed it and stood with his back to it. "Are you still willing to kill the Spider Lord?"

Niall's heart sank. He said: "Of course. Today?"

"That may not be possible. We have to wait for a north wind, so we can use the balloons. We couldn't just march into the spider city—they'd be ready for us."

"Us?"

Doggins nodded. "We couldn't let you do it alone. You might get killed. In that case, someone else would have to try. If we tried to kill him and failed, we'd be worse off than before."

"Then we can do nothing until the wind changes?"

"That's right. But it may change at dusk—on days like this we often get a wind from the mountains. In the meantime, we have to talk to the others. We'd better go back to my house."

"I promised to wait for Merlew."

Doggins grinned sarcastically. "You didn't. She ordered you to wait for her. But we've no time to lose." He slapped Niall on the shoulder. "She'll find you if she wants you."

Reluctantly, Niall followed him out of the room. A moment later, they were blinking in the golden afternoon sunlight. The sun was already low on the horizon. The wolf spider was still standing guard over the collapsed balloons, but the crowd of children had vanished.

Ulic came towards them over the grass. "I was just coming to fetch you."

Doggins took his arm. "Listen. I want you to take a message to Hastur and Kosmin. Tell them to get the spider balloons ready for use. If anyone asks them what they're doing, tell them to say we've agreed to return them to the spiders." As Ulic hurried away he called after him: "And get back as soon as you can."

Niall asked: "Are you thinking of disobeying the council?"

Doggins gave him a sidelong grin. "The treaty hasn't been properly concluded yet. Until it has, the balloons are still our property."

Manetho was waiting for them on the lawn of Doggins' house; he hurried to meet them, asking anxiously: "What's happening?"

Doggins patted his muscular arm. "Nothing much. We're just going to have a meeting to discuss some matters of policy. Would you like to join us?"

His casual tone did not deceive Manetho. "Yes, I would."

Inside the house, Niall excused himself. "I'll be back in a moment." He was beginning to experience a sense of exhaustion, the aftermath of three days of inactivity, and felt the need of the thought mirror to aid his concentration. Doggins and Manetho went into the dining room.

As soon as he opened the bedroom door, he noticed the smell of vegetable decay, like the foul odor of disturbed swamp water. For a moment, he thought the viperweed was no longer there. Then he saw that it had collapsed to the floor. The green stem had turned a yellowish-white and had become limp and soft; the leaves had also become bleached and had contracted and folded, so they looked like shriveled hands. Niall bent over and looked more closely; the plant had obviously been dead for hours.

He closed the window, then sat down on the end of the bed. The words of Merlew came into his head: "If the Spider Lord decides to kill you, nothing can prevent him," and his sense of fatigue suddenly combined with a heavy foreboding to produce a treacherous sinking of the heart, as though the ground had opened up under his feet.

He took the thought mirror from the chair and hung it round his neck; it produced such an acute flash of pain that he hastened to turn it the other way. He closed his eyes, attempting to fight off the feeling of nausea and defeat; he succeeded, but the effort left him drained.

As he entered the dining room, Simeon looked up with a friendly smile; this changed to an expression of concern. "You look dreadful. You ought to be in bed."

Niall managed a smile. "I'm all right. But I'm afraid your plant is dead."

"Dead? Are you sure?"

Niall followed him down the corridor; the smell of vegetable decay came through the open door. Simeon knelt beside the plant and examined each of the serpent-like heads in turn. Doggins stood in the doorway, with Milo and Manetho behind him; his nose was wrinkled with disgust.

From his pocket, Simeon took a small folding knife. He held the largest of the heads in his hand, and sawed it open; the flesh was obviously tough. Looking over his shoulder, Niall could see why he had selected this particular head. Now he looked closely, he could see the needle-like spike that had pierced the flesh from the inside, and which now projected half an inch beyond it.

Simeon took the head in his powerful hands, and twisted it open. Inside there lay a large black mosquito; with its sting extended, it was almost four inches long.

Doggins knelt beside him. "That's just an ordinary swamp mosquito from the Delta. Why should that kill it?"

Simeon used his knife to point to the protruding sting. "At a guess, because this has been smeared with some pretty powerful poison—I'd guess the juice of the devil weed. The slightest scratch would probably bring instant death." He took the cloth from a small table and carefully folded it. He sawed off the head and wrapped it in the cloth, snapping off the sting as he did so, then handed it to Milo.

"Ask Lucretia to burn this, and tell her not to take it out of the cloth."

All were thoughtful as they returned to the dining room; again, Niall had to fight off depression and fear.

Ulic came in as they were seating themselves. "Kosmin says the balloons will be ready in half an hour." Niall could see that he was exhilarated at the prospect of action. When none of them spoke, Ulic looked around at their faces. "Is anything the matter?"

As Niall described what had happened, Ulic's excitement drained away; his face became thoughtful. "It looks as if the Spider Lord is determined to kill you."

Niall shook his head. "I don't think so. If he killed me now, he could ruin the peace negotiations. And that's the last thing he wants."

Simeon nodded. "I agree with Niall. This was intended as a warning—that if we don't make peace, he can destroy us all."

Doggins said quietly: "And if we *do* make peace, he can still destroy us all. But he can do it at his leisure."

Manetho asked hesitantly: "Surely it isn't our decision? It's up to the Master and council to decide whether to make peace."

Doggins nodded. "Which is why we have to decide this afternoon, before they reach a decision."

Manetho looked perplexed. "But what could we *do?*"

Doggins said: "Look, let's examine the facts. The other day, when the Death Lord tried to kill Niall, the Master refused to make peace. He said the spiders had forfeited all right to his cooperation. So I think we can assume he won't change his mind and hand Niall over to the spiders. But he's already agreed to hand back the balloons. That sounds as if he's ready for compromise. The only question now is: will the compromise include making us destroy the Reapers? Because if it does, then we're back where we were before except that the Spider Lord now regards us as enemies. And you know as well as I do that the spiders never forgive anybody who's killed one of their kind. Together, we are responsible for the deaths of hundreds of spiders. So I think we can assume that, whether the council makes peace or not, the Spider Lord is going to look for an opportunity for revenge."

Simeon said: "You are suggesting that we attack the spiders now—even though they are trying to make peace?"

Doggins nodded. "I am suggesting that we try to destroy the Spider Lord before he has a chance to destroy us."

Simeon frowned; his bushy eyebrows almost obliterated his eyes. "But can we be sure he wants to destroy us?" His eyes rested on Niall. "You are the one whose life is most at risk. What do you think?"

Niall said: "The Princess Merlew has been trying to convince me that the Spider Lord wants peace. I must admit that she almost succeeded."

Doggins interrupted: "She *intended* to convince you. That is what the Spider Lord wanted her to do." He made an obvious effort to restrain his impatience. "Of course they want peace. And the easiest way to get it is to kill all their enemies." He leaned forward. "I believe the Spider Lord cannot afford *not* to be treacherous. That is why we must act before he gets the chance."

Simeon was obviously unhappy; he frowned, shaking his head. "You say the Spider Lord cannot afford *not* to be treacherous. But is that true? The Peace Treaty has now lasted for three hundred years, and in all that time there has been no incident of treachery between the spiders and the beetles. You know the Peace Treaty as well as I do. It is a hundred and eighteen paragraphs long. When old enemies draw up a treaty as long as that, they are not prepared to break it lightly."

Doggins nodded. "What you say is true. I also know most of the treaty by heart. But it was drawn up three centuries ago, and many things have changed since then. The spiders have always known that human beings are their most dangerous enemies. That is why they have always tried to enslave us and turn us into cattle. But they could not enslave the servants of the beetles. They had to allow us a certain degree of freedom. Even so, the treaty forbids us to learn to read or write, or to use any kind of machine—even a simple pressure lamp." He tapped the table with his knuckles. "Why do you think I was so anxious to find the Reapers? It was not to attack the spiders, but to force them into bargaining. I wanted to be allowed to use my own mind without having to ask the permission of the spiders. That is surely the right of every man? Well, now we have the Reapers, which means we have the means to claim the right to think for ourselves. The spiders know we are determined to gain our freedom at any cost—and that, sooner or later, we shall succeed. They know they've finally lost their hold on us." He turned to Simeon. "That is why they *must* destroy us if they get the chance. And that is why we cannot afford to trust them."

He spoke with such passion and conviction that they were all impressed; Niall sensed that he was unconsciously using the power of the thought mirror, and that this gave additional force to his arguments. Yet it was obvious from Simeon's frown that he remained unconvinced. He said: "In that case, they must be bound by an even stronger treaty. They must be bound by oaths that they would never dare to break."

Doggins shook his head emphatically. "I do not believe that such oaths exist."

Simeon said: "There you are mistaken. My brother-in-law Pandion has spent his life studying the spiders—he was the assistant harbor master for many years and worked with them every day. Pandion assured me that they believe in their gods and goddesses as much as we do in ours. He told me of an occasion when a wolf spider had gone mad after eating a poisoned assassin fly, and killed four sailors. They succeeded in locking it into the hold of the ship, but when it sailed into port, no one dared to release the spider. Pandion went and spoke to it, and saw that it was mad with pain and close to death. But he promised to release it if it would swear an oath by Iblis, the god of darkness, and Nuada, the goddess of the Delta. And although the spider was in agony, it kept its word and attacked no one. It died in convulsions a few hours later. Surely that proves that a spider can be bound by an oath?"

Doggins said: "An ordinary wolf spider, yes. But do you suppose the Spider Lord can be bound by such superstitions?"

"Yes. Because they do not believe they *are* superstitions."

Doggins shrugged. "Which is still no guarantee that the Spider Lord could be bound by an oath. I'm afraid we could go on arguing like this for the rest of the day without reaching any conclusion. And we *must* reach some conclusion." He looked around the table. "What do the rest of you have to say?"

There was a silence, which Niall broke by asking Simeon: "You say there is a goddess of the Delta. Do you mean the Great Delta?"

"Yes. The Delta is one of their sacred places."

The words caused a tingling sensation in Niall's scalp. "Do you know why?"

Out of the corner of his eye he saw that Doggins was making an impatient gesture; he ignored it.

Simeon said: "Perhaps because the Delta is so full of life. Nuada is also known as the river of life."

Again Niall experienced the feeling like cold water flowing over his skin. "The river or the giver?"

"The river."

Niall turned to Doggins; his excitement was so great that he had to make an effort to control his voice. "Don't you see? *The Delta is the center of the force.*"

Doggins was suddenly alert. "What makes you think that?"

"You remember I said that the force is like ripples on a pond? If that is so, then the ripples must have a center. That center *must* lie in the Delta." He turned to Simeon. "You've been there. Didn't you feel some underground force?"

Simeon frowned and shook his head. "I didn't feel anything—I don't seem to be sensitive to that kind of thing. But my wife was. And she always told me there was some kind of underground vibration in the Delta." The admission seemed to embarrass him. "I always assumed it was her imagination."

"Why?"

Simeon smiled reminiscently. "It's easy to let your imagination run away with you in the Delta. It always made me think of a rotten cheese full of maggots. You get the feeling you're being watched all the time. Spider crabs follow you, and big dragonflies come and inspect you. Even I used to get the feeling there was some kind of presence. . . ."

"Then why couldn't you believe what she said about the vibration?"

"I like hard evidence." He frowned meditatively. "Mind, there *was* one odd occasion. . . . We'd just arrived in the Delta one afternoon—we'd gone to collect ortis juice—when there was a tremendous thunderstorm. We were afraid we'd be washed away. When it was right overhead, there was a great flash of lightning and the loudest clap of thunder I've ever heard—it made my ears ring. And right after that, we both had this strange sensation that something had happened. I can't explain it except to say that things felt different. That sense of being watched had vanished. And when the storm was over, the insects were all blundering about as though they'd been stunned. Even the plants seemed to be confused. We saw a dragonfly blunder into a Venus flytrap and we expected to see it snapped up. Instead, the trap closed so slowly that the fly escaped."

Doggins asked: "What do you think caused it?"

"My guess is that it was something to do with the lightning. But the lightning couldn't have affected every single plant and insect. The situation lasted several hours, and we got our ortis juice with no trouble at all—the plant didn't even try to stun us and nothing tried to attack us, although Valda tripped over a web-foot scorpion. The next day things were back to normal—we felt we were being watched again."

Manetho nodded. "I've had the same feeling when we landed on the Delta for water—a sensation of being watched. It always gives me a prickling feeling in the back of my neck."

Niall asked him: "Did you notice this underground vibration?"

Manetho considered it, frowning. "Yes, I suppose I did—although I haven't thought about it until now."

Doggins asked Simeon: "Did you talk to anyone about this experience in the Delta?" Simeon shook his head. "Why not?"

Simeon shrugged. "It didn't seem important. The Delta's a strange place—anything can happen."

Doggins looked at him with raised eyebrows. "It would have struck *me* as important."

Simeon brushed aside the implied criticism. "One of the first rules of science is: never build a theory on insufficient evidence."

Niall said: "But this morning you told me that viperweeds grow far bigger in the Delta. Wouldn't you count that as evidence?"

"Of what? It could be due to the soil or the heat or the moisture, or a mixture of all three." He added grudgingly: "Although I have to admit that your underground force could explain a great many puzzling things."

Niall said: "For example, a force that makes plants grow bigger could also make insects grow bigger."

Simeon shook his head. "Insects don't have roots."

"How do you know roots are necessary? The squid funguses don't have roots either."

"Squid funguses?" Simeon looked at him blankly.

Doggins said: "Did you know that when spiders die, they change into squid funguses?"

Simeon regarded him suspiciously. "What is this—some kind of fairy tale?"

"No. It really happens. If you don't believe me, go and look at the dead spiders out near the quarry."

Simeon thought about it. "It's more likely, surely, that the squids attack the spiders when they're dead?"

Doggins said emphatically: "No. The spiders really turn into funguses. We've been watching them this afternoon."

As they were speaking, Niall reached inside his tunic and turned the thought mirror. It brought an instant sensation of calm and relief; the almost painful excitement suddenly vanished to be replaced by a new sense of comprehension and control.

He turned to Simeon. "Don't you see what this means? You were saying the other day that you couldn't believe that spiders had ever been tiny creatures. This explains it. The force that made the plants of the Delta grow bigger also affected the spiders. *That's* why the spiders regard the Delta as sacred. That's why they call the Delta goddess the river of life. She *is* a river of life. She makes things grow."

"Then why doesn't she turn human beings into giants?"

"I think I know the answer to that. Because we can't pick up the vibration. We've lost touch with our instincts—we use our minds too much."

Milo asked: "And where do you think this force comes from?"

"I don't know. Perhaps it has always been on earth. Perhaps it is the force that makes all living things grow, but it just happens to be more concentrated in the area of the Delta."

Ulic smiled. "Perhaps it was riding on the tail of the comet."

Simeon ignored this. He asked Niall: "If the spiders have evolved so recently, why is their willpower so much stronger than ours?"

"I believe it's because the spiders have always known about willpower. They spend their lives sitting in their webs, waiting for insects to fly in. And when an insect comes close, they try to will it to enter the web. Human beings have never *needed* that kind of will. We learned to use our hands and minds instead." A new insight came to him as he spoke. "And I can tell you something else. That's why human beings will eventually conquer the spiders. The spiders have no imagination, and willpower is no use without imagination. Because only imagination can tell us *what* to will. After all, what use do the spiders make of their willpower? They just sit in their webs all day long. They haven't even built their own city—they've merely taken over an old human city. Their chief aim seems to be to enslave human beings and prevent us from making proper use of our own powers. They aren't fit to be masters of the earth. That's why we have to fight them."

Doggins nodded with approval. "Well said!"

Simeon asked Niall: "Do you think this force is intelligent?"

"Not in our sense. As far as I can see, its single purpose is to produce more life. And it does that by making things struggle. That's the chief problem with living things—they reach a certain point of discouragement, then they give up. This force stops them from giving up so easily . . ."

Milo said: "So it's really the enemy of the human race?"

The comment puzzled Niall. "Enemy?"

"Well, if it helps the less intelligent forms of life against the more intelligent . . ."

Niall shook his head doubtfully.

Doggins leaned forward. "In other words, if we want to destroy the spiders, we have to destroy this force."

Niall looked at him in surprise. "Destroy it? I don't think you can destroy a force." For some reason, the idea gave him a disagreeable sensation.

Simeon said: "Why not? If it could be paralyzed by lightning, it could be destroyed by a Reaper."

"That's right." Doggins was suddenly excited. "If the center of the force lies in the Delta, then we ought to be able to locate it."

Niall asked: "But how? It could be anywhere."

Simeon was smiling. "I think I can answer that." They all looked at him. "I didn't quite finish my story about the Delta. A few days

60

after we got back, I spoke to the captain in charge of a squad of slaves. She told me something very strange—that a spider had fallen out of its web outside the officers' quarters and been killed. Now you know how unlikely that is—a spider falling out of its web. When Valda and I worked it out, we decided it must have happened at the same time as the storm in the Delta."

Doggins asked: "What time was the storm?"

"About two hours before dark, on a summer day."

"In other words, the human beings would all have been back in their own quarters?" Simeon nodded. "So it could have affected *all* the spiders?"

"That's right."

There was a silence as they absorbed the implications. Doggins said finally: "I think we may have found our solution." He looked at Niall. "Don't you think so?"

Niall shook his head; there was something about Doggins' attitude that deeply disturbed him.

"But how would you find the center?"

"We don't have to. You've seen the power of the Reaper. We could destroy the whole Delta in half an hour."

Simeon said: "That may not be necessary. The storm was almost directly overhead when the flash of lightning came. That means the center must have been fairly close."

"Can you describe exactly where you were?"

"I could draw you a map."

Doggins went to a cupboard and came back with a piece of charcoal. He pointed to the white tablecloth. "Draw on that."

Simeon sketched two wavery lines, which joined to form a V. "This is the junction of the two great rivers running from the south. They spread out into this area between them—which, as you know, is swamp and rain forest. The forest is also here, around the sides of the basin. The best ortis plants grow here, on the edge of the forest and the swamp. Back here"—he indicated the area to the south of the junction—"the forest is almost impenetrable. We were roughly here," he made a cross at a point to the west of the junction, "so I would guess that the center of the force is somewhere within this area of rain forest."

Doggins stood behind Simeon, looking down at the map. "To get into the rain forest, we'd have to cross one of the two rivers?"

"Yes, and that could be dangerous. There are giant water spiders, as big as octopuses, and they hide below the surface."

Doggins frowned. "I didn't realize there were spiders in the Delta."

"They're nothing like the death spiders. As far as I can tell, they're not particularly intelligent. And they don't possess the same willpower." He looked at Niall. "That seems to confirm your theory about the spiders. The water spiders hunt their prey like crocodiles. So presumably they've never developed the same will-force. But they've got jaws like a mantrap."

Manetho said: "Another thing you have to watch out for is the red leech." Simeon nodded agreement. "One of my men waded into the water, trying to spear a giant prawn. He ran out a few minutes later, his legs covered in these huge red things, like big shiny slugs. We couldn't pull them off, but luckily somebody thought of fire—we were burning driftwood from the beach. As soon as the slugs were touched with a flame, they dropped off. But they'd eaten big holes in the man's flesh, right through to the bone. He almost died on the way home."

Milo looked at Simeon with wonderment. "And you went into this place just to gather medicine?"

"Very powerful medicine. You could collect enough in a day to last this whole city for a year. Besides, we never ventured into the really dangerous part. The ortis plant grows on the edge of the hill forest. I doubt whether anyone could venture into this part"—his finger indicated the area between the rivers—"and stay alive for more than a few hours."

Doggins said: "We don't have to venture into it. We should be able to fly over it in a balloon—shouldn't we?" He looked at Simeon.

"There's no reason why not—provided the wind's blowing in the right direction."

They all sat looking at the charcoal lines on the cloth, as if they could somehow force them to yield more information. Doggins asked Niall: "What do you suppose this thing looks like? Some kind of gigantic tree? Or a plant?"

"It may not look like anything. Perhaps it's simply a concentration of force."

Doggins said: "It doesn't matter what it's like. The Reapers should deal with it." There was a grim note in his voice.

The door opened; it was Doggins' youngest son, the five-year-old. He announced in a clear voice: "There's a beetle at the door and he says he wants to talk to you."

"Thank you, son." Doggins caressed the child's head as he went out of the room, and Niall was struck by the tenderness of the gesture.

Doggins was back a moment later. He beckoned to Niall. "The Master wants to see the two of us. The rest of you had better wait here."

Outside, the air had become still, as if exhausted by the heat of the day. The shouts of children could be heard from a long way off. In this peaceful atmosphere, thoughts of death and destruction seemed oddly unreal.

Neither of them spoke as they followed the guard back into the town hall and down the ramp into the underground corridor. As he trod cautiously over the uneven floor, and guided himself in the dim light by touching the rough-hewn walls, Niall understood why the beetles had left this part of the building in an unfinished state. They disliked the human world, with its flat, smooth planes and exact right angles, and dreamed of former times when life was simple and instinctive.

The guard halted and pulled open the door of the council chamber. The dim green light made it look like an undersea grotto. The beetles, each resting against its upright podium, might have been carved statues. Merlew was seated in an alcove in the wall and her hair seemed to glow in the light like precious metal. A black death spider stood before the seat of the Master. It turned to survey Niall and Doggins, and Niall could feel the force of its will as a cold sensation that made the hairs on his arms stand on end. Doggins made a low bow before the Master and Niall followed his example.

The Master spoke in his strange, sibilant voice, with almost no movement of his forelegs, and once again Niall was astonished that he understood it as if it had been in his own language.

"We have asked you to return to learn if you have reached any decision about the murder weapons?" The beetle language had no equivalent of the word Reaper.

Doggins spoke with his eyes averted. "Our decision is to do whatever the council recommends."

He was not being consciously dishonest or evasive. In this atmosphere, before the council of the beetles and under the gaze of the Master, no other answer seemed possible. In spite of the thought mirror, Niall himself felt like a helpless child in the presence of the Master.

The Master said: "Good. Then hear the decision of the council. Subject to the completion of the Peace Treaty, we have decided that the murder weapons shall not be destroyed." Niall resisted the impulse to glance at Doggins. "But they will be held in trust by the beetles, and no human being shall have access to them without the permission of a member of the council. We have reached this decision in view of your concern about the numerical superiority of the spiders. This is a concern that we do not share—the beetles have implicit trust in their allies the spiders. But we also wish to meet the objections of our human servants.

"Subject to the completion of the Peace Treaty, relations between the spiders and the beetles will return to those of the first Peace Treaty. But where our human servants are concerned, the clauses forbidding the possession of books shall be removed from the Treaty. This change has been suggested by the Spider Lord, who has also suggested revising the clause about the use of machines to permit the use of certain simple mechanical devices. I have already expressed my thanks on your behalf for his generosity. The exact nature of these mechanical devices will be decided by a joint committee of all parties concerned.

"The only question that remains concerns the escaped prisoner, Niall. The spiders have agreed that he shall no longer be regarded as a prisoner, but shall be free to decide his own future. I have expressed my willingness to allow him to remain here as a beetle servant." Niall looked up and nodded his thanks. "But the spiders have also invited him to return to their city as the consort of the new female overseer." He glanced at Merlew, who was staring at the floor, obviously unable to understand these strange noises. "If he decides to accept this offer, his safety will be guaranteed by a separate appendix to the Peace Treaty. If he wishes to leave at any time, his freedom will also be guaranteed."

Niall said: "Thank you." Merlew looked up at him and smiled.

The Master looked at Doggins. "Do you have any comments or questions?"

"No, Master."

"Very well. Tomorrow morning, three members of the council and three ambassadors from the spider city will meet to discuss the wording of the Peace Treaty. If you wish to be present, you have our permission."

Doggins bowed his thanks; Niall did the same. Something in the Master's manner told him that the interview was at an end. Both made an obeisance and turned. The death spider watched them impassively; as they left the chamber, Niall felt a clumsy attempt to probe his mind. A moment later they were alone in the corridor.

Neither of them spoke as they made their way back to the main hall; both were preoccupied with their own thoughts. The hall was deserted; outside, it was dusk, and the day's business was at an end. Doggins indicated the door labeled "Director of Explosives."

"Come into my office."

The room was in half-darkness; through the window they could see the remains of the sunset over the rooftops. Doggins flung himself into the chair behind his desk and indicated another chair for Niall. He sat frowning at his desktop, making a clicking noise with his tongue.

Niall asked: "Are you pleased?"

"What?" Doggins seemed to wake up. "Pleased about what?"

"They've given you what you wanted—permission to read and write, and the use of machines."

Doggins snorted. "That's not a concession. All the beetle servants know how to read and write. And they didn't say we can use machines. They said 'certain mechanical devices.' They probably mean egg timers and kitchen scales. And we already use them—without the permission of the spiders."

"But they've agreed not to destroy the Reapers."

Doggins shrugged. "What they've done is almost as bad. If we hand over the Reapers to the beetles, we shall never see them again."

"But at least you can be sure the spiders won't dare to launch a surprise attack."

Doggins made a grudging gesture of assent. "That's true. But if they take the Reapers away, we've lost our bargaining power. We're back where we were before." He gave a sigh of disgust.

"Not quite. If you're allowed to read books, you could learn how to build machines on paper. They couldn't stop you from doing that. You could even learn how to make a Reaper."

"Impossible. For that we'd need a whole nuclear technology. And the spiders will make sure we never get that far." He shrugged. "Oh, well, I suppose we'd better get back to the others and tell them what's happened." He began to stand, then sat down again. "But what about you? What are you going to do?"

"I don't know."

"Why not accept the spiders' offer? If it's guaranteed under the Peace Treaty, you can't come to any harm. And you can always leave if you don't like it."

Niall shook his head. "No. I can't do that. Kazak made me almost the same offer and I had to refuse."

"But why?" The practical Doggins obviously found Niall's attitude incomprehensible.

"You don't understand because you've never lived in the desert. But if you'd spent your life hiding under the ground, you'd understand why. I don't *want* to make friends with the spiders. I don't even want to learn to work with them."

"Then what do you want?"

"I suppose I want to see them all destroyed."

"That may not be possible."

"Perhaps you're right. All I know is that men were once the masters of the earth, and now the spiders are."

Doggins said: "And the beetles."

Niall smiled. "Yes, the beetles."

"So you'll stay here with us?"

Niall shook his head. "I couldn't do that either."

"Why not?" This time there was a note of exasperation in Doggins' voice.

"Because I intend to go on working against the spiders. And if I did that, I'd have to break my word to the beetles."

"So what *do* you intend to do?"

Niall thought about it. "Go back to the desert."

"And what would you do there?"

"I don't know. Perhaps look for other men like myself, men who hate the spiders and want to see them destroyed. There must be other underground arsenals like the one in the spider city. Perhaps we could find more Reapers."

Doggins shook his head violently. "Oh, this is mad!"

Niall looked at him with surprise. "Why?"

"Because I agree with every word you say. I want to see the spiders destroyed. So do the others—Milo and Ulic and Manetho and the rest. None of us want to work with the spiders. We've come too far for that."

"And the treaty?"

Doggins grunted. "The treaty's not signed yet."

"So what do you think we should do?"

Doggins turned to the window. "The first thing we do is . . ." He broke off, and his body stiffened. Niall looked past him, wondering what had caused the reaction. The foreground was dark; all he could see was the fading orange sky and a smoky cloud drifting across it.

Doggins pointed. "That looks like your answer." His voice sounded oddly strained.

"I don't understand."

"The wind has changed." He grasped Niall's arm. "Let's go outside."

The hall was now so dark that they had to grope their way across it. The great wooden doors had been closed; they had to leave the building by a side door. As soon as they emerged on the steps, the wind snatched at their tunics.

Doggins licked his forefinger and held it up. "It's a northwesterly." He turned to Niall. There was an odd expression in his eyes, a mixture of excitement and something like fear. "Don't you think that's a sign?"

Before Niall could answer, Ulic came hurrying towards them across the grass. Doggins placed one arm around Ulic's shoulders and spoke in a low voice.

"Now listen carefully. I want you to go and take a message to Kosmin and Hastur. They are to prepare three balloons. Tell them we shall need food and drink for six people." He glanced over his shoulder. "And tell them we shall need Reapers."

Ulic's eyes brightened with excitement. "When do you want to leave?"

"As soon as it's dark."

"Wouldn't it be better to wait for moonrise?"

"No. We don't want to be seen."

As they walked back towards Doggins' house, Niall experienced a watery sensation of fear and excitement. But at least his doubts and misgivings had vanished; he knew that they no longer had any choice.

PART TWO

The Delta

The lights of the beetle city receded quickly beneath them; within moments they were surrounded by a darkness so complete that Niall could not even see the white glimmer of his own hand before his eyes. During this ascending stage, there were a few violent jerks as the connecting rope became taut; after this, the rope slackened and the ascent became smooth. Five minutes later, the roaring of the wind had ceased; at this height it met with no obstruction and was therefore soundless. Moreover, since they were now traveling at almost the same speed as the moving air, the wind seemed to have dropped so that it was hardly more than a faint breeze. It was a strange sensation: to hang there, apparently motionless, in the total blackness, and to realize that they were hundreds of feet above the ground and traveling at more than thirty miles an hour. At this speed they should reach the Delta in just over four hours.

Gradually, the blackness paled into a gray dusk, so that Niall could see Manetho standing on the far side of the undercarriage, his arms outstretched as he held on to the supports of the balloon. For a moment, Niall assumed that his eyes were adjusting to the darkness, then realized, to his surprise, that the light came from the western horizon, where pink clouds reflected the setting sun. It took him some moments to grasp that their height allowed them to see across the earth's curved surface to a more distant horizon. The light also enabled him to see the two other balloons, each approximately level with his own. The one containing Doggins and Milo was less than fifty yards away, so that the rope that connected them hung in a drooping arc. Doggins pointed and shouted something, but the wind made it inaudible. Ten minutes later the sun had vanished again and they were once more in total darkness.

At least the floor beneath their feet was solid; a large circular board had been installed in the bottom of the undercarriage. On this there were two bulging canvas bags containing provisions, each firmly attached to the supports of the balloon, in case air turbulence caused them to slide about. Between his feet, Niall held a smaller bag containing his Reaper and a supply of firebombs. Blankets had been spread on the wooden floor and tucked beneath its edges to prevent them from moving or folding. Kosmin and Hastur, who had been largely responsible for the preparations, had shown a remarkable amount of care and foresight. And, to their credit, they had betrayed no sign of the acute disappointment they must have felt at being left behind.

Niall was warmly clad; Doggins' womenfolk had provided him with a fur-lined garment that reached almost to his ankles. On his feet he wore boots—a type of footwear to which he was completely unaccustomed—made of canvas with thick rubber soles. At first they felt hot and uncomfortable, but after half an hour in the balloon, he was grateful for the warmth; at this height, the temperature was close to zero.

There was a sudden spark of light which illuminated Manetho's face; he was sitting on the floor, igniting the tinder box. A few moments later, the dry shavings were burning. Manetho used it to light a small oil lamp, whose flame wavered unsteadily; he used this to consult a compass.

Niall crouched beside him. "Are we on course?" Manetho nodded. "What time will the moon rise?"

"It won't." Manetho pointed overhead. "There's a blanket of cloud."

Niall looked up into the blackness; after a moment, he caught a glimpse of a few stars, which vanished immediately. He asked: "What are we going to do?"

Manetho said grimly: "The only thing we can do is hope." He blew out the oil lamp.

"Why are you doing that?"

"We can't risk it overturning. Anyway, there's nothing to see."

"Hadn't we better speak to the others?"

"I suppose so. I'll do it. You stay here, or we'll make the floor tilt."

They had made arrangements for an emergency like this. The rope had been looped around the balloon, as well as attached to each support; if the balloons wished to approach one another, all that was necessary was to pull in the rope, hand over hand. From the vibrations of the undercarriage, Niall could sense that this was what

Manetho was doing. A few minutes later, a faint bump told him that the balloons had collided. He heard Doggins ask: "Any idea where we are?"

"No," said Manetho. "But we must be at least ten miles from the coast. I'm worried about this cloud. If it doesn't lift, we shan't know when we're over land."

"Are you sure we're not still over the land?"

"We can easily find out."

He heard the clink of the firebombs as Manetho groped in the bag. Niall rose cautiously to his feet and looked over the side, leaning on one of the supports. He felt the jerk as Manetho tossed the bomb. For a while, it seemed that nothing would happen; then there was a brilliant yellow flash of light from below them. It continued to blaze as it fell downward, and suddenly its reflection was cast back by the sea. For a brief moment, Niall glimpsed black water and the white of breaking waves; then the flare was extinguished. These few seconds had been enough to show them that the sea stretched in all directions. For the first time since he had climbed into the balloon, Niall felt a shock of fear. Enclosed in the darkness, he had felt secure; now the realization that they were suspended in a vast emptiness suddenly came home to him.

Doggins said: "We could go up above the clouds, but we wouldn't be any better off. What do you think?"

"No point—we still wouldn't be able to see the land when we approach it. The only thing we can do is to keep dropping firebombs when we think we're getting close. How many have we got?"

"A dozen each."

"Good. That's seventy-two—seventy-one without the one I dropped. That's more than enough."

"In that case, we may as well have something to eat. I'm ravenous."

Manetho let go of the rope and sat down on the floor of the balloon. A few moments later there was a faint jerk as the rope reached its limit.

Once again Manetho used the tinder box and ignited the tiny oil lamp; he held on to it tightly as Niall seated himself on the floor. Manetho was at least fifty pounds heavier than Niall, so that the floor was inclined to tilt beneath his weight. With some difficulty and infinite caution, they rearranged themselves in relation to the baggage, until the weight was evenly spread. Then Manetho handed Niall the lamp while he untied the top of one of the canvas bags. From this he took a wickerwork hamper of food. It proved to contain flat cakes of bread, honey, cooked game, goat's cheese, apples, and a carafe of golden wine. They sat cross-legged to eat; the walls of the undercarriage had never been intended as support for the human back and yielded alarmingly to any pressure.

If he closed his eyes, Niall could almost imagine himself back in the burrow. The wine and food induced a pleasant sense of security and optimism; it no longer mattered that he was swinging in empty space a thousand feet above the ocean. Yet it also made him aware how much he had changed; the child who had lived in the burrow seemed to belong to a remote epoch of his life.

A dazzling flash of light startled him into wakefulness. Doggins had dropped another firebomb. It revealed exactly the same prospect as before: the black sea, flecked with white, stretching endlessly around them. They emptied the wine bottle and Manetho tossed the empty bottle overboard; it gave Niall an odd feeling of satisfaction to imagine it plummeting down through the blackness. Manetho once again extinguished the light.

It was soon after this that it began to rain. Niall pulled up the hood of the fur-lined garment and used the drawstring to tie it tight. The garment was made of cured animal skin, and was completely waterproof. But the pattering of the rain on the hood aroused Niall from his somnolence. This in turn made him aware of the danger of allowing himself to drift into a sense of false security. If they were now on course, they should be at least halfway to the Delta. According to Simeon, the junction of the two rivers was about a mile inland from the coast. Traveling at the present speed, it would be easy to overshoot the mark and perhaps land in the desert on the far side of the Delta . . .

To control the nagging sense of anxiety, he fumbled inside his tunic and turned the thought mirror. The drowsiness vanished immediately. At first, this seemed to be of no particular advantage; he merely became more aware of the sound of the rain and the swaying of the balloon. Then his thoughts turned to the porifid a few inches above his head, and he immediately became clearly aware of its presence. It seemed to be a point of dim light surrounded by long threads of energy that reached out into the blackness. At the center of the light, where all these threads joined, there was a steady pulse like a beating heart. As he concentrated on this pulse, he seemed to become a part of it; there was a curious sense that it was trying to communicate with him. Then he himself became the pulse. His own body seemed somehow remote and alien, as if it belonged to someone else.

And now, suddenly, it was no longer dark. He knew his eyes were closed; yet they seemed to be open. He was drifting through a red haze, and when he strained his senses, he could see as clearly as if by daylight. He could see the thick blanket of dark cloud and the three-quarter moon that drifted above them. Far below, he could see the breaking waves. A further effort even allowed him to penetrate under the surface of the sea, and to become aware of the bottom almost as far below as he was above.

He was also conscious of the porifids in the other two balloons; his own energy threads mingled with theirs and their perceptions mingled with his. Now Niall understood why the balloons stayed at the same height, and why they never collided; the porifids were aware of one another and maintained roughly the same distance between them. Niall had the curious impression that they were able to regulate not only the height of the balloon by the quantity of gas they exuded or absorbed, but also—to some extent—its direction.

Now his consciousness had become identified with that of the porifids, he ceased to feel even a remnant of anxiety about his position. His impatience also dissolved; it seemed to make no difference whether he was in the air or on the ground. He felt that he could be content to drift along between the clouds and the sea forever. His human consciousness, with its eternal vigilance and tension, seemed only a distant memory; instead he was suspended in an awareness that was closer to sleep, yet was also fully conscious.

In this state, he became aware that the energy threads emitted by the porifid were, in fact, short bursts of some low frequency energy, and that these were being reflected back from every object they encountered, enabling him to "see" it. He was also surprised to realize that he himself possessed this same capacity, but to a much lower degree. Unlike the porifids, he had never needed to develop it, because he had always preferred to rely on the senses of sight and hearing. The same was true of Manetho, who was now staring sleepily into the darkness. Because he was now rather bored, he had allowed his will to collapse; the result was that his brain had almost ceased to emit the energy threads.

And this, Niall suddenly realized, was the basic problem of all human beings. As soon as they became bored, they allowed the will to collapse. The spiders had never made that elementary mistake. That was why they were masters of the world. They were incapable of being bored . . .

Doggins was taking another firebomb out of his bag, Niall watched him twist the timing device on the side and toss it overboard. He watched it fall down through the red air until it suddenly disintegrated—this time he could see its fragments flying apart. His human eyelids were aware of the explosion as a bright flash of yellow light, but his porifid senses saw only a disturbing release of energy that spread outward like a sound, vibrating and echoing out into the universe.

For Niall, the firebomb was unnecessary; his extended senses showed him that the coastline was roughly twenty miles away to the south. Beyond it lay the desert. On their present course, they would cross the coastline about six miles east of the Delta. Even from this distance Niall could see that the coast they were approaching was bleak and inhospitable, with swampy mud flats that merged a few miles inland into a rocky desert. But a dozen miles further west there was a long sandy beach, protected by a natural harbor bar of coral and limestone. This was the area Simeon had described as the most suitable place to land.

It was unnecessary for Niall to transmit the mental command to the porifid, for its mind and nervous system were an extension of his own. And with the naturalness of a swimmer changing direction, the porifid turned in a long, slow arc until it was heading directly towards the sandy beach. Niall was baffled by the mechanics of the process, for the porifid seemed to be defying the natural forces of the wind; yet, in another sense, it was making use of these forces. As far as Niall could tell, the secret lay in its failure to realize that it was violating a law of nature.

Niall opened his eyes, and was surprised to find that it was no longer dark. Now the rain had ceased, the moon had emerged from behind the clouds. He leaned forward and shook Manetho's arm; Manetho woke up with a start. Niall said: "We're near the coast."

Manetho jumped clumsily to his feet and peered over the side. "I can't see it."

"That's because it's still twenty miles away."

Manetho stood as motionless as a statue, staring at the horizon. Five minutes later, he raised his cupped hands to his mouth and roared: "Coast ahead!" He turned to Niall, smiling with satisfaction. "We're right on course."

When they could distinguish the palm trees against the white sand, Niall ordered the porifid into a slow descent. For the greater part of the descent the moon remained hidden behind white clouds. When it emerged again, they were within a mile of the beach and could hear the sound of waves, then the crash of breaking surf. Spray blew into the undercarriage. Niall licked his lips and they tasted of salt. Moments later, the undercarriage rocked under the impact of a large wave; it gained height for a moment, sped across the beach, then scraped to a halt within a dozen yards of the row of palms. The balloon immediately began to collapse on top of them. Niall pushed his way out from underneath it, tangled for a moment with Manetho's muscular legs, then found himself on his hands and knees in the yielding sand.

It was a strange relief to feel solid ground under his feet again, and to see the waves breaking impotently on the white sand instead of waiting below to engulf him. His legs felt stiff and painful as he walked along the beach towards Doggins and Milo, but each step on the damp sand gave him pleasure. Fifty yards further away, Simeon and Ulic were struggling to pull their balloon clear of two palm trees between which it had jammed itself.

Doggins was in a state of wild elation; he threw an arm round Niall's shoulder and squeezed him, gesturing with his other hand at the moonlit beach.

"What do you think of that? Smack on target!" He chuckled. "I told you I felt lucky."

It took them half an hour to unload the balloons, and then to drag them, folded, into the shelter of the trees. A hundred yards away, Milo found a rocky pool fed by a small stream; in this they deposited the porifids and emptied a container of grubs in after them. After the long journey, they were all beginning to feel a certain affection towards the evil-smelling mollusks.

The palm trees ran along a ridge that formed the limit of the beach. On the far side of this, there was a sandy hollow covered with marram grass; here they dragged their baggage and the sacks containing the Reapers and the firebombs. Milo and Ulic, who were in a state of noisy euphoria, wanted to light a fire to cook a meal, but Simeon advised against this; it could attract unwelcome visitors from the interior of the Delta. Niall, meanwhile, used his knife to scrape a shallow depression in the sand, with a hollow for his hip, and lined it with the plastic garment that he had brought from the white tower. He made a pillow from a folded blanket and covered himself over with another blanket that was still slightly damp from the rain. No bed of leaves or esparto grass had ever felt more luxuriously comfortable; within a few minutes he was sound asleep.

When he opened his eyes again, the sky was gray with dawn, although the sun was not yet visible. The first thing he noticed was the smell, the distinctive smell of the Great Delta. It was not simply the odor of rotting vegetation; here, at close quarters, there was another smell that was harder to define, a smell that made him think of damp black earth and of white funguses. As he concentrated on this smell, trying to define its essence, he became aware of the vibration. It was not even necessary to withdraw deliberately into a state of inner relaxation. Here, on the edge of the Delta, the vibration was clearly perceptible, like the breathing of some enormous animal.

The others were all apparently asleep; but when he pushed himself up on to one elbow, Simeon turned towards him and smiled. He had evidently been awake for some time.

"Hungry yet?" Simeon spoke softly, so as not to wake the others.

"Yes, I am." Niall realized that he was ravenous.

"That's the trouble with the Delta." Simeon pushed off his blanket, stood up, and beckoned to Niall. "Let's see if we can find some breakfast."

From his pack Simeon took a long knife, whose machete-like blade was obviously designed for slashing vegetation. He also took a large canvas bag with a shoulder strap. Then, treading carefully around the sleepers, they made their way to the top of a row of sandhills that lay on the far side of the hollow. Now, as the light increased, Niall was struck by the greenness of the vegetation and by the rich coloring of the flowers; the leaves on the low bushes looked as if they had been sprayed with some glossy green paint, while the red, yellow, and purple flowers that grew abundantly from the sandy ground seemed to be trying to call attention to themselves, like the moist lips of an attractive girl. Niall found the effect at once appealing and curiously repellent.

From the top of the sandhills, the view over the Delta was impressive. From here they could see that it was a lowland basin, about fifty miles across at its widest point, bordered by hills to the east and west. At the moment most of it was in shadow, since the sun was only just climbing above the eastern horizon. A silvery mist lay above its central region, whose main feature was a low, forest-covered hill. He could also distinguish the gleam of a river winding its way among the rich green vegetation. At this hour of the morning the Delta looked at once harmless and romantic; only its distinctive smell seemed to carry a note of menace.

They walked down into another valley, whose sides were covered with a carpet of glossy green vegetation that resembled a kind of overgrown watercress; it crunched under their feet and gave off a pungent, but not unpleasant, odor. On the far side of the valley there were a number of low bushes with heart-shaped leaves and a globular yellow fruit with streaks of purple.

Simeon pointed. "That's what we're looking for—the sword bush."

"Is the fruit good to eat?"

"No. It tastes horrible."

They approached a bush whose dewy leaves glistened in the sunlight. Niall started to reach out towards one of the fruits, but Simeon caught his wrist.

"Wait. If you want to survive in the Delta, never obey your first impulse. Almost everything you look at contains some kind of trap."

Simeon reached into the pocket of his tunic and took out a leather glove. He placed this on the end of the long knife, then reached out with it so it touched one of the fruits. In the depths of the bush there was a sudden movement that made Niall jump; then he saw that the glove had been transfixed by a long black spike. Swiftly, Simeon withdrew the knife blade from the glove and slashed downward. The glove fell at their feet; Simeon picked it up, and pulled out the spike. It was made of a hard, glossy wood, and its point was as sharp as a needle. Simeon replaced the glove on the knife and this time reached out towards a fruit at ground level. Once again, a spike leapt out from behind the fruit and impaled the glove. Once again, Simeon withdrew the blade and slashed off the spike. He repeated this procedure three times more. But when he did it a fourth time, nothing happened. Simeon tried it once more, and when there was no response from the bush, he reached out and picked the fruit. He dropped half a dozen of these into his shoulder bag.

"You see? The plant learns quickly. Don't do that!" Niall had bent down to peer into the bush, to try to see the origin of the spikes. Simeon's warning made him jerk back his head. "It's learned that a hand is dangerous, but it might still try to put your eyes out."

"But what does it do with the things it's killed?"

"Pulls them back into the middle of the bush and lets them go rotten. Then it somehow absorbs them."

Niall looked with distaste at the harmless-looking bush. "It seems somehow . . . dishonest."

"But understandable. How would you like to have both your feet planted in the earth so you couldn't move?"

Niall pointed to the rich green leaves underfoot, with their sappy, slightly medicated odor. "Is this dangerous?"

"Only if you fell asleep on it. This smell is a narcotic. You'd go into sweet dreams and never wake up. Like that thing over there." He pointed to a low mound covered with the glossy vegetation.

"What is it?"

"I don't know—perhaps a warthog—they wander down from the rain forest."

Niall bent and peered at the mound more closely, moving some of the leaves aside. He could see a few fragmentary remains of fur, but the pale white stems had taken root in the flesh, so that most of it was indistinguishable from the soil. Simeon said: "Once they're asleep, this stuff grows all over them within hours. It's eating them while they're still alive."

They moved on back towards the camp. Simeon suddenly halted. "Ah, that's what I was looking for."

He led the way towards a clump of bushes with brightly colored flowers. As they came closer, Niall saw that Simeon seemed to be interested in a twisted gray shrub covered with spiky globes, each one about three inches in diameter.

"What is it?"

"We simply call it the protector."

"Is it dangerous?"

"Only if you blunder into it without seeing it. The spines are poisonous—they cause very painful swellings."

Simeon raised the knife and chopped off one of the globes; it fell to the earth like a decapitated head. Simeon pulled the glove onto his hand, and carefully picked up the globe by one of its spines. Then, holding it against the ground, he proceeded to chop at the spines until every one had been removed or broken halfway. He then dropped it into his bag, and went on to collect half a dozen of the globes. He said with satisfaction: "That's a good morning's work. These things are worth their weight in gold."

"What does it do?"

"Repels insects."

The others were still asleep; they skirted the clearing, and made their way to the beach. The sea was now magically calm, with gentle wavelets breaking on the smooth sand. A dazzling road of gold stretched out to the rising sun.

"What now?"

"Now we try to find some breakfast."

They inspected the pool with the porifids; the creatures immediately swam towards them, the mouths opening to reveal tiny pink tongues. Simeon took one of the yellow fruits out of his bag, peeled off its hard skin, then placed it on a flat rock and chopped it into small pieces. Niall watched dubiously; he felt that it was unlikely that the porifids would be interested in fruit. But as soon as Simeon tossed it into the pool, the porifids rose to it and caught it in their open mouths; within thirty seconds, there was not a fragment of fruit left. Niall picked up the skin and sniffed it, then dropped it with disgust; it smelled exactly like decaying flesh.

Simeon said: "It's not just the smell that does it. It seems to contain some oil that animals find irresistible."

They continued along the beach to a point where weed-covered rocks sloped into the sea. They climbed across these until they found themselves looking down into a deep pool, whose bottom was covered with a seaweed that looked as if it was made of trailing green gossamer. The rocky bottom sloped upward in the direction of the sea, so that it would remain half-full of water even when the tide was out. They sat with their legs dangling above the water, while Niall and Simeon both peeled the yellow fruits. Simeon then chopped each of these into large cubes. He squeezed one of the cubes in his hand, so that the oily juice ran down onto the surface of the water. The juice, like the dense flesh itself, was slightly stained with purple. When Simeon dropped the crushed pulp, it sank slowly to the bottom and disappeared among the seaweed. Almost immediately, there was a movement at the far edge of the pool, then a flash of pink; a strange iridescent creature, more than six inches long, shot out from under an overhanging ledge and vanished into the seaweed above the fragment of fruit. Niall had never seen a shrimp or prawn in his life, so was unaware that this one was a giant. Others followed from other parts of the pool, while from a black cave below the surface emerged a small brown and green squid, which instantly seized a fragment of fruit and vanished back into its hole. Simeon finished chopping both fruits and tossed them into the pool; by the time he had finished, the water was full of shrimps fighting for the pieces.

Simeon, meanwhile, moved round to the seaward end of the pool, the long knife in his hand, and waded cautiously into the water. The shrimps were too interested in their feast to pay any attention as he speared one of them against the bottom and tossed it out on the sand. In less than five minutes he had caught a dozen more. Niall picked them up, still wriggling and twisting, dropped them into the shoulder bag.

Simeon had his knife poised above a particularly large specimen and was waiting for it to sink to the bottom, when Niall observed the shimmer of red at the far end of the pool. For a moment he assumed it to be another shrimp; then, as it emerged into the sunlight, he saw from the wavering feelers that it was a big shellfish. For a moment, its sheer bulk held it trapped in the entrance to the underwater cave. Simeon reacted instantly to Niall's shout of alarm, and leapt towards the shallow end of the pool. The giant lobster followed him with unnerving speed; its fighting claw was closing on Simeon's leg as Niall pulled him out of the water.

Niall was appalled by the apparition that was now scrambling out of the pool towards them; to him it resembled a huge scorpion. But Simeon stood his ground; as the lobster slithered on the smooth rock, he raised the knife and brought it down with all his force. The severed claw fell at Niall's feet, closing convulsively on a rock, which splintered like a cracked nut. Simeon raised the knife again, this time towards the eyes; but the lobster was already in retreat. There was a loud splash as it vanished into the water.

Simeon looked down at the calf of his right leg; the flesh had been torn and it was bleeding heavily. But closer inspection showed that the wound was less serious than it looked. The claw had pinched the soft part of the flesh and torn away a long strip, which was now hanging down; but the damage was only superficial.

Simeon was evidently prepared for such an emergency; he took a roll of bandage from his pocket and expertly wrapped the lower part of his leg. Niall, meanwhile, looked with horrified fascination at the fighting claw, which was still opening and closing. It was almost two feet long and was obviously powerful enough to sever a man's leg. When it had stopped moving, Niall picked it up; he needed both hands to lift it.

Simeon chuckled grimly: "Put it in the bag. We'll have it for breakfast."

In fact, the claw was too large to go into the shoulder bag and Niall had to carry it.

While they were still five hundred yards away from the camp, a plume of smoke told them that someone had lighted a fire. The smoke was rising straight into the air.

Simeon said: "The wind's dropped. I thought it would."

They met Manetho, returning from the stream with a saucepan of clear water. Ulic had climbed a palm tree and was throwing down bunches of dates. Doggins had spread a blanket on the ground to serve as a tablecloth, and was hacking chunks from a long white loaf. When he saw the shrimps he chuckled and rubbed his hands.

"My favorite dish. But I've never seen them that size." His eyes widened at the sight of the lobster claw. "It would take all day to cook that."

Simeon smiled. "Oh, I don't think so."

Tossed into the center of the fire, the claw hissed and bubbled as the heat forced out the water. Meanwhile, the shrimps were pushed into the hot ashes at the edge of the fire and covered with burning twigs. It took about half an hour for most of them to cook; then they peeled off the blackened shells and ate the flesh with salt and butter. Niall decided it was the most delicious food he had ever tasted and consumed two of them with the appetite of a starving man. About an hour later, when the fire had turned to red hot ashes, the lobster claw was raked out, kicked onto the blanket, then dragged across the beach to the sea. The shell, which had withstood the heat of the fire, cracked as soon as it was thrown into the water; Niall was able to remove a splinter-shaped fragment, and allow the sea water to cool the interior. When the claw was cold enough to handle, they took it back to camp, where Simeon smashed the shell with a rock, then served a portion of lobster to each of them. Niall regretted that he had eaten two of the shrimps; the lobster flesh was just as succulent and appetizing; but he had to confess defeat after eating less than half his share. Simeon ate every mouthful with stolid determination; Niall could see that it gave him immense satisfaction to consume the limb that had come so close to amputating his own.

When they had finished eating and washed down the food with an aromatic drink made from herbs steeped in hot water, Simeon found a flat stone and used it as a chopping block while he hacked open the gray spiny globes. Each contained a soft, white fruit with a peculiar, penetrating smell that made the eyes sting. One of these was handed to each of them and they were ordered to strip naked and rub themselves from head to foot with the juice. It produced a tingling, burning sensation that was almost painful on the more tender parts of the body. When told to rub it on the bald spot at the back of his head, Doggins pulled a wry face. "Do I have to?"

"Yes. You'll be glad of it before the day's over."

Doggins shrugged and did as he was told.

Simeon unwrapped the bandage from his leg and squeezed the white fruit on the wound, clenching his teeth with pain as he did so. But when he had rubbed the remainder of the juice into the torn flesh, then wiped it carefully with a handful of grass, the bleeding suddenly ceased and the wound seemed to whiten and contract; the juice obviously possessed powerful healing properties.

Manetho looked up at the sun, which was high in the heavens. "Isn't it about time we got started?"

Simeon, who was rebinding the wound with a clean bandage, shook his head. "No. That's the first lesson you have to learn in the Delta: never hurry. Now listen." He looked around. "This applies to all of you, so sit down for a moment and listen. If you want to get out of here alive, I want you to bear this in mind. Try to remember that a plant is never in a hurry. It's got all the time in the world. And if you want to survive the Delta, learn to think like a plant.

"There's something else I want to say. You may not believe this, but plants can read your minds. That means that when you feel tired and vulnerable, they know you're tired and vulnerable. So the most important thing to remember in the Delta is to try to stay in the right state of mind. If you don't, you may never get out again."

Milo said: "But surely the Reapers should protect us from most things?"

"Perhaps. But I want you to bear in mind that the Delta is like a single living organism. It doesn't seem to mind these things"—he gestured at the machete—"but I think we might get a more violent reaction if we tried blasting a way through. I can't be sure of that, but I've got a strong feeling I'm right." He looked at Doggins. "In a place like this, mind power is more important than fire power."

Doggins said: "You know more about the Delta than any of us. So you tell us what we should do."

"Right. First of all, there's no wind, so the balloons are useless. That means we have to go on foot. Now the Delta's about seventy miles from side to side. The thing we're looking for is roughly in the center and I've never been there. All I know is that it's at the meeting point of the two rivers. But our best approach is to stick to the hills. It's less dangerous there. The higher you go, the safer it becomes. About the only real danger at a thousand feet is the strangler tree."

Manetho said: "I've never heard of that one."

"You've probably never heard of most of the trees and plants in the Delta. Half of them seem to be new species and they haven't even got names. The strangler tree looks like another tree that I used to call the snake willow. That's got a lot of hanging lianas covered in moss, and it seems to be harmless. But the lianas of the strangler tree wait until you're halfway through them, then grab you like tentacles. They don't have nearly so much moss on the lianas. You'll soon learn to tell the difference."

Manetho asked: "What about the river? Is that navigable?"

"Possibly, although it's full of sand bars and muddy lagoons. But it's also full of big water scorpions that could overturn any boat or raft. And there's also a nasty carnivorous dragonfly with jaws big enough to bite off your arm. So I think we'd be safer to stick to the hills.

"Another thing to watch out for are the chameleon crabs. They like to lie in ambush under the leaves of the marsh orchid, and their claws are as big as that one we've just eaten."

Ulic said: "This is only a suggestion . . . but wouldn't it be better to wait until we get a strong wind in the right direction, so we can use the balloons?"

"We could." Simeon looked at Doggins. "But we may have to wait for days or even weeks."

Doggins shook his head. "No. Let's get it over with. If we stay here too long, the spiders might decide to come and find us."

Simeon nodded. "I agree. So the only thing to decide is what to take with us. We can't carry all our supplies. I suggest we try to travel light and fast."

They emptied the canvas bags on the ground. There were large quantities of food and drink—most of it in sealed wooden jars—as well as medical supplies. Each contained one of the long bladed machetes suspended from a belt, a small but very sharp hatchet, and a canvas bucket. There were also light backpacks.

Doggins said: "All right. Each of you decide how much you want to carry. But let's try to keep it light."

Niall packed dried biscuits and a quantity of bread, a container of honey, a box of dehydrated meat, and a bottle of the golden wine. He also packed bandages and the small hatchet. The fur-lined garment in which he had traveled was obviously too warm for the Delta; he left it behind with reluctance. Instead, he wore a wayfarer's tunic, made of coarse gray sackcloth. In one pocket he carried the telescopic rod, and in the other, rolled into its small cylinder, the thin, metallic garment from the white tower.

To leave the canvas bags on the ground would obviously be to invite the attention of marauding animals. They were carefully sealed; then Ulic climbed to the top of a tall tree, carrying a rope, and drew up the bags one by one, tying them securely to the trunk. As a precautionary measure, the folded balloons were also drawn up into the lower branches, to keep them beyond the reach of storms or an exceptionally high tide.

Niall emptied a whole container of grubs into the pool containing the porifids, and was rewarded by a blast of nauseating odor that made him stagger backwards; yet he sensed that this was the porifids' method of showing appreciation. The sea looked so still and the beach so clean and peaceful that it was hard to believe they were about to venture into the most dangerous place in the world.

The sun was close to its zenith when they set out and the heat was already becoming oppressive. Simeon led them to the top of the row of sandhills, and they paused while he pointed out the main features of the Delta. Now the sun was high, the central basin was covered with a blanket of misty cloud, and they could see both rivers, descending from the southeast and southwest, although the point where they joined was

86

hidden in the jungle. The low hill between the rivers was also concealed by the mist. In this brilliant light, Niall observed the many different shades of green that formed a kind of patchwork in the basin; by contrast, the forest-covered hills were the same shade of bluey-green.

Simeon pointed to the east. "What we're going to do is to try to get up close to the top of the hills, where the trees are less dense. It's cooler and it's also less dangerous."

Manetho indicated the forest-clad slopes to the west. "That looks easier."

"Yes, but we'd have to cross the river, and I don't want to risk that."

They skirted the clearing with the sword bushes—Simeon explained that he wanted to avoid the cresslike vegetation underfoot because of its narcotic properties—but before they had traveled another half-mile, they found themselves suddenly confronted by a carpet of the rich, glossy leaves that stretched as far as the lower slopes of the forest. The alternatives were retracing their steps or making a northward detour towards the sea, back into a terrain of sandy soil and marram grass.

Simeon said: "I think we can risk it, if we hurry. But we'll try to stick to the northern edge. If anyone feels drowsy, say so right away."

As they tramped forward through the rich, ivy-colored carpet, they became increasingly aware of the sappy, medicated smell, and their shoes were covered with a white, frothy substance that was exuded from the broken stems. Expecting to be overcome with drowsiness, Niall was surprised when, on the contrary, he began to experience a tingling feeling of intensified vitality. The smell seemed so delicious that he was tempted to dip his finger into the frothy sap and taste it, but he resisted the impulse.

This feeling, he realized, was of increased control—the feeling he experienced as soon as he turned the thought mirror. His mind felt more powerful and perceptive, and his body seemed stronger, so the weight of the backpack—with the Reaper tied across its top—no longer made him sweat. The others obviously experienced the same pleasant sensation, and Ulic suddenly became talkative, pointing out the beauty of the flowers that grew among the glossy leaves.

The foothills of the forest slopes were now about a mile away. Milo pointed diagonally to a spot where the trees seemed thinner and they could see a clearing that might be the beginning of an uphill path.

"Wouldn't it be more sensible to go over there?"

To Niall's surprise, Simeon said: "Yes, I suppose it's a lot nearer."

Five minutes later they were surrounded by a sea of cresslike leaves. Niall began to take deep breaths, and reflected that this air was literally like wine, producing the same glowing euphoria. The sensation was so pleasant that he decided to see whether it could be intensified by the thought mirror. He reached inside his tunic and turned the concave side inward.

The effect made him gasp; there was a sharp, stabbing pain across the back of his skull, and the sense of well-being evaporated as abruptly as the sun vanishing behind a cloud. The weight of his backpack seemed to double. His first impulse was to turn the mirror back again, but he changed his mind even as his hand moved upward. Why should the mirror destroy his sense of clarity and control instead of increasing it? He fought against the headache, concentrating his mind. This made things far worse; he began to experience a feeling of suffocation and dizziness, and his legs seemed to have turned to stone. The temptation to turn the mirror became irresistible; he allowed his hand to creep inside his shirt. At that point, some impulse of stubbornness made him hesitate; because it seemed that relief was only a few seconds away, he deliberately endured the feelings of suffocation and nausea. Past experience told him that if he could bring these to a climax, they would vanish.

It happened exactly as he had expected. The headache increased until his eyes seemed to be about to leave their sockets; then the pain vanished and was replaced by a sense of relief. But his limbs still felt heavy, and breathing remained difficult.

With astonishment, he suddenly realized what had been happening. The sense of euphoria had not been induced by the narcotic qualities of the plant, but by the curious lifeforce that permeated the Delta. In some mysterious way, the cresslike plant was able to accumulate and transmit this vitality, using the light that was reflected from the glossy surface of its leaves. Now he was aware what was happening, he could see that they were surrounded by the same sparkling shower of energy that he had observed in the flowers outside Doggins' window, and that they were breathing in this energy as well as the narcotic vapors of the plant. Because the energy was far more powerful than the vapor, they were unaffected by the drug. But why should the plant deliberately neutralize its own opiate?

The answer came a few seconds later. Ulic, who had been talking incessantly, suddenly came to a halt and looked around at his companions with an air of puzzlement. As Doggins started to ask "What is it?" Ulic became very pale and collapsed at their feet. Niall immediately stooped down and raised his head. Ulic's face was already streaked with the milky froth.

The others were also looking gray and tired. As he saw Doggins blink and try to focus his eyes, Niall understood what had happened. The plant had simply ceased to transmit the sparks of vitality, leaving them at the mercy of the narcotic vapors.

Niall removed Ulic's backpack and handed it to Milo. "Give Simeon the Reaper and carry the pack yourself." He beckoned to Manetho. "Help me pick him up—we'll have to carry him."

Manetho was also looking pale, but he was able to call on reserves of physical strength. Without a word, he bent down, seized Ulic under the arms and heaved him to his feet. Then he slung the limp body over his powerful shoulder.

Niall said: "I'll take your pack." He pulled it off Manetho's back and removed the Reaper, which he handed to Doggins; he slung the pack over one shoulder.

"We've got to hurry. Let's head over there." He pointed to the spot where the forest was closest. They began plunging through the cress, trampling its brittle stems underfoot. As they stumbled forward, Niall had the impression that the vegetation was trying to wrap itself round their ankles. His vision had blurred and he felt like a drunken man who already feels the beginnings of a hangover. He had only one aim: to reach the edge of the forest and escape this clinging weed whose odor now seemed disgusting.

Then his feet ceased to encounter resistance. He saw they were treading on springy turf and that the forest trees were less than a hundred yards away. He threw the backpacks on the ground and sank down with his head between his knees. Manetho dropped Ulic beside him and flung himself face down on the grass. Doggins was the last to emerge from the sea of green leaves; he stumbled as he reached the grass and fell on all fours. Then he wrenched off his pack, turned onto his back, and lay with arms outspread.

They lay there for perhaps ten minutes, until the noonday heat became oppressive; then Niall forced himself to stumble into the shade of the nearest trees. The others soon joined him, Manetho dragging Ulic under the arms. Niall selected a small tree whose trunk was covered with smooth, silvery bark, and sat down with his back against it. The leaves overhead—broad green and red leaves, each one more than a hand in breadth—seemed to rustle, as if a wind had passed through them. But as he sat there, his eyes closed, Niall began to experience once again the cool, refreshing sensation, as if he was sitting in the spray of a waterfall. He opened his eyes and became aware that the tree, like the narcotic weed, was able to transmit a shower of vital energy.

This, he now knew, meant that the tree was dangerous; the purpose of the shower of energy was to tempt him into staying there and perhaps into falling asleep. Alerted to this possibility, he carefully observed what was happening. The outermost branches of the tree were slowly bending in towards him. It was a frightening sensation, like watching the slow movements of a hunting animal. But with the Reaper only a few inches from his fingertips, he felt he could afford to wait and see what happened. The branches drooped lower and lower, until they were almost touching the ground and he was surrounded by a green tent that admitted hardly any sunlight. It was then that he became aware that the smooth bark against which he was resting had begun to quiver slightly, as if stirring into wakefulness. As he stared at it, the texture changed; the smoothness vanished, and tiny holes began to appear. A few seconds later, there was a slight hiss, like escaping gas, and he smelt a pleasant, sweet odor that sent a thrill of pleasure through his body. It seemed to induce a vision of wide grassy meadows and distant hills. This turned into a sensation of delicious lassitude, so that he was tempted to lie down on the grass and fall asleep. Instead, he sat up, and crawled on all fours out of the leafy tent, brushing easily through the lower extremities of the branches. From outside, it looked as if the tree had turned into a small green house. The leaves had come together to form an overlapping pattern; its obvious purpose was to prevent the escape of the narcotic gas. As Niall stood and watched, the branches very slowly moved apart, and rose up from the ground. Five minutes later the tree looked exactly as it had when Niall first sat underneath it.

The others were lying with closed eyes, apparently sleeping off the effect of the opiate plant; the sheltering branches above them looked reassuringly normal. Niall was struck by an idea. He seized Ulic by the wrists and dragged him under the tree with the silver bark. He propped his back against the trunk, then sat down beside him. The branches shuddered, and a few moments later the refreshing shower of life-energy surrounded them like fine spray. Ulic stirred and opened his eyes. He shook his head, then looked at Niall with a beatific smile. He asked cheerfully: "How did I get here?"

"Manetho carried you."

"That was good of him." Ulic's voice sounded perfectly normal. "What happened?"

By the time Niall had explained, the tree was exuding its narcotic gas and its branches were moving slowly and silently towards the ground. Ulic was so absorbed that he did not even notice what was happening. When Niall pointed out that they were now enclosed in a tent of greenery, he looked around him with an air of mild surprise. "What does it intend to do?"

"Probably eat us. You can stay to find out if you want to."

As they crawled out again into the sunlight, Niall observed that the color had returned to Ulic's cheeks and his eyes were bright. His own feeling of lassitude had vanished completely and he felt as though he had just awakened from a refreshing night's sleep.

He went and shook Simeon awake. Simeon's face looked gray and blotchy, and he groaned as he tried to sit up. Niall pointed. "Do you know what that tree is?"

"No. Why?" He stared at it without enthusiasm.

Niall explained what had just happened.

"And you don't feel any ill effects?"

"None whatever. There aren't any if you move before it puts you to sleep. Try it."

Simeon allowed them to help him to his feet, but they had to support him as they moved under the branches. Within moments, they were bathed in the exhilarating shower of vital force. Simeon gave a long, slow sigh, then began to breathe deeply and peacefully, his head tilted back against the trunk. By the time the branches had reached the ground, he was fast asleep. But the color had returned to his cheeks.

Ulic shook his arm. "Time to move!"

Simeon started into wakefulness and followed them reluctantly as they crawled outside, then stood and stared with horrified fascination as the branches rose slowly into the air; there was something hypnotic about their movement, which was so gradual as to be almost undetectable.

Ulic said: "But what does it *do*?"

Simeon took the tip of a branch between his fingers. "There's your answer."

The tip was soft, like rubbery flesh, and ended in a blunt point; but as Simeon squeezed it, the point opened and revealed a tiny circular mouth.

"It's probably a bloodsucker." He shook his head sadly. "What a pity that anything so beautiful should be so treacherous."

"What is it called?" It was Manetho who asked the question; he was sitting up with his head between his hands.

"It doesn't have a name, as far as I know."

Ulic said: "We ought to call it the Judas tree."

Simeon chuckled grimly. "That applies to practically everything in the Delta." He bent down and shook Doggins. "Wake up. We've got something to show you."

As Manetho, Doggins and Milo experienced the revitalizing magic of the Judas tree—joined again by Ulic and Simeon—Niall stood by and watched them. He felt no desire to repeat the experience; it would have been as pointless as eating when he was no longer hungry. The strange force of the Delta could raise his vitality only to a certain level; beyond that, he had to do it himself.

The sun was now well past its zenith; Niall judged that it was about the third hour of the afternoon. As they began to pull on their backpacks, Simeon said: "Before we set out, there's something we ought to consider. You've seen what the Delta's like. Do we really want to go on? Wouldn't it be more sensible to go back to our camp and wait for a wind, so we can use the balloons?"

Ulic said immediately: "I want to go on."

Simeon ignored him; he was looking at Doggins. Doggins frowned, biting his lip. He asked: "Do you think we're likely to meet anything the Reapers can't deal with?"

Simeon shrugged. "That's impossible to say." He added, after a pause: "But probably not."

Doggins said: "All right. Then I think we should go on." He looked around. "What do the rest of you think?"

Manetho, Ulic, and Milo spoke together: "Let's go on."

"Niall?"

Niall said: "I think perhaps we should go back now and set out again early tomorrow."

"Simeon?"

Simeon said: "I agree with Niall."

Doggins said: "That's four to two. So we go on."

Simeon shrugged. "Very well." But Niall could see that the decision troubled him.

With Doggins and Manetho now marching in front, they followed a path that led directly up the hill. Although the undergrowth was spiny and dense, the trees were spaced far apart, so they seldom had to use machetes. The hill was steep, but the shade of the trees made it less oppressive, and when they had been climbing for an hour, it was noticeably cooler. Niall was struck by the change in the nature of the trees. On the lower slopes there was an astonishing variety, so that it seemed no two trees were alike. Niall also observed that the trees seemed to be aware of their presence, so the trunks often gave a slight but distinctive shudder as they passed, while the branches stirred as if in a faint breeze. As they climbed, the variety disappeared and the trees became bigger. Finally, the woodland looked like that in any temperate zone, except for the immense size of the trees, which towered up around them like columns supporting the sky.

Two hours after leaving the valley, they found themselves in a clearing with a view across to the western hills. They were on top of a ridge that ran at right angles to the path they had been following, while beyond this the hillside continued for at least another thousand feet. The trees were thinner here and the path along the ridge looked as if it was used by animals. After resting for a while and drinking from a small stream, they set off along this path. For more than half an hour they had encountered nothing that looked even potentially dangerous. Big mosquitoes and gnats occasionally buzzed around them, but seemed to be repelled by the juice with which they had anointed themselves.

Ulic asked: "Are we going to camp up here?"

Doggins nodded. "I suppose so."

"Pity. I'd like to find another one of those Judas trees."

"It's too high up here."

They tramped on for another hundred yards or so, enjoying the sensation of walking on level ground. Ulic said suddenly: "It's not!"

Doggins was puzzled. "Not what?"

"Too high. Look." He pointed into the low valley that sloped downward to the east of the ridge. There was rich green grass among the trees and bright blue flowers like daisies, in the midst of which stood a larger version of the tree with the silver bark and broad leaves. Ulic turned to Doggins. "Can we try it?"

Doggins was obviously reluctant to break off the march; but after two hours of climbing, they all felt stiff and weary. He shrugged. "I suppose so."

With a chuckle of delight, Ulic threw his pack on the ground, then tugged at Niall's tunic. "I'll race you."

What happened next stunned them all. Ulic was running across the grass towards the tree, like a child going for a swim. The ground was flat and they could see for fifty yards in either direction. Then, with shocking rapidity, Ulic was engulfed by something black that rose out of the ground. For a moment Niall thought it was an enormous black flower with a trumpet-shaped head; then the head split into writhing tentacles which wrapped themselves around Ulic's arms and neck as he screamed and struggled.

Doggins was the first to react; he pulled the Reaper from the top of his pack and pointed it towards Ulic.

Simeon struck down the barrel. "Don't. You'll kill him."

Ulic's screams were horrible, but they ceased as a black tentacle wrapped itself round his head, covering his mouth.

Doggins said: "For God's sake, what is it?"

"A ground squid." Simeon was unsheathing his machete. "They can be killed if you cut the roots."

Followed by Manetho, he ran across the grass. Only Ulic's head was now visible; the rest of him had disappeared into the black shape, whose lower end vanished into the ground. He was still struggling violently. Manetho drew back his machete and slashed at the point where the squid emerged from the ground. The flesh seemed resistant, like rubber. As Manetho and Simeon both continued to strike, the squid began to disappear back into the soft earth. To strike again would be to risk killing Ulic. Manetho threw down his machete and flung his arms round the squid; its arms immediately seized him by the neck. As Simeon tried to drag Manetho clear, he was also seized. The squid seemed to have a subsidiary set of tentacles that emerged from the ground level and which wrapped themselves round Manetho's legs.

Milo ran forward, carrying his Reaper. He moved around to the far side of the struggling mass, to avoid Manetho and Simeon, and carefully pointed the Reaper down at the ground. In the bright sunlight, its beam was scarcely visible; but the damp earth hissed and sent up a cloud of steam. He moved the Reaper slowly from side to side. Then, quite suddenly, the struggle ceased. The squid collapsed sideways like a tall black flower, carrying Manetho and Simeon with it. A moment later, Manetho was dragging Ulic out on to the grass; the squid, cut off at the root, moved with him.

Doggins called: "Are you all right?"

Ulic nodded, choking, then vomited.

Niall joined them and looked down into the hole. A black, shiny mass that looked like the remains of a huge slug was still moving convulsively; it gave off the foul, typically decaying stench of the Delta. The remainder of the ground squid was still writhing on the grass, leaving quantities of a green-colored slime; but it was obviously incapable of doing further harm.

After lying face downward on the grass for ten minutes, Ulic had recovered enough to stand up. He made his way, with slow steps, under the branches of the Judas tree and seated himself against its trunk, closing his eyes. A few moments later he opened them again.

"Nothing's happening."

Niall looked up at the branches; there was not the faintest movement. Milo said: "Perhaps the temperature's too low up here."

Simeon shook his head. "In that case, why is the tree growing here? It would starve to death." As he went and sat down beside Ulic, his face wrinkled with disgust. "You need a good bath, my boy." His expression changed. "Yes, of course! That's it! The tree won't attack you because you're coated with the slime from this monstrosity."

Manetho called: "There's a stream down here."

Helped by Milo, Ulic made his way unsteadily down the slope; he pulled off his clothes and plunged into the waist high water. When he emerged, five minutes later, Milo handed him a spare tunic; it was yellow and too conspicuous, but it was an acceptable alternative to his gray traveling garment, which was already stiffening with the glutinous slime. When he sat down under the Judas tree a second time, the branches gave a slight shudder and began to bend slowly downward. The others went and sat beside him, their backs against the broad trunk.

Niall experienced once again the delightfully refreshing sensation that was like sitting in a shower of very tiny water droplets. The tiredness seemed to drain out of his body, producing for a moment a sensation close to pain. When he smelt the strange, sweet gas, he opened his eyes and saw that the branches were now touching the ground. He shook Doggins, who was sitting beside him. "We'd better move before we get eaten."

Reluctantly, they crawled out of the green tent. Some of the branches made a halfhearted attempt to fix on their flesh, but were easily brushed aside; the tree obviously relied on reducing its victims to a state in which they were incapable of resistance.

Niall's weariness had vanished, but the muscles of his calves ached from the long climb. He asked Ulic: "Do you feel strong enough to go on?"

"I think so." But he said it without enthusiasm.

Simeon said: "It will be dark in a couple of hours. Perhaps we ought to start looking for a camping site."

They struggled into their packs and continued to march along the ridge. But the experience of the ground squid had shaken them all and they kept their eyes fixed on the path in front of them. Half a mile further on, Simeon halted and pointed to a grassy clearing just below the level of the road. "Look, there's another of them."

At first they failed to see what he meant. Then Niall was able to distinguish the irregular dark patch among a circle of blue daisies.

"Are you sure?"

"Quite sure. Look closer."

Cautiously, they edged towards it; Doggins was holding his Reaper at the ready. With a thrill of horror, Niall realized that he was being watched; what looked like small patches of white fungus were actually eyes, which narrowed as they came closer.

Doggins spat with disgust. "I'm going to kill it." As he spoke, the thin blue flame, like an illuminated glass rod, struck the patch of black earth. There was a violent hissing noise, like escaping steam; they all jumped back in alarm as the squid erupted out of the ground, its tentacles waving; the stench of decay struck them like a blow. As the beam of the Reaper sliced it in two, the stench increased. A moment later they were all hurrying away, sickened by the smell of the creature's burnt flesh.

Simeon cried suddenly: "Stop!"

They all halted. Simeon said: "We are going too fast. What if one of these creatures was lying in our path? We are risking our lives." He looked at Doggins. "It is better not to kill until we have to."

Doggins saw the justice of the reproach. "I'm sorry. I just thought the earth would be a better place without that thing."

Simeon shrugged. "That is your decision. But if it makes us careless and imprudent, then it is a bad decision. Let us walk slowly and pay attention to the road."

Already the light was beginning to fail. When half an hour later they reached another clearing, they could see that the sun was touching the top of the western hills.

Ulic leaned with his back against a tree. "Could we stop now? I'm very tired." His face had become pale and he was sweating.

Doggins looked at Simeon. "What do you say? Shall we camp here?"

Simeon scanned the ground. "I think it's safe."

With relief, they threw their packs on the grass. Ulic lay down on his back and closed his eyes; within moments he was fast asleep. While Manetho went to fetch water, Niall and Milo collected firewood in the undergrowth; both of them carried their Reapers at the ready, but encountered nothing that alarmed them. Niall found a bush with wild strawberries; although still slightly underripe, they were delicious. Half an hour later, they were sitting around the fire in the gathering dusk, eating a substantial meal of cooked lobster flesh—Simeon had carefully packaged the remainder of the meat from the claw—goat's cheese, dry biscuits with butter, and wild strawberries. They washed it down with a cup of the golden wine. By the time they had finished eating, they had ceased to feel themselves surrounded by menace, and had again begun to regard this expedition into the Delta as an exciting adventure. Provided they observed proper caution, it seemed fairly certain that they had nothing to fear. Yet whenever he glanced at Ulic—who was continuing to sleep soundly—Niall experienced a twinge of anxiety. His face looked too pale and his breathing was hardly visible. When Milo tried to shake him awake to eat, he opened his eyes, smiled, and shook his head. After that, Niall observed how often Simeon glanced at Ulic's sleeping face, and felt his heart contract with foreboding.

As the dusk changed to darkness, Manetho threw more logs on the fire; soon the clearing was illuminated with the leaping flames. Niall yawned and wondered if he could decently retire into his blankets.

Something plunged out of the darkness with a whirring noise, struck the back of his head, and then flew into the fire. They all leapt to their feet. It was a brightly colored moth with a wingspan of two feet. Singed by the flames, it fell into the fire, and its frantically beating wings filled the air with sparks and ashes. Manetho seized a dry branch and struck the moth to the ground, then killed it with a single blow. But they had no sooner resumed their seats around the fire than two more moths descended out of the darkness and made straight for the flames. Their sheer size meant that they scattered glowing fragments of wood all over the clearing. Above them, more wings flapped in the darkness. But the fire was now merely a mass of glowing embers and hot ashes, and there was not enough light to attract moths. So they lay there in the darkness, which still smelt of woodsmoke and scorched cloth—where embers had fallen on the blankets—and talked quietly about the prospects for the next day, and about how the beetles and the spiders would react to their disappearance. Niall once again spread out the metallic garment on the grass as a groundsheet and wrapped himself in two blankets; he used his spare tunic from the haversack as a pillow. Gradually, the conversation lapsed; then someone began to snore softly.

He was drifting into sleep when Milo's voice woke him up. Milo said softly: "Simeon." There was no reply; it was Simeon who was snoring. Milo repeated "Simeon" in a louder voice. Doggins' voice asked out of the darkness: "What is it?"

"I think Ulic's dead."

They all woke up. Manetho used the tinder box to kindle a flame. But by this time, Niall had placed his hand on Ulic's forehead and he already knew that Milo was right. Ulic was cold and still. The flame showed that his face looked as pale as marble. Niall experienced a wave of pity and sorrow.

Simeon said: "But what killed him?" By the tiny flame of the burning shavings, he examined Ulic's bare arms, then his legs. As the flame hovered over Ulic's knee, Simeon pointed. "That's what did it."

The right knee was swollen and looked bruised. On closer examination, Niall could see the tiny puncture mark in the middle of the swelling. Simeon said: "That damned thing must have had a sting. I thought he was limping . . ."

There was nothing to be done in the darkness. They covered Ulic's body with a blanket and moved it closer to the glowing embers, as if the warmth might revive him. Then, once again, they lay down to sleep. Although he could see and hear nothing, Niall could sense that Milo was crying.

He lay awake, staring up into the black sky. All desire to sleep had vanished. Now, for the first time since they had left the city of the beetles, he began asking himself what they were trying to achieve. The death had shaken him. Marcus, Yorg, Cyprian, and now Ulic. His whole being was convulsed with a feeling of misery and revulsion. It was no use telling himself that their deaths were part of a heroic struggle. They seemed merely a stupid mistake.

The inner turmoil was so acute that he found it hard to lie still. His natural impulse was to get up and walk around, but he knew this would be rash and dangerous. So he concentrated all his willpower on suppressing the desire to move and forced himself to lie rigid under the blankets.

In the distance he could hear the night cry of some animal and the crashing of a heavy body through the undergrowth. He reached out cautiously to make sure the Reaper was close beside him, and experienced a sense of comfort as his fingers closed on the point where the butt joined the barrel. Then he seemed to see an image of Doggins destroying the ground squid, and it crystallized his sense of dissatisfaction. For the first time, he understood the curious mixture of shame and delight that he had experienced the first time he handled the Reaper. The delight came from a sense of power. *But it was the wrong kind of power.*

For a moment, his insight puzzled him. After all, the ground squid was a horrible and dangerous creature; no one could blame Doggins for killing it. Yet there had been no *need* to destroy it. Doggins had killed it because it aroused in him a feeling of fear and revulsion. He had killed it to exorcise this fear, instead of trying to conquer it with his mind.

The weight of the telescopic rod against his thigh reminded him of the white tower. Now, suddenly, he seemed to hear the words of the Steegmaster; they sounded so clear that it was as if they had been spoken inside his own head. "I want to know why you think the spiders deserve to be destroyed and man deserves to survive. Is man so much better than the spiders?"

Steeg had gone straight to the point. What right had man to try and take over the earth from the spiders? His past history showed that he was unfit to be master of the earth. All his achievements had failed to make him happy. By the time he had evacuated earth to colonize the Centauri system, he had already proved himself a failure.

Could this be the answer to Steeg's riddle—to that question of why he could not help Niall to conquer the spiders? The thought made Niall's heart sink. Yet the more he considered it, the more likely it seemed. When he thought of the glue flies, and of how Doggins had forced them to fly until they had died of exhaustion, he felt saddened and ashamed. Yet when he remembered his own joy as he pointed the Reaper at the spiders and pulled the trigger, he knew that he had no right to regard himself as any better.

These thoughts produced a frightening sensation that was like sliding backwards down a slope. He felt confused and strangely vulnerable. Until a few minutes ago he had felt no doubt whatever about his central purpose: to help to free men from the domination of the spiders. Now, suddenly, it seemed highly questionable.

Someone began to snore—it sounded like Doggins—and he found it oddly comforting; it seemed to restore a sense of normality. For a moment he thought that his despair had been some kind of mistake, a momentary fit of discouragement. Then his mind came back to the central fact: that men were no more fitted to be lords of the earth than the spiders; and again he experienced that sense of sliding backwards.

His fingers crept to the thought mirror, then withdrew. It seemed pointless to use it; he felt no desire to concentrate his mind. Then, as if challenging the mirror to make any difference to his sense of hopelessness, he turned it over. There was a sensation like a fist clenching inside his brain, and the despair vanished. Instead, there was again a feeling of power and control. In a flash, he recognized the answer to the problem. Human civilization had been a failure because man had gained control over the material world without gaining control over his own mind. But this did not mean that man had no right to be master of the earth, for the spiders also lacked control over their own minds—this was proved by their cruelty and stupidity and the pleasure they took in exercising their power. At least man had the insight to know that he lacked control over his own mind. In that respect, at least, he could claim to be better than the spiders . . .

The sky above his head was becoming lighter, so he could see the black outline of the treetops against the blue void. Behind the trees, the moon was rising; it was still invisible, but its light was reflected from the single cloud that drifted overhead. Niall also felt that light was filtering into his inner landscape. Its source was still invisible, but the knowledge that it was there brought a feeling of comfort and relief.

As soon as consciousness began to return, he became aware of the vibration of the Delta. Now it no longer reminded him of the breathing of some huge animal; it was more like the distant vibration of a great machine.

The sky above the eastern treetops was lightening, although they were still in darkness; but the swamplands below would already be illuminated by the rising sun. And the urgent vibration of the force, he now realized, was a response to the rising sun. This thought intrigued him. It suggested that, if the force responded to the dawn, it must be awakening from its sleep, like some giant plant or animal . . .

Since he was still drifting in the state between sleep and waking, it was easy to sink into the stillness of deeper awareness. As soon as he did so, he became conscious of the vast presences of the trees and realized that they were also awakening. Suddenly, he understood why they were so big. The underground force was arousing them out of their dim, dreamlike vegetable consciousness, awakening them to greater effort. But because the temperature here was too low to incubate this new consciousness, their effort could only be directed upward, towards the sky.

The vibration was also flowing through Niall, producing a peculiar exhilaration. Yet he felt no desire to experience it more deeply; to have done so would have meant deliberately reducing his intelligence to a lower level. Humankind had already evolved to a higher rate of vibration, and although his body responded to the invigorating power of the force, his mind found it somehow vulgar and unsatisfying. Yet it also gave him courage because it made him aware that he was capable of raising the vibratory rate of his own mind.

The others were still asleep. Niall took his Reaper and made his way over the ridge and down to the stream. At this point it was scarcely knee deep. He removed his tunic and sat down in the stream, experiencing once again the delight of the desert dweller at the sight of an abundance of water. And then, as he stared down into the clear water, which reflected the paling sky, he experienced the illusion that he was back in the shallow stream in the country of the ants. It lasted only for a fraction of a second, but it filled him with a strange feeling of pure joy. And as he splashed the water over his body, he glimpsed the source of this delight. It was as if a door had opened, permitting him a sudden vision of an immense inner wonderland. In that moment, he understood why the vibration of the Delta flowed past him and left him unmoved. It was because he already possessed inside himself this enormous source of joy, and its intensity was far higher than that of the underground force of the Delta. Unlike the trees, his life was not confined to the present moment; every joy he had ever experienced was carefully preserved in his inner wonderland, waiting to be relived with all its original intensity. It was the realization that, unlike plants and animals, human beings are the masters, not the slaves, of time.

As he pulled on his tunic over his wet body, he was indifferent to the cold; in fact, the discomfort was curiously pleasing and interesting. Walking back to the camp, he carried the Reaper upside down by its trigger guard. His intuition told him that, in this state of mind, his life was not at the mercy of some casual accident.

Simeon was already awake and was engaged in sewing Ulic's body into a blanket.

Manetho woke up, looked around with his broad, good-natured smile and yawned. "This place makes you ravenous. I could eat a roast camel."

Simeon said: "There's no time to roast anything. We've got a long day ahead of us. Can you climb trees?"

Manetho looked up dubiously at the hundred-foot columns soaring above them. "I suppose so. Why?"

"I think we should leave Ulic up a tree instead of burying him. In this ground, he wouldn't last long. But if we leave him up a tree, we might be able to return and take him back home for burial."

Awakened by their voices, Milo sat up and pushed away his blankets. He looked pale and tired; it was obvious that he had slept badly. He laid his hand against Ulic's cheek. "Are you sure he's dead?"

"Quite sure. He's as stiff as a board."

As Milo stared down at his friend, his face was stony; it seemed that he had no emotion left.

They ate a breakfast of bread and dried meat, with cups of cold water. There was no time to light a fire; all felt a sense of urgency, and ate as quickly as they could. Milo finished first and took from his haversack a coil of thin rope. To one end of this he tied a heavy piece of burnt wood from the fire. Then he flung the wood with all his strength towards the lowest branch of a tree whose trunk was as wide as a dozen men. It fell short, almost striking Milo on the head. Manetho picked it up and hurled it into the air; it curved upward, over the branch, and fell down on the other side. The rope was more than long enough to stretch double from the branch to the ground. Gripping both strands firmly in his huge hands, Manetho shinned up it, and scrambled up onto the branch. After this, Ulic's rigid body, now encased in its blanket-shroud, was drawn up into the air. Using another length of rope, Manetho tied it firmly to the branch; then he lowered himself back to the ground. They stood for a moment, staring silently upward, and taking a mental farewell of Ulic; then, still without speaking, Doggins led the way back to the trail.

For the next two hours they continued to follow the ridge until it vanished into a tree-lined valley and petered out. From this point, they could look down on the central area of the Delta, with its yellow-green jungle, in the midst of which they could see the gleam of the river. A dozen miles or so to the south lay the junction of the two rivers, and between these the forest-clad hill rose from the flat swampland like some strange monument. At this distance, they could see that it seemed to be surmounted by a construction like a tower.

They were now faced with a choice: either to descend the valley to the jungle below or to journey on up the far side of the valley, continuing in the same direction as the ridge that had brought them so far. Since there was a tacit agreement that their immediate aim was the junction of the two rivers, it seemed, on the whole, more sensible to pursue their present course above the jungle, and to leave the descent to the plain until the last possible moment. So, after refreshing themselves in the fast stream that ran down the valley, they climbed the grass-covered slope towards the nearest gap in the trees.

Even as they climbed this slope, Niall could see that the character of the vegetation was changing. The grass was thicker and more lush than on the other side of the stream, and when he accidentally stumbled and landed on it with both hands, he experienced a curious and unexpected sensation; the grass seemed to be alive against the palms of his hands and to be writhing away from him. It felt thick and moist and, when he gripped it firmly, it was like closing his fingers on a handful of thin green tentacles. He tried to pluck a blade, but it was oddly tough and resistant.

As they drew closer, they could see that the character of the trees had also changed. They were still enormous, but they were no longer broad, straight columns. This was not woodland but tropical forest. The trunks were black and many had a scaly, reptilian appearance. Others were broad at the base, but tapered just below the branches; they also had a twisted appearance, as if some giant had seized them and tried to screw them out of the ground. These trees were unmistakably more alive than those in the forest on the other side of the valley, and their roots seemed to be trying to tear themselves out of the ground. Some of them reminded Niall unpleasantly of crouching spiders. As soon as he stepped among them, he had a sense of being observed, as if invisible eyes were watching him from the branches.

The ground underfoot was covered with bushes and creepers, among which were many exotic flowers. Doggins surveyed this undergrowth with suspicion. He asked Simeon: "Is it safe?"

"At this height, yes. That's the only really dangerous thing." He pointed across the clearing to a strikingly attractive pink flower that reared up out of snakelike creepers. He turned to Manetho. "Lend me your machete."

Simeon crossed the clearing, with a machete in either hand, and approached the flower, which was about two feet wide. The strangely shaped petals might have been the sails of a boat; but it looked harmless enough. He reached out the machete in his left hand and touched the flower. Instantly, the petals closed around the blade and the machete was jerked out of his hand. With a single powerful movement, Simeon slashed with the other machete, severing the broad green neck that supported the flower. The decapitated neck writhed like a snake, and to Niall's astonishment, a red blood-like liquid welled out of it. The pink flower, still gripping the machete, fell into the mass of creepers at the base of the stem. Simeon bent and grasped the machete by the handle; as he did so, creepers suddenly uncoiled and seized his wrist and forearm. He hacked at them with the machete in his right hand and succeeded in cutting through most of them; but, even as he was doing this, a great broad creeper, as thick as Manetho's arm, emerged from the bottom of the plant and wound itself round Simeon's ankle. Simeon turned and called: "Give us a hand." Then, abruptly, he lost his balance as he was jerked off his feet. He roared with alarm as the thick creeper began to draw him into the center of the bush.

The others were beside him in a moment, hacking at the creepers. Niall observed that the headless stem was also attacking Simeon, curling under one armpit and trying to pull him into the broad leaves; Niall severed it with a single blow. But it was more than five minutes before they finally succeeded in pulling Simeon clear. He regained his feet, panting, and looked back towards the decimated plant with a grim smile.

"Let that be a lesson to you in overconfidence. When I was last here—five years ago—those damn things were fairly easy to handle. Now they're far more dangerous. That means they've been changing all the time." He looked around him. "Nothing ever stays the same in the Delta." He wiped off some of the blood-like liquid that was running down his cheek, contemplated the juice on his fingers, then sniffed it. The pink flower was now lying on the ground, its petals still gripping the machete. Simeon freed the machete, and at the same time tore off one of the petals. He sniffed it, then placed a corner in his mouth.

Doggins said: "Watch out—it might be poison."

"Unlikely. This thing already has one adequate defense system." He nibbled. "Mmm. That's interesting. Try it." He held out a piece to Doggins, who shook his head. But Niall accepted it and bit gently into the soft flesh. It was remarkably pleasant. The flesh had the consistency of a very thick leaf, at once crisp and juicy, and a flavor that reminded him of the golden wine.

Niall tore another petal off the flower and offered it to Milo. "Try it. It's very good."

Soon even Doggins had overcome his suspicion and was chewing with obvious pleasure.

Simeon said: "It's a trap, of course. The flower is intended to lure insects into the bush, where they get eaten." He pointed to a snake-like creeper that lay severed at their feet. "And that's obviously intended to capture larger animals."

Milo said: "I haven't seen any animals so far."

"You will."

Manetho said: "Surely there can't be many, with plants like this around?"

Simeon shook his head. "If the Delta was like any other place on earth, you'd be right. But the Delta is a kind of evolutionary melting pot." He gestured around him. "These things are all experiments. If one of them can't survive, it's scrapped and something else takes its place. So there's a continuous turnover of new life forms."

The flesh of the pink flower was particularly satisfying to the stomach; it also seemed to contain some kind of mild stimulant, for it left behind a glowing sense of exhilaration. As they resumed their journey, they were all feeling more cheerful and confident. Although the ground was covered with many varieties of bush and flower and creeper, these formed no real obstacle to their progress. If they raised their feet and planted them firmly, the vegetation crunched underfoot, producing a sweet, sappy odor with a touch of the scent of roses. After the experience of the previous day, Niall was on his guard; but a deliberate effort of relaxation made him aware that this vegetation was making no attempt to transmit the vibrations of the Delta, and was therefore harmless. But he found it difficult to maintain this state of relaxed awareness, for everything he passed had its own type of consciousness, from the drowsy benevolence of giant orchids, whose only purpose was to lure bees to disseminate their pollen, to the baleful menace of the strangler trees, whose trailing lianas, like the tentacles of a Portuguese man-o'-war, twitched with a horrible desire to grip and throttle. At first it was invigorating to experience these many varieties of awareness, and to recognize that his own narrow human consciousness was only one type among many; but after half an hour or so, he felt replete with new impressions and experienced relief as his consciousness returned to its usual restricted and limited state.

It was clear that the path they were following must have been made by animals, or perhaps by one single large animal, for there were places where great trees had been pushed over at an angle, while smaller ones had simply been flattened. After half a dozen miles or so, the path began to curve downhill, and they became aware of a rise in temperature. Now they could hear the continuous faint hum of insects and the vegetation became more dense. A thick purple creeper suddenly wound itself round Manetho's leg and when he hacked it off with one blow, it twitched and writhed like a bisected worm, a dark blue liquid oozing from the severed end. There was a high, whining noise that made them all jump with alarm, and the wriggling segment was carried away by a long-bodied flying insect with green eyes and a pointed sting protruding from the tail. Simeon identified this as a member of the Tabanid or horsefly species. The foot-long specimen that had seized the creeper was a male and therefore harmless to humans—the male preferring to feed on nectar. Simeon described the female, which sucked blood, as one of the most unpleasant pests in the Delta. The juice with which they had rubbed their bodies should afford them protection from horseflies, as well as from the anopheles mosquito; but in case the effect had worn off during the past twenty-four hours, they halted and rubbed more of the juice on exposed areas of skin, as well as impregnating their tunics. They had become so accustomed to the sharp, ammonia smell that they no longer noticed it.

Now, at last, the path between the trees ran directly downhill and they could see across the valley of the Delta. Directly ahead of them, perhaps a dozen miles away, lay the hill with its tower-like projection. Its shape was striking; it might have been a giant head, whose lower part dissolved into a flowing beard and mane that blended with the forest below, while the tower-like projection looked like the spike on some fantastic helmet.

Niall asked Simeon: "Do you know what that is?"

"No. I've never been close enough to find out. In fact, I've never been this close."

As they descended the slope, the smell of rotting vegetation was stronger; the ground under its carpet of leaves became moist and spongy. When another purple creeper grasped Milo by the ankle, Doggins raised his Reaper.

"Why don't we just blast a path through it?"

Simeon shook his head. "Not yet. This place is alive. You can never tell how it might react."

Doggins looked at him with mild astonishment, as if he doubted his sanity; but he lowered the Reaper.

Ten minutes later, they finally saw the creature that had made the path through the trees. The path ahead of them turned a bend and as they approached it, Niall observed a sudden swaying in a tree-top a few hundred yards ahead. He laid a hand on Simeon's arm and they all halted, then advanced cautiously. They rounded the bend and stopped in amazement. The enormous green creature that moved slowly towards them might have been a giant caterpillar, but the reflection of the sun on its green scales revealed that it was a millipede. This was confirmed when it withdrew its head from the vegetation and looked curiously towards them, revealing the blunt head and tiny wriggling legs that arched sideways like the pincers of a crab. Doggins raised the Reaper again, but Simeon gently pushed it down.

"They're quite harmless. Unless it walks over you."

The body of the millipede filled the path, which was about eight feet wide; it must have been at least twenty yards long. The strange, flat eyes regarded them mildly for a few moments; then the creature lowered its head and continued browsing. Its jaws made a continuous crunching sound and the head moved slowly from side to side, gathering the flowers and creepers with the thoroughness of a harvesting machine. It ate so fast that it moved ten feet towards them as they stood staring at it. When some succulent flower lay slightly beyond its normal reach, in a glade beside the path, it simply moved the upper half of its body sideways, and there was a tearing, creaking sound as trees were pushed aside. Then, having cleared the glade efficiently of its carpet of flowers, the millipede would resume its slow forward progress.

They all looked to Simeon for a lead. He said: "We can try getting past it. It won't attack us."

Doggins said: "What if it rolls on us?"

"That's unlikely. Let's try, anyway."

But as soon as they came within a dozen feet of the browsing millipede, it raised its head again and suddenly exuded a stench that sent them staggering and choking back up the path. For sheer foul rottenness, it was worse than anything Niall had ever smelt in his life.

Manetho, still coughing and retching, said: "Let's go around it. Nothing can be as bad as that smell."

Their Reapers at the ready, they stepped off the path into the undergrowth. Creepers writhed underfoot, but made no attempt to attack them; Niall sensed that this was because of the proximity of the crunching jaws of the millipede; the creepers responded to the alarm of the vegetation that was being torn out by the roots. Manetho, who was leading the way, halted when he found his path blocked by a tree whose forest of hanging tentacles brushed the ground; but closer inspection showed this to be a snake willow, the harmless relative of the strangler tree, and they were able to push

108

their way through without difficulty. A dozen yards further on, they encountered the strangler tree itself. To the casual glance, it looked exactly like the snake willow: a trunk covered with strange, hairy scales, and hundreds of yellow green lianas hanging down like a woman's trailing hair. But the lianas looked more fresh and green than those of the snake willow; this was because the snake willow attracted a kind of gray moss, which hung down in trailing beards from the top of the lianas, and which covered them with a damp mold.

While Simeon was explaining the difference, a female horsefly settled momentarily on the back of Manetho's head, the lance-like proboscis poised to drive into his flesh. Perhaps disconcerted by the smell of the protective juice, it paused long enough for Manetho to reach up, grab one of its wings, and hurl it violently from him. It fell to the ground at Niall's feet and immediately flew upward into the hanging lianas. For a moment nothing happened and the horsefly blundered downwards; it looked for a moment as if it was about to escape. Then, with frightening swiftness, the tentacles coiled round its body and vanished into the branches above. The fly gave a despairing buzz as it disappeared. A few moments later the lianas descended and the tree again looked as harmless as its cousin, the snake willow.

"What happened to the fly?"

Simeon said: "There's a kind of mouth in the top of the trunk." The thought made them all shudder.

By now, the sounds of the browsing millipede had receded behind them; and since the tree blocked their way forward, they decided to return the way they had come. They emerged onto a path that had been completely cleared of vegetation, so that it looked almost like a man-made road. The millipede had already moved on a hundred yards uphill.

Milo said: "Look, it's turned round." The millipede's head, which was eating the vegetation at the edge of the path, rose and looked at them, a fragment of creeper hanging from its jaws; then, deciding they were harmless, it continued to eat.

Niall said: "But the other end's eating as well."

They stared with open-mouthed amazement. There could be no possible doubt; the millipede had a head at either end. The head that was now turned towards them seemed smaller and more pointed than the other, but it functioned with the same efficiency. Its partner had overlooked many juicy stems, particularly at the edge of the path; these were now removed with a certain delicate precision, the head at the rear having more time to complete its task. As it chewed a creeper—which writhed frantically as it vanished into the corner of its mouth—the flat, sleepy eyes gave them a sideways glance that seemed to contain such an infinitude of disgust that they all burst into roars of laughter, and then laughed more loudly still as the millipede gave a start of alarm and hurried forward several yards.

Doggins said: "Well, at least the Delta seems to have a sense of humor."

Simeon said: "That thing didn't develop two heads to make you laugh."

They were all in high spirits as they followed the path downhill; the absence of vegetation made walking a pleasure. But Niall was lost in thought and deliberately walked behind the others, so as not to be drawn into conversation. The sight of the double-headed millipede had filled him with wonderment, but also with an underlying excitement. The creature looked comic, though the purpose behind its absurd appearance was deadly serious. Yet even Niall could see that it was an evolutionary disaster. The tremendous life force of the Delta had driven it to grow until it was as large as a row of houses. That meant that it had to devote its whole life to feeding to sustain its gigantic body. This had left it vulnerable to enemies, so it had developed two heads so it could see the approach of enemies from both directions. In that case, why not a series of eyes along its backbone, or all along both sides? The real answer would have been for it to limit its size and develop more formidable weapons. But its lack of brain prevented it from making the sensible choice . . .

All this led him back to the question: what had gone wrong with human evolution? Millions of years of struggle had made man a specialist in the art of survival. His evolution had turned into a broad downhill path. Then why had he been so frustrated and dissatisfied when the comet forced him to abandon the earth? Why did men seem incapable of real happiness?

In a sense, the answer was obvious: because he was incapable of *appreciating* a life without problems. Yet this was obviously an absurdity. Man had created civilization to solve problems: the problem of food, the problem of security, the problem of peace of mind.

110

Why should he feel bored and dissatisfied *because* he had solved all his problems . . . ?

Milo said: "Oh look! There's another of those trees."

As they were approaching the edge of the forest, the woodland had become less dense, so they could see for a greater distance between the trees. Instead of tangled undergrowth there was rich grass underfoot. A dozen yards away, standing in a small clearing on its own, stood a big Judas tree, its pale green leaves reflecting the sunlight. It was at least twice as tall as those they had seen so far and the quivering leaves gave it a festive appearance.

Milo said: "Can we stop and try it?"

Doggins shook his head. "No. We've got a long way to go and it's already midday."

"It would only take five minutes."

"There's just not time."

Manetho said: "I could do with a drink."

Milo said quickly: "So could I."

They halted and removed their packs.

Doggins said: "My God!"

"What is it?"

"Look." He pointed at the ground. Niall could see nothing unusual in the lush green grass. Doggins said: "Watch." He lifted his pack; the earth underneath it was bare. Slowly, he lowered it to the ground a few feet away; as he did so, the grass underneath it moved sideways with a gentle, wavelike motion. When Doggins raised the pack again, the ground was again bare. But the naked brown patch a few feet away was now covered with grass.

"Ever seen anything like that before?"

Simeon shook his head. "Never."

He bent down and picked up a blade of grass; as the shadow of his hand fell over it, the rest of the grass moved sideways. Simeon held the grass blade up against the sunlight. He chuckled. "Look at that!"

Niall peered over his shoulder. At the bottom of the grass blade—which was more than a quarter of an inch thick—there were tiny white roots. When Simeon pinched the blade, these wriggled like a millipede's legs.

"Walking grass!"

Niall knelt down on the ground and seized a handful of the grass; it attempted to escape the shadow of his hand, but was not able to move fast enough. It seemed to writhe in his hand, and as he held it upside down, he could see the wriggling of thousands of thin white legs. He replaced it on the ground in the middle of the path made by the millipede; the grass seemed quite contented to remain there. Niall knelt on all fours and peered at it. The tiny legs had now vanished into the earth. But as soon as he reached for it, allowing the shadow of his hand to fall across it, the grass instantly uprooted itself and moved sideways, establishing itself again a few inches away.

He plucked a single blade, and nibbled it. It tasted exceptionally sweet and juicy, and was tender enough to swallow.

Milo began to laugh. "Can you imagine the expression on the face of that millipede as it tries to take a huge bite and finds it's got a mouthful of earth!"

Simeon said: "It's not fast enough to escape any normal herbivore—look." He moved his hand over it; in its attempt to escape, the grass bunched together into a thick mass. This over-crowding effect produced the wave-like motion.

"Then why does it move?"

"To escape the sun when it's too hot and the shadows when it's too cold. Another example of accelerated evolution." He looked around with grudging admiration. "This place could keep a thousand scientists busy for a century."

Milo said: "I'd rather stay at home." A shadow crossed his face, and Niall could tell that he was thinking about Ulic.

Doggins said: "Oh, well, I suppose we may as well stop and eat here. There's not much shade out there." The terrain ahead of them was obviously swampland; it was covered with rich green grass and flowering shrubs, but there seemed to be few trees.

Manetho pointed. "There's another of those pink flowers. Shall I get it?"

Doggins shrugged. "Be careful." He turned to Niall. "You'd bet-ter go with him."

The bush was among the trees on the far side of the path; as they approached it, Niall observed the faint quiver that ran through its leaves. His grip tightened on the Reaper. But by the time they were within a few feet of the bush, there was no sign of motion. The pink flowers diffused their sweet, heavy fragrance, and the bush looked as harmless as a garden shrub. The whip-like tentacles were hidden behind the glossy leaves. They stood looking at it for a moment, watching for any sign that might reveal that the bush was aware of their presence, but it was motionless.

With a single, swift movement, Manetho raised the machete and sliced off one of the flowers; it fell a few feet away, on the bare earth. At the same moment, Manetho leapt backwards. But he was not fast enough to escape the green tentacle that lashed out of the bush and seized his wrist. As he tried to tear himself away, more tentacles wrapped themselves round his legs. Another attempted to seize Niall, but he was standing too far away.

Aiming carefully, Niall pressed the trigger. The blue beam severed the tentacle that was holding Manetho by the wrist; then, as he lowered the weapon, sliced through the thicker tentacles that held his legs. Manetho fell backwards onto the ground. The severed ends of the tentacles continued to wriggle; the others had retreated back into the bush.

Manetho picked up the pink flower; it immediately tried to close on his hand, but was too weak to exert any grip. Manetho tore off a strip of petal, and put it into his mouth.

"Excellent. Better than the other one."

"It should be. That plant was more dangerous."

They divided the petals among them and ate them with the biscuits and dried meat. The flavor, as Manetho had said, was richer than the one they had tasted earlier. Niall was intrigued to observe that, in spite of the honey-like fragrance, there was a flavor that reminded him of fresh meat. The juicy petals made a delicious accompaniment to the dried meat and biscuits.

Doggins glanced up at the sun. "Time we moved on."

As he spoke, Niall experienced a tingling sensation against his right thigh; he recognized it immediately as the peculiar vibration of the telescopic rod. He reached into his pocket. The electrical tingling was so strong against his fingertips that he almost snatched his hand away. Then, as he was about to take the rod out of his pocket, it ceased.

Simeon had noticed his change of expression. "Is anything the matter?"

"Nothing." Niall decided it must be some freak effect of the atmosphere of the Delta.

Milo stood up. "I'm going to sit under the tree for a moment."

Simeon said: "Hurry up. And take your Reaper."

"Reaper?" Milo looked surprised.

"Never take risks in the Delta."

Niall decided that a few minutes under the tree might dissipate the drowsiness induced by the food. He picked up his Reaper and followed Milo. Manetho also rose to his feet.

As Milo bent to duck under the branches, Niall saw them shudder. His sense of danger was suddenly alert; the shudder was like the eagerness of a hungry animal. He halted and called: "Be careful." But, even as he spoke, the tree shut like a trap. It was as swift as the leap of a trapdoor spider. Milo screamed as the branches closed in on him with a downward movement like the closing of a hand.

Niall raised his Reaper, but checked the impulse to fire. In that writhing mass of branches, which had now closed down against the trunk, it was impossible to know where Milo was situated. But the frantic scream of "Help me!" banished his hesitation. He pointed the Reaper at the top part of the tree, pulled the trigger, and moved the weapon sideways. The tree hissed like an angry snake as its topmost branches suddenly crashed down, and Niall was sprayed with drops of liquid sap. But the lower branches continued to grip and squeeze. They had now closed in so tightly that the roots of the tree were exposed. Niall pointed the Reaper downward, and pulled the trigger. The tree shuddered convulsively, and some of the branches thrashed like frantic arms. As the tree fell towards him, Niall jumped backwards; at the same moment, Milo stopped screaming. One of the branches lashed at Niall, knocking him off his feet. The tree crashed down a few yards away.

The branches resisted as they tried to tear them apart; it was like trying to force steely fingers to relax their grip. Then Manetho pulled one of them aside by sheer strength, and shouted: "I can see him. Give me a Reaper." Niall handed him his own; Manetho took aim, and carefully sliced off the top six feet of the tree. The branches suddenly released their hold. Simeon pushed them aside and dragged Milo clear. His face was blue, and his clothes were soaked in blood.

Simeon bent over him, tearing open his tunic; he bent down and placed his ear against Milo's chest. "He's still breathing. Bring some water."

Doggins brought his water bottle. Simeon splashed water on Milo's face, using his hand to clean away the blood. Niall struck furiously at a horsefly that tried to settle on Milo's chest and knocked it several feet away. Milo opened his eyes and tried to turn his head.

"Are you all right?"

He tried to speak, but his voice choked. The horsefly made a second attempt to settle on him, and was slammed to the ground by a blow of Manetho's huge hand. A moment later, it had been crushed underfoot; the air filled with a peculiar, bitter odor.

They removed Milo's tunic and washed his body in cold water; when the blood had been cleaned away, they could see that his skin was covered with tiny bruises and puncture marks. It looked as if his flesh had been pierced by a thousand thorns. He was also bleeding from both nostrils. As Simeon prodded and squeezed his limbs, looking for broken bones, he gasped and winced; then he fainted.

Simeon looked down at a swollen ankle. "No bones broken, as far as I can tell. But he's not going to be able to walk for a few days."

Doggins gave a groan of rage. "What are we going to do now?"

"We've two alternatives. We could either make a stretcher and carry him back. Or we could leave him here."

Milo's eyes opened. "You go on." His voice was little more than a croak.

They looked at one another. Simeon said: "I'd have to stay with him. He can't stay here alone."

Milo tried to force himself up on to one elbow. "Yes I can. I'll be all right. It's my fault anyway . . ."

Doggins glared at him savagely. "Yes, it bloody well is, you feebleminded idiot."

Niall said: "No, it's my fault. The Steegmaster tried to warn me." They looked at him with incomprehension. "The rod began to tingle a few seconds before he went under the tree." He took it out of his pocket. "I should have realized."

"Warn you?" Simeon looked blankly at the metal cylinder. "How could it know what was going to happen? It's only a computer."

"It can read minds." He dropped it back into his pocket. "But I should have realized myself. I should have known when we sliced the head off that pink flower. It was ten times as fast as the other one. That's because we're closer to the center of the force. So it doesn't need to stun its prey with drugs—it can use sheer speed."

Doggins said: "If you're right, it should get more dangerous as we get closer to the center."

Niall shrugged but said nothing.

They sat in gloomy silence, watching Simeon tending Milo's wounds. These continued to bleed as fast as they were washed. Milo himself looked down at his body with a curious detachment.

"I think that tree injected some kind of drug or venom. I've got a strange, numb feeling."

A few minutes later, he lost consciousness again.

Simeon used up all the bandages in attempting to stanch the bleeding; within minutes, they were soaked. Simeon said: "I'm afraid he's right. The tree must have injected some kind of anticoagulant. If this keeps on, he'll bleed to death in less than an hour."

Doggins asked: "Is there anything we can do?"

"Mud would help. And the leaves of the suva bush."

"What do they look like?"

"Long leaves, with a kind of purple grape in the center."

Manetho said: "I saw something like that back up the trail. Very dark green leaves, the color of ivy."

"That's right."

"I'll go and get them."

"For God's sake be careful. We can't afford to lose anyone else."

When Manetho had gone, they tried to make mud in a canvas bucket with a mixture of earth and water. But the earth was oddly dry and friable, and the result was unsatisfactory.

Niall said: "I could hear a stream near the bush with that pink flower."

Simeon looked despairingly at the blood that now dripped through the bandages.

"All right. Try it."

Niall carried the Reaper in one hand and a canvas bucket in the other. He advanced with extreme caution, and made a wide circuit to avoid the bush with the pink flowers. Beyond this there was a grove of snake willows. He studied them carefully, made sure that they all had gray moss clinging to the branches, and pushed his way through them. On the far side he found the stream he was looking for. It had deep, sloping banks, covered with rich green grass and tiny yellow flowers; the grass moved aside as he slid down the bank, revealing bare earth, and the flowers withdrew into the ground, leaving only the tops of their heads exposed. Niall trod around them carefully to avoid crushing them.

The water was shallow and was full of a green weed with shiny, cresslike leaves; when he stepped on this, his feet sank into glutinous mud. By tearing up the weed in handfuls, he was able to fill the bucket with a mud that had the consistency of sticky dough.

When the bucket was filled, he washed his hands in the muddy water and straightened up. As he did so, he started with shocked dismay; scarcely six feet away a face was looking into his own; it had the protruding eyes and wide mouth of a frog, but was at least twice the size of a human face. His instinctive reaction was to reach out for the Reaper, but it was at the top of the bank. A moment later the face was gone, but Niall caught a glimpse of an upright body, whitish-gray in color, vanishing into the trees on the far side of the stream. He stood staring intently for at least a minute, but saw no more sign of movement. His breath exploded in a long sigh of relief.

He felt angry with himself for being so preoccupied with the mud that he had allowed the frog-like creature to approach so close, and relieved that it had seemed as alarmed as he was. He hoisted the bucket to the top of the bank, scrambled up—now too preoccupied to avoid trampling on the flowers—and picked up his Reaper. For a moment he regretted leaving it at the top of the bank, then reflected that it would have made no difference; he would not have attempted to harm the creature as it fled. Then he tramped back thoughtfully, holding the Reaper in one hand to balance the weight of the bucket.

Simeon gave a grunt of satisfaction when he saw the mud. He wiped clean one of the smaller wounds, then quickly plastered a handful of mud on it. Thirty seconds later, when there was still no sign of renewed bleeding, he gave a sigh of relief and began removing the bloodstained bandages. While he was doing this, Manetho came back, carrying a bucketful of leaves. Each one had a swollen black object in the middle, looking not unlike a small grape; when Simeon broke one of these with his thumb, the air was permeated with a peculiar medicated smell. With the help of Manetho and Doggins, Simeon cleaned the wounds, squeezed the juice of the suva leaf on each, then slapped on handfuls of dark brown mud. In less than ten minutes, Milo was covered in mud from head to foot. But he was breathing regularly and the color had returned to his cheeks.

Niall waited until they had finished before he told them what he had seen. Simeon frowned, shaking his head. "I've heard of such things, but I've never seen one."

Niall said: "It was probably quite harmless—it ran away as soon as I reached for the Reaper."

Simeon grunted. "Few creatures of the Delta are harmless. They can't afford to be."

The position of the sun in the sky told them that it was now mid-afternoon; they had perhaps seven hours of daylight left.

Manetho asked: "Do you think I should make a stretcher for Milo?"

Doggins looked at Simeon. "You know the Delta. What do you think we should do?"

Simeon shrugged. "I think you three should go on. I'll stay here with Milo."

"Do you think you'll be all right?"

"Why not? With the Reaper, I'm more dangerous than any other creature in the Delta." He smiled grimly.

Doggins looked at Niall and Manetho. There was no need to say anything. They all knew what he was thinking. If they left Simeon behind, their journey would be far more dangerous. And Simeon himself would be in considerable danger, left alone to face the night with an injured man. Yet the only alternative was to acknowledge defeat and retrace their steps. Something in Niall was revolted by the idea and he sensed the same mood of stubbornness in his companions.

Doggins said: "All right."

He stooped down and began closing his pack. Niall and Manetho did the same.

Simeon said: "I want you to remember one thing. The Delta is at its most dangerous if you relax your attention. So stay vigilant."

"And you." Doggins placed his hand briefly on Simeon's shoulder. "We'll hope to be back tomorrow. If we haven't returned within two days, try and make your way back. But leave some indication of what you've done."

"I will."

They left without looking back.

The path downhill quickly brought them to the edge of the forest. Now, at last, the basin of the Great Delta lay before them and they could form a more accurate idea of its geography. Ahead of them, perhaps twenty miles away, lay the western range of hills that ran parallel to the range that now lay behind them. To their right, the Delta sloped gradually downward towards the sea, a desolate plain covered with reeds and low bushes. The gentle upward slope continued to their left, but the swampland here gave way to jungle. In the far distance, the double range of hills became lower as they approached one another and descended to the inland plain. A hot, dry wind was now blowing from this direction. Immediately ahead of them there was swampland and now they were in the plain, they could see that it was covered with high reeds, tall enough to hide a man. The only smell was the odor of decay carried from the jungle, the only sound was the moan of the wind through the reeds.

Their objective—the hill that overlooked the junction of the rivers—was immediately in front of them. But there was no obvious path towards it. When they had crossed the intervening area of firm grassland, they found themselves faced with the forest of reeds and bushes. Manetho went first, machete in hand, tramping straight into it, and for at least two hundred yards they met with no obstacle; the ground underfoot was soft, but firm enough to support them. Then the character of the reeds changed; they became higher and thicker, so that it was necessary to use the machete. Some were as tough and hard as bamboo poles. After another quarter of an hour, they had advanced only another hundred yards and Manetho was beginning to breathe heavily. The air was hot and moist.

Doggins said: "Hold on a moment. This is hopeless. We'll be here for weeks at this rate." He unslung the Reaper from his shoulder. "I'm going to try something."

He knelt on one knee, carefully pointed the Reaper at ground level, and pulled the trigger. As he moved it sideways, the thin blue beam mowed through the reeds like an immense scythe, and they collapsed sideways onto the ground. The result was a clear path stretching for several hundred yards in front of them.

Doggins grinned triumphantly. "There. It only takes a little common sense." He led the way forward. But although they were now able to trample the reeds underfoot, instead of hacking them down or pushing them aside, their progress was still slow. The reeds formed a thick carpet, and their feet sank into it, so that almost every step brought them to their knees. And there were places where the reeds were so thick that they held one another upright, and had to be pushed forcibly aside. Twice more Doggins used the Reaper, until they decided to admit defeat. They had been struggling forward for at least an hour; behind them lay a broad, straight path through the reeds. Ahead of them it was obvious that the reeds were thicker than ever. And from where they were now resting, they could still see the campsite they had left an hour ago.

Doggins said: "We need a tame millipede to go ahead of us." He stared gloomily at the surrounding reeds, some of which were eight feet tall. "I think we'd better go back and look for another way."

They sat there for another five minutes, recovering their breath; Niall used a handkerchief to mop the sweat that ran down his face and neck. The air was stifling. Then, as they were about to stand up, Manetho raised his hand to silence them. In the distance, they could hear something crashing through the reeds. The sound gradually came closer, until it seemed to be coming directly towards them. They stood up quietly, raising their weapons, their fingers on the triggers. Then, when it seemed only a dozen yards away, the crashing changed direction. It was accompanied by a faint but distinctive grunting noise and the sound of heavy breathing.

A moment later, they caught their first sight of the creature: an armored back moving above the reeds a dozen yards away. It was humped, and for a moment, Niall thought it could belong to a giant turtle. Then the animal burst from the reeds behind them and crossed the path they had just made. They caught a glimpse of a flat, toad-like face with horny projections above the brows, a massively armored back, and short powerful legs. The feet were very large and webbed like those of a duck, and it moved clumsily, rocking from side to side. The last glimpse they caught of it was a short but powerful armored tail.

Manetho said: "My God, what was that?"

Doggins shrugged. "Most of these creatures don't even have names. But I can see why it doesn't care how much noise it makes. With armor like that, I don't suppose there's anything that can harm it."

They retraced their steps, and halted at the path that the creature had smashed through the reeds. It was no longer visible, but they could still hear distant crashing noises.

Doggins said: "We may as well go that way. It's better than going back."

As they followed in the trail of the armored monstrosity, the going became easier; its weight had crushed the reeds flat against the ground and at one point, it had even uprooted a small bush. So far, they were following a path at right angles to the direction in which they wished to travel. But a quarter of a mile further on, the ground became soggier, and water squelched up through the reeds as they

120

trod on them; at this point, the creature had turned inland and they found themselves once more moving towards the heart of the Delta.

Niall, who was marching in the rear, glanced periodically behind him; this was not because he suspected they were being followed, but simply because he felt that, as the rear guard, he should heed Simeon's injunction to remain alert. But a few hundred yards after they had changed direction, a curious sense of uneasiness made him halt and look behind him. Was it an illusion, or had his eyes caught a glimpse of movement at the point where the trail vanished into the reeds? Unaware that he had stopped, Manetho and Doggins continued to march on; as their footsteps receded and the silence deepened, Niall heard another sound: a stealthy movement in the reeds a few feet to his left. He leaned forward, listening intently, but as he moved his weight from one foot to the other, a reed snapped, and the rustling noise immediately ceased. He felt no alarm; the weight of the Reaper in his hands gave him a sense of being in control of the situation. He stepped forward cautiously, using the barrel of the Reaper to thrust the reeds aside.

With startling suddenness, he was looking directly into the eyes of the frog-like creature. Its face was less than two feet away and it looked as shocked as he was. As he halted, the reeds gave way, and he raised his arms instinctively to prevent himself from falling. The lips of the creature drew back into a snarl and Niall found himself looking into two rows of yellow pointed fangs. There was a hissing sound and a jet of warm liquid struck his cheek and temple. As he recovered his balance, the creature was gone. Niall caught a glimpse of a gray body pushing its way into the reeds in such a way that they remained unbroken, and closed behind it.

Doggins' voice shouted: "Niall, where are you?" The liquid that ran down his cheek suddenly began to sting, and Niall bent down, scooped up a handful of the muddy water, and washed his skin.

Doggins said: "What happened?"

"We're being followed." His skin began to burn; he wet his handkerchief and used it to rub the cheek. "It was that thing like a frog. It spat at me."

They stood there, listening, for at least five minutes, but there was no other sound.

Doggins asked: "Do you still think it's harmless?"

Niall shook his head. "Not after I've seen its teeth. It's definitely a meat-eater."

Doggins looked at the sky. "We'd better get a move on." They were all thinking the same thing: that the marshes were an undesirable place to spend the night.

As they marched on, Niall's face began to sting; ten minutes later, he had to halt and bathe it again.

Doggins looked at it with concern. "It's beginning to turn red. It must be some kind of venom."

Manetho said: "One of the sailors was once attacked by a spitting cobra—it almost blinded him."

The thought of experiencing this burning sensation in his eyes made Niall shudder.

They continued to follow the path through the crushed reeds. The ground became increasingly marshy, and they were all aware that only a thick carpet of reeds and rushes prevented them from sinking up to their knees in mud. This yielding carpet was tiring to the legs, and the sticky heat made them perspire so their garments looked as wet as if they had been swimming.

But the curtain of reeds was now less dense and the reeds themselves were becoming lower. Occasionally, they were able to hear the sound of the armored creature moving ahead of them. Niall glanced back continually over his shoulder, but saw no more of the frog-like animal. He was finding it increasingly difficult to maintain his vigilance; his chief desire now was to find a dry place where he could sit down and rest.

Manetho suddenly crashed through the carpet of reeds and floundered in water up to his waist. He had been marching in front and was the heaviest of the three. They helped to pull him out again, then to recover one of his canvas boots, which had stuck in the mud. As Niall groped among the reeds, he felt a movement on his wrist, and snatched his arm away; a black leech, at least four inches long, was crawling up his forearm. He struck it off with a gesture of disgust, then used a handful of wet grass to rub violently at the slimy patch it had left behind.

It was plain that the route they were following was becoming impractical; yet the thought of retracing their steps filled them with a sense of weariness. As they stood there indecisively, wondering what to do next, they were shocked out of their fatigue by a bellow of agony. There were violent splashing sounds from somewhere ahead of them, then another bellowing roar. Then, quite suddenly, there was silence.

Their tiredness vanished. They stood looking at one another, their Reapers held at the ready. Now they could hear only faint splashing and gurgling sounds.

Niall said: "I'm afraid we'd better go back."

Doggins frowned. "I'd like to see what's happening there." He began to move forward cautiously, testing each step before he placed his weight on it. The other two, equally curious, followed him. Doggins rounded a bend in the path and raised his Reaper. Then, slowly, he lowered it again, turning to warn them to move silently. They joined him a moment later.

Ahead of them lay a marshy pool, whose water had been churned into mud. The hump of the armored creature rose out of the water; its head was turned away from them. This meant that they were unable to see what it was eating; but its movements made it clear that it was holding something between its front paws and gorging itself on its flesh. Alerted by some sixth sense, it turned its head and looked at them. The tiny eyes glared at them from under the horny projections on its forehead; the warty, toad-like face was covered with blood, and blood dripped from its masticating jaws. Niall's finger prepared to squeeze the trigger. But after surveying them for a moment, the creature turned its head away and went on eating. It evidently felt so totally invulnerable in its armor that the presence of these human creatures left it unconcerned.

They looked at one another. The path ahead was obviously closed. Beyond the feeding monster, they could see that the marshes came to an end and the ground rose towards low hills. On the other side of these, perhaps five miles away, rose the hill with its tower-like stump. But at this distance, they could see that the stump was not a man-made tower; it looked more like the broken horn of some big armored creature.

They retreated back down the path and considered their position. To the north, in the direction of the sea, lay more swampland. There would be no advantage in going in that direction. If they wanted to make a detour round the monster, then it would have to be to the south, once more cutting their way through the reeds.

The thought of leaving the marsh behind them raised their courage. Doggins pointed his Reaper and moving the lever to its lowest setting, pulled the trigger. The reeds ahead of them collapsed as if an invisible giant had strode among them. At the same time, there was a hissing shriek.

Doggins chuckled grimly. "We got one of them."

With their weapons raised, they picked their way forward. Within a dozen yards, they found the remains of the creature that had screamed. The gray body had been sliced neatly in two by the Reaper, whose beam had struck it a few inches below the waist. The lips were drawn back from the yellow teeth in a snarl of agony; inside the gaping mouth, above the back of the tongue, Niall could see the narrow tube that spurted the venom.

It was, in fact, a great deal more like a man than a frog; although the feet were webbed, the long legs were thick and powerful. And although the hands were also webbed, it was clear that the fingers were prehensile. The flesh was of a blue-gray color. An unpleasant stench rose from the exposed intestines, so after pausing for a moment, they hurried on. Around them, in the reeds, they could hear rustling noises; they were obviously being followed.

A quarter of an hour later, low hills were visible beyond the marsh. The reeds on either side of them were becoming thinner, so they could see for a distance of at least a dozen yards. Yet although they continued to hear the sounds of moving bodies, they failed to catch even a glimpse of the creatures on either side of them.

Now it was unnecessary to use the Reaper to clear a path through the marsh; the reeds were sufficiently far apart to provide no obstacle. But the ground beneath their feet was also more treacherous, and at one point Niall lost both his boots, and had to recover them from glutinous black mud that gave off the now familiar stench of rottenness. They were so accustomed to it by this time that they had ceased even to notice it.

It was when they seemed to be within sight of solid ground that Manetho gave a cry and disappeared up to his waist. Niall and Doggins each grasped one of his hands and began heaving him out. At that moment Manetho shouted: "Look out," and they turned to see a horde of the frog-like creatures running swiftly towards them from among the reeds. Niall and Doggins let go of Manetho's hands— he immediately sank back into the muddy water—and snatched up their Reapers from the ground. Doggins was the first to fire. The roaring blue flame carved a path through the running bodies and set fire to the reeds behind them. Yet, amazingly the others continued to run towards them. Niall fired, aiming for their legs, and moving the Reaper with slow deliberation. It disgusted him to slice through their bodies, as if wielding a scythe, but he could see there was no other way. It was as if the creatures had no fear and no sense of self-preservation; their one aim was to destroy these intruders, and the death of their companions was unimportant.

And then, suddenly, there were no more of them. The ground was covered with their bodies, most of them cut off at knee level; these were still jerking and writhing. Others were merely charred remains—Doggins had used a higher power-setting for his Reaper. The smell of burnt flesh filled the air. Niall lowered his Reaper, feeling sick. Doggins continued to fire until there was no more movement. As he replaced his Reaper on the ground, the hot barrel hissed against the wet earth.

By now, Manetho had sunk as far as his chest; the more he struggled, the deeper he sank. When Niall and Doggins tried to pull him out, their feet slipped on the muddy ground. Finally, Niall took a length of rope from his pack, and they tied it under Manetho's arms. Then they retreated until they found firmer ground and exerted all their strength; Manetho helped them by clawing at the ground. With a sucking, squelching sound, his body suddenly slid out of the bog, while Niall and Doggins fell over backwards.

They sat there for ten minutes, recovering their breath, while Manetho tried to clean the mud off his lower extremities with handfuls of grass. The sun was now low over the western hilltops; darkness would fall in less than two hours. But from where they sat, they could see that the point where the marsh ended and the solid ground began was only a few hundred yards away.

Niall stood up and pulled on his backpack. The other two heaved themselves reluctantly to their feet.

Manetho looked back at the charred remains of the frog-men. "Let's hope it's the last we've seen of them."

Doggins said: "Amen to that."

They moved forward slowly and carefully, picking their way between the pools of standing water. These were covered with a fine deposit of emerald weed and a scum made of a green, plankton-like substance. To reach firmer ground, they had to choose a winding path among them.

Manetho, who was marching in front, looked back over his shoulder. "Do you know what I'd really like?"

"No."

"A hot bath."

Doggins cackled, gesturing at the weed-covered surface of the pool they were skirting. "Won't this do?"

As he spoke, the green surface broke apart, and a froglike face stared up at them. Manetho saw it and grinned. Then, before Niall could shout a warning, the mouth opened and the jet of green-colored venom shot out, striking Manetho square in the face. He screamed and staggered backward. With a shout of rage, Doggins raised his Reaper and fired. It was a mistake. Suddenly, they were surrounded by a hissing cloud of scalding steam; Niall fell to his knees, covering his face with his hands, the steam forcing its way into his eyes and up his nostrils. For a moment, he felt completely vulnerable and helpless. Then the steam cleared and he could see again. The pool into which he had been staring a few seconds earlier had almost disappeared; in its place there was a crater of slimy black mud, covered with weed and green scum. Water was seeping in from an adjoining pool. Lying in the mud, face upward, was the frog-like creature, its arms and legs flung apart. The body was swollen and very white; the flesh was hanging loosely from one of its arms, exposing the bone. In the blast of hot steam, its body had been instantaneously cooked.

Manetho was howling and screaming, pressing his face into the wet ground. Doggins and Niall threw off their packs, and removed spare clothing, which they soaked in water. Niall, whose own face was still burning unpleasantly—the skin of the cheek had broken out into tiny blisters—knew how much he must be suffering. Manetho groaned as they forced him to hold still while they placed the soaked rags over his eyes; then he sat with the rags pressed tightly to his face, rocking back and forth with pain, while Niall and Doggins looked on helplessly.

Manetho finally found a small degree of comfort by lying flat on his face over one of the pools, with his forehead and his eyes in the water. But when, after half an hour, he finally sat up, the flesh around his eyes was so swollen that he was scarcely recognizable. He forced his eyelids apart with his fingers, and gave a cry of despair. "I'm blind! I can't see anything."

He collapsed on all fours on the ground, sobbing. Niall looked on in misery, wishing that his own pain were greater, so that he might feel less guilty. He felt no contempt for Manetho; only an abyss of pity.

Doggins placed an arm tenderly round Manetho's shoulders. "I know it hurts, but we've got to move on. If we stay here, we'll die."

With an effort, Manetho controlled himself. "You'll have to guide me."

"Yes, we'll guide you."

Manetho stood up. "Which way?"

Doggins looked at Niall. "We're going back."

"Through the marsh?"

"It's the only way. We've got to get him back to Simeon. There's no point in going on if he can't see."

Niall saw that he was right. He looked behind him at the sun. "We'll have to hurry."

Manetho's teeth were chattering; the pain had been succeeded by shock. He said miserably: "I'm sorry."

Doggins said gently: "Nothing to be sorry about. Do you think you can walk all the way back?"

"Yes. But I can't see."

"You'll be all right. We'll guide you. But now we have to go."

They strapped Manetho's Reaper across the top of his pack and placed the pack on his back. Both regretted having to make him carry this burden, but it was the only practical course; if either of them had attempted to carry it, their speed would have been halved.

Now, as they tramped back along the path through the reeds, Niall was surprised that all his fatigue had vanished. The crisis had renewed his strength, allowing him to draw upon hidden reserves of energy. His only concern was to regain the campsite before darkness fell. Each of them took one of Manetho's hands—it was less awkward than trying to hold his arms—and they walked with long, swift strides. Manetho was also aware that their lives depended on speed, and he made no complaint when he stumbled and fell to his knees. Periodically he asked: "Is it dark yet?" and they answered: "No, not yet." When they set out on the return journey, Niall was secretly convinced that they would be overtaken by darkness long before they reached the camp; but their progress encouraged him, until he once again began to allow himself to hope. When they reached the corner where he had first glimpsed one of the frog-men, he knew that they were more than halfway and his heart suddenly lightened. Twenty minutes later, they rejoined their own original path. The sun had just dipped below the western skyline, but the sky was still dusky blue.

Then, suddenly, they were out of the reeds, and Niall saw a flickering light among the trees immediately ahead. He and Doggins both began to shout at once: "Simeon! Milo!" Manetho's horribly swollen face broke into a smile. Five minutes later, they were limping into the clearing that was illuminated by the campfire, while Simeon helped to support Manetho.

Milo, who was lying by the fire, wrapped in a blanket, raised himself painfully on one elbow. "Back already? Did you enjoy yourselves?"

Niall flung himself down on the ground and closed his eyes. For a few minutes he experienced a sense of sheer delight and relaxation, the feeling of total security he had often experienced in his mother's arms as a child. It made no difference that they were still surrounded by dangers and that they might never escape from this terrifying place. For the moment they were safe and he accepted the present moment as a weary man accepts a feather bed.

While Doggins told the story of what had happened to them, Simeon boiled the leaves of the suva bush in water, and bathed Manetho's eyes. Manetho groaned with pain as the liquid ran into his eyes; but after a few moments, he sighed deeply and smiled with relief. Simeon then made a poultice of the suva leaves and bound it across Manetho's eyelids. A few minutes later, Manetho's deep, calm breathing revealed that he was asleep.

Doggins asked quietly: "Do you think he'll see again?"

"I don't know. If it's like the venom of the spitting cobra, then it won't cause blindness provided it's washed out immediately."

Doggins looked pityingly at Manetho's grotesquely swollen face. "I hope you're right."

In the blackness overhead, the first stars were beginning to appear. A cool breeze blew up the valley from the sea, and although they were protected by the trees, they could hear it sighing and roaring in the branches.

Niall asked Simeon: "Why are there no moths?"

"Because it's too dangerous for them down here. They prefer the higher slopes, where the plants don't eat them."

"Do the plants go to sleep at night?"

"Probably. You notice that the grass has stopped moving?"

"No, I hadn't." Niall pulled up a handful of the thick grass and held it up against the firelight; the tiny white legs were motionless.

When he threw it back on the ground, it made no attempt to re-root itself.

"So the Delta's safer at night than during the day?"

"It would be if there were no animals."

Doggins said: "We'd better take it in turns keeping watch." He yawned.

"I'm afraid so. I was going to stay awake all night. So I'll take first watch."

They ate the remainder of the lobster meat with dried biscuits; but Niall was too tired to feel hungry. He ate only a few mouthfuls, then pushed his plate aside and lay down, intending to eat the remainder when he had rested his eyes. Within moments he was fast asleep.

It seemed only a few seconds later that Doggins was shaking him. He said sleepily: "All right, I'll finish it in a moment."

But when he opened his eyes, he saw that the fire had burned down into a pile of white ash and red embers, and that Simeon and Milo were asleep.

Doggins whispered: "Time for your watch."

"What time is it?"

"About two hours before dawn."

Niall yawned and sat up, shivering. The wind was still roaring in the trees and the air was chilly.

Doggins pointed into the blackness. "There's something wandering around out there. But I don't think it will dare to come closer." He tossed another dry branch on the fire—Simeon had collected a pile of them and cut them into convenient lengths with the Reaper—and within a few moments it began to burn. "I'm going to get some more sleep." He wrapped himself in his blanket, lay down beside the fire, and in less than five minutes was snoring gently.

Niall stared uneasily into the darkness. The sound of the wind made it impossible to hear anything else, but he thought he could see the gleam of two eyes among the trees. He raised the Reaper, then changed his mind; if it was a large animal, then its bellowing would awaken the others. Instead he threw another branch onto the fire, wrapped himself in his blankets, then sat down with his back against the trunk of the fallen Judas tree, nursing the Reaper between his knees.

The knowledge that he was being watched roused him to full alertness. He reached inside his tunic and turned the thought mirror towards his chest. This instantly increased his concentration; but it also made him aware that, sitting with his back against the tree trunk, he was vulnerable to attack from behind. He attempted to use his mind to reach out into the darkness around him, to sense the presence of potential danger; but the concentration induced by the thought mirror made this difficult. Reluctantly, he reached inside his tunic and turned the thought mirror again. Then, by inducing the glowing point of light inside his skull, he created an inner silence in which his awareness reached out into the darkness like a spider's web. Now, suddenly, he became aware of the nature of the beast that was studying them from the darkness. It seemed to be neither reptile nor mammal, but a mixture of the two. It was small and extremely powerful; Niall sensed that it could reach him in one single bound. It was attracted by their smell, which filled it with a consuming hunger. But it also sensed that these strange, appetizing creatures were more dangerous than they looked, and that it would be stupid to surrender to its hunger and attack.

Niall felt no alarm or sense of danger; because he was so intimately aware of the creature's needs and desires, he felt as if its identity had blended with his own. It was difficult to realize that he was leaning back against a tree trunk, and not crouching behind a bush, his claw-like hands resting on the ground in front of him. At the same time, he experienced a strange feeling of suffocation and pity. This animal was trapped in its desires and instincts as if locked in a prison cell; it was little more than a killing machine.

Niall was becoming tired of being a mere observer; he wanted to see if he could influence the animal. But his state of receptivity was entirely passive, as if he were little more than a spider in the heart of its web. Very slowly, maintaining this receptive awareness, he reached inside his shirt. As his fingers touched the thought mirror, his receptivity wavered; but an effort of concentration brought it back again. Then, with infinite patience, he turned it until the concave side was facing his chest. For a moment there was conflict as the surge of vitality induced by the mirror threatened to tear the spider web of pure perception. Again, he relaxed and used his breathing to control the surge of tension. Then, quite suddenly, the two were perfectly adjusted; the power of the thought mirror no longer threatened to destroy the spider web of receptivity.

The result of this adjustment was so astonishing that he lost interest in the creature that was lurking in the darkness; it became a peripheral part of his perceptions. What amazed him was that these two aspects of his being—willpower and receptivity—could be brought into such perfect balance, and that the willpower could control the receptivity without destroying it. Without ever consciously considering the matter, he had always taken it for granted that the two were mutually exclusive opposites. Receptivity was for understanding the world; willpower was for controlling it. Now, in this blissful state of harmony, he saw that this was a crude fallacy. Receptivity was simply a way of descending into his own *inner* world.

It was a breathtaking sensation. He felt as though he was standing on the threshold of his own inner-domain, looking down on it as he had looked down on the land of Dira from the top of the citadel on the plateau. The whole of his past life was there before him, as real as the present moment. And if he raised his eyes, he could become aware of even more distant horizons—of other lives beyond the present one, and of the lives of all other human beings. It was the same sensation he had experienced as he sat in the brook a few hours earlier, but raised to a far higher degree of reality.

Now, at last, he could see the answer to the problem that had been troubling him ever since he arrived in the Delta: why man has always been so dissatisfied with his own life. The answer was obvious: because every man possesses within himself the power to transcend the present and to take possession of the vast domain of his inner being. Man was intended to be the lord of this mental kingdom, not a miserable exile trapped in the ever-changing present. And because all men are born with this instinctive knowledge, no human being can ever be satisfied with the present moment, no matter how completely it seems to fulfill his desires.

This insight also brought a sense of deep sadness. It began, oddly enough, with a feeling of pity for the slavering creature that was now crouching behind a bush, longing to leap on them and tear them limb from limb. It possessed no mental kingdom; it was trapped in the material world, like a prisoner behind bars. That was why the Delta was so full of violence and cruelty. It was the frustration of starving prisoners.

Of course, life on earth had always been like this. Left to themselves, living creatures would relax blissfully and sunbathe in the mud. The force behind evolution had learned the trick of goading them with misery and starvation. Man, at least, had been allowed to evolve slowly, over millions of years—and even that was too fast. But these creatures of the Delta were being forced to evolve a hundred times too fast. That was why life in the Delta had become a sickening, horrifying joke. This evolutionary melting pot was like a sadistic dream. These creatures were being forced to evolve merely so they could destroy one another. Just as the spiders had evolved until they could destroy human beings . . .

The whine of a mosquito startled him out of his meditations and made him strike out instinctively. He realized with astonishment that it was already dawn and that the fire had long ago turned into a pile of white ash.

A hundred feet away, he could see the outline of the bush behind which the hungry animal was still lurking. The vibrations of its hunger were like a cry of misery. It would surely be doing it a kindness to destroy it. . . . But even as he raised his Reaper, he knew this was impossible; instead, he fired at the tree behind the bush and sliced off an overhanging branch. There was a flurry of movement; then, with a single powerful bound, the creature vanished among the trees. Niall caught a glimpse of a green, scaly back, and of long legs like the legs of a giant frog.

The others continued to sleep peacefully. Niall picked up a dry branch and stirred the fire until he uncovered red embers; then he coaxed it back into life. The sense of excitement still glowed inside him, but the vision had disappeared. He was back in the present moment, with only a confused memory of that domain glimpsed from the towers of his inner citadel. But as he felt the flow of the underground force that awakened the Delta into life, he experienced a disturbing sensation that was a mixture of anger and excitement: anger at the force that had created this grim joke, and excitement at the power of his own mind to see beyond its shortsighted purposes.

Manetho's face was now so swollen that he was scarcely recognizable; he looked like a man who has been brutally bludgeoned and battered. But when he inserted his fingers into the bloated rolls of flesh that concealed his eyes and forced them apart, he said that he could see the daylight. This raised their spirits; somehow, the thought of permanent blindness was more frightening than the thought of death.

But Milo was still weak and said his legs felt numb; when he tried to stand up, he immediately collapsed. His feet and legs had turned a dull blue color; when Simeon examined them, he looked grave. But he decided to try a remedy that he had learned from his grandmother: boiling the leaves of the tree that had caused the injury and using them as a poultice.

There was no time for Niall and Doggins to wait to learn the result. They knew they had a long day before them and that lingering could be dangerous. After a light breakfast of dried meat, biscuits, and a potation of herbs sweetened with honey, they set out once more towards the strange hill that looked like a giant's head.

Simeon accompanied them to the edge of the forest. The sun had only just risen over the hilltop behind them, and the central basin of the Delta was still covered in silver mist. Simeon said: "A word before you go. I would have preferred to go with you, but that is impossible. So let me content myself with a word of advice. I know there are many dangers in the Delta, but somehow, the greatest danger lies in your own mind. The Delta has a habit of destroying those who are ready to be destroyed, and sparing those who refuse to become victims. Your chief guarantee of survival is determination. So be courageous without being foolhardy. May the gods protect you."

They clasped forearms and Simeon's grip was so powerful that it made Niall wince. Without intending to probe Simeon's mind, he was aware that the old man suspected he would never see them again. Simeon stood and watched them until they disappeared among the reeds.

Before they set out, they had already decided to retrace their steps as far as the western edge of the marsh. What they had not expected was to find the path of the previous day almost obliterated. Where they had used the Reapers to cut down the reeds, new reeds, more than a foot high, had already sprung up to replace them. They were able to trample their way through these without any difficulty. But where the toad-faced saurian had bulldozed a path for them, most of the smashed reeds were already upright again. At least they were less dense than elsewhere and, when mowed down with the beam of the Reaper, could be trampled underfoot. Because they were feeling fresh after their night's rest, they moved forward with slow deliberation, halting periodically to listen intently for signs of pursuit. But there was no sound except the wind among the tall reeds.

It took them more than two hours to reach the place where the feeding saurian had blocked their path. The only sign of the creature's presence was the red stain in the water of the pool where it had eaten its prey; on the far side of this pool, a path of crushed reeds revealed that it had continued on its way towards the edge of the marsh. They wasted no time trying to bypass the pool, but instead turned and followed their previous path to the place where they had been attacked by the frog-men.

And here, where they had expected to see piles of charred remains, they were startled to discover no sign of the conflict. Not a single body remained. There was not even a sign of the grass that had been charred by the blast of the Reapers; only fresh green grass now grew out of the marshy soil.

Doggins frowned. "That probably means there are more of the frogs around—they must have taken the bodies away."

But Niall was staring in puzzlement at a neat round hole in the mud at his feet; what intrigued him was that it was slowly filling with water. He took his machete, drove it into the wet earth, and twisted it in a circle to remove a coneshaped segment of mud, which he pulled out by its grass. What he saw made him jump back. A large white worm, about an inch in diameter, had been sliced in two by the blade, and one of its halves was already tunneling into the mud; as they watched, it disappeared. The other half wriggled helplessly in the bottom of the crater, which was slowly filling with water. Then another worm slid out from the side of the hole and Niall caught a glimpse of a shark-like mouth filled with pointed, backward-sloping teeth. Without hesitation, it attacked the wriggling segment. Lunging forward with its jaws wide open, it bit out a chunk of flesh as large as its own head, which it tore away with a sudden twisting movement. Moments later, two more worms appeared and joined in the feast. The ground under their feet was obviously seething with these creatures. As he watched with disgusted fascination, Niall felt a light touch on the back of his leg and jumped with alarm; another of the worms had emerged from the ground behind him and was coiled like a snake. With a single slash of the machete, Niall decapitated it. As the headless body writhed on the ground, more worms emerged and attacked it.

Doggins spat. "It's a good thing we didn't try to sleep in the marshes. The damn things are like piranhas." In fact, the headless worm had disappeared before he finished the sentence. The mystery of what had happened to the frog corpses was solved.

They hurried on towards the rising ground, pausing to stare with mistrust at the scum-covered pool from which Manetho had been attacked; but no sign of movement disturbed its green surface. Five minutes later, their feet were once again on solid ground.

Here they halted to survey their surroundings. They were standing on coarse, wiry grass, whose dark green color contrasted with the yellow-greens of the marsh; it seemed out of place in the Delta, as if it belonged to a colder climate. In front of them, the ground sloped up to a low ridge, from which granite rocks emerged. To the south, the ground also rose gently, but the dark green of the grass ended about a mile away and gave way to the lighter green of the jungle, which seemed to be exhaling a silvery mist. Beyond the jungle they could see the gap in the hills that formed the southern limit of the Delta. To the north, the ground sloped gently towards the sea, and the dark green grass soon gave way to a marshy terrain. In the distance, the sea reflected the sunlight. They seemed to be standing on a kind of island of dry, rocky ground in the middle of the Delta basin.

Doggins looked round distrustfully; he was holding his Reaper at the ready.

"I can't believe it's as quiet as it looks. There's got to be a catch somewhere." He looked at the rocky ridge, half a mile away. "I wonder what's on the other side of that."

Niall said: "According to Simeon, the Delta gets more dangerous as you get closer to the center."

135

Doggins grunted. "How does he know? He's never been to the center."

Niall stooped and tried to pluck a blade of grass. It was unexpectedly tough and he had to wind the blade around his index finger to gain more purchase. As he gave it a second tug, he experienced a twinge of shock which made him let go. It was like the faint tingle he experienced when he handled the telescopic rod, but stronger.

Doggins asked: "What is it?"

"Try plucking a blade of grass."

Doggins bent down, grasped a blade firmly between his thumb and forefinger, and tugged. He let go with an exclamation of astonishment, looking at his fingers. "The damn thing gave me a shock!"

Niall bent down and placed his hand, palm downward, on the grass. It was a mistake. The shock was so powerful that it made him snatch his hand away with a shout of pain. They stared at one another. Niall asked: "What is it?"

"Electricity. Ever come across an electric eel?" Niall shook his head. "It gives the same kind of shock."

"Then why don't we feel it through our feet?"

"Because you're wearing rubber soles."

Niall looked down at the grass with an expression of puzzlement. "Then why didn't I feel it the first time I touched the grass?"

"Perhaps because you hadn't tried to pluck it then."

Niall took a few cautious steps forward.

"Do you think it's safe to walk on it?"

"So long as we're wearing boots, yes."

But as they advanced towards the rocky ridge Niall trod warily, unable to believe that the soles of his boots could afford protection. He asked: "Why should the grass want to give shocks?"

"For protection, I suppose. Ordinary grass can't defend itself."

A hundred yards further on, they passed the moldering corpse of a large bird; Niall guessed it to be an eagle. They could see that its talons were still clenched in agony, while the wide-open beak in the eyeless face looked as if it was screaming.

"But what's the point of killing a bird? Birds don't eat grass."

"But their corpses replenish the soil."

Niall looked at the wiry grass with distaste. "It's not as attractive as ordinary grass."

"That's the price you pay for self-defense."

Now, at last, they were climbing towards the top of the ridge. Some of the broken fingers of granite were large enough to conceal an animal; so they advanced warily, their Reapers held at the ready. But when they reached the top, it was clear that their caution had been unnecessary. The ground before them sloped down for perhaps a mile before it was replaced by a belt of jungle that was rich in colors. Beyond this, they could see the nearer of the two rivers that flowed from the southern end of the Delta; in places, this was apparently no more than a meandering stream, winding its way through jungle and marshland. On the far side of the stream, immediately ahead of them, stood the hill with the tower-like protuberance. Now it was hardly more than three miles away, it no longer looked like a head, and the protuberance was obviously not a tower. At this distance it might have been some kind of vegetable extension of the hill, or the shattered remains of a mighty tree.

Doggins said thoughtfully: "Looks as if it's been struck by lightning."

From this vantage point, they could also look down on the junction of the two rivers at the foot of the hill's northern slope. The more distant of the two, invisible on the far side of the hill, was evidently swifter and stronger than the one they could see, for beyond the junction, the two united into a broad and powerful stream.

Doggins pulled out his handkerchief and wiped his brow. "I feel stifled." He blew out a long breath. "The temperature must be a hundred and ten."

Niall also felt suffocated, although they were standing in the shadow of a tall finger of granite. The sudden change in temperature surprised him; on the far side of the slope it had been warm, but not oppressively so. Struck by a sudden suspicion, he reached inside his tunic and turned the thought mirror. The instant sense of concentration was succeeded by a feeling of relief; suddenly, the heat was no longer stifling.

"Have you got your thought mirror on?"

Doggins said: "Of course."

"Turn it over."

Doggins did as he was told, and looked at Niall with surprise. "What happened?"

Niall said: "It wasn't the heat. It was the underground force."

"I don't understand. How can it make you feel hot?"

"By lowering your resistance. If you feel stifled, you automatically think it's hot."

"Do you think it's aware of our presence?"

"I don't know." It was a question that troubled Niall deeply. The force seemed to be as unconscious and impersonal as the wind. Yet at times it could behave intelligently—as when it resisted their control of the squid funguses. The possibility that it might be aware of their presence made Niall's heart contract.

Doggins said: "I'd like to sit down for a rest, but I don't think we can risk it. I don't fancy being electrocuted. So we may as well get on."

They marched on down the slope. The air no longer suffocated them, yet there was an unpleasant quality in the atmosphere, as if the sun itself was throbbing like a beating heart.

Doggins said: "What's that?"

To their left, a granite boulder projected from the earth, and below this there was a hollow. Something white gleamed against the blue-green grass in its depths.

Niall said: "Bones."

Doggins walked closer. "My God, it must have been a monster!"

They could see the immense ribcage and a skull that was pointed like that of a giant rat. Behind the skeleton, the vertebrae of the long, powerful tail were laid out neatly, as if the flesh had simply dissolved from the bones.

A shimmer in the air made Niall shake his head and blink; it was as if someone had shaken a transparent curtain in front of his eyes, blurring his vision. Suddenly alerted, he raised the Reaper.

Doggins looked at him in astonishment. "What are you doing?"

As he looked back, his face drained of color. The bones were moving. The vertebrae of the tail stirred and braced themselves against the ground, the ribs heaved, then the whole skeleton twisted as it moved into the upright position. The bony jaws opened and emitted a deafening sound that was a combination of a roar and a shriek.

Niall and Doggins fired together. Since the Reapers were set on their lowest power level, the thin blue beams were almost invisible; but as they struck the skeleton where the chest joined the neck, the roar ceased as abruptly as it had begun. Carried forward by its own momentum, the creature toppled towards them; both jumped back instinctively. It struck the ground with a crash—not the rattle of bones that they had expected, but the solid thud of flesh on hard earth. The neck twisted in the reflex agony of death and they stared appalled at the hate-filled eyes that met their own for a moment. Both were prepared to shoot again, but it was clearly unnecessary; the energy beams had almost severed the creature's neck.

Now that it lay still, it was apparent that it had a neck. But the flesh was as transparent as jelly, and they could see the network of veins and the powerful tendons that had been torn apart by the blast of their weapons. The body was also semi-transparent and inside the ribcage they could make out the outline of the heart, as large as a man's head.

They walked cautiously around it, starting nervously as the legs gave a convulsive twitch. Now that the monster was dead, it was impossible to understand how they had failed to see that it was a living creature and not a heap of whitening bones.

Niall reached out and touched the tail; the skin was hard, cold, and leathery. In death, the jelly-like flesh was taking on a purple tint, and they could see that the animal was a giant lizard. The muscular development of its back legs suggested that it had been able to walk upright.

Doggins shook his head in bafflement. "But how did we fail to see it?"

The question seemed unanswerable. The semitransparent flesh might have been invisible in cloudy water or in semidarkness, but not in the glaring sunlight of mid-morning. The blood that ran from the gaping wound in the neck was almost as clear as water, but was still perfectly visible. And the long, curved claws on the front legs were covered with a crust that was obviously dried blood.

Staring at the body provided no answer; so they moved on down the slope. When they were less than a hundred yards away, they were startled by a flapping of wings; a large bird of prey was swooping towards them. They raised the Reapers, then lowered them again; the bird was interested only in the dead saurian. It landed on the head and attacked the eyes. Within moments, other birds were swooping down on the carcass, tearing with their claws and beaks.

Niall was struck by a sudden insight. "They're getting their own back."

"Their own back?"

"That's obviously how it catches its prey. It lies there looking like a heap of dead bones. A vulture sees it and flies down to see if there's any flesh left on the bones. Then snap. One vulture less."

"But how does it do it?"

Again, Niall's intuition supplied the answer. "My guess is that it somehow affects the mind. It *wills* you not to see it. If a spider can will a fly into its web, why shouldn't a lizard will a bird not to see its flesh?"

Now they were approaching the edge of the forest, they could see that its richness of coloring was due to a profusion of flowers. From a distance, it looked like one of the cultivated gardens in the city of the beetles, with its colors arranged for effect: yellow, purple, red, orange, and every shade of green. This impression vanished as they came closer; it was obviously a tangled wilderness, yet it still gave the impression of being an overgrown garden.

They were approaching cautiously, their weapons raised; but there seemed to be no obvious cause for vigilance. The nearest bush was covered with large, yellow trumpet-shaped flowers, with a distinctive odor not unlike roses. A furry bee, the size of a clenched fist, crawled out of one of the trumpets and buzzed away into the forest; it evidently had no cause for alarm. As soon as they came close to the trees, the character of the grass changed; it became rich and green, and when Niall bent down and plucked a stalk, it broke without resistance.

They surveyed the ground, looking for the telltale signs of the black squids, and studied each tree, watching particularly for that slight trembling motion that would betray awareness of their presence. Everything looked completely normal. The trees and bushes were sufficiently far apart for them to be able to see between them. There were many bees and some other insects, but nothing that seemed to pose a threat.

Doggins said: "I don't trust that smell. It could be a drug."

Niall shrugged. "Let's wait here and see what effect it has. I need a drink anyway."

After the encounter with the lizard, his throat felt harsh and dry. They sat down on the grass a dozen feet from the nearest bush. Niall had filled his water bottle from the stream before they set out; now the water was warm, but at least it quenched his thirst. He was tempted to drink some of the golden wine—the flask was still half full—but decided that it might not be wise in the mid-morning heat. He chewed a biscuit and ate an apple—Doggins also ate sparingly—and when he had finished eating, sat cross-legged and deliberately induced the sense of inner calm. In these surroundings, it was not difficult. The scent of the flowers and the richness of their colors made the woodland seem like an enchanted garden. In this state, the bush with the yellow flowers made him feel oddly lighthearted, as though its trumpets were sounding clarions of joy.

Doggins had been watching him. He said: "Well, what do you think?"

"I don't sense any danger. I think perhaps we should . . . What was that?"

They both listened. Niall asked: "Did you hear something?"

"I thought I heard a shout."

A moment later it came again. This time there could be no doubt. "Niall!"

Niall's flesh crawled with apprehension and foreboding. The voice was that of his brother Veig and it seemed to be coming from the other side of the woodland. He stood up and cupped his hands to his mouth; but before he could speak, Doggins jumped to his feet and clapped his hand to Niall's lips.

"Don't! It could be a trap."

"But it's my brother."

"That makes no difference. Don't shout."

"Niall!" The voice was unmistakably Veig's.

Doggins said urgently: "The spiders must have brought him here."

"But we have our Reapers."

Doggins gripped his arm. "If they're holding your brother hostage, we can't use the Reapers. That's what they're relying on." Niall shook his head helplessly. "Listen to me. What would you do if they threatened to kill your brother unless you gave yourself up? You'd do it, wouldn't you? That's why you mustn't answer."

"But perhaps he's alone."

"Niall!" There was a note of urgency in the shout. It seemed unnatural not to reply, but Niall restrained himself with an effort of will that was like a sharp pain.

Doggins said: "How can he be alone? Think it out. He didn't know where you were, and even if he did know, he couldn't find his way to the Delta alone. Somebody must have brought him."

Niall's cheeks were burning with a dry heat; he felt confused and vulnerable. "Perhaps we ought to go back."

"What would be the point? We've got to go on."

"Yes." But he said it without conviction. His heart felt as if it had turned to lead. The voice of his brother had filled him with longing and it had drained away all his inner certainty.

They pulled on their packs and advanced warily into the trees. It was cooler there and the air was heavy with the scent of flowers. The colors that surrounded them were so vivid that it was as if some of the flowers glowed by their own inner light. But the rich scents only induced in Niall a feeling of nausea. His cheeks were burning feverishly and his legs felt as if they had no strength. His mind was clouded with doubts and fears. What if they had his mother there, too? And perhaps even the children? The thought made him want to cry out in despair.

He reached inside his tunic and turned the thought mirror. There was an excruciating flash of pain in the back of his skull and he had to restrain the impulse to turn it back again. But as he concentrated, clenching his teeth, the pain disappeared, and he became aware of how far his strength had been depleted by fear and anxiety. Then, like a fist clenching inside him, resolution began to return, and this in itself brought relief. Suddenly, he could see that, no matter how great the problems, it was sheer stupidity to allow them to drain away all his strength. That would be as if a man dying of thirst should deliberately empty his last drops of water into the sand.

The feeling of nausea vanished like a bad dream. Now, at least, he could look at the problem objectively; and as he did so, his courage returned. If Veig was now being held captive by the spiders— and it seemed a reasonable assumption—then the spiders had probably seen them as they came over the brow of the hill. In that case, they were probably lying in wait. When Niall remembered how swiftly he had been taken captive by the wolf spider in the desert, he realized how easy it would be for the spiders to leap out from behind a bush or rock, and overwhelm them before they had time to resist. Then why had they allowed Veig to give away their presence by shouting? It seemed completely senseless. Now they were forewarned, they were unlikely to be taken by surprise.

There could be only one answer. The spiders were terrified of the Reapers and were unwilling to do anything that might provoke them to fire. And if that was true, then there was still hope. It meant that the spiders were willing to negotiate . . .

These reflections revived his optimism and he was appalled at the thought of how close he had been to total surrender. He was also intrigued to observe how quickly the renewal of hope replenished his vital energies. Now, suddenly, he noticed the beauty of the flowers, with their incredible array of colors. There were the yellow, trumpet-like flowers, with their smell that reminded him of roses. There were orange blossoms that had the pleasant tang of citrus fruit. There were bushes covered with a purple flower whose shape reminded him of an open mouth, and whose rich, sweet smell was somehow cloying and disagreeable. There were even green flowers that looked like dog roses, although each petal had a broad band of white; these had a smell that reminded him of coconut or honey. In the grass there were pink and white daisies whose clean, sweet scent filled him with a feeling of innocence. He also observed that where flowers were hidden in the shade of trees, the flowers seemed to glow as if they were phosphorescent.

His sharpened senses soon became aware that each flower seemed to affect him in its own individual way. He had already noticed the curious sense of joy induced by the yellow, trumpet-like flower, but had assumed that this was due simply to its bright color. Now he could see that the whole bush was emitting some vibration that produced this feeling of lightheartedness, and that it was as distinct as a musical note. The deep red flowers produced a thrill of excitement that somehow aroused a flash of cruelty, like a desire to hit someone in the face. The orange flowers brought a sharp feeling of delight that reminded him somehow of Merlew and Dona and Odina; it seemed to contain the essence of femininity. And some great white blossoms, shading into lilac at the tip, filled him with a peculiar sensation of nostalgia that seemed connected with an unknown country whose winds were cold and bracing, and whose streams were covered with ice from autumn until the spring. It was strange to walk among them and to experience all these sensations, and many others that were indescribable, as if swimming through water whose temperature changed from moment to moment.

Doggins said: "What's that?"

They stopped, listening intently. Niall had heard nothing; the air was filled with the drone of bees and other insects. But as he strained his senses, he seemed to hear a sound like distant voices. Then a bee emerged from one of the purple flowers and buzzed past his ear; as soon as his concentration wavered, the sound of voices ceased.

"Can't you hear it?" Doggins sounded strained and tense; Niall saw that his face had become very pale.

"Voices?"

"Children's voices."

Niall listened intently and again seemed to catch the sound of distant voices; but it might have been the sound of running water or the cry of some bird. "I can hear something, but it's a long way off."

"Long way off?" Doggins looked at him in astonishment. "What are you talking about? It's just over there." He seized Niall's forearm and tried to propel him in the direction of the voices.

"No, wait." Niall resisted the pull; Doggins halted reluctantly. He was obviously in the grip of some powerful emotion. "First, tell me what you can hear."

Doggins looked baffled and frustrated. "You already know. Voices."

"Are they close?"

Doggins stared at him as if doubting his sanity. "Can't you hear them?"

"I could hear something. But it's stopped now."

Doggins started. "You mean you can't hear that?"

Niall said: "Listen to me. I think this is some kind of illusion."

"Then why could you hear it too?"

"I don't know. I think I was tuning in to your mind."

"And you really can't hear them? You're not joking?"

"Of course not. What do they sound like?"

Doggins was now puzzled and worried. "Children's voices."

"Your children?"

He shrugged. "All children sound alike." But Niall was not deceived by the casual tone. He placed his hand on Doggins' shoulder.

"There are no voices. They're inside your own head."

It was obvious that Doggins only half believed him. "Then what causes them?"

"I don't know. But I think I know how to make them stop." He pointed to the bush with the purple flowers, whose rich, heavy scent made him feel oddly breathless and depressed. "Try cutting that down with your Reaper." Doggins stared at him blankly. "Do as I say."

Doggins shrugged and took several paces backward. He raised his weapon, made sure it was on the lowest setting, then fired. In the woodland shade, the beam looked like blue ice. The bush was so close to the ground that they could not see its trunk; but as Doggins moved the Reaper sideways, it shuddered, then slowly toppled to the ground. As it did so, Niall was suddenly overwhelmed by a series of emotions, a kaleidoscope of pity, terror, rage, grief, wretchedness—and, underlying them all, a hard tinge of cruelty. Then, as the bush struck the ground and ceased to vibrate under the impact, these feelings passed, like a clamor of angry voices dying into the distance; suddenly, he felt strangely free and light-headed.

Doggins was staring at him in amazement. Niall said: "Well?"

"It's stopped! What did you do?"

"You did it by cutting down the bush."

Doggins stared at it. "What difference does it make?"

Niall shook his head. "I don't understand. All I know is that these things can somehow get inside our minds—like that lizard creature. They can make us imagine things that aren't there."

He could see that Doggins found this very hard to accept; to his practical mind, "things that aren't there" was a contradiction in terms.

"Why did you tell me to cut *that* one down?"

"Any one would have done. They're like the spiders—if you destroy one of them, they all feel it."

As he was speaking, it struck Niall that he could no longer smell the scent of flowers. He leaned forward and sniffed one of the orange blossoms; it was odorless.

"You see? Even the scent wasn't real. It was inside your mind."

It was a disturbing realization: that his senses could be so easily deceived. It made the solid world around him seem unreal and treacherous. Yet as they walked on through the wood, he also felt oddly exhilarated, as if he was breathing cold, clean air. It was as if a burden had been lifted from his senses.

"Your brother's voice—was that an illusion too?"

"I think it must have been." His feelings found it difficult to accept, but logic told him it must be true.

"*Why* do they do it?"

Niall shrugged. "I think they were trying to make us go back."

"But why?"

Niall made no reply. They were again descending a slope, and it was so steep that they had to walk slowly, leaning backwards to avoid slipping. The trees and bushes were now further apart. And then, quite suddenly, they had passed a line of trees and were out of the forest, looking down a bare slope that terminated in another area of woodland. And over the tops of the trees, less than a mile away, they could see the upper half of the great hill.

To Niall, it was as if he was seeing it for the first time. It had a distinctly rounded appearance, and at this distance it was obvious that the projection at the top was neither a tower nor a tree stump. It was twice as wide at the base as at the top and it resembled the broken stalk of a vegetable, as if the hill were a giant bulb that had been half-thrust into the earth by some careless gardener. But the almost vertical upper slope on the northern side of the hill resembled a forehead, so the projection looked like an absurdly small hat. Now he knew why the hill produced a strange sense of foreboding; it looked like a living creature. As soon as he saw it, Niall knew beyond all doubt that this was what they were looking for. The wave-like vibration was no longer confined to the ground under his feet; he could feel it pulsing in the air around him, even though the air was perfectly still.

It was a curious sensation and in Niall it produced a mixture of excitement and antipathy. The excitement was due to the sheer power of the vibration, which seemed as impersonal and as exhilarating as a storm at sea. The antipathy was a feeling that the force lacked delicacy or subtlety; it was like music played too loudly.

When he glanced at Doggins, he was intrigued by the expression on his face; he looked as if he had encountered an unexpected and unpleasant smell.

"What is it?"

"Something . . . bad." Doggins spoke with uncharacteristic hesitation. "Can't you feel it?"

Niall was curious. "What does it feel like?"

Doggins started to speak, shrugged, and gave it up. He pointed at the dome-like hill. "That's what we're looking for." He looked at Niall. "Isn't it?"

"It's possible."

Doggins' lips twisted into a mirthless smile. He raised the Reaper and adjusted the power to the maximum level. "This ought to do it, even at this distance."

Niall said quickly: "Wait."

"Why?"

"It could be dangerous. Remember what happened when you fired into that pool."

Doggins lowered the weapon. Niall knew he was deferring to the power of the thought mirror rather than to his argument. He was surprised at his own sense of relief.

They moved on down the slope. The ground was smooth and hard, like volcanic lava, and its surface was made more treacherous by thousands of tiny channels worn by rivulets of rain.

The wood that faced them was quite different in character from the one they had left behind. The tree trunks were so twisted and distorted that few of them seemed to grow upright, and were so close together that their exposed roots were entangled. This meant that their branches and foliage—which was of a very light green color—were so interwoven that they gave the impression of being a continuous roof. The wood stretched for several miles in both directions and seemed to form an impenetrable barrier.

Halfway down the slope, Niall observed a curious phenomenon. Every step forward was becoming increasingly difficult, as if they were wading through water. Doggins glanced at him but said nothing. Both recognized the signs of an opposing will. A dozen yards further on, the resistance had become so strong that they no longer had to lean backwards against the slope; they had to walk bending forward, as if into a strong wind. Their feet slipped on the smooth surface as they tried to push their way forward. Finally, when they were within a hundred yards of the trees, further advance was impossible. It felt as if an invisible gale was holding them at bay. Niall bent double and tried to creep forward, but it was as if hands were resting on his shoulders, pushing him back. They both sat down on the ground and looked at one another. Both were breathless and perspiring heavily.

Doggins grinned defiantly. "It looks as if something doesn't want us to go on." He glanced towards the treetops, but the hill was no longer visible.

Niall said: "It's the trees."

Doggins stared with surprise. "Are you sure?"

"Quite sure." Niall could sense that the will-pressure was somehow being exerted by the tangled branches.

Doggins looked at them curiously. "They must be using some form of MRI." He picked up his Reaper. "It should be easy enough to find out."

This time Niall made no attempt to stop him. The opposing will-force had aroused in him a feeling of furious resentment. Doggins set the power lever to its lowest level. Then he trained the weapon on the nearest trees and pulled the trigger. The thin beam sliced through the trunks as if they had been as insubstantial as air; as the barrel moved sideways, half a dozen were severed at ground level. Yet the trees remained upright, held by their interlocked branches. Doggins raised the weapon higher and turned up the power. This time, the central part of the trunks was blasted away with a smell of charred wood. Some of them crashed down; others, held by their branches, hung suspended. A fine yellow dust descended from the treetops like pollen. But the resistance was as strong as ever; if anything, it had increased.

Doggins turned to Niall. "Are you sure you're right about the trees?"

"I think so." Even as he spoke, Niall could sense the power emanating from the twisted branches.

"All right. Let's try this." Doggins increased the power again and this time fired close to the ground. The blue beam roared like a flame and the tree trunks dissolved away; suddenly, a path was open through the wood. Then, quite abruptly, the resistance ceased. It was so unexpected that they were both thrown forward and slipped several feet down the slope.

Doggins looked at Niall; his face was shiny with sweat. "Yes, you *were* right."

Some of the trees had burst into flame; the smoke smelled of sap and living wood. The yellow pollen was descending like rain, covering the blackened ground. The sight of the charred alleyway between the trunks aroused in Niall a curious feeling of pity and regret. There was something about the power of the Reaper that worried him; it was too absolute.

Doggins stood up and made a gesture of invitation. "Shall we go on?"

But Niall hesitated. "I'm worried about that yellow stuff. Let's wait until it stops falling."

Doggins walked forward to the edge of the trees and sniffed. "It's just pollen dust." He began to sneeze violently and continued for several minutes. "My God, you're right. It's like pepper." His eyes were streaming.

They sat and waited; periodically, Doggins sneezed again. As the smoke cleared, they could see that the Reaper had opened a pathway through to the far side of the trees. At the far end of the tunnel of overhanging branches, water gleamed in the sunlight.

Doggins opened his pack and took a long drink of wine; he sighed with satisfaction. "I'll be glad when we're back home. There's something evil about this place."

"Evil?" The idea struck Niall as strange. "No, I don't think it's evil. It just doesn't care about human beings."

"Same thing." He took another drink, then put the flask back into his pack. "Let's get started. We'll never get home if we sit here all day."

Niall stood up reluctantly. "Don't forget what Simeon told us—never hurry in the Delta."

They advanced to the edge of the wood. The path cleared by the Reaper was about eight feet wide. As he looked down the tunnel-like opening through the trees, Niall became suddenly aware of the terrifying power that had cut this road through the forest. Some trunks had been divided lengthwise, as if cloven by an axe; others hung suspended above their heads, held in place by interlocking branches. Underfoot, the Reaper had scored a furrow in the earth, and this was as flat as a man-made road. The ground, like the blackened tree trunks, was covered with a thick yellow layer of pollen.

But as soon as they began to walk on this yellow dust, they discovered that it was as slippery as mud; Niall almost lost his footing and had to clutch at a tree trunk to keep upright. The dust made his nose and eyes sting. A moment later, they were both sneezing. Where the pollen settled on his damp flesh, it produced a sharp irritation that made him want to scratch.

Niall retreated back up the slope and sat down again. "I think we ought to look for another way through."

"Another way? There's no other way." Doggins gestured at the line of trees stretching in both directions.

"If we went north, we'd reach the marshland."

Doggins shook his head stubbornly. "I'm not going to be beaten by a bit of pollen." He scratched furiously at his cheek. "Even if it does give me hay fever."

Niall took his spare tunic from his pack and tore a strip off the bottom; it was made of a very thin cotton. He soaked it in water from his flask and washed the pollen off his hands.

Doggins said: "I know the answer." He also tore a wide strip from his spare tunic and soaked it in water. Then he tied it round his face, forming a mask that left only his eyes visible. "That should keep it out."

Niall did the same; the mask felt pleasantly cool against his face. Then, as an afterthought, he took from his pocket the tube containing the metallic garment. As he unrolled this, Doggins looked at it with mild astonishment.

"What's that for?"

"To keep the pollen off my skin."

Doggins pointed. "There's water down there. You can wash it off in five minutes."

"I'd rather keep it off my skin. It stings."

He pulled the slide fastener and clambered into it. As a garment it was cumbersome and voluminous. The rolls at the wrists and ankles proved to be rudimentary arms and legs, but they were less than a foot long. When the garment was fastened at the neck, Niall looked like a silver-colored bat. It was unpleasantly warm, and his perspiration made the thin material stick to his skin.

Doggins said ironically: "Ready?"

He nodded, pulling up the hood. It was impossible to put his arms through the straps of the haversack, and he was forced to carry it in one hand, with the Reaper in the other. He asked Doggins: "Why don't you wear your cloak? It would cover your arms and legs."

Doggins said shortly: "I'll risk it."

It was not easy to walk, with the folds of the garment flapping between his legs; he was forced to move with a kind of crablike shuffle. Doggins watched him with an amused sideways glance but said nothing.

As they walked between the trees, their feet stirred up clouds of the yellow dust. In spite of his mask, Doggins began to cough. He turned to Niall. "I'm going ahead. See you at the other end." He walked on with quick strides, the dust rising in clouds round his feet. Using his gloved hands, Niall tucked the wet linen more firmly under his chin; but the dust made his eyes sting and caused a prickling sensation on his damp forehead. He tried tugging the mask upward so that it covered his eyes and forehead, and discovered, to his relief, that he could still see through it; the water made the cotton semi-transparent. He breathed through his open mouth, aware that it was safer than breathing through the nose, since each intake of breath drew the material tight against his lips and prevented the yellow dust from entering. The heat in the garment was stifling, rising in waves to his neck, but he resisted the temptation to hurry, even when the stinging made his eyes water so that he was unable to see. Then, suddenly, he was in the sunlight again.

Doggins said: "Are you all right?"

"Yes. Are you?"

"I shall be when I've washed this damn stuff off me."

Niall pulled down the mask and found that the outside was covered with a thick layer of pollen dust. It was hard to resist the temptation to rub his streaming eyes with his gloved fingers, but he could see they were also thick with pollen. Coughing and sneezing, he unzipped the garment and struggled out of it. His cheeks and forehead glowed with a prickling heat.

They were standing on an expanse of hardened mud that sloped down to the river, which was brown and slow moving. On its far side, a mass of rich vegetation extended up the lower slopes of the hill, with lianas so thick that they looked like pythons. The hill itself rose out of the ground like an immense boulder; in the flat surrounding terrain, it looked as if it had fallen out of the sky.

Niall stared with dismay at Doggins' face. It was red and swollen, as if he was suffering from severe sunburn. Doggins was scratching frantically at his forearm and his nails left streaks of blood.

He grimaced. "You were right. This stuff really hurts." He threw his Reaper on the ground beside his haversack and hurried towards the river. Niall ran after him.

"Wait! It could be dangerous." He seized Doggins by the back of the tunic and had to dig in his heels to prevent him from running straight into the water. "Stand still."

As Doggins stood there, cursing and massaging his eyes, Niall took his spare tunic from the pack, soaked it in water, then handed it to Doggins, who clapped it to his face with a moan of relief. Niall's own forehead was burning as if it had been scalded, so he knew what Doggins must be suffering. He took the canvas bucket from the bottom of his pack, punched it into shape, and dipped it into the water. As he did so, he noticed the swirl just below the muddy surface that told him their presence had been observed. He made Doggins bend over and poured the brown lukewarm water over his head and shoulders.

Doggins groaned. "It's no good. I've got to get into the water. My arms and legs are on fire."

"No. There's something in there. Wait."

He picked up the Reaper, made sure it was on its lowest setting, then fired at the disturbance in the water. There was a hiss of steam that made him jump backwards; as it cleared, he caught a brief glimpse of wide-open jaws and pointed teeth. He fired again, moving the Reaper slowly from side to side; the hiss of the steam almost deafened him; for a few seconds, it was like being in the midst of a thick fog. When it cleared, the surface was still and smooth.

"I think it may be safe now. Try it." With a cry of relief, Doggins plunged into the water; he immediately sank up to his knees in soft mud. Niall watched the surface, prepared to fire again, as Doggins stooped down and immersed his shoulders in the water. Within ten seconds there was another swirl of water upstream, moving towards them. Without hesitation, he fired. A few seconds later, Doggins gave a scream of agony.

"It's boiling!"

Niall grabbed him by the wrist and helped him out of the water. He said grimly: "Better to be boiled alive than eaten alive."

Doggins was covered in brown mud. But when Niall looked more closely, he saw that it was moving. He wiped some of it away with the wet cloth, and saw that it was full of tiny crab-like creatures, almost as transparent as ice, and that Doggins was bleeding from dozens of tiny bites; his pain was so great that he had not even noticed them. Niall filled the canvas bucket with water over and over again, and poured it on Doggins until the mud had been washed off; as soon as they were on the ground, the crab-like creatures made for the river.

For the next half hour, Doggins lay on the ground, his eyes closed and his teeth clenched, while Niall poured bucket after bucket of water over him. As his skin turned red and began to swell, Doggins writhed and cursed. Then, suddenly, he stopped moving. Niall dropped on his knees and placed his ear against his chest; to his relief, the heart was pounding fast. Doggins had evidently fainted. Now, for the first time, Niall realized that he was also in pain and that his forehead was swollen. So was the left side of his face, still sore from the poison of the frog-like creature. But it seemed unimportant.

When Doggins woke up again, he was delirious. He seemed to think that Niall was Simeon, and kept asking for Lucasta and Selima. When Niall tried to soothe him by pouring water over his arms, he screamed that it was boiling. Then he began to twist from side to side; there were flecks of foam on his lips, and his eyes were like the eyes of a terrified animal. On three occasions Niall had to prevent him from rolling into the river. Finally, he became unconscious again. After a while, his breathing grew more regular.

The burning sensation in Niall's forehead was now diminishing, so he guessed that Doggins was no longer in agony. Half an hour later, Doggins was sleeping normally, with only an occasional convulsion; but his arms and legs had swollen to twice their normal size and his face looked like an overinflated balloon.

Niall realized suddenly that it was dusk. This surprised him; he had lost track of time and assumed it was still mid-afternoon. Now, for the first time, he began to assess their situation. To spend the night there would obviously be dangerous; the river was full of living creatures. Niall was aware constantly that they were being observed; but at least this kept him in a state of alertness. But even if he could carry Doggins on his back, there was nowhere they could go. A hundred yards behind them there was the woodland, with its thick layer of yellow pollen. Twenty yards ahead of them was the river, with its unseen predators. But even unseen predators were less dangerous than the yellow dust; at least they could be destroyed with the Reaper, while the dust seemed indestructible. To the south, the river vanished into mangrove swamps and jungle; to the north, it meandered into the marshes before it reached the sea. They had no alternative but to stay where they were.

As the dusk deepened, a cool breeze blew from the sea. Niall laid out his own blankets on the ground, pulled Doggins on top of them, then wrapped them around him. After that, he went to collect Doggins' haversack and the metallic garment, which still lay close to the trees. Some instinct of caution made him carry his Reaper at the ready. He used a damp cloth to wipe the haversack free of the pollen, then began to wipe the metallic garment. As he did so, he glanced back towards Doggins, and saw to his astonishment that he was moving, sliding towards the river. For a moment he suspected it was a trick of the half-light; then, when the movement became unmistakable, he began to run. From his present position it was impossible to use the Reaper; Doggins lay between himself and the river. Doggins was now within a few feet of the water and seemed to be moving of his own accord, as if sliding gently down a slippery slope. Niall raised the Reaper, took careful aim, and fired. There was a hiss of steam and Doggins ceased to move. When Niall reached him a moment later, he saw that Doggins was still asleep, breathing regularly; the movement had been so gentle that he had not even felt it. A few feet away, on the foreshore, lay a severed tentacle. It was very thin, about four feet long, and glistened with slime. When Niall kicked it into the water, it felt as tough as leather and as steely as a whiplash.

Out in the middle of the river there was a splashing sound and the swirl of water. Overcome by a sense of rage and frustration, he raised the Reaper and fired into the river, moving it slowly from side to side, and ignoring the steam that swirled around him and scalded his face. The surface of the water boiled and bubbled; any living thing in its depths would be cooked alive. His teeth still clenched with rage, Niall stared at the dark water for any sign of movement. Filled with a desire to strike and destroy, he was tempted to push the lever to its maximum power level and fire straight into the hill that towered above them. His hand was on the lever when he remembered Doggins; if his action provoked some backlash of violence, Doggins would be helpless. Reluctantly, he lowered the Reaper. The rage evaporated slowly, but it left behind it a curious sensation of latent power tingling in his blood.

He pulled on the metallic garment, then went and sat cross-legged beside Doggins, the Reaper cradled in his lap. He experienced no desire to lie down and sleep, nor any sense of hunger; the emergency seemed to have called upon some deep reserve of endurance. As the light faded from the sky and the first star appeared in the north, he listened intently to the noise of the river, trying to distinguish its normal sound from the swirl that indicated the presence of living creatures. His heartbeat slowed and finally became so soft that he could scarcely feel it. Once again he experienced the sensation of being a spider in the center of its web, aware of every vibration of the night. At this depth of inner stillness, he seemed to be at the heart of an immense silence.

Yet there was something about the silence that puzzled him. It was some time before he understood what it was. He was no longer being watched. Ever since they had arrived in the Delta, he had felt that he was being observed. It was not an uncomfortable or oppressive sensation, such as he had occasionally felt when being watched by an unseen enemy; merely a feeling that the Delta was aware of his presence. Now this had suddenly vanished.

He reached inside his tunic and slowly turned the thought mirror. This time there was no conflict; only a feeling of intensity and power that blended perfectly with the stillness. Then, as his concentration hardened and his senses expanded into the night, he understood what had happened. The silence was a reaction to his sudden rage. The Delta was afraid of him. As he sat cross-legged, cradling the Reaper in his lap, he was like a poisonous snake, coiled and ready to strike. The Delta was holding its breath, terrified of what he might do next.

Then, suddenly, he knew what he had to do. He stood up and pulled down the slide fastener of the metallic garment, allowing it to fall around his feet. Then he picked up both the Reapers and walked towards the river. As he did so, his logical self rebelled, pointing out to him that what he was about to do was suicidal. Some deeper impulse overruled it. He stopped at the edge of the water, then, one after the other, threw both Reapers into the center of the stream. In the strange silence the splashes sounded very loud. Then he stood there waiting for what would happen next.

What happened was at once unexpected and banal. There was a gurgling sound in the river, as if some large creature had been disturbed, and a few drops of water struck his face. Then the night was full of normal sounds: the flow of the water, the rustle of leaves in the wind, the squeak of bats, the distant cry of some nocturnal animal. Outwardly, nothing had changed; he was still a solitary human being in the heart of the Delta. But he sensed he was no longer an intruder. His gesture of good faith had been received with approval. The Delta had accepted him.

He groped his way back in the darkness and again sat down by Doggins. Now he felt curiously calm and patient. He had done his part; there was nothing to do but wait. He sat with his hands on his knees, listening to the sounds of the night without concern or anxiety. The Delta had made a truce with him and he knew he had nothing to fear.

Half an hour later the moon rose and he was again able to see his surroundings. The sky was cloudless and the stars very bright. The light was so bright that he could see the marshes to the north and the jungle to the south, both looking calm in the moonlight. The southern face of the hill was also clearly visible and from this angle it again bore a resemblance to a face. As he looked at it, he became consciously aware of something he had known for the past twenty-four hours: that this was not a hill but a giant plant and that he was looking at the creature Simeon had called Nuada, the goddess of the Delta.

The command came about an hour later, when the moon was high in the sky. He was sitting there, relaxed and receptive, when he experienced an impulse to stand up and remove his boots. If he had been an animal he might have accepted this as his own decision; but because he was human, another part of him looked down with detachment on the animal that responded to its own desires, and recognized that it was obeying an order.

After he had removed the boots, he took the thought mirror from round his neck and laid it down beside them. Then he took the expanding rod from his pocket and placed it on the ground. Doggins was fast asleep, lying on his back; his face looked pale in the moonlight, but was no longer badly swollen. He wheezed slightly as he breathed. Niall covered him over with the metallic garment and tucked it under his chin. Then, still obeying the command, he began to walk parallel to the river.

He tramped along the sun-baked mud for perhaps a mile. To his left the twisted trunks of the trees looked as if they were made of iron; their branches were perfectly still in the faint breeze and made no sound. On his other side, the river flowed sluggishly in the moonlight, with occasional gurgling noises as some large creature came close to the surface and dived again. He saw only one living thing: a big caiman that seemed to be floating rather than swimming downstream, its nostrils just above the surface of the water; its wicked eyes followed Niall as he went past, but he had no sense of danger.

He reached a point where the river became wider and was partly blocked with leaves and branches. Without hesitation, Niall stepped into it. His feet sank for about six inches in the slimy mud, then reached hard shingle. Small creatures wriggled between his toes. He waded in slowly, leaning forward, until the water was above his waist. A branch twisted under his foot and scratched his leg, and some lithe and soft creature shot out from under it and slid past his leg, making his heart beat faster. He waded on slowly, a few inches at a time, until the water became shallow and he struggled out onto the opposite bank.

Here the same inner compulsion made him turn north again and return in the direction from which he had come. The vegetation on this side of the river was thick, and in many places came close to the water's edge; in the black shadows cast by the moonlight he had to step cautiously. A startled bird flew out from a bush and flapped into the trees with a curious whirring noise, and some heavy body began to crash through the undergrowth; Niall ignored them. When he could once again see Doggins sleeping in the moonlight, he experienced an impulse to turn left into the trees. Here the moonlight was unable to penetrate and he had to grope his way forward by touch alone; yet he was able to move almost as fast as in the moonlight. A sixth sense seemed to warn him when he was about to fall over some twisted root or walk into a bush.

Then, suddenly, the ground at his feet was clear, and felt again as solid as the baked mud of the river bank. He began to ascend. Within a few minutes he was out again in the moonlight, looking down on the river and on the treetops. He was about halfway up the southern face of the hill. On his other side there was a tangle of thick undergrowth that looked impassable; but soon he was high enough to see beyond it to the river that flowed to the west of the hill. This was far broader than the river he had crossed and the ripples on the moonlit surface revealed that it was flowing more swiftly.

As he climbed higher the path became steeper; he was forced to clamber with the aid of bushes and tufts of grass. Half an hour later, as he approached the top, the ascent became so steep that he decided to look for another way. He moved cautiously sideways until he found a place where the vegetation was thick enough to afford hand and foothold. This final ascent was about fifty feet high and was so steep that, when he turned and looked backwards, he felt dizzy and afraid, aware that the will that was directing his movements had no power to prevent him from falling and breaking his neck.

Then, suddenly, he was at the top, scrambling over the edge of a sloping plateau, at the center of which was the object he had mistaken for a tower. Now he could see that it was neither a tower nor a broken tree. There were no visible roots and no clear distinction between its base and the ground on which it stood. It seemed to be made of some gray, fibrous material and, when he ran his hand over its rough surface, felt like the bark of a tree. On its western side, which was bathed in moonlight, a long strip of this "bark" had been torn away and had curled up at the foot of the stump; it was brown and scorched, and the deep furrow from which it had been torn looked like a wound. This damage had clearly been caused by lightning. The ragged splinters at the top, some thirty feet above his head, were also twisted and scorched.

Far below, on the northern side, he could see the confluence of the two rivers. This side of the hill—which looked in profile like a face—was far steeper than the slope he had ascended, so that the water was almost directly below him. He could see the course of the river as it flowed through the marshes towards the sea, often invisible among high reeds. To the south, rising steadily to the gap in the hills, lay the jungle, looking very peaceful in the moonlight. But even as he watched, some bat-like creature, many times larger than a bird, winged up into the moonlight, then dived into the trees with a strange, harsh cry. There was a frantic scream of some animal in pain.

Through the gap in the hills beyond he could catch a glimpse of the silvery gray desert—the desert that he had crossed on his way back from Kazak's city. For a moment he experienced an overwhelming pang of nostalgia and had the curious illusion that his father was standing beside him. It vanished as quickly as it had come, leaving a feeling of emptiness.

Now that he had arrived at his objective, he felt a sense of anticlimax. During the past hour, he had allowed himself to be carried along passively by the impulse that had moved his feet, his own will in abeyance, like a leaf drifting in a current. That impulse had now vanished. He still remained passive and receptive, waiting for further orders, but none came. Since there seemed to be nothing else to do, he walked round the foot of the stump, examining it carefully. The base curved down smoothly to the ground, like the foot of a large tree, but there was no obvious point at which it disappeared into the ground; in fact, the ground under his feet was hard and gray, like the material of the stump. All this only verified what he already knew: that he was not standing on a hill, but on top of some giant plant. On the stump itself there were rough protrusions, suggesting that leaves had once grown there; if so, they had long ago withered away.

He sat down at the base of the stump and stared out towards the sea. Half an hour later, when the moon was in the mid-heaven, he was yawning. The sense of urgency had evaporated and he was beginning to wonder if he was mistaken to believe he had been brought there for some purpose. Perhaps the climbing of the hill was a purely ritual act; perhaps he had been made to repeat the ritual as a sign of trust and acceptance. In that case, his task was completed and there was nothing to do but return. But when he went to the edge and looked down, he decided that it would be safer to wait until daylight.

His position at the foot of the stump was not particularly comfortable; since the base curved downwards, he was forced to sit with his back at an angle. But when he allowed himself to slip downward into a less awkward position, he found that the curved portion made an excellent pillow; there was even a slight depression for the back of his head. He sighed with fatigue and closed his eyes. As soon as he did this, he experienced a wave of peace that ran down from the top of his head to the soles of his feet. His hands and bare feet, which had been cold, now began to glow with warmth. Once again he experienced a sense of being controlled; but this time the unknown force was urging him to relax.

The first thing he observed when he reached the level of inner silence was that he was no longer aware of the rippling, wave-like motion of the force. For a moment he was puzzled, then he understood; he was at the center from which the waves emanated, and the center was motionless.

Now, strangely enough, he was no longer tired. He was aware of the quiescence of his resting body as a glow of self-enjoyment, but the desire to sleep had vanished. Instead, he was possessed by an alert but muted excitement. For the first time, he understood clearly how the heaviness of the body limits the freedom of the mind. Now his mind felt bright and clear, like a still summer morning, and it seemed that he was contemplating his own life and the lives of all human beings from a great height. Yet the relaxation of his body continued, and had soon reached the point at which his consciousness normally melted into images and dreams. It was as if he stood on the threshold of some antechamber of the unconscious; voices and images over which he had no control began to invade his personal identity. But while he refused to be drawn over this threshold, he could still return to full awareness.

160

He was surprised by this ability to prevent himself from drifting into sleep, aware that his normal self-control was not equal to the task. The inner force that had brought him here was now providing the guidance and discipline that his own mind had not yet achieved. What astonished him was that this force was not manipulating or controlling him, but was treating him as an equal, respecting his individuality.

Then he was drawn into the world of living images that he had encountered so often on the borderland between sleep and waking. This was the dream world he had entered every night since he was born, and it was as familiar as the landscape around the burrow. Yet this was the first time he had seen it with his waking consciousness. The normal curtain of amnesia that separates sleeping and waking had been drawn aside, and he became aware of inner landscapes which, under their shifting dream imagery, were as real and permanent as the world of external reality.

As his own dream images faded, he understood why he was being allowed to linger at this gateway between waking and sleeping. This was the level of the consciousness that was trying to communicate with his own. The being whom the spiders worshipped as the goddess of the Delta lived permanently on a level that in human beings would have been called the subconscious. That was why she had been unable to communicate while Niall remained awake; to his conscious mind, the speech of the goddess would have been as meaningless as the sound of waves breaking on a beach.

Now, in the half-dream state, it was as clear as if it had been in spoken language. But it was a language without words. It reminded him of what had happened the first time the Master had addressed him directly; there had been no sense of a "voice" inside his chest, only a sense of direct communication. Now again the meaning was perfectly clear. The goddess was offering to answer any question he cared to ask.

Niall's first reaction was a kind of inner paralysis; it seemed almost blasphemous to question a deity. But even this nervous reaction drew an immediate response. In images that spoke as clearly as words, he was informed that she was no more a goddess than he was a god. In fact, she had no gender. On her planet of origin, there were no sexes. This planet—known to astronomers of the late twentieth century as AL (Alpha-Lyrae)$_3$—was the third in the solar system of the blue star called Vega, in the constellation Lyra. Being slightly larger than our own sun, AL_3 exerts a gravitational pull about a hundred times greater than earth, so a man on its surface would weigh ten tons and would be unable even to lift his eyelids. Sexual reproduction is therefore impossible and life on the planet proceeds by a kind of self-generation.

Because of its immense gravitational pressure, life on AL_3 has proceeded at a far slower pace than on earth. Life first appeared on the planet about five thousand million years ago, as compared to a mere three thousand million on earth. Three and a half billion years later, AL_3 produced its first intelligent life form. On earth, they would not have been regarded as living creatures, since they resembled terrestrial mountains; but on AL_3, the evolution of a thought takes as long as a human lifetime.

Half a billion years later, evolution had produced its highest form so far, the species to which the "goddess" belonged. On earth, these giant globular creatures would have been called vegetables. Unlike the "mountain" life form, they had achieved a certain individuality (although to Niall's bewildered senses, the goddess seemed as impersonal as the sea). Moreover, each member of the species was in mental contact with every other member and had access to the memories of all its ancestors.

In answer to Niall's unspoken question, he was shown a picture of conditions on the surface of AL_3. The first impression was of brilliance; with its great blue star blazing in the heavens—fifty times as bright as our own sun—it looked as if everything was illuminated by a continuous lightning flash. In this blinding light, the great flat plane seemed to stretch to infinity in every direction—since AL_3 is so much bigger than earth, its horizon appeared to be almost infinitely distant. Our own planet seemed absurdly tiny by comparison. Halfway across this plane, mountains a thousand times greater than those on earth— the dead remains of earlier life forms—looked like symmetrical cones. And in the foreground, the monotony of this blinding plane was broken only by the presence of a few dozen hemispherical plants, each one surmounted by a stalk—far taller than the stump against which Niall was now reclining—through which it communicated with others of its kind.

A hundred and fifty million years ago, there occurred below this flat, unchanging surface, an explosion that tore an immense crater and hurled into space enough material to constitute all the planets of the earth's solar system. This explosion was caused by the gravitational pull of a stellar fragment ejected from an exploding galaxy. Some of the material caught in the "tail" of this comet-like fragment was dragged on through space for many thousands of years. During this time, the life trapped in the tail—in the form of microscopic cells—remained inert, traumatized by the shock of its ejection and frozen by the icy cold of space. When it again came to consciousness, it found itself trapped in the tail of another comet—not this time a star fragment, but a ball of gas with a diameter of fifty thousand miles—and was on its way to our own solar system.

When the explosion had first hurled these living cells into space, our earth had been dominated by the great dinosaurs of the Jurassic era. When the tail of the comet Opik brushed the earth and deposited some of these spores in the earth's atmosphere, most of the human race had already been evacuated from the planet in giant space transports and was beginning its long journey to the Centauri star system and the planet labeled New Earth.

Most of the spores fell into the ocean and perished; others landed in deserts or polar regions and were forced to retire into defensive hibernation. Only five succeeded in germinating: two in central Africa, one in southern China, one on an island off the coast of Borneo, and one in the Great Delta.

Even for these survivors, life was appallingly difficult. They had become accustomed to developing slowly, over thousands of years, but such development was dependent on a powerful gravitational field. In earth's low gravity, all their molecular processes were accelerated, so they expanded like balloons until they were in danger of exploding. In similar circumstances, any earth organism would have perished. But the giant plants had achieved a degree of control over their bodies that men would have regarded as miraculous; they adapted to earth conditions—although growing ten times larger than on their own planet—fed on its energies and its atmosphere, and achieved within a few years a development that would have taken centuries on AL_3.

And so these five globular plants found themselves trapped on a tiny green planet, ninety-three million miles away from an unremarkable star called the sun. The struggle to survive had developed in them a far higher level of consciousness than in those left behind on their own planet. They were aware that, compared to other living forms on earth, they were at an immense disadvantage. On earth, only plant life is unable to move about freely; in our low gravitational field, locomotion comes easily. When these five alien plants began to develop, their flesh was tender and delicious, and many species of bird and insect would have found it palatable. There was only one way for the plants to defend themselves: by using their telepathic powers to establish direct control over the minds of these predators. And so the tiny spore that landed on the soft mud of the Delta developed into the empress of the Delta, the absolute controller of all its life forms.

So far, Niall had been able to follow the story without difficulty; it had been presented in a series of images that were as simple as a child's picture book. But now he wanted to know why the giant plants had found it necessary to broadcast waves of pure vitality to other life forms—the vitality that had enabled the spiders to become masters of the earth—and he found this altogether more difficult to grasp. For the answer seemed to be that these aliens found the earth boring because of its lack of variety. In view of the monotony of their own planet, this seemed absurd. Then he began to understand. On their own planet, each plant was confined to a single place; yet their minds could travel anywhere, merely by identifying with the mind of another member of the species. Evolution itself was a tremendous community effort in which every individual played its part. This is why their evolution had come to a standstill on earth. There were simply not enough of them to build up the necessary thought-pressure.

Even without being told, Niall could see that there was only one solution. If they were to evolve, the plants needed the companionship of other superbeings like themselves. If such beings did not exist, then they would have to be created. Animals, birds, even trees and plants, would somehow have to be imbued with *more life.*

It seemed an impossible task. But the plants possessed endless patience. Since their telepathic powers enabled them to communicate with the minds of other living creatures, it was merely a question of raising their powers by transmitting pure vitality—the life force of the earth itself. The "empress plant" and its fellows became, in effect, immense broadcasting stations.

All creatures that could receive these vibrations began to evolve at an accelerated pace. Unfortunately, these did not include man, whose intelligence had already developed too far to benefit from this crude vitality. But many other creatures were filled with a sense of power and reckless energy—in many cases so great that they were not afraid of death itself. (Niall remembered how the frog-like creatures had continued to attack even when they saw their fellows destroyed by the Reapers.) Many kinds of insect developed into giants—insects seemed particularly receptive to these waves of vitality. Even the simple tree fungus, a relative of the toadstool, developed into the mobile squid fungus. Many ordinary plants became carnivorous, like the viper weed and the strangler tree. The garden pest *limax*, the common slug, developed into the ground squid, which conceals itself in the earth as the octopus conceals itself on the bed of the ocean.

But the most spectacular success story had been that of the spiders. These had always been an adaptable species, ranging from the tiny crab spider to the enormous birdeating spider of the tropical jungles. Spiders were highly receptive to the vibrations of the empress plant; their cellular structure—identical to that of the squid fungus—was a particularly good conductor of the life force. They possessed many of the same qualities as the plants—patience, caution, determination; and as they grew in size they also developed formidable intelligence and willpower.

During these early days, the greatest enemy of the spiders was man himself. When the radioactive tail of the comet Opik brushed the earth, ninety percent of the remaining human beings had been destroyed. Many of those who were left suffered from radiation sickness and from unfavorable mutations—one group in central Asia even developed claws on their hands and feet. Traumatized by the catastrophe, man reverted to barbarism. He moved from the cities back to the countryside, and as his atomic blasters and Reapers and laser pistols wore out, he discarded them and returned to the spear and the bow and arrow. Yet even so, he remained a formidable enemy. One great leader, Ivar the Strong, conquered most of his human neighbors and used slave labor to build the walled city of Korsh, which became as powerful as ancient Thebes or Babylon. He drove all the spiders out of the land of the two rivers and became the ruler of a thriving farming community. His grandson, Skapta the Cunning, ambushed the spider general in the ravine called Mursat and killed eight thousand spiders with an avalanche. After this, he attacked their capital city on the shores of the great river and burned it to the ground. But Skapta was cruel as well as cunning and murdered so many of his own subjects that he was finally assassinated by his own minister, Groddig of Kos, whose son Trifig became the ruler. After Trifig came the greatest of all the warrior kings, Vaken the Wise, the son of a poor peasant who lived on the edge of the desert. A man of tremendous physical strength, he was seen by the king's daughter Masya when she was out hunting; she fell in love with him and married him. In the reign of Vaken, which lasted for sixty-eight years, man almost conquered the spiders; they were driven back beyond the borders of Vakenland, and were even hunted by men for their poison, which could preserve animals in a state of paralysis through the long winters when food was scarce.

The turning point came after the death of Vaken, in the reign of the Spider Lord Cheb. The legend tells how Cheb learned the secrets of the human soul from the renegade Hallat, who betrayed his own kind for the love of Princess Turool. But the truth was less dramatic. The spiders had learned from their defeats under Vaken the Wise that their real enemy was not human boldness and aggressiveness, but human intelligence. Among the advisers of the Death Lord was an ancient counselor named Qisib, also known among his own kind as "the wise." (It came as a surprise to Niall to learn that the spiders also had their thinkers and "wise men.") Qisib was fascinated by the secrets of human behavior and began to devote his days to studying a group of human prisoners. His great discovery came about by accident, when he took into his household the newborn son of a woman who had died in childbirth. The baby—whose name was Jurak—was tended by one of Qisib's daughters, who treated him as a pet. To Qisib's astonishment, the child became deeply attached to this daughter and to Qisib himself, and seemed to regard himself as a spider rather than a human being. It was through Jurak that Qisib began to understand the human heart and the human soul, and to recognize how easily men could be dominated through their affections and their craving for security.

So the spiders began to make a practice of taking newborn babies from their human mothers and bringing them up among baby spiders; in this way, they developed a class of human servants who were totally loyal to the spiders and who despised their fellow men. Vaken the Wise had used the gray desert spiders as spies; now the

Death Lords used their human servants in the same capacity. Those human communities who still resisted the spiders were betrayed. Within a few generations, the legacy of Vaken the Wise had been destroyed and all the men in the country of the two rivers had been killed or enslaved.

Niall was shocked to realize that the spiders owed their triumph to their human servants; but there was worse to come. He learned how, in the time of Qisib's successor Greeb, there had been a revolt of the slaves; it had been carefully planned, and before it was suppressed thousands of spiders and their human servants had been destroyed. The Death Lord asked Greeb to devise some method that would prevent such a catastrophe ever happening again. Greeb's first suggestion was that all the slaves should be killed, so that the only human beings who remained would be the faithful servants of the spiders. But this was impractical; there were too many slaves. Besides, the spiders wanted to maintain a class of slaves because they found human flesh tasty and were naturally unwilling to eat their loyal servants.

It was one of Greeb's human servants who suggested the solution. The name of the traitor has not been preserved; all that is known is that he was skilled in the breeding of cattle. It was this man who suggested that the spiders should breed the slaves by the same method as cattle and carefully select the fattest and most stupid to propagate their own kind. Any who showed signs of unusual intelligence should be destroyed long before they reached manhood. These ideas were adopted, and within a single generation the spiders achieved their aim: the total submission of their most dangerous enemy. Human beings came to regard the spiders as their lords and masters; defiance—or even resentment—became unthinkable.

As he listened to all this, Niall's anger grew until he felt choked by it. It was directed against the giant plants as well as the spiders; the plants were responsible for making the spiders masters of the earth. When he thought of the spiders, with their poisonous fangs and evil eyes, Niall experienced a wave of loathing and revulsion. How could anyone favor a species that murdered, devoured, and enslaved their fellow creatures?

His anger seemed to arouse a more personal response in the plant and its reply was as unambiguous as human speech. It addressed him directly, as if speaking aloud, and seemed to be saying:

"Then how can you favor your own kind? They were murdering, enslaving, and devouring their fellow creatures long before the spiders. They murdered and enslaved their enemies and bred animals for food. How can you say they are better than the spiders?"

For a moment Niall was alarmed by his own temerity. Then he realized this was absurd. The empress plant was superhuman and therefore unoffendable. Besides, she could understand his thoughts whether he spoke them or not. He was also emboldened by the feeling that he was not entirely in the wrong; when he thought of the spiders, and of what they had done to his own family, he still felt enraged.

"At least men have always respected intelligence. The spiders know that men are as intelligent as they are, yet they want to destroy them."

"As you would destroy the spiders."

He said defiantly: "Yes, I would."

Then his anger evaporated. As he looked into the soul of the empress plant, he saw that it was irrelevant. The concern of the giant plants was not for individual species, but for evolution. It made no difference to them who were the masters and who the slaves.

Besides, the story was not yet finished. In the century after the enslavement of man, the plants realized that something was going wrong. The evolution of the spiders was slowing down. They were becoming lazy, contented to remain all day long in their webs, catching flies for sport and gorging themselves on human and animal flesh. The plants tried increasing their injections of vitality, but it made no difference; the spiders seemed to accept it as a free gift.

Then the plants understood their mistake. On their own planet, life was so difficult and harsh that the struggle to evolve had become second nature. By comparison, the earth was full of variety. The result was that its creatures only evolved when they had something to fight *against*. During the first ten million years of their evolution, the spiders had hardly changed at all; now, in a few centuries, they had become masters of the earth. They were happy and secure; why should they make any further effort?

The plants decided to try an experiment. The bombardier beetles had always regarded the spiders as their hereditary foe. A bombardier beetle defends itself by producing a tiny explosion of hot gas, and this deters most of its natural enemies. But if a beetle wandered into a spider's web and the spider began to spin a cocoon of silk around it, the beetle would allow itself to be trussed up into a helpless parcel, for its firing mechanism was activated only by direct attack. It was a slave of its instinct.

Now the giant plants decided to concentrate their efforts on the bombardier beetles. They determined the precise wave length of vitality to which the beetles responded and transmitted this with increasing intensity. And as soon as the beetles became "more alive," they learned to overrule their mechanical responses. When a spider tried to entangle a beetle in its silk, it was promptly driven off by a burst of scalding gas.

The spiders had become accustomed to having their own way and were infuriated by this defiance. They were so angry that they decided the beetles deserved to be exterminated. (Niall smiled grimly; it was exactly what he would have expected.) But the beetles had gained a new confidence from their immunity and fought back with courage and determination. When the spiders redoubled their efforts, the beetles redoubled their resistance. In the centuries during which the two sides fought for supremacy, both evolved new levels of willpower and intelligence. And finally, intelligence and common sense prevailed. When the Master of the beetles proposed a truce, the spiders accepted eagerly. But then, as both sides settled down to the pleasant existence of successful conquerors, their evolution began once more to mark time.

The experiment confirmed what the plants already knew: that on earth, creatures evolve only when they have to struggle. In that case, the attempt to create superbeings was apparently a failure.

Yet there was still one more possibility . . .

The Death Lords had made one serious mistake. They had been confident that man was no longer a danger to their species. It was true that the men of the desert remained free; but they were useful for breeding and the spiders were convinced they posed no real threat.

And now, too late, they realized the full extent of their stupidity. The realization had come with brutal suddenness on the day after the raid on the Fortress. More than three thousand spiders had died; many more lived on in agony, their torment experienced by every spider in the surrounding area. It was on that day that the Death Lords knew that their struggle to become masters of the earth had ended in failure.

The thought filled Niall with a feeling of grim triumph and he recalled his own exultation as he had pointed the Reaper at a spider and pulled the trigger. Then, as he sensed the revulsion of the empress plant, the feeling evaporated and he felt like a child who has been detected in some forbidden activity. He tried to hold his thoughts in suspended animation, as if holding his breath. When this effort became too much, he asked finally: "What do you intend to do?"

The reply startled him. "Now it is in your hands."

It took several moments for Niall to digest this astonishing communication. His thoughts were in a turmoil. Did the plant mean . . . ?

He asked: "Do you mean we can do whatever we like?"

"We cannot prevent you."

To Niall this seemed absurd. "You could prevent me from leaving. You could"—it was impossible to conceal the thought—"kill me."

"No. You came here in good faith because we made a compact. We cannot break that compact."

He shook his head in bewilderment. "But what do you *want* me to do?"

The answer was as clear as if it had been spoken. "You must reflect and then make up your own mind. You are free."

The thought made him slightly nervous. It seemed impossible that he was being offered total freedom. Yet the plant's mind was open to him; there could be no deception.

"We are free to use the Reapers against the spiders?"

"If that is what you decide."

Niall envisaged returning to the city of the beetles and mobilizing the menfolk to fight against the spiders. He imagined the attack on the spider city and the destruction of the headquarters of the Death Lord. He could picture the spiders fleeing to the countryside in panic and then being hunted down one by one. And then men would unite in freedom to rebuild the city. With the aid of the white tower, they would rediscover the secrets of the past, so they need never again be afraid of the spiders. Lights would blaze in the tall buildings. Happy children would play in the parks. Men and women would throng the pavements, going about their daily business, and there would be no sinister spider webs overhead. Man would once again resume his rightful position as the lord of the earth. . . . It was a dazzling vision and it filled him with almost ecstatic delight.

"And what then?"

The question interrupted his train of thought, so that for a moment he failed to take it in. He repeated blankly: "What then?"

"What will men do when they are masters of the earth?"

The question struck him as pointless. Surely the answer was obvious? They would build a new civilization and live in peace.

"As they did in the past?"

Niall found these questions disturbing. Since the empress plant could read his mind, why was she bothering to ask?

"To make you reflect. When you leave here you will be free to do whatever you please. But before you decide, I want you to think of the consequences."

Niall shook his head. "It is true that men of the past fought endless wars. But in the century before they left the earth, there were no wars."

A silence followed; Niall waited for the next question. But when none came, he found himself thinking about what he had just said. It was true there had been no more wars; the old man in the white tower had told him that. But the old man had also said: "By the time men left the earth, they had still not solved the secret of happiness." The words echoed in Niall's memory as clearly as if they had just been spoken. So did another sentence: "A famous biologist wrote a book asserting that men would finally die of boredom."

Niall said: "*I* shall not die of boredom. I shall use the thought mirror to learn to control my own mind."

"You will. But what about the others?"

This question was accompanied by an image of Doggins. It was then that Niall understood why the plant was asking questions: not to learn what he thought, but to make him aware of what he thought.

He said: "Surely they can also learn?" But he recognized his lack of conviction as he spoke.

"Do you think they will learn more easily if they become masters of the earth?" Niall was silent. "You have seen what happened when the spiders and bombardier beetles became too successful. What makes you think men are different?"

Niall said slowly: "Men *are* different. They are not as lazy as the spiders."

"Perhaps so. But that is because their freedom is limited. Have you never noticed that men are at their best when they have only a limited amount of freedom? Then they fight and struggle for more.

171

When do you make your greatest efforts—when you have to struggle for what you want, or when you are free to do exactly as you like? If men are suddenly presented with too much freedom, they feel confused and lose their sense of purpose."

Niall said nothing; he knew it was true.

"What do you think would happen if men destroyed the spiders? Try to imagine what it would be like. At first they would be delighted with their freedom. They would rebuild their cities and burn all the spider webs and hold great celebrations. Then they would begin to teach themselves all the things the spiders have forbidden—how to make airplanes and ocean liners and space transports. But within a few years they would forget what it was like to be a slave of the spiders. They would begin to take their freedom for granted. And their grandchildren would go out looking for adventure because they were beginning to feel bored. You know that it has all happened before. Do you want to make it happen all over again?"

Niall shook his head; his inner certainties were beginning to evaporate. "Not all human beings are like that."

"Do you know any who are not?"

When he thought about it, he had to admit that he didn't. He thought of Kazak, with his desire for power; of Ingeld, with her haughtiness and vanity; of Merlew, with her egotism and love of her own way; and it was obvious that the plant was right. Even the good-natured Doggins had his curious limitations: a kind of crude self-assertiveness and total blindness to his own shortcomings.

"Then what do you *want* us to do?" But even as he asked the question, he knew what the answer would be.

"You have to decide for yourself."

"But you are saying that we must learn to live with the spiders?"

There was no reply and he took this for assent.

As he thought about it, he was struck by an idea. "If we drove them out of the city, perhaps we could force them to make a truce, just as they did with the beetles?"

"No. That is impossible."

"Why?"

"Because to drive them out of the city you would need to use the Reapers. And as soon as you use the Reapers against the spiders, you will be starting a process that you cannot control. You will be forced to go on until you have destroyed them."

Niall could see that this made sense. In the eyes of the spiders, a man with a Reaper was like a deadly snake; he would inspire fear and loathing. Sooner or later, the spiders would react with aggression and then men would be forced to destroy them.

"But if we cannot use the Reapers, how can we force the spiders to give us our freedom?"

"I cannot answer that. You must reflect on it until *you* see the answer."

Niall felt a wave of anger and frustration. He seemed to be trapped in a spider web of logic, in which every possible solution contained a flaw. His deepest impulse was to destroy the spiders. But if the spiders were destroyed, man would become master of the earth. And man was not yet ready to become master of the earth. For that, he would need far greater control over his own mind. And he would achieve that control far more easily if the spiders remained on earth, to remind him that he must strive to retain his freedom. It seemed an absurd paradox, but man needed the spiders more than the spiders needed man.

If man used the Reapers, then the spiders would be destroyed. But if man destroyed the Reapers, what would prevent the spiders from taking their revenge and destroying the creatures who had come so close to destroying them?

There seemed to be no solution; Niall made an effort to control an increasing sense of desperation. "Is there *nothing* you can do to help?"

There was a silence, but this time he felt a flicker of hope; it was as if the empress plant was reflecting on his question. Then he experienced a faint tingling sensation in the skin of his forehead. It reminded him of something; for a moment he was unable to remember what. Then, as the tingling increased, he remembered. It was the sensation of felt pads pressing against his forehead in the white tower. Suddenly, he was aware of his body lying on the ground, with his head pillowed against the foot of the stump. Then there was a sensation as if he was floating clear of his body, while the tingling increased until it became an intense glow of pleasure. This time, he was aware of what was happening. The plant was making an immense effort to raise the level of the life-vibration, until it could be absorbed directly by the human organism. But it was almost impossible; the plant itself was not on a high enough level to transform the crude life-force of the earth into the intense vibrations required to stimulate the human brain. There was something heroically self-destructive in its efforts to raise him to a higher level of perception.

Then something happened; as the plant's energy flagged, another force seemed to take over. With absurd ease, it filled Niall's brain with a flood of white light, in the midst of which there was a sound not unlike the vibration of a gong. Then, once again, it was as if the sun had risen from below some horizon of his inner being, and he was flooded with a sensation of overwhelming power, surging up from his own depths. This immense power was attempting to force itself through the narrow doorway of his body, as some roaring torrent might try to force its way out of a narrow canyon. Mixed with the exultation there was the recognition that if this continued, his body would be destroyed. But this appeared unimportant; his body seemed a mere encumbrance.

Then, because he knew the power had its origin inside himself, Niall took control of the force and deliberately terminated the experience. He had seen all he wanted to see. As the power ebbed, like a wave returning on itself, his body throbbed with exhaustion. He sighed deeply, allowing the fatigue to bathe him like a warm bath, then to obliterate his awareness.

As consciousness returned, he was aware of sunlight on his face and bare arms, and of a peculiar, lightheaded sensation in the top of his skull. He opened his eyes and shrank with alarm. A huge bird was standing a few feet away, regarding him with mild astonishment; the curved beak looked big enough to peck his head off. But what startled Niall was that he was looking at two birds, and that although they were quite distinct, they were standing in the same place. He could clearly see this fierce creature, with its bald head and powerful claws; but superimposed on it was another bird, slightly larger and semitransparent. This second bird was not at all fierce; it was obviously an amiable, good-tempered creature, and at the moment it was rather unsure of itself. As Niall stirred and sat up, the bird rose and flew away, disappearing over the jungle with slow flaps of its great wings.

Niall jumped to his feet and looked towards the east; the sun's disc was halfway above the top of the mountain ridge, which indicated that it was at least an hour after dawn. A silver mist was rising above the trees and it seemed to him that the jungle was exhaling a sigh of pleasure at the coming of the sun.

When he shaded his eyes and looked down towards the east river, he could clearly see the gap in the trees that Doggins had blasted with his Reaper, and the stationary object lying on the expanse of yellow mud was unmistakably Doggins.

A strong breeze was blowing from the sea and he was glad of its clean freshness; although he had become accustomed to it, he still disliked the decaying stench of the Delta. He walked round the eastern edge of the hill until he found a place that was less steep than the others and lowered himself down. In the bright sunlight it looked even more dangerous than by moonlight; at this point, a slip could plunge him down a thousand feet into the trees that edged the river. He took care not to look down, and instead concentrated his attention on each hand and foothold. Moving diagonally, he worked his way round to the south face of the hill, and at last found himself standing on the curving track that led down into the jungle.

During the descent, his mind had been so concentrated that he saw nothing but what lay before his eyes. But as soon as he relaxed, he again became aware of the peculiar effect of double exposure. To begin with, he was aware of the surging force that flowed in waves through the earth, and he felt as if he was walking across the head of a sleeping giant. It was this force that made him conscious of two worlds at the same time, for as it flowed through the earth, he could follow its progress; this meant that, in some strange sense, the earth was transparent. It was exactly as if he possessed two sets of eyes, one of which saw the solid, material world, while the other could see through it to a deeper world of reality. As he reached the level of the treetops, birds flew up in alarm and hovered round him, squawking and flapping their wings. They were big and looked dangerous, but if he looked at them with his second set of eyes, they became as harmless as domestic animals; he could see that they were merely putting up a show to defend their territory, and had no intention of coming closer. A bat-like creature that regarded him balefully from the fork of a tall tree was altogether more dangerous; it had the face of a demon and a soul that was full of savagery and violence; but when it met Niall's gaze, it looked away. It sensed that he, too, was dangerous.

As he picked his way along his own trail through the jungle, he was astonished that he had found his way in the dark; there were many fallen trees and the ground was full of deep ruts made by rainwater gushing downhill. He deliberately ignored his second pair of eyes, concentrating his attention on the ground. At one point, he was surprised to find his path blocked by a thick liana, more than a foot high; he had no recollection of climbing over it the night before. Then, as he came closer, it began to move, and he saw that it was a green snake, its mid-portion grotesquely swollen by some recently swallowed prey. By using his second pair of eyes, he could see that this prey was a piglike creature, covered in black bristles, which were being slowly dissolved away by the powerful digestive juices of the snake. The python itself was curiously unfrightening; its consciousness was only slightly greater than that of the trees, and its life on the ground made it feel continually vulnerable. At the moment, it merely wanted to be allowed to sleep in peace.

176

This double vision, he realized, was merely an extension of his normal ability to still his soul and project himself into the minds of other creatures, but it had been developed to a new pitch of sharpness by the experiences of the past few hours. The communications of the empress plant had at first struck him as strange and ambiguous, but he had soon become so skilled in interpreting them that he seemed to hear them in human language. This same skill was now permitting him to grasp and interpret vibrations from the world around him so swiftly and spontaneously that he was not even aware that there was any interpretation involved. It seemed like direct vision. It also opened to him new worlds of possibilities, for he could sense that even double vision was a form of unconscious self-limitation. If he wanted to, he could have seen other levels of reality—treble vision, fourfold vision, even fivefold vision. He had never realized so clearly that normal human perception is a form of blindness.

When he emerged from the trees, he found himself standing on the bank of the river and looking directly across at Doggins. The water looked calm and smooth, but his double vision showed him that, a few feet below the surface, a big caiman was lying, staring up at the dim outline of his figure and hoping that he would come close enough to be dragged into the water. For a moment Niall wished that he still had his Reaper. Then it struck him that this was unnecessary; the reptile's soul-mechanism was so crude that it was easy to implant into its mind the suspicion that this two-legged creature might be far more dangerous than he looked. The caiman sank quietly into the mud at the bottom, where it felt safely concealed.

Niall walked south along the river bank until he reached the place where he had crossed the night before. Here, where the water was shallow, there were no big predators; only hundreds of tiny creatures that lived under the fallen tree that partly blocked the stream at this point and which looked like a horde of many-colored fireflies as they darted around their home. But as Niall waded slowly across, his arms held above his head for balance, he was aware of the presence of some larger creature, a few hundred yards upstream, which launched itself gently out of the mud and began to swim towards him. This one failed to respond to his suggestion that he was dangerous; but its nervous system was so crudely constructed that it was easy to confuse it with false messages that made it proceed very slowly. As Niall scrambled up the opposite bank—falling for a moment on all fours—he looked back and caught a brief glimpse of something that looked like a writhing mass of gray weed, caked with glutinous mud, which broke the surface for a moment as the current lifted it over the concealed log.

Doggins was lying on his back, his mouth open slightly, snoring softly; the metallic garment, which covered him from head to foot, cast a shadow over his face. Gently exploring his sleeping mind, Niall could sense that he was still suffering from exhaustion and needed many more hours of sleep. But this was out of the question. This place was too dangerous.

Niall opened his pack, which was covered with dew, and took out his water bottle. The water was refreshingly chilly; the night must have been colder than he had realized. Then he chewed a hard biscuit, and took stock of the situation. The line of trees, with their tangled branches and interlocked roots, extended in both directions for many miles; to the south, they merged into the jungle, to the north, into marshland. Making a detour round them might take most of the day; it would be simpler if they could return by the way they came. The metallic garment would protect one of them. Would it be possible to use all the spare clothing to devise some makeshift garment that would protect the other? He laid out his blanket and spare tunic on the ground, then decided, regretfully, that it was beyond their skill. A good tailor might meet the challenge, but they did not even possess a needle and thread.

When he walked across to the gap in the trees, his hopes lifted. The breeze had driven the pollen into heaps, like drifting sand and, on these, beads of dew had formed in glistening droplets. It was just possible that the dew might have the effect of emulsifying the dust and preventing it from rising in clouds. Niall bent forward and cautiously touched the nearest heap with the tip of his index finger, then massaged the fine yellow dust between his finger and thumb. It felt oddly slippery, but he was delighted to observe that there was no stinging sensation. Cautiously stooping down, he took a pinch of the dust between his finger and thumb and rubbed some of it on the back of his hand. Although he massaged it into the skin, he still felt no discomfort. He waited patiently for several minutes until he was convinced that there was no delayed-action effect, then, as a final test, took another pinch of the dust and cautiously breathed it into one nostril. It made him sneeze, but there was no burning sensation and no aftereffect. As he stood up again, he laughed with exhilaration.

He went and shook Doggins by the shoulder. "Hey, Bildo, wake up!"

Doggins grunted, sighed, and slowly opened his eyes. For a moment he stared at Niall without recognition; then he remembered where he was and sat up suddenly.

Niall asked: "Are you all right?"

"I think so." He looked down at his arms, which were still covered with red spots. "Bloody sore, though. Hand me a drink, would you?" He took a long swallow from his water bottle, then pushed back the metallic garment and struggled to his feet. He tilted back his head and looked up at the empress plant. As he stared at it, his lips twisted into a thin smile that had more than a touch of malice. He pointed. "That's what we're after."

"What makes you so sure?"

"I don't know. I just feel it." He looked down at the ground. "Where are the Reapers?"

Niall, who was refolding the metallic garment, said: "I threw them in the river."

"Come on. Where are they?" He assumed Niall was joking.

"I told you. I threw them in the river."

Doggins looked at Niall's face and saw that he was serious. He stared incredulously. "But why, for God's sake?"

Niall said patiently: "Because it's the only way of making sure we get out of this place alive."

"Alive!" It was a cry of anguish. Doggins rushed to the edge of the river and for a moment Niall was afraid he meant to jump in. There was a swirl in the water, and the snout of the caiman appeared above the surface. Doggins recoiled and stood staring, prepared to retreat, until it sank back again. He turned to Niall with a gesture of despair. "And how do you think we're going to get out of this bloody place without weapons?"

"It may be easier than you think."

Doggins was struck by the confidence in his tone. "Why?"

"It may want to get rid of us." He pointed at the line of trees. "What purpose do you think they serve?"

Doggins gave a snort of unamused laughter. "To stop us from getting away!"

Niall said quietly: "No. To stop us from getting in. They want us to go. Look." He went to the gap in the trees and took a handful of pollen, allowing it to run through his fingers to the ground. "It's harmless now." He came back and rubbed some of the pollen on Doggins' arm. "See, it doesn't burn any more."

Doggins jerked his arm away and stared at it nervously. Slowly, his face relaxed into a smile of relief. He said with grim exultancy: "Come on—let's get out of this place before it changes its mind."

They gathered their possessions together quickly; a few minutes later they were picking their way slowly between the trees. Caution proved unnecessary. The pollen now seemed to be inert and even where it lay thick on the ground, no longer rose in choking clouds as their feet sank into it. But Niall was relieved when they reached the far side; with his sharpened perceptions, he could sense the hostility of the trees towards these violent interlopers.

Ahead of them lay the steep gray slope, scored with thousands of water channels. These made walking difficult; it would have been easy to slip and twist an ankle. By the time they were halfway up the slope, Doggins was breathing heavily and his face had become very pale. He gave a gasp and pressed his hand against his side.

"I'll have to stop. I've got a stitch."

They sat down together on the hard ground, but it was difficult to find a comfortable position and they had to dig in their heels to prevent themselves from slipping. Doggins looked exhausted; his cheeks were hollow and his cheekbones seemed more prominent than they had been on the previous day.

Niall said: "Do you want to know how to recover your energy?"

Doggins shrugged, his eyes closed. "How?"

"Use your thought mirror."

Doggins said dully: "That would only make things worse."

"No, it wouldn't. Turn it inward and try to concentrate your energies inside yourself."

Wearily, Doggins reached inside his tunic and turned the mirror over. A moment later, he gave a gasp of pain. "That hurts!"

"I know it does. But keep on, all the same."

Doggins clenched his teeth and screwed up his eyes; drops of sweat stood out on his forehead. Yet in spite of obvious pain, he continued to make the effort. After about a minute, he breathed in sharply, then slowly exhaled. As his face relaxed, the color returned to his cheeks. He opened his eyes and looked at Niall with a smile of astonishment.

"That's amazing! What happened?"

"It wasn't just tiredness you were feeling. You were getting depressed and discouraged, and that made you feel twice as tired as you really were."

Doggins was impressed. "Where did you learn that?"

"From experience."

Doggins heaved himself to his feet. "Oh well, let's get a move on."

Half an hour later, they reached the outskirts of the wood. After the uniform grayness of the slope, its rich colors were a relief to the eyes. It was a delight to feel the thick, soft grass under their feet. Niall observed that the scents were more varied than ever. But whereas on the previous day they had seemed heavy and exotic, like some oriental garden, they now had a quality of lightness that caused a strange exhilaration, a desire to laugh aloud. Niall found it almost impossible to believe that this symphony of fragrance existed only in his own mind. Then he made an effort to see them with double vision—he was finding this more difficult to induce as the day wore on—and immediately understood. The plants were exhilarated because these strangers were unarmed and were pouring out their relief in a flood of high spirits. As he looked at them with his second pair of eyes, their colors seemed to fade away; instead, he became aware of the roots and branches, and of the sap that flowed through them like green light. He could also see that the air was full of a sparkling shower of happiness which descended on them like the mist from a fountain, and that it was this happiness that his senses interpreted as a continually changing fragrance.

When he glanced at Doggins, he received a shock. Doggins had also become transparent, so that he could see through his flesh to the structure of his skeleton. He could clearly see the veins and arteries and the action of the heart as it pumped blood. But he could also see that the heart was responsible for a flowing web of color that suffused the whole body and extended slightly beyond it. This color contained a mixture of red, orange, and yellow, but was mainly blue and apple green, and it seemed to be sustained by the beating of the heart. As Doggins responded to the joy that filled the air around them, the colored tide flowed further and further beyond the limits of his body, until it extended six inches from the surface of his skin. Niall perceived this for only a few moments; then his double vision left him, and the world once again became solid and normal. He understood that this was necessary—he was merely wasting energy by seeing two worlds at once—but it left behind a tinge of regret.

On the far side of the wood, they were faced with the slope of tough, wiry grass, at the top of which fingers of granite stood out against the skyline. As the rich, tender grass of the wood blended into this coarser grass, Niall observed a change in his own feelings. It was as if he was responding to a cold, bracing wind. Last time they had been on this slope, both had experienced a sense of oppression and suffocation, which Niall had recognized as the deliberate action of the grass upon their nervous systems. Now the grass was sending up waves of a powerful force that was at once crude and invigorating; to Niall's mind, it contained a curious element of brutality. A brief flash of double vision made him aware that this force was being gathered from the earth itself; it was like a black wind rushing up from the granite substructure of the hill. Their own life energies were normally too subtle to respond to this brutal current but, because they were tired, their bodies were readjusting themselves to take advantage of its crude energy. It was somehow as distinctive as a smell and it made Niall think of hard rock bathed in the spray of a high waterfall. It seemed to carry to him a scent of the earth itself—not the surface, but the rocky, burning interior, where tremendous tensions created a whirlpool of magnetic energy. For a moment, he experienced a feeling of indignation and misery; it seemed absurd that man's senses were so limited, so that he was blind to the incredible variety of the forces that surrounded him. But this was replaced immediately by a recognition that this limitation was self-chosen and could be replaced at will by this richer and more complex form of awareness.

As they passed the hollow where they had killed the giant saurian, Niall experienced a momentary rush of panic when he saw the same white bones gleaming in the sunlight. But when he used his second pair of eyes, he saw with relief that this was exactly what it seemed: the skeleton of a dead animal. Not the slightest vestige of flesh remained on the bones; they had been picked clean.

When they reached the top of the slope, they paused for a breath. Niall, without thinking about it, sat down on the grass. It produced a faintly pleasant tingle where it touched his damp flesh, but seemed otherwise like any normal grass.

Doggins gave him an odd look, then also sat down. "Did you forget?"

Niall shook his head. "Not exactly."

It was true that he had forgotten; yet he had also known, sub-consciously, that the grass was now safe.

They were staring out over the brown marshlands, with their high reeds, to the distant hills where the others were waiting for them. It was encouraging to be within sight of their objective.

Doggins gave him a long sideways glance. "You know something that I don't. What is it?"

Niall did not pretend not to understand. In a sense, he had been waiting for the question ever since they set out two hours ago. He pointed over the great bowl of the Delta, with its steaming jungle and swampy marshland.

"The spiders and beetles regard this as a sacred place, the temple of the goddess Nuada. We came into it armed with weapons of destruction and the Delta was prepared to destroy us. Now we've abandoned the weapons and the goddess is allowing us to go in peace."

Doggins said slowly: "There was a time when you'd have been burnt as a sorcerer."

Niall shrugged. "It isn't sorcery, just common sense." He stood up. "We'd better move if we want to get back before dark."

The second part of their journey was oddly uneventful. In the marshes, they followed the trampled path through the reeds. The sun beat down on them from a blue sky that seemed to ripple with its own energy, yet neither of them felt tired; they seemed to be sus-tained by some inner force. Dragonflies more than a yard long buzzed down towards them then flew upward again, creating a welcome draught with their powerful wings. In one place where the ground was swampy, green gnats, each one as big as a finger-end, made a shrill noise as they whirled around their heads, sometimes making them wince with alarm when they flew too close to their ears. Yet neither of them sustained a single bite.

As the sun dipped towards the western hills, Niall observed that the insects were becoming less active, and that even the sounds of the birds had taken on a drowsy note. He himself was experiencing a pleasant heaviness in his limbs. The empress plant was withdrawing its energies, allowing them to sink with the sun; Niall's drowsiness was an indication of how far he had become reliant on the vibration of the plant. But by turning the thought mirror, he was able to restore his alertness and concentration. Unlike the other creatures of the

Delta, he was not dependent on the energies of the empress plant; his source of energy lay inside himself.

By the time dusk fell, they could see over the tops of the reeds to the green space that ran between the marsh and the treeline at the foot of the eastern hills. And as they emerged from the reeds, both of them saw the rising sparks that marked the presence of a campfire. Doggins halted, cupped his hands to his mouth, and shouted, "Simeon!" The sound echoed back from the hillside and alarmed birds flew up from the treetops. A moment later, there was a faint shout in reply. As they hurried up the green slope towards the trees, they saw a light advancing towards them; this soon resolved itself into Simeon, carrying a burning torch in front of him. When they were ten yards apart, he laid it carefully on the ground, then ran forward to embrace them. He hugged Niall so fiercely that Niall thought his ribs would crack.

"Thank God you're back. We didn't think we'd see you again."

The voice was as gruff and controlled as ever, but Niall could sense that it concealed immense depths of relief.

The leaping flames of the bonfire made the clearing almost as bright as day. But Niall could see at a glance that little had changed since they left. Milo was lying on a makeshift couch of leaves and grass, wrapped in blankets; Manetho was standing beside the fire, smiling, but when he moved towards them he did so with the uncertain steps of a blind man. As Niall embraced him, he caught a glimpse of white eyeballs below the grotesquely swollen eyelids.

Half an hour later, Niall was relaxing on his own improvised couch of branches, sipping a cup of wine as he watched Simeon chopping vegetables for a stew. Nearby, on the ground, lay the skin of an animal Simeon had shot that morning and whose flesh was now simmering in the cooking pot; it had the snout of a pig, but was covered in soft gray fur and had the long, powerful hind quarters of a hare. The smell from the cooking pot made Niall's mouth water.

Doggins asked Milo a question; when there was no reply, they saw that he had fallen asleep. Simeon said quietly: "It's been like that since you left. He's spent most of the time asleep."

"When do you think he might be well enough to travel?"

"Not for several days, at least."

Doggins said: "Then we'll have to make a stretcher and carry him. We can't spare that much time."

Simeon poured the plateful of vegetables and roots into the simmering cooking pot. "Are we hurrying back for any reason?"

Doggins shrugged and shook his head. It was the first time he had admitted, even tacitly, that the expedition had been a failure. "We can't stay away too long. You can never tell what the crawlies might do."

Niall found himself falling into a doze; the heat of the fire made him drowsy, and it had been forty-eight hours since he had slept. Yet even as his mind filled with the voices of sleep, some element in him refused to abandon consciousness. For a moment, he seemed to hover in a dark limbo, as featureless as outer space. Then he realized that he was again slipping into the half-dream state and was aware of the vibration of the empress plant. This time there was no communication; the plant did not even seem to be aware of his presence. But its soft nocturnal vibration filled him with a sense of peace. This, he realized, was the purpose of the vibration: to bring relaxation and refresh the vital powers.

Then his consciousness seemed to reach out to the others and he began to experience an acute sense of discomfort, as if a cold wind was draining away his warmth. After a moment, he was able to grasp that this discomfort proceeded from two sources. One was Manetho, who was sitting quietly by the fire, listening to the conversation. Because he could feel the firelight, but was unable to see it, Manetho was suddenly gripped by a black despair; the thought of spending the rest of his life in this darkness drained away all his courage.

The other source of discomfort was Milo, who was fast asleep. Now, suddenly, Niall was aware of what was wrong with him. It was not poison that was draining his vitality, but some form of living fungus in his bloodstream. The fungus was part of the sap of the Judas tree and it was a parasite. As fast as Milo renewed his vitality with food and sleep, the fungus drained it away again. And Milo was helpless against it since his own vital forces were on a higher level than those of the parasite and lacked the power of retaliation.

For Niall, the answer seemed obvious. All that was necessary was for Milo to tune in to the vibration of the empress plant, which was capable of attacking the parasite on its own level. But Milo was totally incapable of doing this; he was unaware of the power of his mind to control his vital responses.

But at least his mind was now passive, sunk in exhausted slumber. Niall allowed his own vital forces to blend with Milo's, until the two were synchronized. Then he set out to soothe Milo's overstrained nerves and discordant spirits into a state of relaxation. Milo's problem was that he was little more than a child; he had spent his life in the cozy security of the beetle city without any need to call upon his deeper resources; now he felt helpless and vulnerable. Yet because his mind was childlike, he was surprisingly easy to influence. As his breathing became soft and regular, his being relaxed until it had reached the same vibration rate as the empress plant. Then the power began to flow quietly into his bloodstream, awakening the resistance of his own vital forces. At this point, Niall knew he could safely leave him to his own devices.

Then someone was shaking him by the shoulder. Simeon was leaning over him. "Ready to eat?"

He yawned and forced himself into a sitting position. Simeon handed him a bowl of hot stew and a chunk of bread torn from the loaf. The fire was now a mass of glowing embers, in the midst of which a few recently thrown logs were bursting into flame.

"How long have I been asleep?"

"About two or three hours."

A voice from the shadows said: "Don't I get anything to eat?"

Simeon looked round in surprise. "You awake, Milo? There's plenty of stew. How hungry are you?"

"Ravenous!" Milo's voice was firm and clear; Doggins and Simeon exchanged glances. Simeon began to spoon broth into a bowl.

"Stay there. I'll bring it to you."

"I don't want to stay here. I've been lying down long enough." Suddenly, he was standing in the firelight. His tunic was creased and rumpled, and his hair was disheveled; but the color was back in his cheeks. He suddenly began to laugh. "What's that horrible-looking creature?" He was looking at the skin of the animal.

"That's what you're going to eat. It may look funny, but it tastes all right."

Milo took the bowl, picked out a leg with his fingers and bit into it. "Mmm, delicious. Better than rabbit."

It was true; the flesh of the strange creature had a curiously nutty flavor and the texture of roast lamb.

Doggins asked casually: "Think you might be ready to set out tomorrow?"

Milo swallowed, nodding enthusiastically. "That would be marvelous. I've had enough of this place."

"Good. We set out at dawn."

Simeon and Doggins stared at Milo as he ate, unable to believe in the transformation. Milo, unaware that he had just returned from the brink of death, concentrated on his food with the absorption of a hungry child.

Niall finished his own soup, drinking the last dregs out of the bowl, then lay down and pulled a blanket round his shoulders. Within moments he had plunged into a deep and dreamless sleep.

When he opened his eyes, the moon was still overhead and the sky was blue with dawn. The others were packing their haversacks and folding their blankets; they had obviously let him sleep on.

They ate a light breakfast of hard biscuits and fruit, sitting around a small camp fire. As the sky lightened, birds began to sing, and the treetops rustled with a dawn wind. Simeon and Doggins looked thoughtful; Niall guessed they were thinking about what would happen when they got home. Milo wore a cheerful smile, he was evidently elated at the prospect of returning. Manetho stared straight ahead of him as he ate and spoke only when spoken to; when Niall looked at the expressionless face, his heart contracted with pity.

Simeon asked: "Have we decided which route we're taking?"

Doggins said: "Back the same way we came, I suppose."

Niall said hesitantly: "Why not straight down the valley?"

Simeon frowned. "It's more dangerous. There are swamp adders and ortis plants and vampire bugs and God knows what." He glanced towards Manetho and the look implied: with a blind man in the party, we have no right to take risks.

As if he read Simeon's thoughts, Milo said: "I don't mind the risk."

Doggins turned to Niall. "What do you think?"

Niall thought about it. "I don't think we'd come to any harm if we went along the valley."

Simeon looked questioningly at Doggins.

Doggins said: "If Niall thinks it's safe, I'm willing to try it."

Simeon shrugged; his look implied: in that case, don't blame me.

They set out ten minutes later. By now the sun was above the tall conifers on the hilltop and the mist was rising from the marsh and the jungle beyond. The empress plant looked like a great face staring seaward, with long hair descending to its shoulders. As he looked at it, Niall experienced a curious sensation of power; it flowed through his skin, causing an almost breathless feeling of delight and a sudden vision of other places. The experience lasted only for a moment, but it left behind a glow of confidence and exhilaration. It also made Niall aware that his attitude towards the force had changed. Two days ago he had found it somehow vulgar and unsatisfying. Now he was aware that it was not being transmitted for his benefit, he could enjoy its sheer power as impersonally as he could appreciate the power of the wind or the sea.

They were now marching north, towards the sea, along the strip of grass that separated the tall reeds and the forest.

They walked in single file, with Simeon in front, followed by Doggins, then Manetho, then Niall and Milo. Their progress was slow, for where the ground was uneven, or where shrubs and bushes impeded their way, it was necessary to take Manetho by the arms and guide him. None of them wanted to show too much concern; Manetho insisted that he could see dim shapes in the sunlight and obviously wanted to believe that his sight was returning, but his stumbling and lack of direction made it clear that he was totally helpless.

A mile further on, the reeds gave way to swampland with pools of scum-colored water and clumps of prickly dark green grass; the ground underfoot became soft and spongy. The character of the forest also changed; the trees to their right became twisted and stunted, and there were many prickly bushes, among which Niall recognized the dangerous sword bush, with its yellow fruits streaked with purple. These were interspersed with a larger bush with yellow fleshy leaves and dark green, pumpkin-shaped fruit, each one as big as a large grapefruit. Some of these fruit had split open, revealing a coral-colored interior with large seeds and a syrupy liquid that dripped on the ground. The smell was rich and inexpressibly pleasant.

Niall asked Simeon: "Do you know what these are called?"

"No, but I wouldn't trust them."

"Why not?"

"Because they smell too good."

They had come to a halt, enjoying the rich odor. As they stood there, one of the fruits burst open with a faint plopping noise, and its two halves slowly separated like an opening mouth. A stick insect, lured by the delicious smell landed delicately on the skin of the plant and lowered its head to taste the syrupy juice. Suddenly, the fruit had become a globe again and the insect was struggling wildly, its head trapped inside the mouth that had closed as swiftly as the blink of an eye. The plant could evidently exert suction for, as they watched, the insect was drawn inside inch by inch, until its struggling back legs vanished.

Milo said: "Surely they couldn't harm human beings?"

Simeon shook his head. "I wouldn't bet on it."

Niall made an effort to see the bush with double vision. What he saw made his skin crawl with alarm. The bush suddenly exuded an air of menace, like a death spider prepared to sink its fangs into its prey; he could see that, beneath the large, fleshy leaves, which presented such a harmless exterior, the branches were flexible and prehensile, like tentacles, and that each one of them had a concealed sting at the end. As they moved away, he could sense its disappointment; it had been waiting for one of them to try and pluck its fruit.

The ground had become increasingly soft, and as they descended into a broad, shallow basin, was so spongy that they sank in up to the ankle with every step. It was necessary to tighten the straps around the tops of their boots to prevent them from being sucked off. They could have moved on to firmer ground by simply walking up the slope into the trees; but all felt instinctively that this would be dangerous. Most of the ground under the trees was hidden under a tangle of undergrowth, yet in other places, the earth was covered only with a light layer of pale green moss. Niall already knew enough about the Delta to guess that such places almost certainly concealed a trap. It was safer to squelch on through the relative safety of the marsh, even though each step released an odor of decay. When he made the effort to induce double vision—which became increasingly difficult as his tiredness increased—he felt that they were being studied by unseen eyes. Yet apart from birds and the occasional snake, they saw no living creature.

Two hours later, with the sun high overhead, fatigue had made their progress so slow that Niall began to wonder if the valley had been a wise choice after all. Then they noticed that the ground was becoming firmer as it sloped gently upward, and that the spiky swamp grass was giving way to the coarse marram grass that grew on sandy soil. Suddenly they found themselves on top of a low eminence, looking down on a pool of brown peaty water; it was about five hundred yards across, and was surrounded by gorse bushes.

Doggins threw his pack on the ground, and sank down beside it with a sigh of relief. "Oof! I think we deserve a rest."

Milo pointed. "What's that?"

At the edge of the forest there was a twisted tree with gray, prickly leaves, and its dull colors emphasized the brightness of an orange-red creeper that grew around the trunk; with its almost luminous color—it also had streaks of green and yellow—this looked like some exotic fungus. From the top of the creeper, where it vanished into the branches of the tree, hung several bunches of a semitransparent green fruit, not unlike bunches of grapes.

Simeon caught Milo's arms as he advanced towards it. "Careful!"

"Don't worry." Milo picked up his Reaper and held it at the ready as he walked towards the tree. Niall, also intrigued by the striking colors, went with him. Simeon came and joined them. The creeper was undoubtedly beautiful; its tints were as rich and varied as trees in an autumn landscape.

Simeon leaned forward to peer at the grapes. "I wonder if they're edible?"

As he spoke, Niall made the effort to induce double vision; his fatigue made this difficult, and he had to screw up his face and concentrate before he could bring about the gear-change of inner-perception. But as soon as this happened, he was overcome by a sense of danger; both the creeper and the tree were living creatures that were fully aware of their presence.

As Milo stepped forward, reaching out towards the grapes, Niall seized his arm. "Don't go near!"

As he spoke, the bottom of the creeper—which had seemed firmly embedded in the ground—uncoiled from the trunk and snaked out towards Milo; appendages like hairy roots coiled round his wrist. Milo jerked violently backwards and the roots lost their grip. Then the tree shook its dry leaves, as if quivering with disappointment.

Milo said: "Filthy creature!" and raised the Reaper. But as his finger tightened on the trigger, Niall pushed the barrel down. "No!"

Milo said irritably: "Why not?" He tried to raise the barrel again.

"Don't." With both hands, Niall forced the barrel down so it was pointing at the ground. Milo gave way with a bad grace.

"I don't see why not!" He shrugged angrily.

Niall said: "Do you want to get back to the coast alive?"

Milo dropped his eyes. "Of course."

"Then don't use your Reaper."

Milo grunted and went and sat down.

Simeon asked Niall: "Why do you say that?"

"Because all these plants are aware of one another. If you kill one, they all feel it."

"But would that matter? It would only make them more cautious."

"That's not true. They're more destructive than wild animals because they lack power of movement. As soon as one of them is killed, they all begin to look for ways of destroying the interloper."

They were seated now, opening their packs. Simeon asked curiously: "How do you know all this?"

Niall shook his head. "It's hard to explain. I just feel it."

"Is that why you told us it would be safe to use the valley?"

"Yes."

Doggins smiled with a touch of irony. "Is that why you threw our Reapers in the river?"

Milo gaped at him. "You threw the Reapers in the river?" Niall nodded. "But why?"

"Because . . ." He found it difficult to select the right words. "Because if you want to stay alive in the Delta, you have to become part of the Delta. It has to learn to trust you."

"But what happens if something attacks you?"

Niall was finding it difficult to argue; their minds were too far apart. He said, shrugging: "I can't make you understand."

But Simeon was looking at him with a curious expression. "Why not try?"

Niall took a deep breath. He was not sure where to begin. "Everything in the Delta has its own weapons of defense and attack. But the Reapers . . . are too absolute." Milo started to interrupt, but Simeon waved him to silence. "They're so powerful that they give us a sense of . . . false security." He felt he was expressing himself badly.

Simeon said: "False power?"

"That's right!" He was relieved to find himself understood. "Yes, it's false power. They make us feel more powerful than we really are. And so they stop us from becoming aware of our real power . . ." He tapped his forehead.

Simeon said quietly: "But the spiders have developed more of that power than we have."

Niall shook his head. "If that were true, they'd deserve to be the masters. But it's not true."

Doggins, his mouth full, said: "Let him eat his food."

But Simeon was looking at Niall with deep interest. He asked: "What do you mean about the spiders?"

"They don't really possess greater powers than we do. It's just that we haven't learned to use ours." He shot a defiant glance at Milo. "And we never shall while we rely on the Reapers."

Simeon asked: "But how can we fight the spiders without the Reapers?" He added: "Or perhaps you don't think we ought to fight them?"

Niall said: "We have to fight them. But on their own terms. And sooner or later, we have to learn to live with them."

Doggins looked at him with astonishment. "I thought you wanted to destroy them."

"I did. But that was before I came to the Delta."

Simeon asked: "So now you don't think we should use the Reapers?"

Niall said: "We *mustn't* use the Reapers."

"Why?"

"Because if we do, we can't help destroying them."

Milo asked: "And what do you think we should do with the Reapers?"

Niall shrugged. "If you want to know what I think . . ." He hesitated.

Simeon said: "Yes, we do."

"I think we should throw them in that pool."

Milo gave an exclamation of astonishment. Simeon gestured him to silence, and asked quietly: "And what good do you think that would do?"

Niall found himself looking into Manetho's blank eyes. "It might cure Manetho's blindness, to begin with."

Even as he said it, he was startled by his own words, and immediately regretted them. They seemed to have slipped out before he could stop them.

Doggins looked at him sharply. "Do you really think that's true?"

"Yes." But Niall felt like a child who is trying to save face. He felt ashamed to look at Manetho.

Simeon said slowly: "In that case, perhaps we ought to try it." He looked round at the others.

Niall's heart sank; he wanted to protest that he hadn't meant it.

Then, for the first time, Manetho spoke. "I don't want anyone to make sacrifices for me."

His voice was flat and expressionless; but his words revealed that Niall had aroused his hopes.

They looked at one another, then at Manetho. Each one of them felt guilty that Manetho was blind while he was still able to see.

Simeon raised his eyes towards the sea. "The worst of the journey is behind us. With luck, we should reach the sea in two hours."

They all looked at Doggins. He pretended to be preoccupied with his food; but all knew he was aware that he was being asked for a decision. Finally he shrugged. "All right. Do as you want to."

Milo said incredulously: "I think this is mad!" No one answered him. He turned to Niall. "Do you think this will help Ulic?"

Niall shook his head, but said nothing. Milo gave a helpless shrug and turned away.

Simeon held out his own Reaper to Niall. "Will you do it?"

Niall took it without speaking. As he walked towards the pool, he uttered a mental prayer, and looked towards the empress plant. From this angle it looked curiously anonymous, like any other hill. He walked to the eminence overlooking the pool, raised the Reaper above his head, and threw it as far out as he could. As he did so, he experienced a strange exhilaration that contained an element of malice. Then he turned round. Simeon handed him the second Reaper. Again, Niall threw it with all his strength. It struck the water with a splash and vanished immediately. Simeon took the third Reaper from Milo's hands; Milo relinquished it unwillingly. Niall sent it spinning towards the center of the pool. As it vanished with a splash, the surface was disturbed by a bubbling noise, followed by a sudden swirl of movement.

Doggins said grimly: "There's something in there."

Milo said: "Let's hope it's not hungry."

They all looked at Manetho, whose blank gaze was turned towards the center of the pool. Then Simeon took him gently by the arm.

"Wash your eyes in the water." Manetho started to kneel, unaware that the water was six feet below him. "No, not there. Come over here." They led him to a spot where the ground sloped into the pool. Manetho knelt down and lowered his spread hands until they touched the surface. Then he bowed his head and splashed some of the brown water into his eyes. He gave a scream of pain.

"It stings!" He recoiled, massaging his eyes frantically with his hands. Milo ran and brought a piece of cloth, which Manetho pressed tightly against his face, clenching his teeth. Niall stooped and took some water into his palm, then splashed some into his own eyes. The pain made him cry aloud; the water was salty with minerals that stung like acid. A drop ran into his mouth; it was horribly bitter.

Doggins handed Manetho a bottle with a few inches of wine left in it. "Here, drink this." Manetho shook his head and pushed it away; he was obviously in agony.

Simeon knelt in front of him, and grasped his wrists. "Here, let me look."

Manetho lowered his hands unwillingly, but had to screw up his eyes; he was still groaning. Simeon murmured soothing words, placed his fingers on Manetho's swollen cheek, and gently pulled down the lower eyelid.

Manetho suddenly became still; a look of incredulity crossed his face. "I can see you!"

With an effort, he opened both his eyes and stared at Simeon. Then he began to laugh hysterically, mopping at his eyes to brush away the tears, which were streaming down his cheeks. He stared around him. "Yes, I can see again." Manetho jumped to his feet, flung his arms round Niall, and squeezed him so hard that Niall gasped with pain. His rough beard scratched Niall's ear. "You were right! It worked."

Simeon asked: "Can you see us clearly?"

Manetho blinked at him. "Not very clearly. But I *can* see." He gazed around with delight and astonishment.

Milo was looking at Niall with awe. "How did you do it? Was it some kind of magic?"

Niall shrugged. "I doubt it. Probably the water. It must have counteracted the poison."

But he could see that Milo thought he was simply being modest.

Manetho now accepted the wine and drank it without lowering the bottle from his lips. After this, they sat down and finished their meal. They were all feeling euphoric; what had happened seemed a good omen. Niall himself had the curious sensation that he had just recovered his sight, so that he looked at everything with a feeling of delighted incredulity; when he thought about it, he realized it was probably due to some kind of empathy between himself and Manetho.

When they resumed their march they were all in high spirits. The ground under their feet was firm again; the sea was noticeably closer; at this speed, they should reach it by late afternoon. Now, once again, they were marching through a terrain of marram grass and low bushes, many of them covered with bright berries; they took care to give these a wide berth. To their left, the land sloped towards the river, which now wound its way towards the sea through flat marshes. At mid-afternoon, a rainstorm descended from the western hills; the wind changed suddenly, low black clouds streamed over the hilltops like an invading army, and ten minutes later, they were blinded by rain that fell in sheets. Flashes of lightning were followed immediately by deafening crashes of thunder, and the ground at their feet dissolved into mist at the fury of the downpour. There was no point in halting; the bushes afforded no shelter and the ground under their feet had turned into a torrent that flowed down the slope towards the river. Within seconds, they were all soaked to the skin, in spite of their cloaks, and their boots were full of water. They staggered on, buffeted by the wind, blinded by the rain which ran down their bodies as if they were naked. At one point, when Niall almost fell to the ground, Manetho's powerful hand caught him and dragged him to his feet; then Manetho placed his arm round Niall's shoulders and gave him a squeeze. Niall looked at his face and saw that Manetho was laughing exultantly, his face upturned into the downpour. Once again, he shared Manetho's joy in being able to see as well as feel the rain.

Then, suddenly, everything was still again; the clouds vanished over the eastern hilltops and the sun warmed their cold flesh. The only sound was the splash of their feet through the water that continued to run downhill. They halted and removed their boots, then marched barefoot, with their boots suspended upside down from their packs. Soon their garments were steaming in the heat and the marram grass had ceased to be waterlogged. Ahead of them, the sea was glittering in the sunlight, as if the rain had washed it clean.

Doggins, who was marching in front, halted suddenly and stared intently. Niall asked: "What is it?"

Doggins pointed. "Snakes."

Between two gorse bushes, something white was emerging from a hole in the ground. The same thing was happening all around them. They stared in dismay, and for a moment Niall regretted throwing away the Reapers. Then Simeon said: "That's not a snake. It's a mushroom!"

Niall leapt backwards as something touched his shin. Then he saw that it was a wavering stalk, pushing its way up out of the ground with motions not unlike those of a worm or a centipede. All around them, flowers, mushrooms, and toadstools were pushing their way out of the soil like tiny reptiles. Puff balls swelled up like balloons, then suddenly stopped growing; others exploded, filling the air with the odor of damp woodland.

Niall was reminded of the blossoming of the desert in his childhood; but all this was happening far more swiftly. In less than a quarter of an hour, they were marching through a sea of flowers and multi-colored fungi, and the air was filled with a mixture of scents, some delicious, some oddly unpleasant; one liver-colored fungus smelled like rotten meat. But even the unpleasant smells did nothing to dispel Niall's feeling of delight. It was as if his childhood had returned and they were again living in the cave at the foot of the plateau, and his father and Hrolf and Thorg were still alive. Once again, he experienced his excitement as he bounced along on his mother's back on their way to their new home. He could taste the faintly bitter flavor of the succulent tuber that his mother had dug up with a knife, and smell the charred odor of creosote bushes, and the peculiar, distinct odor of the tiger beetles that hung around the burrow for so many months. It was astonishing to realize that the seven-year-old child was still there inside him and that every one of his memories was preserved as perfectly as if no time had elapsed. As he tramped through the flowers, whose stems were cool against his legs, he felt that the Delta had given him back his childhood, and that this was a farewell present from the empress plant.

Two hours later, they were close enough to the sea to hear the cry of gulls. Once again they were surrounded by the green vegetation like overgrown watercress and by the bushes whose glossy leaves looked as if they had been painted. They had to make a wide detour to the east to avoid the ivy-like plant with its narcotic properties, and an impenetrable clump of sword bushes that stretched in a wide arc for more than half a mile. This detour brought them to the foot of the eastern hills and past the point at which they had started their journey up through the forest. Niall thought about Ulic, and for the first time that afternoon, was oppressed by a cloud of sadness.

Then the wind brought them the smell of the sea, and a few minutes later they were tramping through the warm sand and listening to the crash of waves on the beach. Niall flung down his pack with a groan of relief, and experienced an absurd feeling of lightness, as if his feet were about to leave the ground. He ran across the beach and waded into the water until the waves were heaving around his waist; as he stood there, his eyes closed, being rocked backwards and forwards by the movement of the sea, the fatigue drained out of his body and was replaced by an exhilaration that made him laugh aloud.

A shout from Milo made him look round. Milo was pointing up the beach. For a moment, Niall was unable to understand why he was looking so excited. Then he saw the plume of smoke that rose from behind the palm trees, half a mile away. He waded ashore as quickly as the water would allow him.

Simeon was looking grim. "It may be servants of the spiders. If so, the spiders must have brought them."

Niall shook his head. "I don't think so."

"Why not?"

"They think we're still armed with Reapers. They wouldn't risk a direct confrontation."

Manetho looked around at their faces: "Then it may be our own people, come to search for us."

They moved in close to the palm trees and advanced slowly along the beach. The wind was blowing from the northwest, but it carried no sound of human voices. When the rising smoke was only a few hundred yards away, they came to a gap in the trees, and clambered cautiously over the ridge. From there, they could see that the fire was burning on approximately the same spot where they had camped during their first night in the Delta. Nearby, in the shadow of the trees, a man was lying, apparently asleep.

Milo turned to them. "I think it's Ulic."

Doggins said: "Don't be silly. He's dead."

"But he's got a pack like ours."

It was true; the pack beside the camp fire was undoubtedly like the ones they were carrying.

Suddenly, Milo was running as fast as his legs would carry him. They heard him shout. The man jumped to his feet and stared. Then Milo turned round, waving his arms. "It is Ulic!" The two ran towards one another, embraced, then began to perform a clumsy dance of sheer joy.

It was Doggins who voiced the thought that struck them all at the same time. "Thank God we didn't bury him."

Moments later, they were slapping Ulic on the back and shaking his hands until he winced. He was pale, and had several days' growth of beard on his chin; otherwise he looked exactly as when they had last seen him.

This was no time for explanations; their relief made them incoherent. Their stories were told in jumbled fragments, which were only assembled into some kind of connected sequence many hours later, as they lay round the campfire in the dark. Meanwhile, Niall climbed the tall tree and lowered down their canvas bags and the spider balloons; Manetho took a fishing line and went to the rocks to catch their supper; Ulic and Milo went off with a container of grubs to feed the porifids, who greeted their arrival with ecstatic bubbles of foul-smelling gas. Doggins, who was suffering from exhaustion and blistered feet, lay down in the shade of the palm trees and slept without stirring until dusk. Niall bathed in the sea, dried himself in the sun, then went and sat beside Manetho, who had already caught three large mullet, and would catch four more before they decided they had enough for a celebratory meal.

The fish were encased in leaves, then in a layer of mud, and baked in the hot ashes. While Manetho cooked, the others stared at the emerging stars, and gave themselves up to the curious magic of the Delta, in which the smell of danger seemed to blend with a marvelous sensation of freedom. Then Manetho raked the fish from the ashes with a forked twig, and the air was suddenly filled with the delicious aroma of fish that had been freshly caught and immediately cooked, and of bread molded into flat cakes and baked between hot stones. The reflective mood was banished by the food and by draughts of wine, and was replaced by exhilaration as it dawned on them, for the first time, that they had returned unscathed from the heart of the Delta, and that they were all together again.

As they ate, Ulic caused gales of laughter as he described how he had awakened and found himself tied to the branch of a tree, fifty feet above the ground, and how he had shouted indignantly for his companions, convinced that they were playing a practical joke. It was not until he noticed that he was wrapped tightly in a blanket, which had been secured around him by long thorns, that it finally dawned upon him that he had been left for dead. After long struggles, he had succeeded in freeing his right arm—Manetho had tied him very tightly in case birds of prey tried to dislodge the body—and eventually untied the double knot on his chest. It had cost him a considerable effort to free himself without falling off the branch; the blanket, finally unpinned, had fallen to the ground, and he had saved the rope only just in time—"otherwise I'd still be up there." (They continued to laugh—no longer out of mere amusement, but also out of admiration for Ulic's sheer good humor as he recounted an episode that he must have found grimly serious.) Finally, after crouching in the fork of the tree, allowing his circulation to return, he had tied one end of the rope round the branch and lowered himself to the ground. There he had found his pack propped against the base of the tree, and the ashes of their camp fire, which had obviously been cold for many days and which showed footprints of wild animals. After eating a meal and drinking some wine—which had restored his spirits—he had set out on the long journey back to the beach, which, fortunately, had been uneventful.

Niall asked: "When did all this happen?"

"Yesterday."

"What time did you wake up?"

"At dawn—the birds woke me."

It made Niall thoughtful. So Ulic had regained consciousness at the same time that he himself had awakened on top of the empress plant . . .

Doggins asked Ulic: "What did you do with your Reaper?"

Ulic looked surprised. "I thought you took it."

None of them could remember precisely what had happened to the weapon; to the best of Milo's recollection, he had left it beside Ulic's pack, leaning against the foot of the tree.

Ulic shook his head. "Well, it certainly wasn't there."

They looked at one another. Niall said: "Fortunately, you didn't need it."

Doggins shrugged gloomily: "He might have done."

Niall said: "I doubt it."

Simeon gave him an odd look, but said nothing.

Niall fell asleep long before the others; the food and the night air made it impossible to keep his eyes open. Periodically, he was awakened by their laughter, or by a sudden brightness when dry branches were thrown onto the fire. Fragments of their conversation—"the biggest millipede I've ever seen," "they looked like oversized frogs"—mingled with his dreams. Finally, there was only the sound of the waves breaking on the beach and the wind rustling in the palm leaves.

Then Simeon was shaking him by the shoulder. "Wake up. The wind's blowing from the southwest. We've got to get the balloons inflated."

As the Delta receded beyond the horizon, Niall once again experienced the sense of hanging motionless in a windless space between sea and sky. The sky above them was deep blue and cloudless; the sea stretched endlessly around them, its blue surface fading to misty gray where it met the skyline. Only the coolness of the air revealed that they were moving fast. It might have been a clear day in midwinter.

The three balloons were again linked together; but this time, Niall was sharing the undercarriage with Simeon, whose familiarity with the coastline made him the natural choice as navigator. Until they were out of sight of land, they stood on opposite sides of the undercarriage, to maintain an equal balance. Although they had been airborne for more than an hour, neither had spoken a word; they were hypnotized by the immensity of the circular horizon and awed by the tremendous drop beneath them. Here, in the daylight, the flight seemed more dangerous than at night.

When Niall began to feel cold, he sat down cautiously on the floor and wrapped his cloak around him. He opened his pack and took out a biscuit and a slice of dried meat; there had been no time to eat before they left the beach. Simeon joined him and for a few minutes they ate in silence.

Then Simeon said: "There's something I've been meaning to ask you. Something strange happened the other night, while you and Bildo were away. I was sitting on guard, listening to the sound of some wild animal in the forest. I knew it was watching us, waiting for the opportunity to attack. Then something happened. I can't describe it except to say that I lost the feeling we were in danger. In fact, I felt so certain about it that I lay down and went to sleep." He took a draught of water from the bottle. "Do you know what happened?"

Niall said: "That was when I threw the Reapers into the water."

"Why did you do that?"

Niall had been expecting the question and had not been looking forward to it. For the past two days, he had experienced a deep reluctance to speak of what had happened to him; it was as if some invisible force was ordering him to remain silent. Yet now, as Simeon spoke, he felt this inner prohibition dissolve and knew he was permitted to speak. He described how he had lost his temper and fired into the river, and his skin became icy cold as he recalled how close he had been to destroying the empress plant. He told of the sudden impulse that had made him throw the Reapers into the water, and of how he had obeyed the order to cross the river. As he was speaking, many things became clear for the first time. Now he recognized that the goddess could have destroyed them at any time after they landed in the Delta, and that she had taken a calculated risk in allowing two armed men to approach so close. But he also understood that the impulse that had drawn him to the heart of the Delta was a summons from the goddess herself.

It was as he tried to describe his encounter with the empress plant that he began to experience an increasing sense of frustration. The words seemed to falsify what he was trying to say. Simeon listened without interruption, for which he was grateful; even so, he felt as if he was trying to maintain his balance on slippery ice. When he concluded: "Then I woke up and it was morning," Simeon looked startled.

"And that's all?"

"That's all I can . . . explain."

"So you didn't learn anything that will help us against the spiders?"

Niall was disappointed; he had hoped Simeon had understood. "No. I've tried to explain—we have to learn to live with the spiders."

Simeon shot him a glance of mild irony. "And did you learn what we should do if the spiders decide to conquer us?"

Niall struggled for words; he said finally: "No."

Simeon said: "Then it seems to me that we're back where we started, only worse off."

"Why do you say that?"

"Because we no longer have any bargaining power. We've left our Reapers behind in the Delta, and by now the beetles will have confiscated the rest. The spiders can do what they like."

"Provided the beetles agree. And the beetles would not allow us to be enslaved."

"They may have no choice." He laid his hand on Niall's shoulder. "Look, I've had a lot of opportunity to think about this over the past few days. The beetles have always allowed their servants a lot of freedom, and the spiders have always said that's a mistake. The spiders say men won't accept just a little freedom—they always want more. According to them, men are always dangerous unless they're kept enslaved. And now it looks as though they were right. How can the beetles defend themselves against that kind of logic? They'll have to admit that men are murderous and dangerous." He shrugged gloomily. "And we've thrown away our only bargaining counter."

"Nevertheless, we were right to destroy the Reapers. There was no other way."

Simeon thought about it, his gray eyes averted. He said finally: "I daresay you're right. But I don't like to think what the consequences will be."

They were interrupted by a shout. They stood up cautiously and moved to either side of the undercarriage. In the next balloon, Doggins was pointing towards the northern horizon; when Niall shaded his eyes, he saw the dim outline of the coast, with mountains in the distance.

A quarter of an hour later, they could clearly discern the coastal landmarks: a line of high, gray cliffs, and, further to the north, a brown island that rose out of the sea like a fortress, with pinnacles of pointed rock.

Simeon said: "We're heading too far north. The harbor's on the other side of that." He pointed to a distant headland in the south.

"Does it make much difference?"

"It means a day's march back to the city. I hope we don't meet any spiders."

The cold air was making Niall shiver. He reached up inside the cloak and turned the thought mirror. The sudden concentration made him feel better; as he focused his mind, he discovered that he could induce a warm glow in his hands and feet. He closed his eyes and allowed his consciousness to relax and expand. After a moment, he became clearly aware of the porifid above his head and of the threads of energy that stretched around it into space like an immense spider web. He deliberately allowed his own consciousness to merge with that of the porifid and with its companions in the other balloons. The result was fascinating: the world around him seemed to change into a gigantic pattern of energy, like a spider web. Space itself seemed to vanish and to be transformed into energy.

What astonished him were the colors. The energy web had a violet color, while the porifids seemed to be small blue patches, with trailing threads of transparent blue. Other energies, rather less intense, were streaming up from the sea; these were of a very pale blue color. Above the distant land, there was a haze of green energy, which changed to gray over the mountains. Simeon, standing a few paces away, was a red mass of energy; but when Niall looked more closely, he could see that this energy was diffused, like smoke, and that it was continually leaking away, so Simeon had to keep on replacing it from his own body.

It now struck Niall that until he had turned the thought mirror, his own energies had also been leaking away. Now his mind was concentrated, he was able to control this waste of his vital force. He was also aware that he was able to absorb energy from the violet web, as well as from the earth and sea. The source of the violet energy lay beyond the southern horizon, and he was aware that this source was the empress plant. It absorbed the green energy of the earth, concentrated it, and then transmitted it, so it could be absorbed by living organisms like the porifid. But the porifid was far too small and inefficient to make proper use of the energy; it could only store up a little at a time. And Simeon, who could have stored large amounts of energy, was almost totally unaware of its existence.

Yet Niall himself could store the energy. He merely had to absorb it, like a fish eating plankton, and then prevent it from escaping again. As he mastered this trick, the glow of warmth inside his body increased, until he felt as if he was sitting in front of a large bonfire. When he looked down at his body, he could see that it had ceased to be a pale, diffused red, but had been transformed into the rich, glowing color of a ruby.

Simeon touched him on the arm and brought him back to consciousness of the physical world.

"I'm going to start releasing pressure. The wind should be less strong down there. There's no point in being carried too far out of our way." He reached up towards the release valve.

Simeon's anxiety struck Niall as absurd. He was aware that the wind was merely a crude form of energy and, as such, merely a part of a vast energy pattern of which they themselves were, for practical purposes, the center. So if they wished to change the pattern, they merely had to make a spontaneous effort of will, like a bird changing direction in flight. Even the porifids knew how to do it.

Niall closed his eyes and fixed his mind on the headland to the south. Then he made an effort to absorb and retain more energy. It was exactly as if he was increasing his own weight, so the spider web of energy began to sag underneath him. This created a vortex of controlled power, which sucked in the surrounding energies like a whirlpool. Their balloon shuddered violently, so the connecting rope jerked them sideways; they were forced to cling on to the sides of the undercarriage.

Simeon said: "Sorry." He was evidently under the impression he was responsible for the turbulence. A few minutes later, he gave a grunt of satisfaction, and slapped Niall on the shoulder.

"Good, I think it's working." He waved triumphantly at Doggins in the next balloon.

Niall said nothing. Like a yachtsman, he was concentrating on steering into the crosscurrents of energy, preventing them from sweeping him further than he wanted to go. He found this easier if he kept his eyes closed; then he was aware of precisely how much energy he was controlling. When he opened his eyes again, he could see beyond the headland, with its lighthouse, to the massive stone walls of the harbor. Twenty minutes later, they crossed the coast north of the headland; down on their right they could see the harbor and the docks. They were low enough to see men and spiders moving around on the quays; the men paused in their work to stare at the strange sight of three balloons linked together, while Niall experienced the cold sense of discomfort that came from the concentrated gaze of many spiders. But he was also aware of a different quality in the probing beams of will that surveyed them—a quality of caution, even of anxiety. The spiders were learning to fear and respect human beings.

To the northeast, they could see the buildings of the spider city, lying in its shallow depression of hills, and, on the far side of the hills, the twisted red towers of the beetles. Soon the spider city lay below them and Niall's heart rose as he saw the white tower glittering in the sunlight. Then, once again he was aware of being watched, and once again he sensed doubt and caution. But from the headquarters of the Spider Lord he was aware of a different quality of observation: a malevolent gaze that surveyed them as a hungry animal watches its intended prey. Here there was no sense of fear: only hatred.

Further inland there was only a light breeze; they were sheltered by the range of coastal hills, the feature that had led the men of old to choose this site for their city. As they began the long descent towards the city of the beetles, steering was almost unnecessary; the wind carried them directly towards the green space of the central square. When their approach was observed, men and women began to run towards the square, and a crowd formed on the steps of the town hall and on the surrounding pavements. Now the ropes between the balloons were untied and allowed to hang suspended. When they came close enough to the ground, men jumped up and caught them, steering the balloons towards the center of the grass. Niall felt the bump as they touched the ground, then suddenly found himself lying flat, being dragged along with the balloon on top of him. Moments later, hands pulled him clear and helped him to his feet. A girl flung her arms round his neck and pressed her lips to his cheek. It was Dona. He saw, to his astonishment, that there were tears in her eyes.

"Why are you crying?"

"I didn't think I'd ever see you again . . ."

It felt strange to be standing on solid land, as if the ground was pushing up against his feet. The air was pleasantly warm and the scent of flowers was like a caress.

The others were also being overwhelmed by embraces; Doggins was almost pulled to the ground by his children. Milo, Ulic, and Manetho were surrounded by a crowd of admiring young men and women.

Crispin clasped Niall's forearm, embracing him with the other arm round his neck. He asked in a low voice: "Is it true you went to the Delta?"

"Yes. What's been happening while we were away?"

Crispin glanced over his shoulder. "The Master was furious that you left without permission. Hastur and Kosmin have been in prison ever since. And the spiders have been in and out of the town hall every day."

"What about the Reapers?"

"They've been taken away."

"But not destroyed?"

"No. But I believe they're talking about it."

A beetle guard was advancing through the crowd towards them; Niall guessed what he wanted.

Dona placed her lips close to Niall's ear. "Is it true that you're going to marry Merlew?"

"Who told you that?"

"Everyone's heard the rumor." She added with a touch of irony: "I think she probably started it."

Niall laughed. "Then she forgot to tell me about it."

Dona smiled with relief.

Doggins said in Niall's ear: "Here comes trouble. Better let me do the talking."

The beetle guard halted and addressed Doggins in signal language. Doggins replied in the same way, at the same time speaking aloud for Niall's benefit.

"Tell the Master we shall be there." He turned to Niall. "We're being summoned before the council in an hour."

As the beetle turned to go, Niall attuned himself to its mental vibration. "Wait!"

The beetle turned and regarded him with astonishment. With its eyes looking into his own, Niall found direct communication as natural as speech.

"Please tell the Master that I wish to speak to him now."

Doggins asked: "What's going on?" The beetle guard was looking at him questioningly. Niall said: "I've told him that I want to speak to the Master immediately."

Doggins looked at him with raised eyebrows. "But why? You'll only get all the blame."

"That doesn't matter."

Doggins shrugged. "Well, I don't suppose it can do any harm." He turned back to the guard and made a signal with his hands; the guard acknowledged it and returned towards the town hall. "I hope you're not going to try to take the blame?"

Niall shrugged. "There shouldn't be any blame. We have a right to go wherever we like." He started to follow the guard.

Doggins looked alarmed. "Here, wait a minute!"

Niall ignored him and hurried after the guard. The beetle walked with enormous strides, its long legs carrying it comfortably over the heads of the crowd. Niall had to apologize as he pushed people aside. The beetle had turned left and already vanished around the corner of the town hall; but when Niall reached the corner, he was in time to see it coming to a halt in front of one of the twisted red towers. As he hurried down the street, the guard disappeared inside. A few moments later, Niall halted in front of the doorway and paused, glad of an opportunity to regain his breath.

The doorway before which he was standing was a low arch, carved in a wall that was more than a foot thick. Inside, he could see an ascending ramp. Leaning inside the door, against the wall, he could see a door made of the same heavy, waxy substance. Niall found it intriguing that the beetles should have failed to avail themselves of the human invention of hinged doors, but should have preferred this thick, clumsy slab that had to be carried into place. He also observed that the arched doorway was scarcely higher than himself; the beetle guard had been forced to flatten its stomach against the ground as it entered. These observations helped to calm his sense of anxiety; they revealed that, in spite of their intelligence, the beetles were still tied to their evolutionary past.

He made an effort to relax, and found it surprisingly easy: there was an instant release of tension that made him feel almost drowsy. Then he experienced a sensation of warmth, and realized that he was surrounded by a glow of energy that seemed to emanate from the house itself. It was like a blue-green flame that burned gently upwards. Now he understood why each beetle-house was surrounded by a narrow moat; it prevented the flame from spreading sideways and therefore increased its intensity. The energy bathed him in a gentle glow, like a breeze, and made his skin prickle with warmth, not unlike a mild sunburn.

The guard beetle squeezed its way out of the doorway—it was obviously an operation to which it was accustomed—and beckoned Niall to go inside. Niall stepped into the dark interior and halted. After the bright sunlight, he felt as if he had been blindfolded. But after about a minute, his sight cleared and he was able to see by the dim blue light of the flame. He walked up the ramp, treading cautiously—for to his leather-shod feet it seemed slippery—and found himself in a large hallway. Except for the dim light of the blue flame, it was in complete darkness. Around the hall were rooms with semicircular doorways; he could sense the presence of other beetles, and from one of the doorways, a tiny bombardier beetle with a silvery-green skin watched him with eyes that were bright with curiosity.

He was facing another ramp, at the top of which there was a wide arch; Niall sensed that this was the entrance to the Master's chamber. As he started to mount the ramp, the voice of the Master seemed to address him from the air.

"Humans should remove their shoes before entering the dwelling of a Saarleb."

These words were accompanied by a feeling of irritation that was like a cold wind. Oddly enough, this aroused in Niall a curious feeling of satisfaction; it revealed that the Master was subject to emotions and that therefore he was not completely superhuman. Without bending down, Niall kicked off his boots and left them on the floor; then, in his bare feet, he mounted the ramp.

He stood in the center of the archway, sensing that to enter the room without invitation would provoke further offence. The Master's chamber was shaped like a large sphere, and its shape seemed designed to capture the blue energy, which followed the curvature of the walls and concentrated in the middle of the ceiling. The curved floor was covered with a carpet of green leaves and grass, and with a thick layer of moss or lichen. There were large rocks in the room and a huge decaying fragment of log; these apparently served the same function as furniture in a human household.

The Master was lying in the center of the room, his legs folded underneath him. Even so, his eyes were on a higher level than Niall's.

The invitation to enter the room was not forthcoming; instead, the Master said: "Why did you ask to see me?"

Now Niall made an interesting discovery. On the previous occasions when he had spoken with the Master, he had replied in human language, and relied upon the Master's ability to read his thoughts. Since his encounter with the empress plant, the words had become unnecessary; he was able to convey his meaning by thought alone. He said: "I have come because I need your help."

The reply was like an icy blast. "You have no right to my help. You have led my servants into disobedience."

Before replying, Niall made a deliberate effort to control any sense of dismay or alarm.

"I did not say I had come to ask for your help. I said I have come because I need your help." He paused to allow the meaning to become clear. "You have no choice but to give it."

The words might have been expected to arouse the Master's anger; in fact, they had the opposite effect. The Master became alert and attentive. He asked: "Why do you say that?"

Niall said: "You have to make your peace with the spiders and you have to decide what to do about your servants. For both these things you need my help."

It was a strange sensation. Before he had entered the room, he had no idea of what he intended to say. Now the words seemed to be rising up from inside him, as if governed by some inner logic of their own. All that he had to do was to control his emotions, so that no personal feeling entered into what he said; then he understood precisely what he had to say.

The Master asked: "How can you help to make peace with the spiders?"

Niall said: "I must go to see the Spider Lord. He and I will make peace."

"If you place yourself at his mercy, the Spider Lord will kill you."

"That is true. That is why I need your help."

"Explain yourself."

"You are now in possession of the Reapers. If the Spider Lord kills me, you must hand them back to your servants, so they can avenge me. If you make that promise, the Spider Lord will not dare to kill me."

"You have your own weapons. Why do you need the others?"

"Our own weapons are destroyed. We left them in the Delta."

Niall could feel the Master's surprise, followed immediately by suspicion. "Why?"

He resisted the Master's attempt to probe his mind; again, it was a sign of their changed relationship.

"Because they were too dangerous."

As he sensed the Master's bewilderment, Niall suddenly knew that he had won.

There was a silence. Then the Master said: "I am aware that something has happened to you since you last stood in my presence. Now you speak with authority. I had intended to order your immediate banishment, and the punishment of Bildo and my other servants. Now I can see that this will not be necessary." He surveyed Niall thoughtfully, but abandoned the effort to probe his mind. He said finally: "I will do as you ask. One of my servants will accompany you into the presence of the Spider Lord, and he will deliver a message that you are under my special protection. The Death Lord will understand. When do you intend to go?"

"I would like to leave immediately."

"Very well."

The Master made no signal, but a moment later a young beetle, scarcely more than a child, appeared in the room. Niall was unable to understand the words that passed between them; they seemed as meaningless as the rustle of dry leaves. Then the young beetle withdrew.

The Master said: "One more thing. The Spider Lord is cunning and malicious. But he is not dishonest. If he makes you a promise, he will keep it. If you can reach a peaceful agreement about the fate of my human servants, we shall all be grateful to you. Perhaps you will succeed. I sense that you are in possession of a secret." Niall said nothing; he had learned to control his responses so that his mind seemed blank. "Now go. My chief adviser will go with you."

"Thank you."

Niall turned and left the Master's presence. He was halfway down the ramp before he recalled that he should have bowed or shown some other sign of respect.

Outside, the sunlight dazzled him and made him close his eyes. As he stood there, hesitating, he felt a touch on his shoulder. A beetle was towering above him, regarding him quizzically. It made signs with its forelegs, accompanied by sibilant noises. Niall replied by projecting his thought: "I cannot understand your language. Please try to communicate with your mind."

The beetle gazed at him with its expressionless black eyes and made more signs, this time slowly and deliberately; it was evidently unable to express itself in human language. Niall shook his head and repeated his thought message. The beetle finally made a signal for Niall to follow; they set off together in the direction of the square.

The crowd had now dispersed; only a group of children stood and watched as Ulic and Milo folded the balloons. A cart with four charioteers at the shafts was waiting outside the town hall. The beetle signaled Niall to climb into it; as soon as he was seated, the charioteers began to move.

"Hey, wait a minute!" Doggins was running down the town hall steps, waving his arms. The charioteers halted. "What's happening?" Niall thought Doggins was looking tense and harassed.

The beetle turned to Doggins and addressed him in beetle language. Doggins went pale. "He says you're going to the Spider Lord."

"Yes."

Doggins' face was grim. "Has the Master ordered you to do it?"

"No. I made the decision."

"But why? Are you mad?" He was interrupted by the beetle. Niall sat and watched as the two of them exchanged signals. Doggins turned to Niall, shaking his head in exasperation.

"That won't make any difference!" He made a visible effort to control himself. "He says he's going with you to tell the Spider Lord you're under the protection of the Master. But that won't make any difference. He's already tried to kill you in front of the Master."

Niall placed his hand soothingly on Doggins' shoulder. "Don't worry. If I die, the Master has promised to hand over the Reapers, so you can take revenge."

Doggins stared incredulously. "He promised you that?"

"Yes."

Doggins thought about it for a moment, then shook his head. "It's still mad. Why do you want to go alone?"

"I caused these problems. Now I must try to solve them."

"In that case, I'll come with you." He started to climb into the cart. Niall restrained him with a hand on his shoulder.

"No. I have to go alone."

Doggins stared into his eyes as if trying to read his thoughts. He said finally: "I hope you understand what you're doing."

"I think so." Niall hoped that his eyes did not betray his lack of conviction. "Now I must go. I think the Master has cancelled that meeting of the council. But try and get Hastur and Kosmin out of prison. Goodbye until we meet again."

He leaned forward and made a signal to the leading charioteer; they set off at a trot. As they turned into the main street, he saw Dona running across the grass and calling to him. He decided not to stop; the thought of more explanations filled him with dismay.

The beetle followed on behind them, walking with long, unhurried strides; it cost it no effort to keep up with the charioteers. Ten minutes later, they had passed beyond the limits of the town and were in the open countryside. It was a clear, pleasant morning, with a faint breeze, and the air had the smell of approaching autumn. Since he had last come this way, the leaves on the trees had started to turn brown. The road through the woods was shady and the stream that ran beside sparkled invitingly; its sound lulled him into a state of calm and soothed away his doubts.

When he thought back to his interview with the Master, he felt at once astonished and baffled; it seemed incredible that he had addressed the Master with so little respect. When he tried to re-create his state of mind during the interview, he realized that his words had been based upon a deep sense of inner conviction. But what precisely was that conviction? The more he thought about it, the more it eluded him.

One thing was clear: that in spite of their power and wisdom, the beetles lacked insight into the human craving for freedom. They were less ruthless than the spiders; yet they treated their human servants like children. It never seemed to strike them that a man might be discontented to be a servant, no matter how kindly he was treated. Without even realizing it, they were inviting rebellion . . .

They were now within a mile of the outskirts of the spider city. On either side of the road there were cultivated fields and orchards, and in one of the fields he could see a party of men hoeing potatoes, supervised by a female overseer. In this mellow sunshine, it seemed an idyllic world. He found himself reflecting on the basic paradox of human nature: that men crave freedom, yet they also crave comfort and security, and that these two basic desires seemed to be in conflict. It was a baffling and disturbing thought.

Then the charioteers reached the top of the hill that marked the outer limit of the spider city, and once again Niall experienced a feeling of awe as he looked down on this vast collection of human dwellings. It seemed almost unbelievable: that this great city had once been occupied by hundreds of thousands of human beings who were their own masters, and who owed no allegiance either to spiders or to beetles. Now they were once again traveling downhill, the charioteers moved at a brisk trot; over their heads, the empty spider webs vibrated gently in the warm breeze. As the cart rattled on down the broad avenue, with its distant glimpse of the river, Niall tried to calculate how long it had been since he first saw the city of the spiders. This time yesterday they had been struggling through the marshes of the Delta; the day before that, he and Doggins had been returning from the banks of the great river; the day before that . . . When he had finished his calculation, Niall realized with astonishment that it had been a mere two weeks since he had landed in the harbor. And only three days before that, his father had been alive and they were still living in the burrow. It seemed incredible: in a mere seventeen days he had lived through enough experience to last most men a lifetime.

It was then, as they entered the slave quarter, that he suddenly knew the answer to the question that had troubled him so much. *That* was why men craved freedom more than security and comfort: because freedom meant a certain richness of experience, and experience in turn meant discovery of their own possibilities. Without richness of experience, there could be no discovery of their inner powers. That was why man hated slavery: because it meant inner stagnation . . .

The familiar smells of the slave quarter, and the sight of tattered garments hanging on lines, and of rats scavenging for food in alleyways, brought a sudden feeling of nostalgia; once again, he had to remind himself that it had been less than two weeks since he had first set eyes on these untidy streets. Again, he was astonished at the changes that had taken place in himself in such a short period.

They were approaching the bridge over the river. At the end of the avenue beyond it, he could see the white tower, and beyond that, the headquarters of the Spider Lord. He observed with grim satisfaction that his involuntary twinge of alarm was controlled and arrested before it could flood his nervous system. A moment later, he noticed the cart that was waiting in the middle of the road at the other end of the bridge. The shafts were held by two charioteers who stood to attention: the red-clad figure who sat inside it was unmistakable. As Niall approached, she waved and climbed out of the cart. Niall's charioteers halted of their own accord and bowed their heads respectfully. Under the impassive gaze of the two wolf spiders who guarded the bridge, she came over to Niall's cart, made him move over with a small imperious gesture, then climbed in beside him. She leaned over and tapped the nearest charioteer on the shoulder. "Go on, but slowly." She had completely ignored the beetle, whose bulging black eyes seemed to express amazement.

Niall said: "How did you know I was coming?"

"We women have our secrets." Merlew flashed him a charming smile. "Have you decided to take my advice?" She made it sound as if they were resuming a business discussion.

"You mean about marrying you?"

"No, silly!" She colored and glanced quickly at the charioteers, hoping they had not overheard. "About coming to terms with the Spider Lord."

He shook his head. "I don't think so."

Her eyes widened with astonishment. "Then why . . ." She made an effort and lowered her voice. "Then why have you come here?"

"To try to bargain with the Spider Lord."

"That's absurd!" Her cheeks had flushed with the effort of keeping her voice low, and her eyes had become very bright.

The wind was tugging aside the thin material of the red dress, revealing her shapely bronzed legs. A part of Niall responded with dazzled admiration to her beauty; another part looked on with ironical calm. Seen through the eyes of his emotions, she was maddeningly desirable. But with his second pair of eyes, he saw a spoilt schoolgirl, accustomed to having whatever she wanted, and determined to annex him for herself. Even the thin dress was being worn for his benefit; she knew that, in this bright sunlight, it made her virtually naked, and that no man could resist her when she put forth all her attractions. He was intrigued to notice that she seemed to be exuding some electrical force that made his heart beat faster. But while his emotions found her adorable, another part of him regarded her with almost cynical detachment. This other person, who looked through his second pair of eyes, saw her as a delightful but willful child, and knew that any long-term emotional involvement with her would end in disaster.

She leaned forward and called to the charioteers: "Take us to my palace."

Niall shook his head. "No. I have to see the Spider Lord."

"I know that." Her voice became coaxing. "But come and talk to me first."

"I'm sorry. I must see the Spider Lord." He knew she would use all her arts of persuasion, and did not relish the thought of having to resist them.

"All right." Her submission almost made him relent. "But please listen to what I have to say." She caressed his hand with her slim fingers, looking into his eyes. Her breath smelt sweet. "You know the Spider Lord has reached an agreement with the beetles?"

He said with surprise: "No, I didn't."

"They made an agreement as soon as you left—you shouldn't have left, by the way. That made the beetles very angry, and it was stupid to make them angry when you were trying to get them on your side."

He asked patiently: "What was this agreement?"

"They agreed that they allowed their servants far too much freedom, and that this only made them ungrateful and disobedient. They agreed to take charge of those horrible guns, and promised that they wouldn't, under any circumstances, give them back."

Niall asked: "How do you know all this?"

"I know everything that goes on."

He asked: "What would happen if the servants decided they didn't want to be servants any more?"

She shrugged. "That's stupid." It was evident that the idea struck her as absurd.

"Why?"

"Surely I don't have to tell *you* that?"

They had reached the far side of the square, facing the white tower and the headquarters of the Spider Lord. Black smoke was rising from a bonfire on the far side of the tower: a crowd of slaves were standing around it, throwing things into the flames. Other slaves were pulling carts across the grass. A number of overseers and servants looked on from a distance.

Niall asked: "What are they burning?"

"Just books." She gestured at the crowd. "Look at them. What would they do if they weren't servants? They're perfectly happy. Even Massig and the others are enjoying themselves now they're settling down. I'm sure your people are exactly the same."

Niall said: "I don't want to be a servant."

"You don't have to be!" She squeezed his hand fiercely. "You're like me. We are natural rulers." She lowered her voice and her lips came close to his. "That's why we belong together." Then she remembered that they were in a public place and withdrew her face. She squeezed his hand again. "Do be sensible."

"If what you say is true, I don't seem to have any alternative."

"That's right." She smiled at him. "No one could blame you."

He asked: "Why are they burning the books?"

She shrugged. "It's the latest idea of the Spider Lord. He suddenly realized that this place is full of books, hidden away in old houses."

"But his servants can't read."

"Of course not. But they might be tempted to learn." Their charioteers had been forced to halt to make way for a cartload of books;

they were all in blue leather bindings, with gilt lettering, and were evidently from some library. Merlew said: "The beetles have promised to do the same over in Crashville. Their servants have been disobeying the law for generations. Now they're going to be made to hand over their books. I think that would probably be a good thing."

"Why?"

"I wish you wouldn't keep asking me why! Isn't it obvious? It's part of the peace treaty that human beings shouldn't be allowed to read. The beetles have been allowing their servants to break the treaty. Now they've agreed it's got to stop. I think it's rather a good thing."

"Why?"

She said patiently: "Because it doesn't do servants any *good* to read. You can't read, and it hasn't done you any harm, has it?"

"But I *can* read."

"Can you?" For a moment her eyes reflected alarm. "Oh well, I don't suppose it matters, so long as the spiders don't find out."

Niall said: "That's why I don't want to be a servant. I want to be allowed to make up my own mind about these things."

"Yes, I know." Her eyes were abstracted; she was evidently thinking of something else. "I don't suppose they'll really care. In any case, there won't be any books left when they've finished."

They had halted in front of the headquarters of the Spider Lord; two wolf spiders stood on guard under the portico. Merlew suddenly realized where she was: she leaned forward and tapped the nearest charioteer angrily on the shoulder. "I thought I told you to go to my palace."

Niall said: "No. I must see the Spider Lord first."

"They should still do as they're told!" She glared angrily at the charioteers. Once again, Niall caught a glimpse of the spoiled child, and felt saddened.

The bombardier beetle hurried forward towards the main doors. As he did so, they opened and a black death spider came out. It was short and squat, and its crooked legs gave an impression of great strength. As it stared at Niall, he experienced a powerful sense of danger. Merlew said in his ear: "That's Skorbo, the captain of the guard."

The sense of hostility that emanated from the spider was almost suffocating. Niall was tempted to use the thought mirror to express his defiance, but dismissed the idea immediately; it would be point-less to provoke it further.

The spider and the bombardier beetle conversed for a moment; then the beetle turned and beckoned to him. As he started to climb out of the cart, three more spiders emerged from the building and surrounded him. To Niall, this seemed pointless; he had no intention of trying to escape. Then he understood: their purpose was to make him feel that he was a prisoner and that he would be lucky to escape with his life. He could feel their hostile willpower beating down on him, like some intolerable pressure.

Merlew climbed out behind him. The spider-guards tried to stand in front of her, but she pushed her way firmly to Niall's side.

Niall said: "You can't go in there with me."

"I can go where I like. I am the princess." She glared haughtily at the nearest spider-guard. Its reaction was one of fury: it was being defied by a mere human being. But the presence of the captain of the guard forced it to restrain its anger. Niall, who was aware of all this, and who was afraid of his own reaction if the spiders harmed Merlew, took her by the hand.

"Please go now. I have to deal with this alone."

Her mouth set in a stubborn line. "I'll go when I'm ready."

One of the spiders prodded Niall on the shoulder and urged him towards the door. Merlew walked beside him as they entered the dark interior, oblivious of the detestation of the spider-guards. The captain of the guard stood on one side and watched them with a curiously speculative gaze; Niall felt instinctively that it was far more danger-ous than the other spiders. This mindless, brutal hostility was mak-ing him angry; but he knew it was important to keep his emotions under control.

He could also sense that the bombardier beetle was unhappy and unsure of itself. According to protocol, it should have been treated with respect and consideration; in fact, the spiders made it obvious that it was regarded as an unwelcome intruder. This, in turn, was a gesture of disrespect towards the Master. Yet there had been no open discourtesy, and it was not sure whether it should show its resent-ment or remain tactfully silent. As he sensed its bewilderment, Niall again experienced a surge of fierce hatred towards the spiders.

He had expected to be escorted up the stairs; instead, they were made to stand in a dark corner of the hall. The three guards stood close around them; their bodies gave off a peculiar acrid smell which Niall found disgusting. Physically speaking, they looked less menacing than the hairy wolf spiders; yet they seemed to exude their own peculiar air of violence.

Merlew was becoming impatient. Daily familiarity with the spiders had made her bold. She pushed imperiously past the guards and confronted the captain. "Why are we being kept waiting?"

The spider merely stared back at her, pretending not to understand; this was its own way of showing contempt. Merlew flushed angrily and came back to Niall. "I shall complain to the Spider Lord. They have no right to treat us like servants."

Niall said gently: "No one likes to be treated like a servant."

The doors opened and another spider entered. Now his eyes had become accustomed to the dim light, Niall could see that this spider was old, and that its long, thin legs had some difficulty supporting its large body. Merlew stared at it with newly awakened interest. As it mounted the stairway and vanished round the corner, she whispered in Niall's ear: "That's Dravig, the Spider Lord's chief adviser. They must think you very important." With sudden wry amusement Niall realized that she was impressed.

The captain now made a gesture to the guards; the nearest guard gave Niall a gentle nudge in the back, to indicate that he was to move; it made him stumble.

Merlew turned furiously on the spider. "Don't you dare to touch me!" Then she realized that the captain was standing in front of her, barring her way. She stared back defiantly: "I'm going with him."

She tried to move forward, but seemed to be held back by some invisible barrier. The captain was exerting just enough willpower to prevent her from moving. Her eyes became bright with anger.

Niall laid his hand on her arm. "Please wait here. I'd rather go alone."

She made an effort of self-control. "Very well." She glared at the captain, then turned and walked out of the half-open door. Niall sighed with relief. He felt he had problems enough without having to worry about Merlew's impulsiveness.

They mounted the stairs. The last time Niall had been in this building, it had seemed full of activity; he recalled that some kind of drill sergeant had been shouting orders at the wolf spiders. Now the place seemed strangely silent. Niall closed his eyes and made an effort to relax. As soon as he did so, he understood the silence. The whole city was in mourning for the hundreds of dead spiders, and for the many spiders who, at this moment, were dying of severe burns. It had never struck Niall that the spiders could mourn one another like human beings, and for a moment he experienced a wave of sympathy. Then he stumbled and the spider behind him prodded him in the back of the neck. The sympathy evaporated and was replaced by disgust; yet the disgust was less intense than before.

As they crossed towards the black-studded door, it swung open, revealing the dark hall with its network of cobwebs. Niall reminded himself that he was here as an ambassador, not as a prisoner, but it was difficult to control the sudden feeling of panic that squeezed his heart. For the first time, the three guards stood aside, and allowed Niall to enter alone. The captain of the guard walked in front of him, the beetle-ambassador behind. The captain halted, then moved aside, standing a few feet away. Niall and the bombardier beetle stood there side by side, staring into the shadows. Niall tried to pierce the darkness with his double vision, but it was as if some kind of curtain was obstructing his gaze.

Then the familiar soft voice sounded inside Niall's chest. It said mockingly: "Now you are able to hear me."

Niall said: "Yes." He used only his mind to convey the word, directing it at the invisible presence in the darkness.

There was a pause. The voice said softly: "And this time you understand me?"

"Yes, I understand you." His inner-voice was calm and assured as he spoke the words, and he sensed that the Spider Lord was surprised.

The Spider Lord addressed the captain of the guard. "He is wearing something round his neck. Take it from him."

Niall had no desire to feel the spider's claw fumbling around his neck. He reached up, removed the thought mirror, and handed it to the captain. But he experienced a twinge of regret to lose it.

The beetle-ambassador spoke. "May I deliver the message with which I am entrusted?"

The Spider Lord sent an impulse that signaled his permission. The ambassador said: "The Master wishes me to say that this human being is under his protection, and that he knows you will treat him with courtesy."

The reply of the Spider Lord, couched in the unaccustomed vibration of the bombardier beetles, sounded like a stutter of rage. "This human creature is the murderer of many of my people. He deserves death a thousand times over. I think that my claim upon him is greater than that of your Master." The web itself vibrated, as if shaken by some huge body.

"That may be so, but . . ."

"You have delivered your message. Now go."

The menace conveyed by this order was formidable; it made Niall's skin crawl. He expected to see the ambassador leave the hall; no other response seemed possible. To his surprise, the ambassador stood his ground.

"As his escort, I demand the right to remain."

It spoke quietly and without bluster; yet behind the words, Niall could sense a steely determination. He suddenly understood why the spiders had made war on the bombardier beetles, and why they had finally been obliged to make peace.

The captain of the guard had taken a step forward: he seemed prepared to make a physical assault on the ambassador. A wordless order from the Spider Lord made him withdraw. When the Spider Lord spoke again, its voice seemed quieter and more reasonable.

"I have asked you to leave. Your presence is not required."

The ambassador spoke in a clear voice. "Your discourtesy forces me to speak frankly. The Master wishes you to know that if you kill this human being, he will be forced to hand over the stolen weapons to his human servants, and allow them to take revenge. That would mean more deaths among your people."

Even before he had finished speaking, the room seemed to be filled with a cold and violent rage; it was as powerful as a storm at sea, and Niall braced himself instinctively and prepared for a brutal blow. When he looked at the beetle-ambassador, he saw with amazement that he seemed to be unaffected by it, and was gazing quietly and calmly into the darkness of the cobwebs. Niall was overcome with admiration, which in turn allowed him to reestablish control over himself.

The Spider Lord also seemed to recognize that this rage betrayed a lack of self-control. When he spoke again, the voice was unexpectedly calm. "I have no intention of killing him. Death would be too easy. Now do me the favor of leaving me alone with him."

The beetle stood his ground. "I am sorry. I must stay."

Again the captain made a menacing move forward; again he was halted by a wordless command. There was a silence, then the Spider Lord said: "Very well, remain. But since this is my domain I impose the conditions. You must promise to remain silent. Is that agreed?"

"It is agreed."

"Good. If you break your word, you have also broken our agreement, and the prisoner's life will be forfeit."

The ambassador said stiffly: "I cannot agree to that."

"It makes no difference whether you agree or not. Now be silent." Niall had the uncomfortable feeling that the Spider Lord's temper was close to breaking point. Then the voice spoke again inside his chest. "It seems I have been forced to spare your life. But a crime like yours cannot go unpunished. Therefore I have decided that you should also taste the pain of bereavement. Your family must die in your place."

Niall said nothing, but his heart seemed to turn to ashes.

The Spider Lord addressed the ambassador. "You agree that you have no right to object to what happens to my other prisoners?"

For a moment the ambassador was silent; then he made a gesture of acknowledgement.

The delay had given Niall time to think. He said: "You want my cooperation. If you harm my family, that will be impossible."

"Nothing is impossible." The voice was soft, but there was a hard edge of brutality. "Allow me to prove it to you. You will bow down on the ground and acknowledge me as your lord."

Niall stood there, waiting. He had no intention of bowing before the Spider Lord; the very idea filled him with angry contempt. Then, to his horror, he felt the will of the Spider Lord take possession of his body. He tried to resist, but it was impossible. This will was like the coils of some gigantic snake, winding around him and squeezing him until he felt breathless. His body was totally incapable of movement; at the same time, it became numb, as if he had been frozen inside a block of ice. Even the muscles of his eyes were paralyzed, so that he could not glance sideways towards the ambassador. Not a nerve or a muscle was capable of obeying his volition.

Then he felt his knees bending as he knelt down on the floor. His head bowed in a gesture of submission. His hands stretched out in front of him and he touched his forehead on the floor. His lips moved, and he heard his voice say: "You are my lord, O great one."

The voice said: "Good. Now stand up and ask the ambassador to leave the room."

Like a glove puppet, obedient to the invisible hand inside it, Niall's body stood up again, and turned towards the beetle-ambassador. His voice said: "I am asking you to leave me alone with the Death Lord."

He felt the beetle's mind trying to probe his own; but it was incapable of tuning in to his wavelength. As he stared into its black eyes, Niall was aware that he was incapable of changing even the expression in his own eyes.

The beetle replied: "I am sorry, but I would be disobeying the Master if I left you alone here."

Niall sent out an impulse of gratitude, and felt relief as he saw that the beetle-ambassador had received it. The slight tremor of its feelers was unmistakable. The knowledge that he had succeeded in communicating helped to free him from the sense of impotence that was numbing his mind into submission. But as he tried to send another message, his brain itself was gripped in the vice of the Spider Lord's will, so that even the mental impulse was frozen.

The voice of the Spider Lord said: "Now tell me what you came here to say."

Niall heard his voice replying: "The Master has asked me to say that he wishes to reestablish peace between his people and yours. I am willing to do whatever I can to bring that about."

"Even if it means swearing to become my servant?"

"Yes."

"Good. Then kneel down and say: from this moment I am the servant of the Death Lord and swear to obey all his commands."

Niall struggled to establish control and to throw off this grip of steel that controlled his body and brain. For a moment, he succeeded; his eyes expressed defiance and his lips remained closed. Then the pressure became more than he could bear. He heard his voice say: "From this moment I am the servant of the Death Lord and swear to obey all his commands."

Yet even as he spoke, his mind continued to express defiance. It brought a peculiar feeling of triumph: the knowledge that his will remained free and unbroken. From the increased pressure, he could tell that this infuriated his enemy. Only total submission could satisfy the Spider Lord. He longed to break Niall's will and to force him to cringe and beg for mercy. And in spite of his helplessness, Niall knew that his will was beyond the control of the Spider Lord.

The beetle-ambassador was puzzled. He was only half convinced by Niall's apparent surrender, suspecting that Niall had reasons of his own for pretending to submit to the will of the Spider Lord. But he was determined not to be persuaded to leave without Niall. For this Niall was deeply grateful.

The Spider Lord said: "Good. I accept your oath of loyalty. Now I shall submit you to your first test. You must tell your family that they are to die to expiate your crime against my people." He addressed the captain of the guard. "Bring in the prisoners."

The ambassador said angrily: "This is going too far."

The Spider Lord said: "You have broken your oath of silence." The room was suddenly full of a heavy atmosphere of menace. Although he was unable to turn his head, Niall could sense that the ambassador had decided to obey.

The captain of the guard had gone to the door; Niall heard it open. Then footsteps came into the room. His brother Veig walked past him; but for a moment, Niall failed to recognize him. Veig was wearing a kind of fur hat that covered his face like a hood, and his hands were tied behind him. Siris came next, with Runa and Mara on either side of her. All three were wearing the same fur hoods, and their hands were also tied behind them. Siris, Runa, and Mara were joined together by a cord connecting their wrists. The captain ordered them to halt, and they stood there passively, facing the shadowy web. Niall thought they seemed to be oddly listless, as if drugged. Then the captain ordered them to turn round; when they did so, Niall could see that the hoods were masks, with holes cut for the eyes, and a broad slit for the mouth. Through these slits, Niall could see that they had all been gagged. There was something horribly chilling in the sight of these fur hoods, and in the expressionless eyes that looked out from behind them. Suddenly, Niall was glad of the icy grip that squeezed him so relentlessly; it numbed the despair that rose up inside him. For the first time, he suspected that the Death Lord was planning some unimaginable cruelty.

Yet in spite of the anger and misery, a part of him remained calm; this was the lesson he had learned in the past few weeks. As he stared into the web, he imagined that he still had the thought mirror suspended round his neck; then he imagined that he had reached inside his shirt and turned it. The anger galvanized his will; once again, he experienced the sudden sensation of concentration and power. The feeling of helpless misery evaporated and was replaced by a savage determination. It was like waking up from a deep sleep. He realized with a shock how close he had been to surrendering his will, and knew that this would have been the supreme stupidity. His will was the only thing about him that could not be broken or controlled.

His body remained in the power of the Death Lord; his eyes stared straight past his mother, into the darkness of the web. He could sense that the Death Lord was enjoying this moment, savoring his sense of total power. This gave Niall time to consider his position. The Spider Lord intended to force him to pronounce the death sentence on his family, perhaps even to execute them. He believed that this would destroy Niall's will and remove the last vestige of his freedom. Therefore it was imperative that Niall should refuse to allow this to happen. His only way of defying the Spider Lord was to refuse to surrender his will. This thought gave him a certain grim satisfaction.

It was then that he suddenly understood the final message of the empress plant. He had asked: Is there nothing you can do to help? The response had been a *revelation of power.* It was as if the plant had said: You don't need my help; you can do it yourself.

The answer lay in this refusal to surrender. While the will remained unbroken, the mind remained unconquerable. Hope lay in this strange power of the mind over the external world: a power that the mind itself failed to understand.

Yet how could this power help him in the present circumstances? As he peered into the darkness, he summoned his double vision, and tried to penetrate the shadows that concealed the Spider Lord. It was impossible: some force had been interposed between them like a curtain.

The Spider Lord said: "Speak to your family."

Niall's face turned towards Veig and saw there was no one there. His family had disappeared. The spot where they had been standing a moment ago was empty. The rigidity of his nervous system prevented him from feeling surprise; the power of the Spider Lord controlled even the beating of his heart. Suddenly he understood what had happened. He was continuing to look through his second pair of eyes, and they showed him that his family were empty shadows, delusions conjured up by the Spider Lord. As soon as he allowed his double vision to fade, his family reappeared. They stood facing him, their eyes staring from behind the eye-slits in the hoods. He marveled at the completeness of the illusion. His mother was dressed in the same shabby animal skin that she had worn last time he saw her; the children still wore their blue nursery uniforms, now crumpled and grubby. The Spider Lord was reaching into his brain and making him dream.

He heard his voice say: "I am ordered to tell you that you have been sentenced to death, in order to expiate my crime against the people of this city. You are all to die immediately. Which of you wants to be the first?"

Mara tried to run towards him, then tripped and fell as she reached the limit of the rope. Involuntarily, Niall tried to reach out to save her, but found himself unable to move. Her fall made Siris stagger slightly, and she half-turned and bent down, trying to help Mara with her tied hands. Now Niall understood why they were wearing the fur hoods; a single glimpse of their faces would have made him aware that they were phantoms of his imagination. The Spider Lord lacked the subtlety to make a human face reflect a human soul. So he had covered their faces and gagged their mouths so they could not speak. But now that he knew they were illusions, Niall could see that even this touch was unconvincing. Even a gagged person can make some kind of noise; these phantoms were silent.

The Spider Lord said: "If no one is willing to volunteer, you will have to make the choice yourself. Which one is to die first?"

Niall felt his hand rise up and point to Veig. The Spider Lord said: "Very well. Since you have chosen."

A blow made Veig stagger forward, so he half-fell to his knees. Then his body was lifted clear of the floor. His limbs writhed in agony as an invisible iron fist closed around them. A muffled scream came from behind the gag. Then there was a sound of cracking bones. A moment later, his ribs caved in, and his body began to distort. The muffled screams suddenly ceased. Blood began to drip from the broken limbs. It was as if a sponge was being squeezed until it contained no more moisture. Blood splashed on the floor; then the crushed body was allowed to fall. It lay like a trampled doll, the head twisted backwards on the broken neck, the eyes still staring through the eye-slits of the mask.

The voice of the Spider Lord said mockingly: "Now, who shall be next?"

Niall was horrified and enraged; even though he knew it was a delusion, the violence still shocked him. If he had possessed the power, his fury and hatred would have destroyed every spider in the city. As it was, the anger reinforced his determination that nothing would break his will. Vulnerability came from within; while his will was unbroken, he was indestructible, and the Spider Lord could be defied forever. His vital powers clenched inside him like a fist, and the result was a kind of inner explosion of rage and contempt.

All at once it was as if he had contracted beyond some inner limitation. The fury freed his nervous system from the iron grip of the Spider Lord, and his heart was suddenly like a dynamo driving the blood through his veins. What happened next was already familiar to him. There was a flash of perception, a recognition of the nature of freedom—that it meant that he was free *here and now*—followed by a surge of pure delight. Then, once again, another force seemed to rise up from his inner depths, sweeping aside the normal boundaries of personality and bringing again the absurd recognition that he was not himself. This force dissolved the paralysis in his limbs, so that he could move again. He felt the will of the Spider Lord flinch, as if trying to avoid a blow. His lips remained tightly closed, yet it was as if his whole being had uttered a shout of triumph, which seemed to illuminate the room like a flash of light. Then, for the first time, his gaze was able to penetrate the tangled forest of the web.

What he saw made him breathless with astonishment and incredulity: not the mighty shape of the Death Lord with a hundred eyes, but a host of smaller spiders whose black bodies covered the web like entangled flies. Some of these were already moving nervously towards the corner of the web, causing it to tremble and vibrate. For a moment, he suspected that this was some further illusion of the Spider Lord. But as he stared, unable to believe his eyes, the light slowly increased, so that he could see the innermost depths of the web, and the spiders, as if recognizing that further concealment was impossible, halted and stared at him with their beady black eyes. As he sensed their fear and bewilderment, it was no longer possible to doubt their reality.

He took a step towards the web, and the captain of the guard made a sudden movement. But as Niall turned and prepared to defend himself, the spider cringed away. He seemed to be illuminated by a pale blue light, which made the fine hairs on his body look as if they were covered with a chalky dust. Niall took another two steps, until he was standing on the spot where, a few moments before, the body of his brother had been lying. From there he could see into the web, whose crossed strands seemed to have become transparent. Facing him, in the heart of the web, was a small, shriveled spider, whose body was gray with age, and whose size revealed her as a female. Unlike the others, she was standing her ground, staring back at him with a certain nervous defiance. She was obviously far older than any of the other spiders in the web—who, on closer inspection, Niall could see were also females.

He said with incredulity: "So you are the Death Lord?"

She made no reply; but when he took another step forward, she flinched and raised her jointed palps to cover her eyes; the blue light was causing her pain. He turned his head and looked for its source; but the light seemed to bathe the whole room in its pale, even glow. It also seemed to fill the room with a strange stillness, a silence that produced a sense of exhaustion and suffocation. It was as if the whole world had stopped like a clock. Then, as he looked down at his body, Niall realized with astonishment that he himself was the source of the blue glow; even his hands were shining as if they were made of white-hot iron. It was only then that he recognized why the glow seemed familiar: it was the light he had seen on the planet of the empress plants, the light of the star called Vega.

The room darkened and seemed to contract. At the moment this realization dawned upon him, the light began to fade. Then the last glow vanished and suddenly it was as if time had resumed its forward flow. The oppressive stillness disappeared and the air seemed full of life and motion. It was then that Niall understood his feeling of suffocation: while the light was shining, the vibration of the Delta had ceased. At the same time he understood the curious feeling of inner certainty that had possessed him during the past few hours, and that had imparted to his actions the confidence of a sleepwalker. His decisions had been directed and controlled by the goddess.

He peered into the web; there was no movement. When he turned and looked at the beetle-ambassador, he was startled to see that he was lying prostrate on the floor; so was the captain of the guard. As Niall bent over the beetle, placing his hand on the gleaming shell, the ambassador stirred. Niall asked: "Are you all right?"

To his surprise, the beetle answered feebly: "Yes, lord."

The captain of the guard was lying with his legs bunched underneath him; Niall's thought-probe established that he was suffering from shock and exhaustion. When Niall said: "Stand up," he made no movement. Niall gave the spider a push with his boot in the soft part of its underbelly; it scrambled hastily on to its legs.

Niall went back to the web. "Come out, all of you."

There was a pause, then the web began to vibrate. The shriveled female was the first to emerge; she moved awkwardly, as if her limbs were stiff. The others came out after her, one by one, and formed up in a row behind her, like a squad of soldiers. The last spider to emerge caused greater vibrations than the rest; its legs seemed bowed under the weight of its heavy body. This was Dravig, chief adviser to the Death Lord.

Niall walked forward until he stood in front of the ancient female spider. She was only slightly taller than he was, and at close quarters he could see that her skin looked shiny and cracked, like old leather. Although he knew that she could kill him with a single bite of her fangs, he experienced no apprehension. He could sense that she was badly shaken and demoralized. He was also aware that she regarded him with superstitious fear.

Niall said: "Send the others away. I want to talk to you alone." As Dravig took a step towards the door he said: "No, you stay."

The other spiders filed out of the room—he counted twelve of them—and as they did so, Niall gently probed their minds. They were aware that he was doing it and made no attempt to prevent it. These twelve females were, he discovered, the ruling council of the spider city. All were far younger than the Death Lord, the youngest being the spider equivalent of a middle-aged woman. Although their official position was that of councilor, each was, in effect, a ruler in her own right, for their minds were able to unite together into a single mind. To be ordered to leave the room like this was a humiliation; but because they believed it was the will of the goddess, they accepted it without question.

The Spider Lord—Niall continued to think of her under this title—was by far the oldest among them; among human beings she would have been a centenarian. Now that her mind lay open before him, Niall could see that she had both the faults and virtues of an old woman. She was imperious, bad-tempered, and rigidly set in her ways; she was also cunning, wise, and more farsighted than any of her subjects. Even so, she would have been incapable of exerting the force that had held Niall's body in its grip of steel. This had been the joint effort of all the council, and the effort had been coordinated by Dravig, whose mind was capable of acting as a catalyst that united all the others.

It was Dravig who interested Niall most of all. There was something about his mind that was curiously abstract and impersonal; Niall could sense in him the same kind of wisdom he had sensed in the Master. The Spider Lord was totally self-absorbed, obsessed with her own private purposes; Dravig's mind seemed to be directed towards the universe outside himself. Yet there was an element of strangeness about his thought-processes that Niall found totally incomprehensible.

When the door closed behind the captain of the guard, it was Dravig who spoke first. Niall could sense his nervousness.

"Are you a god or a human being?"

Niall laughed. "A human being, of course."

The Spider Lord said: "But you are a messenger of the goddess." It was a statement, not a question.

Niall said: "Yes." In a sense, it was true.

Both spiders made a peculiar movement, raising the jointed feelers at an angle of forty-five degrees, and at the same time lowering their bellies to the floor while the position of the legs remained unchanged. Niall inferred that it was a ritual gesture of homage. The Spider Lord said: "What is her will?"

Niall said: "First of all, that all my people should cease to be slaves. Human beings must be given the same freedom as the spiders or the beetles. If they should choose to serve you of their own accord, that is their business. But all must be allowed to make the choice."

When they made no reply, he asked: "Well?"

The Spider Lord said: "It shall be done."

It was then that Niall understood that their silence had been a gesture of assent. To reply would have been a sign of disrespect, since it implied a choice.

He said: "Next, it is the will of the goddess that there shall be a peace treaty between spiders and human beings, like the treaty between the spiders and the bombardier beetles. This treaty must be strictly observed by both sides, and whoever breaks it will bring severe punishment upon himself and his people."

After a silence, the Spider Lord replied: "It shall be done."

It was slightly disconcerting. Niall had been expecting some kind of resistance or, at least, a sign of reluctance or resentment. This total submission left him feeling unsure of what to do next. To cover his indecision, he went to the window and tore aside some of the thick cobwebs that covered it, admitting a beam of sunlight through the dusty glass. Both spiders flinched at the light. As Niall's eyes became accustomed to the brightness, he saw clouds of smoke billowing into the air above the bonfire. The square below was full of people; another cartload of books was trying to force its way through the crowd. A huge pile of unburned books lay at the foot of the white tower, waiting to be consigned to the flames.

Niall turned to the Spider Lord. "Order them to stop burning the books."

Without speaking, Dravig went out of the door. He returned a few moments later, and silently resumed his place by the Spider Lord. And now, in a flash of insight, Niall understood why they obeyed his orders without resentment or reluctance. They had just witnessed a miracle. They had looked upon the face of the goddess and she had spoken to them directly. This room would henceforth be a holy place. Compared with this awesome miracle, nothing else was important. Mere personal feeling would have been a blasphemous absurdity. And since Niall was the instrument of the revelation, anything he said or did was beyond question.

But they had also treated the envoy of the goddess with brutal disrespect—a disrespect that, according to their own barbarous scale of values, merited the most agonizing death. This, he now realized, was why their sense of awe was tinged with apprehension.

Niall stood in front of the Spider Lord. "Do you expect me to take revenge?"

"Yes." She answered without flinching.

He turned to Dravig. "And you?"

Dravig hesitated, then, to Niall's surprise, answered: "No."

"Why not?"

Dravig said dryly: "Because you would not ask the question if you intended to take revenge."

Niall laughed and his respect for Dravig increased. It was true that his hatred of the spiders had almost vanished since he was no longer at their mercy.

"You are right. Revenge would be pointless." He could sense their relief; they made no attempt to close themselves to his scrutiny, as if they regarded it as his right to probe their minds. "It is true that I am responsible for the deaths of many of your people. But you are responsible for the deaths of many of my people. Now the time has come for peace. There must be no more deaths and oppression must cease. You must learn that man has an appetite for knowledge that is as strong as his appetite for food. His deepest and strongest desire is to be free to use his mind, for he knows instinctively that all power comes from the mind, and that he must learn to explore its possibilities. It is because you have tried to prevent him from satisfying this appetite that he regards you as his enemy."

He waited for them to speak; when they remained silent, he said: "Please speak your minds freely."

It was Dravig who answered. "The spiders have always wanted peace. It was man who forced us to become the masters, because he gave us no peace. While man was free, he spent all his time making war on us and trying to destroy us. That is why we were forced to enslave him."

The Spider Lord added: "And for the past two centuries, there has been no war."

Niall was silent; he knew that what they said was true. He said finally: "But now it is the will of the goddess that men and spiders should learn to work together. If we can do this, we shall have lasting peace under the protection of the goddess." As he spoke, he felt that the words carried an authority that was greater than his own.

Again the spiders made the strange and slightly absurd ritual movement of homage.

Niall sensed that he had said enough. He turned to the door. "Now I must go to my own people. But be prepared for my return. Then I shall bring a council of free men to draw up the terms of the peace treaty; for the treaty must be as fair to your people as to mine. From now on, men and spiders shall be equal."

The Spider Lord said: "So be it."

Dravig threw open the door for him. As Niall stepped into the hall, he was startled when the two spider guards sank to the floor, their legs bunched underneath them; the movement was as abrupt as if they had fainted.

Niall turned to Dravig. "What is wrong with them?"

"They are showing veneration for the envoy of the goddess."

As he descended the stairs, preceded by Dravig, Niall had to struggle with a sense of unreality. On each landing, spider guards lay in the same attitude; down in the main hall, dozens of them were collapsed on the floor, giving it the appearance of an improvised mortuary. If he accidentally brushed against them, they made no movement; even their minds seemed passive and immobile, as if all life had been suspended.

It was a relief to step out into the sunlight; after the cold darkness of the building its warmth was like a benediction. The square in front of the building was crowded with people; as he emerged, there was a murmur of excitement. Then, at a gesture of command from Dravig, all fell to their knees and made a movement of obeisance. Even Merlew, who was standing halfway down the steps, knelt and bowed her head.

Niall felt himself blushing with embarrassment. He turned to Dravig. "Please tell them to stand up."

Dravig said respectfully: "That would be unlawful. As the ruler of the city, you must be treated with the same veneration as the Spider Lord."

Niall looked at him incredulously. "The ruler?"

"Of course. As the envoy of the goddess, you command the lives of all who depend on her."

Niall looked at the kneeling crowd, whose bodies were as rigid as those of the spiders, and was overcome by a sense of absurdity. Then he looked at Dravig, and abandoned the idea of ordering them to stand up; instead, he hurried down the steps towards the waiting charioteers. But as he passed Merlew, she raised her head, and he caught her glance of ironic amusement. He was grateful to her for that.

Six weeks after the signing of the peace treaty, Niall embarked from the harbor in a vessel captained by Manetho; he was also accompanied by Simeon and his brother Veig. His purpose was to fulfill the vow he had made on the day he had sealed up the burrow: to return to the desert and give his father a warrior's burial. When he had announced his intention to the Council of Free Men, they had immediately voted that Ulf's bones should be interred in a marble tomb in the city's main square. But Niall had resisted their suggestion that he should sail with a flotilla of ships, and that their return to the city should be accompanied by a torchlight procession. So, to avoid argument, he had slipped away at dawn, informing only his mother of his destination.

The morning was bright and cloudless, but the northwesterly breeze had the indefinable scent of autumn. The adjustable lateen sail enabled them to sail due south—a course that, according to Manetho, should carry them directly to the beach from which Niall had embarked three months ago.

Niall stood with his arms resting on the gunwale, staring out across the sea, whose choppy wavelets reflected the sunlight. He was experiencing again the strange feeling of delight that was always induced in him by sheets of water, as if water was, in itself, a magical substance that concealed in its depths the secret of happiness. As he gazed at the receding coastline, his whole being seemed to relax with a sigh of deep contentment, and he was flooded with a delightful certainty that life is infinitely rich and rewarding.

But it was the first time in many weeks that he had experienced this sensation, or even had the opportunity to think his own thoughts. Life as a ruler had proved to be more exacting than he had anticipated. For three days after the signing of the peace treaty, the people of the spider city had indulged in a riot of celebration, with carnivals that lasted all night and an orgy of feasting. For the first time in two centuries, men and women had been able to mingle freely, and the children had been released from the nurseries to join in the festivities. Runa, Mara, and Dona had been missing for twenty-four hours, and had returned to the palace with their faces painted in bright colors and garlands of flowers round their necks. Veig had been so drunk that he had slept throughout the third day, and had awakened the following morning with a headache that convinced him he was dying. But Niall had taken no part in the celebrations; he had spent most of the three days closeted with the Council of Free Men trying to devise a working routine to replace the compulsory labor of his fellow citizens.

At first, it had seemed simple enough: now men were free, everybody should be allowed to do whatever he liked. But someone pointed out that, in that case, there would be no one to do the unpleasant jobs, like operating the sewage farms or disposing of rubbish. So it was finally agreed that, for the moment, everyone should stick to his present job, and that any change should be made at the discretion of a tribunal. But it was unanimously agreed that the men should make their own way to work, instead of marching in squads under the command of wolf spiders or female overseers.

This debate was followed by a discussion about the future of the slaves—were they also to be regarded as free men and allowed to live where they liked? After all, it was not their fault that they were mentally subnormal. But it was finally decided that the slaves would be happier in their present area of the city, and that it would only confuse the issue if they were offered a free choice of jobs. The only difference was that, from now on, they would not be referred to as slaves, but as "nonvoting citizens."

On most other issues—the status of commanders, the right to travel, the creation of a public transport system—it was also decided to leave things as they were. The only major innovation was that couples should now be allowed to marry and set up a home together, and that the nursery system should be abolished. When Niall communicated these decisions to Dravig, the chief adviser was clearly relieved, and congratulated Niall on his wisdom and moderation.

The commander of Niall's personal guard was a statuesque, dark-haired girl named Nephtys. On the morning after the carnival, she woke Niall at dawn to tell him that almost none of the work force had reported for duty. When Niall went outside to investigate, he stumbled over a drunken man who was asleep in the doorway; half a dozen more were lying in the gutters. He told Nephtys that today should be proclaimed a public holiday, but that all workers would be expected to report at dawn the following day. The next morning, about a quarter of the work force presented themselves. Again Niall told Nephtys to proclaim a public holiday, but to add that anyone who failed to report the next day would be punished. But when, the following morning, only about a third of the work force appeared, Niall went to consult Dravig, and in less than an hour, unshaven workers were being driven into the streets by commanders with whips, and marshaled into squads by wolf spiders. From then on, the commanders and wolf spiders were again placed in charge of the workers, and there was no more absenteeism. Oddly enough, the workers themselves seemed perfectly content to return to the old arrangement.

Later that day he had been faced with a far more difficult decision. A dead man was found lying in an alleyway, the knife that killed him still embedded in his chest. In a basement nearby, someone noticed that the garments of a sleeping man were stained with blood. He was a charioteer named Otto and admitted freely that he had stabbed his best friend in a fight over a girl.

Niall sent for Simeon and asked his advice. Simeon said that according to the law of the beetles, a man guilty of willful homicide should be condemned to die at the hands of the headsman. Niall was shocked at the idea. But he agreed with Simeon that if the murderer was pardoned—on the grounds that he had killed his friend in a drunken brawl—it might set a precedent. There had been no case of murder in the spider city within living memory. Niall brooded on the problem for most of the day. Meanwhile the killer was locked in a temporary prison in an empty house—the spider city had no official jail, since most offences had formerly been punished by death. The idea of executing a fellow creature struck Niall as barbarous; the idea of building a prison and confining him for the rest of his life seemed even worse. He asked Dravig whether it would not be possible to send the man into exile in some distant place; Dravig pointed out that this would mean almost certain death, since remote areas were full of dangerous wild creatures. After a sleepless night, Niall was relieved to learn that Otto had saved him from making a decision by hanging himself in his cell. But when Nephtys brought him the news, he realized that he felt as if he had aged ten years since the previous morning.

During these first weeks as lord of the spider city, Niall seemed to devote most of his time to administration and planning. He was awakened at daybreak by Nephtys, and often received officials and councilors while he was eating his breakfast. He usually spent the rest of the morning touring the city and surrounding suburbs, deciding how best to employ his squads of workmen. (He estimated that repairs to the harbor would take five years.) In the afternoon he attended a meeting of the Council, which often continued until late in the evening. When he arrived home, he was usually too tired to stay awake for more than an hour; he listened politely and tried to stifle his yawns while Siris told him about the events of the day and about her domestic problems. More often than not, he fell asleep on a pile of cushions, and Siris covered him with a blanket, blew out the candles, and ordered the servant girls and musicians to tiptoe out of the room.

Yet this new life had its compensations. He had chosen for his palace an imposing building on the corner of the main avenue, directly opposite the headquarters of the Spider Lord, and a squad of fifty men worked from dawn to dusk repairing and redecorating its crumbling rooms. Siris was in charge of the household; Sefna, her sister, supervised the workmen. Dona took charge of the education of Runa and Mara. The women radiated contentment. So did Veig, who also lived in the palace. He had chosen a suite of rooms on the other side of the courtyard, where he could lead an independent existence. As the brother of the ruler, he was in an enviable position, obeyed by all the men and admired by the women. With his curly black hair and bright blue eyes, he was regarded as one of the most eligible bachelors in the city, and was constantly in the company of some attractive woman. It was rumored that the hundred members of the Corps of Commanders had made a wager amongst themselves about which of them could persuade him into a more permanent arrangement. Veig seemed determined to give them all fair consideration before he made up his mind.

What Niall enjoyed most of all was to stroll through the streets at dusk and observe men and women as they walked arm-in-arm through the torchlit thoroughfares. The streets were always crowded at that hour; small groups of men sat on the pavement playing dice, while others brought their supper outdoors and ate it with their backs propped against the area railings. They no longer glanced nervously at the spider webs stretched over their heads. There was only one drawback. As soon as they recognized Niall, they knelt face downward on the ground, and remained in this position until he was out of sight. He tried issuing a proclamation that he wanted to be ignored, but it made no difference. Veig told him about a conversation he had overheard between two men, one of whom insisted that Niall was a magician, while the other preferred to believe that he was a god or some kind of supernatural being. Instead of being flattered, Niall felt saddened and depressed.

His dissatisfaction reached a climax on the day he announced his intention of returning to North Khaybad to bring back his father's remains. The Council immediately passed a resolution that Ulf's bones should be interred in a magnificent marble tomb in the center of the main avenue. Then, in spite of Niall's protests, they voted that Niall should be accompanied by a thousand armed men, and that their return should be greeted with a torchlight procession in which everybody would take part. As soon as Niall left the Council meeting, he sent a secret message to Manetho and Simeon, and the next morning they slipped out of the city and embarked on the ship that was waiting for them.

These were the thoughts that preoccupied Niall as he leaned on the gunwale and watched the shoreline fade into the sea. Yet his mood of depression now seemed an absurd piece of self-indulgence. The fresh breeze and the open sky filled him with a sense of freedom and excitement, and he found it hard to understand how he had ever allowed himself to become so frustrated and dissatisfied. None of the problems that had faced him in the past few weeks had really been insoluble. The real problem, he could now see, lay in the limitations of his own consciousness.

Veig came up on deck, chewing an enormous roast beef sandwich and holding a cup of mead in the other hand. "There's breakfast down below."

"Aren't you coming?"

"No. I'd rather eat in the fresh air." But his eyes strayed involuntarily towards the pretty, bare-breasted overseer, who was now consulting with Manetho.

Simeon was alone in the captain's cabin, removing the backbone from a steaming broiled trout. The table was covered with dishes of cold meat, pickled vegetables, and jars of jam, marmalade, and honey. Niall carved himself some underdone roast beef from a joint and poured a cup of papaya juice. Simeon glanced up at him from under his bushy eyebrows.

"The Council is going to be upset when they find you've gone."

Niall shrugged. "It can't be helped. I didn't want to take a thousand men and twenty ships."

Simeon squeezed a lemon on his trout. "They were only trying to please you. They hold you in great esteem."

Niall said gloomily: "I know."

Simeon shook his head. "You see, it's the duty of a ruler to allow himself to be revered." It was obvious that Simeon had been awaiting the opportunity to say this. "He's not just there for his own pleasure. He's there to give the people something to look up to. A happy country is a land with a ruler that everybody can honor and respect. That's the way he serves his people."

"That's not the way Kazak served them."

"And they didn't respect him as they respect you. Don't you realize you're the first human being who seems to have got the better of the spiders? You've become one of their heroes, like Ivar the Strong and Vaken the Wise. What else do you expect?"

"It was the goddess who got the better of the spiders, not me."

"But the goddess couldn't have done it without your help." He laid down his fork and spoke with emphasis. "What's happened in the past few weeks is a kind of miracle. I can hardly believe it myself. When Bildo told me you wanted to free men from the spiders, I thought: poor young chap, he's got to come to terms with reality. And now you've actually done it. It's just like one of those legends. You've got to be willing to take the credit."

Niall said: "I wanted men to be free—as we were free in the desert—not to beat their foreheads on the ground every time I go past."

Simeon sighed. "Men don't want too much freedom—it makes them feel confused. You can't give them more than they want. Look what's happened in our city. The beetles have told us we're all free, and we can go anywhere we want and do anything we like. And not a single person has taken advantage of it—including me. It takes time for men to get used to freedom."

"Do you think they'll ever get used to it?"

"Oh yes, provided they're given it in small doses." He peered sympathetically at Niall. "I thought you hadn't been looking too well lately. Is something the matter?"

Niall thought about it, then laughed. "I suppose I just don't like being the ruler, that's all."

Simeon buttered a chunk of bread. "What would you rather do instead?"

"Well, to begin with, I'd like to spend more time in the white tower. I've only been in there twice in the past six weeks, and that was to ask Steeg's advice. I'd like to spend days in there—yes, even months or years—just learning about the past. That's far more interesting than getting the sewers repaired or talking about the housing shortage. It's the most fascinating place in the world—I'll take you there when we get back. But I never have time to use it."

"There's nothing to stop you spending a couple of hours a day in there."

"I don't seem to find the time. But that's not all. I just want to have time to think my own thoughts. I'm enjoying this trip because I'm not surrounded by people. I want time to learn to use my own mind. You're right about men not knowing how to use their freedom. But that's because they don't know how to use their own minds. When they're free, they get bored and look around for something to do. And just as I'm beginning to learn to use my mind, I have to spend most of the day in Council meetings."

Simeon nodded slowly. "Well, I could think of various solutions. If you don't want to be the ruler, you could resign and move to our city. Or you could train a deputy to do the boring jobs. Or you could marry Merlew and leave it all to her. She's just like her father—she loves giving orders."

Niall laughed. "That's why I don't think I'll marry her."

They were interrupted by Manetho, who came into the cabin with the pretty overseer; Veig was immediately behind them. The subject was tacitly dropped. But as Niall went on deck half an hour later, he was feeling strangely lighthearted; talking to Simeon had made him more conscious of the problem, and therefore brought the solution one step closer.

In less than two hours, the mountains of North Khaybad seemed to rise up out of the sea. Half an hour later, they were close enough for him to be able to recognize the pass between sandstone cliffs

from which he had caught his first glimpse of the sea; his heart contracted with a mixture of delight and sadness. It was like returning to
the world of childhood. Somehow, it seemed appropriate that the
golden sunlight had the mellow tinge of autumn.

By mid-afternoon they were securely anchored in the bay. As he
was rowed ashore, with the pretty overseer at the oars, Niall found
himself wondering why returning to familiar places brings a curious
sense of exaltation. Then he saw the answer: because it makes us feel
that we are the masters of time, not its victims.

Since there were still several hours of daylight, they decided to
begin their inland march immediately. Six men bore the empty coffin
that had been made by the finest carpenter in the city of the beetles;
it had been enveloped in sackcloth to protect it from scratches, and
was carried on a litter. Six more sailors, armed with spears and bows
and arrows, came along as guards. Half a dozen porters carried food
supplies. Niall, Simeon, Veig and Manetho made up the rest of the
party. Veig stood looking with regret as the pretty overseer returned
to the longboat. Niall was unable to understand the attraction. He
could see that the girl was physically desirable, but when he tuned in
to her mind he found it full of boring commonplaces, and completely
incapable of any kind of sustained thought. Veig knew this too, but
didn't seem to mind.

For the next four hours they marched across the fertile coastal
plain towards the mountains. Wasps and dragonflies buzzed past
them, and grasshoppers chirped in the undergrowth. Niall remembered how, a few months ago, this place had struck him as a para-
dise; now, compared to the green, leafy countryside around the
spider city, it seemed barren and unwelcoming. Yet the warm air
brought back memories of Hrolf and Thorg and of his father, and he
was haunted by a troubled sense of loss.

When they halted, an hour before dusk, the mountains rose up
in front of them. This was close to the spot where Niall had been captured by the wolf spiders. His dinner that night, he recalled, had been
dried rodent flesh and stale bread, washed down with coconut milk.
Now they dined off roast fish—caught by the sailors in their passage
across the sea—fresh bread, goat's cheese, and green vegetables, and
washed it down with mead that had been kept cool in a pannier
stuffed with straw. But although it was delightful to drowse by the
campfire, and listen to the sailors as they sang sentimental ballads

about Shenandoah and the Rio Grande, he was too tired to indulge in self-congratulation, and fell asleep long before the sailors had exhausted their repertoire.

They were awake two hours before dawn and began their march while the stars were still in the sky. This was the hardest part of the journey—the ten miles or so to the top of the pass—and they wanted to accomplish it before the sun made the climb intolerable. Dawn rose as they reached the foot of the final steep slope. Although the sailors were men of magnificent physique, and all were in excellent physical condition, they were beginning to show signs of fatigue.

Niall glanced at Manetho, who was also breathing heavily. "Don't you think we ought to give them a break?"

Manetho said cheerfully: "That's up to you. You're the chief."

It suddenly dawned on Niall that they regarded him as the leader of this expedition, and as the man who gave the orders. He found himself blushing as he said: "In that case, I think we'll stop for breakfast." Manetho shouted the order, and they sat down at the side of the road to refresh themselves with coconut milk and bread and cheese. And Niall reflected with amusement that, even after two months, he had failed to accustom himself to the idea that he was "the chief."

Between the great sandstone cliffs of the pass, they paused again to enjoy the sea breeze that was funneled between its walls. Now they could look down on the desert landscape in which Niall and Veig had spent most of their lives, and—in this clear air—even catch the distant gleam of the inland sea called Thellam.

Niall turned to Veig. "It's a pity we didn't bring Massig with us. He would have enjoyed looking down on his homeland, even from this distance."

Veig shook his head and laughed. "Oh no, he wouldn't. I asked him if he'd like to return and he said he hoped he'd never see the horrible place again. Most of the others feel the same. Even under the spiders, they were happier than when they were living underground."

Niall shook his head sadly; for him, there was a poignant magic in the sight of the plateau and the glint of the great salt lake. They brought memories of unalloyed happiness, of his first taste of real freedom.

The descent was easy enough; but since the mountains cut them off from the sea breeze, it was hot and exhausting. When they reached the red plain, with its strange columns of windworn rock, their faces were streaked with dusty sweat. But since there was no shelter and the sun was now directly overhead, there would have been no point in stopping to rest; they plodded on with slow steps over the red sand. Then Niall recalled the granite cistern by the side of the road; when he told them about it, their feet quickened, and they began to sing a marching song. Again Niall was struck by the paradox of the human will: that it can be strangled to death by boredom, then resurrected in a moment with a single word of encouragement.

But as they rounded the corner that brought them within sight of the cistern, the sailors halted in dismay. Lying coiled at its base, taking advantage of a tiny area of shadow, was a huge centipede. The vibration of their tread had already alerted it to their approach, and it was looking towards them, its horn-like feelers erect. Since the cistern was on the east side of the road, and there was a steep rocky face on the other side, it would be difficult to avoid the centipede by making a detour.

Niall advanced towards it slowly, with Veig on one side and Manetho on the other; he was hoping that it would retreat in the face of so many. But perhaps the creature had only just found the cistern, or perhaps it was simply unwilling to relinquish the only cool spot for many miles. Their approach only made it raise the front half of its body off the ground, so it reared menacingly; at the same time it made a hissing, strident sound that was unmistakably a threat. It was at least eight feet long, and the eyes were as blank as those of a coiled snake. Veig and Manetho halted, while Niall took another step forward. Simeon muttered a warning, and suddenly the creature was rushing towards them, moving with frightening speed on its tiny legs.

Something hissed in the air, close to Niall's shoulder; then an arrow embedded itself in the open mouth. The centipede gave a strange squawk of pain, not unlike the harsh croak of a bullfrog. Another arrow glanced off the shiny brown armor plate of its back. It reared threateningly, the tiny legs moving like a hundred angry arms. This gave the archers a chance to fire their arrows into the soft underbelly; one of them struck with such force that it disappeared as far as the feather, and they heard the sound of it striking the armor plating from inside. Amazingly, the creature still came on, carried forward by the rush of its rear legs. Then the biggest of the sailors leapt forward and hurled his spear with all his force between the open

243

jaws. Niall's brain caught the flash of its instinctive response: the sudden recognition that death was inevitable. It suddenly halted, then turned and scurried with remarkable speed in the opposite direction, leaving behind a trail of light pink blood, and drops of a green liquid. They watched it scrambling over the rocks at the edge of the road, the projecting arrows impeding its progress. Suddenly he remembered the unknown animal that had tried to attack him when he slept under the nearby rock, protected by a thorn bush; some intuition told him that this was the creature that was now seeking a place to die.

They were all euphoric; the heat no longer seemed oppressive, and the tiredness disappeared from the muscles of their legs. The sailor who had fired the first arrow was congratulated repeatedly; the others explained in detail how they had awaited the precise moment to fire, and the exact angle at which their arrows had entered the underbelly. They drew jars of icy water from the cistern and drank greedily, then poured the remainder over their heads and chests. Then they sat in the narrow band of shadow at the foot of the rock face, and made a meal of bread, cheese, and onions.

Simeon was thoughtful. "I wonder what made it attack us when it could see it was outnumbered?"

Niall shrugged. "It probably regards this place as its own territory."

Simeon shook his head. "Wells and drinking holes are never the territory of any individual animal—everyone uses them." He looked out over the desert, with its shrubs and cacti. "I suspect it has encountered humans before, and found they were easily frightened."

"What, in this place?"

"Why not? You lived in the desert."

It was true. Niall stared at the heat waves that shimmered over the sand, and wondered if these rocks and shrubs concealed entrances to underground burrows. And how many other human beings cowered in underground caves or even underground cities— in the barren regions of the earth? He made a resolution: one day, he would find a way of contacting these outcasts and telling them that they could once again live in the open air as free men.

An hour later, relaxed and refreshed, they resumed their march. By mid-afternoon, the red desert had given way to black volcanic pebbles and irregular chunks of basalt, and the road wound between bushes of thorn and tamarisk; to the west, they could see the volcanoes that lay on the far side of the country of the ants. Four hours later, with the sun close to the western horizon, they were walking on sand, and Niall recognized that they were approaching home territory. The men were weary; but when Niall told them that their goal was so close, they marched with renewed vigor, heartened by the thought of turning their faces homeward on the morrow. The emptiness of the desert induced in these city dwellers a sense of futility.

The first stars were appearing in the eastern sky when Niall sighted the familiar group of organ pipe cacti. Veig was so excited that he ran on ahead. Ten minutes later he waved to them from under the euphorbia cactus that stood near the entrance to the burrow.

"It's still sealed."

When they joined him, he was using a flat stone to dig into the sand that had accumulated over the entrance. There was so much of it that the burrow was virtually buried—evidence of a recent sandstorm. The porters, who were carrying shovels, took over the task of digging, while the others were sent in search of fuel. (Niall advised them to remain in pairs, in case they disturbed a tiger beetle or a scorpion—few desert creatures would attack more than one man.) As the first flames of the fire leapt into the night air, a shovel struck against rock, and Niall found himself looking at the big flat stone that covered the entrance to the burrow. He could see at once that the stones with which he had sealed the entrance were still in place. Manetho and Simeon held torches while Niall and Veig loosened stones and dug with their hands. Niall braced himself for the stench of decay. But as they tore aside the final rock that sealed the entrance, they were met only by the familiar odor of tiger beetles, mingled with the distinctive smells of human habitation. Niall took the torch from Manetho's hand and scrambled down into the darkness. Everything was exactly as it had been on the day he left it. On his father's bed lay a human form, still shrouded in a sheet of cloth. But when Niall steeled himself to pull aside the cloth, he found himself looking into the eyeless sockets of a skull. In the heat of the burrow, the flesh had decayed quickly from Ulf's bones, leaving only a skeleton covered with a few rotting fragments of clothing.

The coffin was lowered into the burrow; then Niall and Veig lifted the whole bed, with its mattress of esparto grass, and carefully transferred it to the silk-lined interior. Niall did this without emotion, concentrating on preventing the skeleton from falling apart; but when the torchlight reflected on the front teeth, and he recognized the slight gap that had given his father's grin a mischievous quality, he was suddenly overwhelmed by a sense of loss; he sat beside the coffin, buried his face in his hands, and cried as he had not cried since he was a child. Veig made no attempt to comfort him; his own cheeks were wet with tears. But when Niall had dried his eyes, and arranged the bony hands in the form of a cross, he experienced a sense of relief and comfort, as if he had been in contact with the spirit of his dead father.

The coffin was passed out through the entrance; Niall wanted his father to lie under the stars before the lid closed down on him forever. But he took the sheet of cloth from the burrow and drew it over the coffin, leaving only the skull exposed; it seemed somehow indecent to allow the night wind to blow through his father's bones.

Ever since he had set out on this journey, Niall had entertained the notion of spending a final night in the burrow, sleeping on his own bed. But as he sat in front of the campfire, wrapped in a blanket—for the night was already cold and a wind had sprung up from the northwest—he knew that he would find it impossible to sleep underground; he had become too accustomed to the sensation of the wind against his face. He and Veig sat apart from the others, eating and drinking sparingly, finding it hard to believe that they were back in the desert, and that so much had happened in the three months since this place had been their home. But as the sailors sang their melancholy ballads—their own way of showing respect for the man whose white cheekbones now reflected the rising moon—their eyelids drooped, and memories of the past blended pleasantly with daydreams of the future. They drew closer to the fire, pulled their blankets round their shoulders, and sank into dreamless sleep. And the sailors, weary from their long day's march, soon lapsed into silence, then into slumber.

Niall was awakened by the crackling of flames. Someone had tossed a creosote bush into the dying embers of the fire. It was Simeon, who was now sitting cross-legged, a fur cloak wrapped around his shoulders. Somewhere out in the darkness, a large creature moved across the stones; from its clumsy movements, Niall guessed it to be a large male scorpion, weighted down with oversized claws. It had probably been watching them, wondering if it was safe to attack; now it retired discreetly into the night.

Niall turned on his back and looked up at the stars. The Steegmaster had taught him to distinguish the major stars and constellations: the pole star, the Great Bear and the Little Bear, the Dog, and the Lion. The pole star was now close to the northern horizon, with the Great Bear above it: that meant that it was about two hours to dawn. He traced a line through the central stars of the Bear, and found Vega, also close to the horizon. It glittered in the clear desert air like a blue diamond. A hundred and fifty million years ago, the great explosion had hurled the spores of the empress plants towards the solar system. What had happened to the plants that remained on AL_3? Had they now achieved the ultimate goal of their evolution and become superbeings? Or had they vanished and been replaced by some other species?

On the southern horizon he could distinguish Scorpius and Libra; just below the horizon lay Centaurus. Niall thought of the men who lived in that distant constellation. According to the Steegmaster, the climate of New Earth was in many ways similar to that of our own planet, and the ratio of oxygen to nitrogen in its atmosphere was almost exactly the same. Its men had set up colonies on other planets of their system, and even built a domed city on its airless moon.

But Steeg had so far told him nothing about the history of these pioneers, and it had not occurred to Niall to enquire. Now, as he lay staring at the sky, he was suddenly consumed with curiosity, and he formulated a hundred questions. Were there other intelligent life forms on New Earth? Were its men and women able to live without conflict? Had they remained physically unchanged in their new environment? Had they any natural enemies? Did they have trees and plants like those on Earth? And seas and rivers? But above all, had they succeeded in solving those persistent problems of human nature that had made man's history such a disappointing record of brutality and stupidity? Had the flight from Earth and the hardships of creating a new civilization taught them to shake the mind awake, and to prevent it from falling asleep again?

For this, he could now see, was the central problem of human beings. When they were faced with perils and difficulties, they fought magnificently. But as soon as they had conquered, they lost all the ground they had gained; they sank into laziness and became the victims of triviality. They seemed to be unable to maintain a sense of urgency. It was as if they were all suffering from sleeping sickness. If the men of New Earth had solved this problem, they would be more like gods than human beings . . .

Simeon threw more wood onto the fire. Niall pushed himself up into a sitting position. Simeon asked: "Like a hot drink?"

Niall nodded. He crawled over to the fire and huddled there with the blankets wrapped around him; the desert wind was like a knife. Simeon was spooning a mixture of dried herbs into boiling water. A pale light was already appearing on the eastern horizon.

"Have you been awake all night?"

"No. Something woke me up—something with red eyes." Simeon gestured towards the organ pipe cacti.

"Probably the brown scorpion that lives under the rock. It nearly ate Mara when she was a baby."

Simeon grimaced with disgust. "I think I prefer civilization."

They sat warming their hands on the hot mugs, breathing in the fragrant steam. The wind was blowing the underside of the logs into an orange heat and the effect was hypnotic. For a while, each was involved in his own thoughts. Then Simeon said: "Have you ever wondered why the Spider Lord took so much trouble to pretend she was a male?"

"Because a Spider Lord is more frightening than a Spider Lady."

Simeon grunted. "I find them both about as bad."

"All the same, we all think men are more capable of evil than women. And for some reason, human beings seem to admire people who terrify them."

Simeon said dryly: "That's a sad admission."

"I learned it in the white tower. The chief thing that struck me about human history is that most of the great leaders were homicidal maniacs. They even gave them names like Ivan the Terrible and Abdul the Damned, and it was supposed to be a compliment. The more frightening they were, the more people admired them. Human beings can be incredibly stupid."

Simeon gave him an amused sideways glance. "Then wouldn't it have been better to leave them under the domination of the spiders?"

"No. Because no matter how stupid men are, they still need freedom. It's only through freedom they can become less stupid. They learn through trial and error. They need to be allowed to make their own mistakes. They need to think out their own problems. Do you *really* think they'd be better off as slaves of the spiders?" There were times when Simeon seemed to enjoy being exasperating.

"No. But you said yourself that you were sick of them banging their heads on the pavement every time you walked past."

"Yes, and that's the strange paradox of human nature. They want freedom more than anything in the world, yet as soon as they've got it, they want to give it away to some leader. They're always looking around for somebody to admire." The subject had been on Niall's mind a great deal during the past few weeks. "It's because all human beings crave a sense of purpose. And because they don't have a purpose of their own, they want to hand over their freedom to somebody who can give them one. But that doesn't mean they're better off without freedom. It only means they've got to learn to look for purpose inside themselves."

"And how do you teach them to do that?"

"I don't know. Sooner or later, I'll find a way."

Simeon said blandly: "I thought you didn't like being the ruler?"

Niall shrugged. "I don't. It's hard work. But somebody has to do it. Somebody has to show them how to organize their lives and rebuild their city and educate their children. The spiders tried to breed the intelligence out of them. I suppose my job is to try to breed it back into them. If I could do that, they wouldn't need a ruler."

Simeon shook his head firmly. "They'll always need a ruler. Because a ruler's an excuse for laziness, and even intelligent men can be lazy. I'm not being cynical. The more you do for them, the more they'll revere and admire you, and insist on looking up to you. They *enjoy* banging their heads on the pavement. Why do you think they want to put your father's bones in a vast mausoleum? So they've got somebody else to revere and admire."

The remark startled Niall. He turned and looked at the coffin. Its handles of polished gold were glittering in the first rays of the rising sun. But the empty eye sockets of the skull were still pools of darkness. Niall laughed suddenly and stood up.

"Yes, of course you're right. I was stupid not to see it."

Simeon glanced at him in perplexity. "See what?"

Niall leaned over and shook the nearest man by the shoulder. It was one of the coffin bearers. "Wake up the others. Tell them to go and gather more fuel."

Simeon guessed what he had in mind. "Do you think that's wise?"

"I'm sure of it. Besides, he wouldn't sleep comfortably in the middle of a city."

"But what about your mother?"

"She'll understand."

Veig, awakened by all the activity, sat up and rubbed his eyes. "What's happening? Time to leave?"

"Not yet. Get up and give me a hand with this."

"What are you going to do?"

Niall said: "This is where he belongs, here in the desert. Do you really want to see our father resting in a marble tomb?"

Veig looked at him in perplexity for a while, then finally shook his head. "No. As a matter of fact, I always disliked the idea."

He heaved himself to his feet. Together they lifted the coffin into the center of the fire; its weight crushed the half burnt creosote bushes, and it subsided into the midst of the flames. As red sparks rose around it, the enamel began to blister, then burst into flames. Niall hurled the coffin lid on top of the blaze. As the men returned with creosote bushes and dry wood, Niall ordered them to throw them into the flames. Ten minutes later, the heat was so great that they had to stand at a distance. By now, the coffin was no longer visible in the midst of the crackling blaze.

As he watched his father's remains turn into smoke and ashes, Niall experienced a surge of exultation. Sorrow and regret belonged to the past, and men were too fond of clinging to the past. These flames made him dream of the future.

When the fire had subsided into a heap of glowing ashes, Niall turned to Manetho. "Order the men to gather their belongings. It's time to go home."

T H E   E N D

Coming in Volume 3

Spider World:
The Magician

By the will of the goddess, Niall has become the master of the Spider City. Now his task is to try to mold his fellow human beings, whose genetic stock has been enfeebled by generations of slavery, into a third force that will galvanize the spiders and the beetles to reinvigorate their own evolutionary impulse, which has been weakened by centuries of unchallenged domination.

At the end of his first year as ruler, Niall's task seems to be a straightforward matter of politics and social engineering.

What he is not aware of is that the spiders have a far older enemy than man, an enemy who has observed their humiliation with satisfaction, and who now sees the opportunity to expand his domain into the lands between the Grey Mountains and the southern ocean. . . .

Shortly before dawn he was awakened by a cold so intense that it reminded him of the desert night. He lay there, the bedclothes pulled around his face, and his breath formed moisture on the blanket as he exhaled. He had chosen this room because it faced east, and he liked to be awakened by the sun. Today there was no sunlight; the dawn came like gray mist, until the room was filled with a cold, even light. No birds sang.

Something about the strange silence disturbed him. He crossed to the window, treading on the soft woolen rugs, and found himself looking out on a white landscape. White rooftops seemed to blend into the pearl-gray sky, and the great square was carpeted in the same featureless whiteness. It had even found its way into the corners of the window frames, and a few fine flakes had frozen on to the outside of the glass.

Niall had heard about snow and read about it, but this was the first time he had ever seen it. Nothing had prepared him for this cold, beautiful whiteness that seemed to blanket the universe. He was suddenly filled with a magical excitement which, although he was unaware of it, had filled thousands of generations of children at the first sight of the winter snow.

Possessed by a longing to touch this strange substance, he pulled on a sheepskin mantle over his tunic, thrust his feet into shoes lined with rabbit fur, and hurried out of the room. The palace was silent and its corridors empty; Niall was usually the first awake. He mounted the staircase to the top floor, passing the sleeping chamber shared by his cousin Dona and his sisters Runa and Mara, then climbed the narrow stairs that led up to the roof. As soon as he opened the door, a rampart of snow tumbled in and deluged his bare legs. He jumped back with an exclamation; he had not realized snow would be so cold. Then he took off his shoes—the snow had fallen into them—and one by one shook them out; the fur now felt cold and wet to his ankles. Yet the morning air seemed surprisingly warm; this was because there was not the faintest breath of wind.

The space between the parapet and the steep roof was deep in snow; it crunched underfoot as he trod in it. He picked up a double handful and molded it into a ball; but it froze his fingers, so he threw it away. With the sleeve of his mantle he carefully brushed the snow from the parapet, then stood leaning on it, gazing out over the milky whiteness that extended as far as the distant hills. In the center of the parkland on the far side of the square, the white tower rose like a finger of ivory, but now the surrounding grass was white, it was no longer the most striking feature in the landscape. This distinction belonged to the river, whose blackness split the cold plain like a current of ink; it made him feel colder merely to look at it.

The city seemed empty; there was not a living thing in sight. Then, as he turned to go indoors, his attention was caught by a movement in the square below. Something black was lying in its northeastern corner. From this distance it might have been an uprooted bush. Then he looked more closely and saw the red stains in the snow; at the same time, another faint movement made him aware that he was looking at a badly injured spider.

He hurried back down the stairs, holding the balustrade because the snow on his shoes made the marble treacherous. For a moment he was tempted to return to his room to put on warmer clothes; but his sense of urgency overruled the discomfort. He pulled back the bar that locked the main door, and tramped out into the deep snow, ignoring the cold wetness that ran down inside his shoes. The snow had turned the steps into a smooth ramp, so that he had to tread with extreme care; at one point he fell and plunged in up to the elbows. But as he struggled to his feet and waded unevenly across the square, choosing a route where the snow lay thin, his mind was obsessed by a single problem: how a death spider could have met with serious injury in such a wide-open space.

As he approached, the spider saw him, and it made a convulsive attempt to rise; but its jointed legs were not strong enough, and buckled under its weight. The black, hairy body was covered in snow, evidently it had been lying there for some time. Niall found this puzzling; spiders are telepathic and can send an instant distress call to others of their kind. And since this one lay within a few hundred yards of the headquarters of the ruling directorate, on the far side of the square, its presence should have been sensed the moment it was injured.

When he came close enough to see the far side of its body he saw why it had been unable to rise. Three of its legs had been smashed to a pulp; the bottom joint of one of them, with its black claw, was almost completely detached. A trail of blood smears, partly obliterated by snow, showed that the spider had dragged itself for about fifty feet before it collapsed. It was obviously dying.

"What happened to you?" Niall spoke the words aloud, but knew that his meaning would be carried directly to the spider's brain.

The reply that sounded inside his chest made him wince; it was a blur of pain, and the directness of the communication made Niall experience its misery and exhaustion, so that he himself felt drained and nauseated. It was impossible to distinguish what the spider was saying, but the "voice" was one that Niall instantly recognized. It was Skorbo, the captain of the guard. Now Niall understood why its communication was an incomprehensible chaos of feeling. The ability to communicate with human beings was a difficult art—the equivalent of a human being learning to read. In spider terms Skorbo was an illiterate peasant, a creature whose chief value to his masters was a certain brutal strength and the ability to dominate others. Niall had always found him repellent; yet now that Skorbo was injured and dying, he felt overwhelmed with pity.

He said: "I'll go and get help."

It was impossible to hurry through the snow; each step plunged him in up to the knee, and if he tried to withdraw the foot too quickly, he left his shoe behind. To avoid discouragement, he deliberately averted his eyes from the expanse of snow that stretched in front of him, and treated each step as an individual effort. It was a pleasant surprise to find himself suddenly at the foot of the steps in front of the headquarters building. Two wolf spiders would normally have been on guard outside its great double doors; the cold had evidently driven them inside. Niall beat on the door with his fists, not because it was locked, but because he knew he would risk being attacked if he rushed in without warning. There was a movement inside and the door opened; Niall found himself looking up into the enormous black eyes of a brown wolf spider, whose height was at least two feet greater than his own. The chelicerae (or pincers) were extended, so he could see the folded fangs. A moment later, the spider recognized him, and sank down in a gesture of homage, lowering its belly to the floor.

Niall turned and pointed. "Quick. Skorbo has been injured. Go and fetch him." Again, the words conveyed his message directly to the spider's brain. Followed by the second guard, it loped across the square towards Skorbo, its enormous strength unaffected by a mere foot of snow. Niall knew there was no point in trying to follow; his whole body felt drained. Instead, he sank down on a bench outside the door, and watched as the guards gently lifted the injured spider. As they approached, he observed the way the legs dragged in the snow and knew that Skorbo was dead.

They placed the body on the floor, scattering snow on the black marble. Skorbo was still bleeding; his blood was thicker, more viscous, than human blood, and it spread slowly, like a pool of oil. It was running from the spider's head, which lay sideways on the floor, and now Niall was able to see that there was a hole in the skull, about a foot above the single row of eyes that extended in a band around its head. Unlike human beings, spiders have no internal bone structure; the armored shell is itself an external skeleton. Skorbo's skull had been shattered by a blow. What puzzled Niall was that there seemed to be fragments of broken armor in the hole, as might have been expected if some tremendous blow had been delivered from above. A large segment seemed to be missing. Blood oozed from the hole as from the socket from which a tooth has been pulled.

The wolf spiders were standing there, too respectful to ask questions. Niall said: "Please notify Dravig of what has happened. Tell him I shall be at home."

But as he plodded back through the snow, curiosity overcame his weariness. What had happened struck him as completely incomprehensible. The hole in the skull made it look as if Skorbo had been attacked. By whom? Another spider? That seemed unlikely. Unlike human beings, spiders seldom fought amongst themselves. Yet it was equally difficult to envisage some accident that might have caused the damage.

The obvious way to find out was to go and look. Niall retraced his steps, and took the diagonal route across the plaza, where the forward rush of the wolf spiders had churned up the snow like some enormous plough. When he came to the place where the injured spider had lain, he realized that Skorbo had lost a great deal of blood; his life had oozed away into the snow as he lay there, his brain too damaged to send the signal that would have brought help. In front of Niall, along the eastern side of the square, there were a number of empty houses in various states of disrepair. The city was full of such houses; spiders often made their homes in the upper stories. But they preferred houses on either side of the street, so they could weave their webs between them; this is why the houses bordering the square had remained empty.

The trail of blood had been obliterated by falling snow; but by bending until his face was within a few inches of the surface, he was able to make out the darker patches. These, he could now see, led back towards the second house from the corner, a tall building whose rusty balconies suggested that it had once been a hotel. Like the others, its windows had been boarded up, and its door was closed—all houses in this square had been forbidden to human beings. Niall tried the door; it seemed to be locked. Yet when he brushed aside the snow on the doorstep with his shoe, a damp bloodstain told him that this was the house in which Skorbo had met his injury. He rammed the door with his shoulder; it seemed completely immovable. But a sheet of plywood covering a window proved to be less solid, and caved inward when he pushed it with both hands.

He leaned in with caution. If something—or someone—powerful enough to kill a spider was lurking inside, he was going to take no risks. In fact, he found himself looking into a bare hallway whose wooden floor was covered with plaster and rubble; it smelt of decay and damp. Recognizing that his tension was blocking his perceptions, he deliberately relaxed, exhaling deeply and closing his eyes; then, as he achieved inner stillness, he concentrated intently. A point of light glowed inside his skull, and the silence seemed to deepen. In that moment, he knew with absolute certainty that no concealed enemies were lying in wait; the building was deserted. Yet this deeper perception also made him aware of another odor, musky and slightly sweet. It was familiar, yet its significance escaped him.

He pushed the plywood violently; the nails that held it to the window frame tore loose, and it fell into the building. Niall clambered inside. By now he was regretting that he was not wearing warmer clothes; his hands and feet were frozen. But since he was here, it seemed pointless not to explore. The light from the window gave him a clearer view of the hallway. He observed rat droppings among the dust and plaster on the floor. That indicated clearly that no spiders used the building; they regarded rats as particularly appetizing delicacies, and would wait for hours in the hope of catching one.

As he expected, there were more bloodstains on the floor, and clear signs in the dust and rubble that a wounded spider had dragged itself across the floor. The marks continued across the hallway to an open door beyond a collapsing staircase; this admitted light and a draft of air. Beyond this, a corridor led down to an open space that had once been a garden; there were more bloodstains on the floor. The door at the end, which stood half-open, had obviously been forced; its lock had been smashed, and marks on the outside woodwork, made by a chisel or a crowbar, looked fresh.

Niall peeped cautiously into the weed-grown garden, then looked upward at the wall above the door; it rose, vertical and windowless, to the roof, where the guttering was still intact. This disposed of his theory that the spider had been struck by some heavy object—perhaps a piece of masonry—dropped from above. Yet when he brushed aside the snow on the threshold, he saw signs of blood. This garden clearly held the secret of the spider's death.

To Niall's untrained eye there were no obvious clues. The layer of snow on the ground had covered any footprints. The garden, which extended as far as the rear wall of the next building, was divided from the gardens to the right and left by high walls. A dozen feet from the door stood a young palm tree; beyond this, there was a tangle of weeds and shrubbery, which offered a great deal of concealment. When Niall studied this more closely, he observed a number of freshly broken twigs, which indicated that someone had been there recently. But the hard ground had retained no other indications.

He penetrated the shrubbery as far as the rear wall; here the overgrown grass convinced him that no one else had been here for months. But as he was about to turn back, he noticed something that made him pause. In a corner of the garden wall there lay a heap of palm leaves, some of them spreading out from a common center. They looked so natural in that setting that he almost failed to notice them. But why should there be palm leaves lying in a corner? Then he looked up and saw that the young palm tree had no leaves. In fact, someone had hacked off its top, leaving a bare trunk. And within a foot of the top of the truncated palm, there was a length of rope.

Now at last he understood. The tree was about twice the height of a man—precisely the distance from the foot of the tree to the rear door of the building. A further search of the shrubbery revealed the stunted tree to whose base the other end of the rope had been tied. The young palm had been bent backwards like a catapult. When the spider had stepped out of the doorway, hesitating as it faced the dark garden, someone had cut the rope, and the tree had snapped over like an immense spring. Skorbo had evidently been standing slightly to one side, or had started to move at the last moment; the tree had smashed his legs and battered him to the ground . . .

Niall returned to the doorway and looked down at the blood-stains. They showed clearly that his reconstruction was correct. The blow had caused blood splashes which were some distance from the original stain, and other splashes had struck the wall at an angle so they were elongated, with tadpole-like tails. And a few feet away, half-buried in the snow, there was a triangular fragment of the spider's skull, with brain-fragments still adhering to its underside. But the original blow had shattered the legs, not the skull. This could mean only one thing: that while the spider was stunned, someone had deliberately smashed the top of his skull, with the intention of penetrating the brain and destroying his capacity to send out a distress signal.

Niall shivered. He had no liking for Skorbo, but the sheer savagery of the attack horrified him; he felt as if he had been there to witness it.

His shiver reminded him of how cold he was; his facial muscles had lost all feeling, and his eyelids felt as if they were frozen. He retraced his steps back through the empty building. The front door had been wedged shut with a baulk of timber. He heaved it loose and went out into the square.

As he plodded back through the snow, walking in the deep footprints he had left earlier, he recalled his excitement on first seeing the snow from his bedroom window. It had made the world look like a fairyland. Now it was merely cold and uncomfortable, and somehow too real.

Hampton Roads Publishing Company

. . . for the evolving human spirit

Hampton Roads Publishing Company
publishes books on a variety of subjects,
including metaphysics, health, integrative medicine,
visionary fiction, and other related topics.

For a copy of our latest catalog, call toll-free
(800) 766-8009, or send your name and address to:

Hampton Roads Publishing Company, Inc.
1125 Stoney Ridge Road
Charlottesville, VA 22902

e-mail: hrpc@hrpub.com
www.hrpub.com